I0700198

A DOSE OF INFIRMITY

C.M. LOKKEN

Published by:

Spotted Boogin Press

I dedicate this book to my incredible and wonderful child.
You fill my heart with more joy than I ever thought possible.
I love you, buddy.

CHAPTER 1

Seven years ago, I stumbled into the biggest mistake of my life, and as I reflected on my failures sitting in the tub, I found myself contemplating a bigger one. I lifted my arm from the soapy lukewarm water and picked up the razor blade. The metal was cold in my hand, and I heard the voice in the back of my head ask: *What would it feel like? Would it hurt much? I could just let it all go...*

I threw the blade across the bathroom and listened as it clanged around the counter. This wasn't the first time I had these intrusive thoughts, but they had been happening more frequently lately. Growing up being abused by my father, I had a few scars to prove that this wasn't my first bout. These last few years had brought me back to that dark helplessness, feeling like nothing I did was ever good enough.

I wanted to forget the island and everything that happened, but that's hard to do when it brought one of my lovers and our child into my life. Also there's the tattoo running down my skull and neck that glare at me in the mirror even from behind the flowers and mantises I tried to cover them with. Most people can't see the strange symbols anymore, but I can. It's all I see when I look at myself. I could still feel the scars from Khan's hack job through the new professional work even if no one else could tell they were there.

I picked up my glass bowl from the edge of the tub, summoned a flame to the tip of my finger to light the herb and took a long drag. It was a shit habit, but honestly it helped to numb the bad thoughts more than the good ones. I laid my head back and held the smoke in my lungs for a minute before releasing my breath. One hit would be enough, weed was way stronger than it was when I was a teenager. I grabbed the plug chain with my toes and pulled to let the water drain while I sat in the tub, trying to visualize the negative thoughts running down the drain with the rest of the filth.

Minutes later I wiped the condensation from the mirror and stared eye to eye with my reflection. A few lines from drying tears ran down my cheeks. I ran my hands along the artwork emblazoned in my flesh. Blue, pink, and purple hydrangea blossoms dotted along lattice like patterns to cover the larger symbols, and the leaves housed a variety of praying mantises. My favorite was the orchid mantis that peaked out from behind my ear. The flowers spilled down my neck and onto my chest, while the symbols down my back were hidden under a traditional Japanese-style phoenix: a symbol of rebirth and new beginnings. At the time, I felt the phoenix represented how I had escaped the island and started a new journey, but I was questioning that more and more each day.

I picked up the hair trimmer, and stared at the long red hair that grew from the parts of my head not destroyed by the mystical patterns forced into my skin. I flicked the switch, buzzed off my mohawk, and felt a weight lift from my head that was more than just wet hair. Each pass of the buzzing blades seemed to free my mind from heavy thoughts and memories. I set the trimmer down and picked up a shaving razor to finish the job. I wet a hand towel and wiped away the remnants of the hair stuck on my skin and then rubbed my head with lotion to moisturize the fresh skin.

I dried off, wrapped myself in my towel, and stepped out into the large dark bedroom to find myself alone. I picked up my phone and swiped the screen lock code to see if Star texted me, but there were just the usual hundreds of emails and social notifications. I cleared them all without checking what any of them were. The towel dropped to the floor as I walked towards the pile of what I hoped were clean clothes. I hadn't let the housekeeper in our bedroom for a while, and it was a mess. I pulled out a pink and black t-shirt dress that read 'Dead Inside' across the chest. It passed the sniff test, so I tugged my body into it and slipped into my last pair of clean panties in my drawer.

I took a deep breath and opened the bedroom door, stepping out into the hall for the first time in a month, maybe two, I had lost track. The rest of the house was immaculately clean, and I almost retreated into my den of comfortable funk. I shook it off, I was tired of being in this hole of depression. It was time to decide, time to shit or get off the pot as it were. I couldn't let my failures keep holding me down and I was finally ready to act.

After the wedding, we exhausted every lead we had trying to find Bach so we could put a stop to his scheme to push Opulentia worldwide, but everything turned up with nothing. Even dedicating some of my tech centers to a team of researchers and private investigators got us nowhere. We were looking for the wrong things as it turned out. Everything we knew about Bach and Paradigm was a lie, a façade he made up to con us into being his playthings. There were a few times I thought we were close, and then suddenly our lead investigator would quit or vanish and show up in the morgue.

I spent hundreds of thousands of dollars trying to get something that would let me put my hands around the weasel's neck, but every time wound up in a dead end. Much of my lottery winnings were gone, but thankfully we had enough invested and steady business to keep us from falling back onto the street. I would give it all up for the chance to get revenge but forced myself to be responsible and provide a life for our kid. That drive for vengeance still eventually burned me out and I fell into a deep depression cycle. Some days I was okay, but for most I was back in that dark bathroom, sitting in a tub of tepid water, contemplating ending things.

I leaned up against the doorframe looking into Cherry's room. She was an angel, and I loved her as much as if I had given birth to her myself. She and Callie had moved in with us after the escape and watching her grow up has been one of the few things keeping me grounded.

The walls of her room were full of music posters and books, her two favorite hobbies. She was just like a regular teenager, except for the powers of course. She was physically mute but has somehow learned to speak telepathically. We still taught her sign language so she could communicate at school without freaking people out too much. It's been a struggle to battle the hormones and her abilities but she's mature for her age, a side effect of the trauma.

We got the privilege of giving her a taste of a real childhood though, which has been great. Despite my obsession with Bach, we always found time to let Cherry experience the real world. Road trips, amusement parks, riding bikes on the pier, shopping, fast food, spending time with the people that loved her and trying to let her move past the dark place she came from. She was about fourteen years old now, though we didn't know for sure and had to go by her doctor's estimate. We let her pick her birthday, and being obsessed with anime, she chose March 27th which falls near the start of the annual Cherry Blossom Festival in Japan. We took her to see it the very next year to celebrate.

I moved down the hall to the other largest bedroom, the one we shared with Callie. Star and I both fell in love with Callie, and the arrangement works well for us. Callie wasn't home, she had been out for the last year trying to find who she really was. Bach had erased a lot of her family records after he trapped her, and finding out where she came from was rather difficult. DNA tests were inconclusive thanks to the changes from the experiments, and even after Cherry removed her powers, we never got clear enough results to get her much information. She had fractured bits of memories from landmarks, and with some long google sessions, we managed to find a few places that seemed to match what she could remember. She decided to go look for herself and see if anyone recognized her. She called us every week to give us updates and tell us how much she misses us and to make sure we are eating right.

I made my way downstairs and heard the TV on in the living room. My heart fluttered, as it often did when I thought about my best friend and wife. The reason I waded through hell and back, the person I would give everything for over and over again, my Star. I entered the room and there she was engrossed in a documentary about people escaping some religious cult. She paused it and rushed over to me.

"There you are, I thought I heard you bumping around. Oh! Your hair! What happened!?" she said holding me in place.

"It was time for a change, I cut it all off." I replied leaning into her embrace.

"It looks great! Caught me off guard, but I love it. Very metal. I'm glad you are up and moving around. You want some of my ice cream?" She said, holding me close and kissing my cheek.

"Yeah, sounds great."

We sat on the couch and Star fed me some ice cream until she got sucked back into her show. Being close to her again made all the negative feelings wash away. It felt like she just radiated healing rays that melted away the darkness surrounding me. I felt safe, I felt at home. I loved her more than life itself, and nothing could ever change that. I sat on the couch and watched her drip ice cream on herself and smiled. She was my world.

Star understood my depression better than most. She had a rough childhood just like mine, different extremes but traumatic just the same. We bonded over our shared experiences and managed to heal a bit thanks to support from each other. Anytime that one of us faltered the other was there to pick them up and mend the pieces. We shared everything, and I couldn't ask for a better partner. Adding Callie to the picture only enhanced our relationship: in those scarce moments where we couldn't meet each other's needs for one reason or another, Callie stepped in and bridged the gap. She was there for both of us in a way that no one else in our lives had ever been.

I often struggled with myself looking at my life and where I was and feeling as though it wasn't really me. I should be happy, I told myself, trying to ignore all the terrible things we went through, but it never worked. I knew I should go back to therapy and try to process myself. Soon, I thought, maybe next month. I still had a score to settle, but it felt less possible by the minute.

I wasn't sure if I was ready to give up chasing him just yet. I just needed something to grab on to, something that would lead somewhere for a change. Something had to go in my favor eventually, right? Maybe I was just fooling myself.

I felt my eyelids drooping and the voice droning on the TV was making it harder to keep them open. Star had shifted to lay on top of me and already cuddled herself to sleep so I was stuck there. The couch was incredibly comfortable at least. I let my eyes close, and I could hear the rain starting outside, the first drops from a tropical storm rolling in from the sea. It wasn't anything dangerous, not that I wasn't used to facing down a storm.

My dreams always take me back to that damn island. It's not always the same events, but I'm always on the island and the sky is raging. Sometimes I'm fighting the monster, sometimes I see my friends dying, sometimes I'm strapped to the table in the basement, and sometimes I'm making sandwiches for the president but we're still on the island for some reason. I haven't figured that particular one out, but it's happened more than once.

Tonight was no different. No sooner had my eyes closed than I found myself standing on a cliff, looking out at the tumultuous waters feeling lost and alone. Lightning cracked through the clouds, and I spread my arms wide and screamed. The scene shifted and I was standing in the rubble of the collapsed building. The monster stood before me, though it looked more human than I remember. He held out his hand and I fell through the ground and then into the sky. I was above the ocean now, storm raging around me with nothing but crashing waves below. My neck tattoos flared a blue glow, and I began to fly, using my fire like jet propulsion like I was *Iron Man* or something. After a moment I flew up through the clouds into open sky, and the fire engulfed me searing my flesh.

I screamed and opened my eyes just in time to see the water hit me. Gasping for air I sat up and wiped the water from my eyes.

"Oh my god Tri! Are you okay!? I came to check if you wanted breakfast and your whole head was smoking!" Star blurted.

I looked down at the soggy pillow and saw the symbols from my tattoo had burned themselves into the pillow I was laying on.

"I… think I'm fine. I was dreaming." I said. I ran my hand along my neck, and it felt warm to the touch but unharmed.

"On the island again?" Star asked soaking up some of the water with a towel.

"It's always the island, so yeah. I dunno I was flying and then just caught on fire and started to burn up." I explained picking up the pillow to show her.

"That was your favorite pillow. I'll try to find another one later. Are you sure you're okay?" She asked, setting the pillow aside to hold my hands.

"Yeah, just a little rattled. You mentioned food? I'm starving."

"Oh, yeah… I made French toast!"

She tugged at my arm to get me off the couch and lead me to the kitchen. Cherry was already sitting at the table with her nose buried in a manga. She smiled as I entered.

G'morning Mommy! Sleep good?

The voice chimed in my head, and I smiled. Her voice sounded like any other teenage girl would, which made it a little less weird that she was speaking in my head and not from her mouth. I stood next to her and gave her a kiss on the head.

"Well enough, little one. What are we reading today?" I asked, taking my spot at the table. Cherry set the book down to take a sip of her orange juice.

It's about a girl that gets saved by a local gang leader and falls for him even though she doesn't like bad boys. He's got a really cool tattoo on his back, reminds me of yours a little bit.

"Hmm, that sounds interesting. Let me know where it goes." I said patting her on the head.

"Okie dokie girls! It's ready!" Star announced.

She stepped in carrying a large platter, set it down on the table, and then handed us plates. Each one was stacked with golden brown slices of French toast drenched in syrup and sprinkled with powdered sugar. There was also a plate of bacon and scrambled eggs, and some fresh fruit which was Cherry's preferred breakfast. She still had some of the toast though, it looked too good to pass up.

I checked the time on my phone and realized Cherry should have been at school already. I washed a bite of food down with some milk and then signed at her 'Are you late for school?'

She shook her head.

I've got a late start today; teachers needed some prep time for exams, so they have us only coming for half the day. Mama is going to take me shopping at the bookstore and then drop me off.

"Time for more already? You go through those quick!" I laughed.

She just nodded and went back to her book as she munched on some fruit.

"Most of the new manga she reads release new issues weekly, so we go pretty regularly." Star said, pouring herself a glass of juice.

"Makes sense, I always struggled to read comics because I had to wait a week between issues. I like to let a run finish and then get them all at once so I can binge through them. Well, hope you guys have fun while you're out today. I'm going to try to get back to my office and figure some stuff out."

"Don't stress yourself out too much, take it easy. I don't want to hear about the house burning down while I'm getting my nails done."

"I'll be fine. I'm going to medicate and blast some music so I can center myself before I get started." I said, chewing on some bacon.

Please remember to open the window, that stuff stinks worse than a skunk.

"Sure thing. I'll put the vent fan in, so it all goes outside."

We sat and finished our meal together. It was so nice to have almost everyone together like this. Callie said in her last call that she would be home soon with an interesting surprise, and I was eager to hear about the trip. Coming out of the fog of depression into a warm loving environment was helpful to say the least. I helped Star clear the plates and followed her upstairs to get dressed.

"Are you sure you'll be okay? You know I worry about you..." Star asked.

I wrapped my arms around her and kissed her on the cheek.

"I'll be fine. I'm coming out of it again, and I'm ready to get back to the swing of things. You go have fun; you've done enough worrying for me lately."

"I'll never do enough, but thanks. I need to get out and pamper myself some." She said, leaning her head against mine.

"Call me if you need anything and I'll be right back." She said.

"If I'm *calling* you then something terrible has already happened and I might need bail." I joked. She knows I detest talking on the phone. She jabbed my ribs with her finger.

"You know what I mean. I love you, take it easy... mean it."

"I will, love. I will."

We shared a kiss and I let her get dressed so she could leave while I made my way to the basement where I built my office. She was right, she needed today for herself as I had been taking up too much of her energy lately. I hated that I made her worry so much.

CHAPTER 2

Half the basement was our home theatre where we watched movies together in big comfy loveseats, it had a small kitchen attached for making snacks. The other half was my personal space. I had set up a nice area with lights and supplies to print, build, and paint miniatures. It was a great way to relax, and I wound up with something cool I could put on the table for games. Sometimes I got the family to play Dungeons and Dragons with me for game night, but usually I went to the local game store and played with some old friends there.

The rest of the basement was my office, and where I had my custom computer rigs set up. There was one that was strictly for gaming and had my other systems all hooked up to a big TV with a comfy chair for long sessions. The other was work oriented and was loaded with cutting edge security tech to keep me safe and hidden while browsing the shadier parts of the internet looking for leads. Proxy server connections, VPNs, encrypted hard drives, I couldn't explain how all of it works, but I know enough to use it. I paid my best techs to put it together for me and teach me what I needed to keep it running. I had access to lots of information and tools to sort through the usual algorithms and really get to the good stuff when needed.

My favorite part of the whole setup though was the sound system. I had each room in the house equipped with its own blue tooth system that I could control from my phone, but down here I had a really unique system. Fully immersive 7.1 surround sound with top quality amps and speakers set up by a professional sound engineer I met backstage at an EDM show a few years ago. I spent a small fortune on this system and the quality shows. The sound is crystal clear, and the room is soundproof to boot so I can jam out and forget about the rest of the world without bothering the rest of the house.

I also set up security monitors so I can keep an eye on the house and make sure no one is sneaking in while I'm occupied. I flicked on some heavy music, activated the ventilation system, and pulled out a decorative box where I hid my stash of good weed. While I'm normally a death metal girl, today I opted for some Deftones, still heavy, dark, and full of just the vibes I needed to clear my head after a long funk. I packed a bowl, summoned a small blue flame, and got a good toke while only choking a little bit. I sunk into my comfortable chair and let the music flow through me.

Once I felt the high kick in, I turned to my computer, checking the security cameras while waiting for the network encryption to start up. Star and Cherry had already left, and the house was empty except for the housekeeper, Beatrice, and our cats: Echo, Ginger, and Nipsy. Echo was my Siamese baby even though she was getting old and wanted nothing to do with the two kittens. Ginger was a tortie, and Nipsy was a mostly white, orange tabby. They were currently destroying what I hoped was a toy mouse in the hall while Echo napped peacefully in the living room window. Everything was otherwise calm and normal.

I needed to check in with my team and see if anything had surfaced while I was away. It had been at least a month since I checked in with any of them, but they knew what I was going through. All this time searching and failing to find anything was wearing on me, and I hated feeling so helpless knowing that such a terrible person was out there doing who knows what to another innocent victim. I needed to stop him, but I was afraid that I was running out of time. My only solace is that we hadn't seen him make any major moves yet, but I couldn't be certain that was entirely good.

As soon as I connected to the network, my notifications light up like fireworks. I had automated scripts set up that watched for keywords in various news outlets and pulled stories to me if they matched the criteria we set. Of course, looking for things like magic and monsters brought up tons of gaming news but we filtered that out. These were different and before I had a chance to look through them my secure VOIP line rang. I answered, but the line immediately went dead. A moment later it rang again, and I answered and again it went dead and rang again. This was code for an emergency, I answered the final time.

"We have something you need to see. Patching it through now." A male voice spoke.

I think it was my head tech Matt, but a lot of these guys sound the same on the phone when they are worked up.

A video came through and started to play. I was waiting for some choppy web footage or shaky phone camera video ripped from social media but to my surprise it was a news outlet from Florida. The anchors were discussing a story about a drug raid and mentioned that police stated some of the dealers were setting things on fire with their bare hands while others pelted the officers with small rocks. It resulted in a shootout but there were no casualties. They showed some security footage that wasn't clear but showed a shirtless man setting fire to a crate full of something from his bare hand. I studied the image; he didn't have any tattoos on his head or neck but it was clear he was producing the flames himself.

"What the fuck? Drug dealers?" I asked.

"It's not the only one. Similar stories have popped up all over the country, areas where known criminal rings operate. It's not just the U.S. either, we have pings out of China, Japan, Russia, and Mexico amongst others. That's just within the last week. Whatever it is, its Global." Matt said.

"Why the fuck didn't anyone call me sooner!?" I yelled.

"You told us only to use secure lines, and you haven't been answering. We were starting to fear that you had already gone looking." He replied.

I pinched the bridge of my nose in frustration, but it was my own fault so I couldn't be too mad. I flicked through the notifications from my searches and sure enough, tons of sightings of people seemingly using magic in small robberies, drug deals, and gang turf disputes. I knew Bach had planned to distribute globally, but drug cartels didn't seem like his style. This was strange and I had a feeling there was more going on.

"There's more. Some of the bigger gangs have been seen buying property on the outskirts of major cities and opening tattoo parlors. No reports of magic from those spots but given what you told us about the tattoo ritual it seemed like too much of coincidence."

My hand was autonomously rubbing the scars on my neck as he spoke.

"This is great, I mean… it's awful, but we finally have some kind of a lead. Do we have any idea where they are getting the Opulentia?"

"It's unclear if they are, there's no mention of that word anywhere in any of the reports or rumors. The drugs don't seem to be coming from anywhere new, the supply chain appears to be the usual places. Cartels, Triads, probably the feds too. I'm not trying to track all of the drug runners on the planet, but what we've seen seems unchanged since the first reports of magic started appearing. Two months ago."

His last words stung a little, I hadn't realized it had been that long since I checked in. I was furious with myself, I let my feelings get in the way and now it may be too late to stop him. I took another hit from my bowl to calm my nerves.

"Do we have any connection to Bach or Paradigm, or any other strange corporations?" I asked through the smoke.

"Nothing. Whatever their connection is its locked up tight and untraceable with our current resources." He said, sounding a little distracted.

Another alert went off, and I opened the other secure line into our call.

"Tri? Thank goodness you're back. Are you up to speed on the drug situation?" A female voice this time. Constance, a private investigator that has been working on the case for about two years now, the longest we've kept one.

"Yeah, do you have an update."

"I've been surveilling one of these tattoo shops for a couple weeks. Noticed a pattern in their deliveries. There's a lab above the tattoo shop cutting and packaging cocaine, it was already part of the Triad distribution before they opened the parlor. They don't sell out of that warehouse, but I noticed a dealer I recognized came and dropped off payment, got a shiny new tattoo while he was there."

"Any weird symbols or designs in the ink?" I asked eagerly.

"Nah, just a bit of gang flair, flowers, and guns sort of thing. But I had someone follow up with him and see what he was pushing. Get this, he's selling cocaine, but the power has a light red tint to it. Not long after, his gang shows up in a bust, start setting things on fire with their bare hands. It's wild looking, but I have to say it's nothing like what you showed us you can do. Looks like a party trick almost, they still doused stuff with liquor to make it burn." Constance said.

"So, they are cutting the drugs and putting the Opulentia in it? Could be why its weaker, its diluted by the drugs." I thought out loud.

"That's not all. This stuff is causing some bad withdrawals and overdoses. Not just the usual drug problems, seems like whatever they are adding in is creating a bigger chemical dependency and so the addicts are dropping like flies. It's almost as bad as Fentanyl." She added.

I leaned back into my chair to think. This was nefarious on a whole other level. Something about it all felt off but I could put my finger on it.

"We need to keep digging, keep an eye on these tattoo shops. It may just be the start of something bigger. I know that bastard is up to something, and we've got to figure it out before it gets any worse." I ordered.

"We've got twenty-four seven surveillance on a few locations already, and the team is scrolling the footage for clues. We'll keep a close eye on the situation. Will you be available for direct contact. I can set up the secure line to your phone if you want." Matt said.

"Yeah, what do you need me to do?" I asked.

"Plug in the USB and then run this program I'm sending you. I'll do the work from here. It will allow you to take our secure calls but it's not going to secure the whole phone like we did your system, so don't save anything you want to keep a secret." Matt replied.

"I'll put some more feelers out, see if I can get a trail on this weird coke product. It's probably got a fancy new name in the designer circles already, might give us new leads." Constance added.

"Sounds great, I need a break to let this all soak in. Let me know as soon as you guys find anything new. I need to come up with some kind of plan once we know a little bit more." I said, rubbing at my temples.

I disconnected the call and sat back in my chair again. My phone was plugged in, and I could already see Matt working his magic. Finally, after so many years of dead ends things were moving, but the whole thing felt wrong. This didn't have the pompous air or twisted elegance Bach carried himself with, this was dirty and basic. There had to be something else going on behind the scenes and I had to find it before it was too late. I turned the music back on and lost myself in my thoughts as it raged on.

I glanced at the security monitor, and swore I saw something for a split second before Beatrice stepped into frame to dust off some shelves. I rolled the footage back a little but saw nothing out of place. I told myself it was nothing, but I wasn't sure I believed it. It was probably just the weed making me paranoid, along with the stressful information I just received. It was probably nothing.

Right?

CHAPTER 3

I sat in my chair for a while, watching the security monitors like a hawk. I moved the feed to my main screen so I could see more clearly and slowly flicked through the various cams. Beatrice was cleaning, the cats were playing, and everything else sat quiet. I couldn't shake the feeling something was wrong. I was also thirsty, and decided I should walk through the whole house on my way to get some water.

I tried to digest the information from the call as I walked. I needed to understand the plan better to figure out what was happening. Selling drugs was certainly profitable albeit dangerous, the risk of it had me questioning the intention. What did Bach stand to gain from selling a weak version of his drug after all his work trying to make the effects permanent. Why were all these dealers suddenly opening tattoo shops? I clenched my fist.

"There has to be more to it!" I shouted, which startled Beatrice who I had accidentally snuck up behind.

I apologized and continued my tour of the house. It was angering that I wasn't finding anything in the house or my thoughts. I took some deep breaths and sat down in the window next to Echo, gently patting her back in the spot she likes. It was surprisingly nice outside after the small storm passed, and there was a flock of gulls looking for food down on the beach. I decided I needed to get some sun, I hadn't been outside in a month or more.

I kissed Echo on the head and gave her one more scritch before heading to the kitchen to get a drink. I filled up a large water bottle with cold water, grabbed a protein bar for a snack and made my way out the back door. I told myself I had to be content that I didn't find anything out of place in the house. I grabbed the basket we keep on the back deck with supplies for the beach and made sure to cover my pasty skin with sunscreen before stepping out into the sun. I was incredibly pale for someone that lived on her own private beach, partly genetic but mostly because I spent so much time inside in the dark like some kind of cave troll.

The beach was completely private, which meant we never had to worry about other people making a mess of things. There were the occasional nosy folks passing by in boats, or looking for hidden spots but our groundskeeper, Beatrice's husband Gerald, would politely ask them to leave. Mostly we just shared the beach with wildlife. Sometimes we even got nesting turtles and I would go out at night when the eggs hatched to make sure all the babies made it to the water. It was always so adorable to watch their little legs flop through the sand into the waves.

I walked to the large parasol we set up over our beach chairs and worked it open to help shield me from the sun. I took off my nightgown and panties, letting the breeze flowing in from sea dance across my skin. I always loved being naked outside, there was something about it that just felt so free. It felt refreshing as the wind passed over the light perspiration on my skin, and it felt strange on my newly bald head. I was used to feeling the wind in my hair, but without hair the sensation was a bit different like a gentle caress on the freshly exposed skin.

I pulled the bluetooth speaker from the basket and connected my phone so I could continue my music. Music has always been like therapy for me. Anytime I need to think or relax I turn on some tunes and let the sound rattle my brain until it functions the way I need. I prefer heavier music, but my taste really does vary into most genres. The older I get, the more I just want to experience new music as much as possible. I didn't want to be one of those old people that listened to the same bands they did in high school and made fun of anything the kids were enjoying.

I grabbed a brush from the basket and cleared the sand from the chair before I sat down. I laid back and watched the ocean for a while as the speaker played some Lofi instrumentals. The storm last night had churned up quite a bit of driftwood, seaweed, and other detritus on the shore. I noticed some gulls and crabs picking through it all looking for tasty snacks. I should bring Cherry down later to look for seashells like we used to do when we first brought her home, I thought.

Cherry loved the beach. I think it helped her remember her parents and friends from the island. She could spend hours reading or playing in the sand. A few times she's brought friends home from school for little beach parties. She didn't have tons of friends, but the ones she did have seemed to be great for her. We made sure that she knew not to use any of her powers around folks from school, but I was sure she talked to her best friends telepathically. She was taking to her new life better than we expected.

I was often worried about her fitting in, growing older, being rebellious. Teenagers were already a handful, and I wasn't looking forward to adding magic powers to the equation. We did our best to meet her needs and give her space, but I always feared Bach would show up and take her from us. I don't think he knows how special she is, and I wanted to keep it that way. She had more talent with her magic than Star or me and she was clearly different from any of the others that Bach tortured. I could sense a strength in her that felt familiar, it reminded me a little of the monster but calm and collected.

Star and I had decided to keep our powers in case we came across Bach or another one of those creatures, but Callie decided to let Cherry take hers away. That was something truly incredible about Cherry that we definitely didn't want Bach to know about. As far as we knew she was the only person that could not only control all the elements but separate the blood of the monster from a person and remove their powers. Callie laid down on the kitchen table, and we made a small incision on her palm while Cherry set up candles like Devon had taught her. I don't think the ritual added anything to the process, but Cherry insisted it helped her focus so that the removal wasn't as painful.

We watched as Cherry lifted Callie's hand and touched her blood. She closed her eyes and focused on her task. The air in the room changed, there was a weight to it, and the candles began to flicker. The flames grew taller, and the lights in the house dimmed for a brief moment before Cherry began to make a motion with her hand. A stream of dark blood rose out of the wound and began to swirl around Cherry's hand as it waved through the air. Callie seemed to be in a trance and fully unaware of what was happening. Cherry gathered up the blood into an orb and then summoned flames around it which caused it to congeal and dry like a scab before dropping it with a wet thud into a bucket we had waiting next to the table.

Callie sat up from her trance and everything went back to normal. She said it was like being asleep and she dreamed that she fell apart and someone was putting her back together. Sadly, it didn't do much to bring Callie's memory back, but it did completely remove her magic abilities. Callie said it was a relief to put that darkness behind her so she could focus on living her new life while she tried to figure out her old one. Part of me envied her for letting go.

I was unable to let go of the past, my mind held on to every shred of memory from the island against my will. I felt so driven to stop the man that had done this to us, that I let it consume me, and when it spit me out I was in a depression so deep I nearly gave up everything. I was just thankful that Star understood, and even though it was hard, she continued to love and support me. She was truly special.

I lost track of time sitting in the chair, and actually dozed off for a short time. I woke up when I felt something crawling and looked down to see a crab curiously inspecting some of my tattoos.

"If you pinch me, I'm having crab for dinner." I grumbled, startling the crab.

I watched it tumble off the side of the chair and scurry away to hide in the sand. I sat up and stretched which made my back pop in that really good way that makes everything tingle for a second. I checked the time on my phone, it was almost five pm. Cherry should be home from school, probably doing homework. I wasn't sure what all Star had planned for the day or if she would even be home yet.

I pulled my clothes on quickly in case Cherry had a friend over and gathered up my things into the basket to head back inside. As I turned to walk away, I felt something watching me. I spun back around, sure that someone was standing on the beach but saw no one. My buzz had worn off during my nap, so I couldn't blame the weed this time. I clenched my fist and it blazed with blue flames. I could feel my tattoos flare as well, I was ready to fight but there was nothing. I blasted an orb of fire into the water's edge spraying foam and sand into the air and scaring away the sea gulls.

"Something is fucking with me…" I thought out loud.

I waited for a moment, letting the heat forming in my body cool down with my emotions. Nothing, no one but me was on the beach. I shook it off and headed back towards the house. The stress was getting to me again.

Inside I could hear music from upstairs. Cherry was listening to some Japanese pop rock band; she was absolutely obsessed with Anime and Japanese culture. We told her we would take her to Japan again this summer if her grades were good, but her grades weren't really a concern and Star had already made the reservations. I was looking forward to the sushi personally.

I looked around for Star, but it didn't seem like she was home yet, Cherry must have had a friend drop her off. I checked the driveway for a car, but only saw my truck and Cherry's bike. No guests, nothing out of place, everything is fine. Beatrice was starting to cook dinner and smiled at me as I stepped into the kitchen.

"Did you enjoy the beach dear?" she asked.

"Yes, almost brought you some fresh crab." I replied. "Have you noticed anything strange today? Anything moved around or anyone snooping?"

"No, it's been a quiet day. Gerald is out with some friends and won't be back until later, so I've been keeping busy up here. Why, should I be expecting someone?" she asked, setting down her knife.

"No... must have been a dream I guess." I answered.

"Well, I'm happy to see you up and about at least. I cleaned your bedroom while you were outside, there's some of your favorite incense burning to cleanse the smell and your clothes are in the laundry room."

"Thanks, B., you're a treat. What's for dinner?"

"Smash burgers and fries for you and Star, roasted veggies for Cherry. Cookies for dessert, snickerdoodles." She said going back to her cooking.

"My favorite. You're the best, B!" I said and gave her a shoulder hug.

I walked to the living room and sat on the couch to watch some TV. I grabbed my phone and texted Star.

Hey. :) Hope you're having a good day.

Yeah! I got my nails done, met up with an old client for coffee.

Nice. B's making smash burgers and some cookies.

She's happy to see you out of the bedroom too!

Be home soon!

<3

<3<3

I set the phone down and turned on the TV. I scrolled through the streaming apps for a while and then turned it off. I just wasn't in the mood to search through the abundance of options for something to watch. I found it hard to watch anything but YouTube most days. I liked to watch other people play games and see stories I might otherwise miss. I had a few channels I really enjoyed: Markiplier, Jacksepticeye, Game Grumps. I usually watched them when I needed to laugh and wind down, but my mind was elsewhere.

No matter how much I dwelled on it, I couldn't put together Bach's plan with the information I currently had. It was really eating at me. We had the best lead we've had in years though. Something was definitely happening, and I just hoped we could get ahead of it. I tried reporting the event to the police when we got back, but of course they thought I was just making up stories. No one took me seriously until I showed them the magic, but I wasn't about to trust the police with that and get locked up or experimented on again.

My phone buzzed; Callie had texted me.

> *Hello love! I heard you were out of your gloom. I should be home in about a week. I miss you all so much. <3*
>
> That's great! Can't wait to see you! We miss you too <3

I smiled. I couldn't wait to see her; it's been a year since she left and I just wanted her to hold me again. She was one of the only women I'd ever met that was taller than me, and I loved that about her. Star was the shortest of us and I always enjoyed being in the middle, especially in bed. I was also looking forward to that again when Callie got back.

I heard the front door and looked up to see Star carrying in some bags from shopping. I stood up and took a few from her giving her a kiss on the cheek.

"Thanks, Cherry got a ton of books this week there's another bag in the car too. I got some new clothes and plenty of snacks." She said, relieved that I took some of the load.

"Callie said she's coming home next week!" I chimed.

"Yeah, she texted me a little while ago. I'm so excited to see her again!" Star replied.

We carried the bags to the dining room table and set them down so Star could sort through it, and I went out to grab the other bag of books for Cherry. It was a huge stack of manga, several different series. I closed the door with my hip, and stopped in my tracks when I turned around. There was someone standing in the driveway.

Not standing, walking. There was someone walking in my mile long driveway towards my house. I set the books down and could feel the heat rising, my neck tattoos were starting to glow, and I stepped out of the garage, eyes locked on the shadowy figure. I raised my palm ready to blast the man with fire, almost certain that it was *him.* The figure raised his arm as well and waved.

"Sorry to scare you miss Triana, just little ol' me!" Gerald said.

It was my grounds keeper, carrying a bouquet of flowers. I sighed heavily and dropped my arm to my side.

"Sorry Gerald, B said you would be home late I thought you were an intruder." I said.

"Be kind of strange for an intruder to carry flowers up the driveway…" Gerald replied.

"I have some strange enemies."

Gerald walked up to me and gave me a hug.

"Glad to see you movin' around Trianna! Nice haircut, look good on ya!" He said. "My friend had to leave early; babysitter got sick. Beatrice in the kitchen still?"

"Yeah, she's making smash burgers for us tonight." I said, picking up the bag of books.

"She makes a mean burger. I'm gonna sneak in and give her these flowers. It's the anniversary of when we first met you know?" he said, gently patting the bouquet.

"You're such a sweet man, Gerald. You two warm my heart."

"You not so bad yourself, got a good head on your shoulders. Doing good raising that kid and loving them two women you got. I just try hard and hope for the best." He smiled.

I smiled back and watched him start to sneak around the back of the house to surprise his wife. They were good people. They didn't judge anything about our life, which a lot of people would consider unusual. They loved us like we were their own flesh and blood, and we always treated them like family not servants. I made sure they were paid more than their job was normally worth, and always had anything they needed. I paid for their son to go to college so he could follow his dreams. They didn't were a little confused about the magic, but after we explained everything that happened, they went right back to loving us.

Cherry met me in the living room as I came back in with her books, apparently this bag had the next issue she was waiting for. I handed them off and told her dinner would be ready soon and she just hugged me and flopped on the couch to read. I caught up with Star still sorting things in the dining room.

She had done a lot of shopping for Cherry, aside from the books there was quite a bit of clothes and school supplies. There were at least two bags full of snacks for the pantry, bulk boxes of some of our comfort snacks for when periods rolled around. Chocolate, crackers, cookies, all a good mix of crunchy, chewy, sweet, and savory. A couple jars of peanut butter, and two big jars of pickles for me. Peanut butter and pickle sandwiches were one of my favorite snacks, high or not.

"Good day?" I asked, wrapping my arms around her.

"Very, how about you?" she replied, leaning back into my hug.

"Not sure good is the word. But not bad either. Got a new lead, strange activity and some people using magic but really weak. Something off about the whole thing. Been paranoid all day for some reason too." I said.

"Oh, Tri that's a lot! Are you serious?" She exclaimed.

"Yeah, but it's a bit dry. Matt and Constance are looking into it more. Waiting to hear back from them so I can come up with a plan."

"But you found people using magic? For real? Is it Bach's people?"

"Nah, it's a bunch of small thugs and drug dealers, linked back to something from the major cartels. Cocaine with a red tint to it, but it's like it's really watered down. They don't look to have the powers we saw back on the island. Bach's nowhere to be seen either, but he's got to be up to something. No way someone else found a way to make that stuff, right?" I asked.

"Probably not. Maybe he wants to muddy the waters, throw people off his trail before he starts pushing the real deal. Make it seem like he perfected it after there's a market for it?" she replied, turning to face me.

I furrowed my brow. "Hard to say 'til I get something more solid. Smells fishy to me though. The whole thing just doesn't seem like his style, so there's got to be something else going on that we haven't seen yet."

"I'm kind of surprised we didn't hear about it sooner, people suddenly using magic should be a bigger deal. Why isn't it in the news?"

"It's hit a few small local outlets, but I bet Bach is paying to keep it suppressed. Could just be getting swept under the rug because it's all drug related."

I helped her put stuff away while we waited for Beatrice to call us for dinner. I heard her shriek and then laugh while I was talking with Star, so Gerald's surprise had worked out. We came back downstairs just in time to see them carrying the food to the dinner table and helped set places. Cherry floated into the room a few moments later, ready to eat as any of us.

Dinner was delicious, the cookies were perfect, and we all had a nice big family dinner together. I wanted to enjoy it more, but I was only thinking about Bach and his scheming. After dinner I gave everyone a hug and then headed back down to the basement. I scanned through the day's security footage, trying to prove to myself that something had been there but found nothing. I packed another bowl and sat brooding in my chair staring at the screens.

I checked through the data Matt had sent over, looking at the locations of all the tattoo shops and other points of interest trying desperately to see a pattern. I got an alert from Constance.

Got a lead. Club near Charlotte.
Designer drug crowd getting ahold of the powder.
Some are calling it Pink Wiz. I dunno.
Wanna take a field trip?

I stared at the phone and thought for a moment. If I could get a sample of the drug, I could see if Cherry could pull any Opulentia out of it and know for sure. Then we could try to trace the source back to Bach and deal with him. It wasn't much but it was something. I pulled up the Charlotte tourist page online to see what events were going on in the area. Perfect, there was an Anime convention this weekend. I could bring Star and Cherry, have a little fun there and then meet up with Constance for some reconnaissance.

Yeah, I'll take the girls to the anime show there this weekend.

Sounds good.

I'll head there tomorrow to get info. Where you want to meet?

We can meet at the hotel and then hit the club.

Send me your location when you're ready.

I set the phone back down and took a hit from my bowl. I watched the security monitors through the smoke while my music rattled my thoughts away. Star was back in the living room watching her show, Cherry was heading to her bedroom to get ready for bed. Beatrice and Gerard were holding hands and walking down to the beach to spend some time together. The cats were asleep in the dining room. Everything was calm and normal, just as it should be.

My body was tingling from the weed, and I felt a pleasant warm feeling washing over me. I set the bowl down and opened up another locked drawer. Inside was my other relaxation helper: my Magic Wand. Nothing cleared my thoughts better than an orgasm, and it had been a while since I had one. I knew I was ready to break out of my spiral if I was ready to masturbate.

I pulled up some porn, took another hit, and let my wand work its magic. It didn't take long, and I let myself enjoy a couple of consecutive O's. Masturbation is great for the body and mind, add in a little buzz and it's exquisite. After the fourth orgasm I put the wand away and melted into my chair. I was out of breath, but fully relaxed and mostly thought-free for the first time all day.

I swapped the porn over to YouTube and then ordered three VIP tickets to the anime convention in Charlotte. The hotel hosting the event was full, but I booked a nice suite at a fancy place a few blocks away with shuttle service. Cherry was going to be so excited when I told her about it, and that she could bring one of her friends. I'd let Star chaperone them, because she would probably like to see some of the panels, and I could track down some 'Pink Wiz' and get things in motion.

I checked the cameras one last time, and then dozed off in my chair to the soothing screams of Jacksepticeye playing through some underwater exploration game.

CHAPTER 4

A few days later, I was piling bags into the back of a Dodge Caravan I rented for our trip. It felt weird being excited about driving a minivan, considering I usually drove sports cars, or my custom truck built by my old friend Jackson who ran his own custom vehicle business now. I helped him get it off the ground a couple years back and now he builds all kinds of customer vehicles for famous people, and the occasional friend. This van was huge, with plenty of space for luggage, and each section had its own air controls. The sound system was almost as good as mine, and the seats were so comfortable, perfect for a road trip.

Star was on her way back from picking up Cherry's friend Savannah to take with us, they were both ready to explode with excitement. They each had a few costumes to wear for the event, some Sailor Scouts that I was familiar with and then some other more obscure manga characters that I'm sure I would be chastised for not recognizing. All morning Cherry had been filling my head with ramblings about the con and how excited she was. I was thrilled she was going to enjoy herself. Star loved the idea too and was glad I was getting out of the house even if it was going to be work for me.

I had told her about the plan, and she agreed it could be a good place to start. She was always supportive of my ideas, even if they made her worry. I know she wanted revenge on Bach too, but she didn't feel quite as strongly about it as I did. She wanted to put it behind us but agreed that he needed to be stopped from harming more people. I hated making her worry. She always urged me on though and was always there to ground me when it got the better of me.

I got all of our bags in, and left space for Savannah's just as Star pulled up to the house in her Volkswagen Bus, another custom-built Jackson special. It was painted with a beautiful blue body and white top, the classic look, with a very 70s inspired interior. The seats in the back two rows could even fold down into a bed, with a hidden mattress stored on the roof. I had a rack installed on the back that could carry her old scooter too, restored and painted to match. I thought she was going to die when I brought it home for our anniversary, she had always wanted one since she was little.

We loaded the last of the bags, grabbed a few road snacks and headed off. It was a great ride to Charlotte, we sang songs, played silly word games, and just had a blast. You would never know that three quarters of the car's inhabitants could bend elements to their will and were secretly on a mission to stop a nefarious madman's evil plot. Today, we were just family and a close friend taking a road trip.

With traffic, it was only about four hours to Charlotte, so we drove for a few and then stopped to have lunch. We found a nice Asian buffet with good reviews and ate until our bellies hurt before piling back in the van for the rest of the journey. We stopped at a gas station to grab some drinks and top off the gas tank and then resumed. Star and the girls fell asleep, and I happily continued to drive.

I loved to drive, always have. Partially because I got motion sick easily if someone else was driving, but mostly because I just loved the sensation. I felt connected to the car and the road and it unlocked some feeling of adventure inside me. I could go anywhere, see anything, and all I needed was a tank full of gas and four wheels on the asphalt. To be honest, I probably also needed a GPS and someone to tell me I was still going the wrong way because my sense of direction was only getting worse with age.

I pulled into the hotel and the valet service was already waiting with a cart for our luggage. I woke the girls up and handed the keys to the valet before we walked inside to check in. We got our room keys, and our luggage was carried up to the suite for us. The suite had three rooms, one for Star and myself, and one each for the girls though I suspected they would probably share one to spend more time together. I wanted to make sure they had the option of personal space though.

Registration for the con started the next morning, so we had the evening to unwind from the trip. We ordered a pizza and watched a couple movies until the kids started to doze off and went to their room together. Star and I did the same.

We got into our jammies and collapsed into the bed together to enjoy the end of our day.

"Do you think they're making out?" I asked.

Star gasped and chuckled. "I don't know if they like each other like that. Savannah's dad might have a fit."

"They're probably making out." I said. Star poked me in the ribs.

"Not everyone has your libido, Tri. Also, Cherry told me she has a crush on some boy in her history class." she said.

"So? I used to date boys and make out with other girls." I retorted.

"Stahhhp!" Star said, almost shoving me off the bed.

"I'm just teasing. They're pretty tired from the trip, sugar crash probably has them passed out in there." I said, running my hand across Star's arm.

"I'm pretty worn out too. Are you meeting with Constance tomorrow?" she asked.

"Yeah, I'll walk you guys to the shuttle in the morning, find somewhere with a decent cup of coffee and wait for her to pick me up. We're going to get some nice club outfits and then try to mingle and find a connection for the drugs." I explained.

"Sounds like a fun date!" she teased.

"Nah, Constance isn't into women. I'm not sure she's into men either. Really job focused that one. Probably works too much to spend any time on a real relationship."

"Well, as long as she's happy."

"Mhm." I mumbled.

My eyes were already drooping, and I was dozing off. I barely noticed Star cuddling up against me and turning on the TV. She couldn't sleep in a strange place without the TV on, she said it calmed her nerves. I could sleep through just about anything, so it didn't bother me. It wasn't long before I was completely asleep.

The next morning, we all got dressed and headed downstairs for breakfast. The hotel had a full restaurant in the lobby, and they served a full breakfast menu. We had eggs and fruit and something that passed for coffee, but I needed something stronger. I walked the girls to the shuttle stop and told them to have fun as they left. I pulled out my phone and looked for a real coffee shop, and lucked out that there was one nearby. I had already texted Constance to let her know I was ready whenever she was.

I sat in the coffee shop for a little while, sipping something that was probably closer to chocolate flavored tar than a beverage and flicking through the news on my phone. Every day that passed there was less talk about the mystery magical drug dealers. Most I could find now was a few subreddits with the comments disabled. Someone was going through a lot of trouble to keep this hushed.

Constance appeared almost out of thin air and sat down at my table with coffee and donut in hand. I looked at the donut and she grumbled.

"Don't say it. I'm not a cop."

"I wouldn't be here if you were." I said, taking another sip of my coffee.

"I'm not sure about this shopping idea Trianna, I haven't gone clubbing since I was twenty-one." she said.

"You'll be fine, we'll look cute and if somehow we don't... well it's usually dark." I explained.

I was confident that we could fit in well enough. I was thirty-five, Constance was almost forty, but all sorts of people do all sorts of drugs these days. Some cute dresses, a little make-up, and some confidence and we'd have our connection in no time. There's no age limit on partying as long as you can match the vibe. I just had to figure out how to get her out of her head and into character enough to pass.

We finished up and then hopped in her rental car, a blacked-out SUV. It was a smart choice for blending in and not drawing attention while still looking important. We went to the mall and spent a few hours trying on dresses until we had something I could convince her to be seen in. She settled on a dark green evening dress that showcased her figure pretty well. She was built like someone that worked out a fair amount but spent just as much time sitting in a dark car watching people. Both were true.

I found a sleek black outfit with black stones and gold accents. It fit me like a glove and really showed off my assets, sure to turn heads as soon as I walked in. I saw Constance eyeballing the price tags and starting to sweat.

"Relax, I've got it. My op, I'm footing the bill." I said.

"You sure we can't get something cheaper? I feel like I'm being gawked at, and I don't even have it on yet." She mumbled.

"No, if we've gotta do it then we do it with style. We'll be back to grungy shirts and jeans soon enough. Enjoy yourself a little." I teased.

She mumbled some more and waited for me to check out. I picked up some matching clutches and some light jewelry to round out the outfit.

"Do you even wear make-up?" I asked curiously.

"Not usually. Used to, but I got decent genes and clear skin, so I don't wear it often. It's probably been a decade since I last painted a whole face." she replied.

"Not a problem, I've got a plan. Let's get lunch, and then we'll go hit the salon and have some professionals give us a makeover. Should fill enough time before the clubs open."

She sighed, I laughed. It was going to be fun for me at least.

The day went by quickly as we prepared. Lunch at a nice deli with some fantastic sandwiches, afternoon spent at a high-end salon getting makeup and hair done professionally, and then a light meal in the car on the way back to her hotel to change. We looked amazing, and I couldn't help but notice Constance checking herself out in the mirror. I think she surprised herself a little bit with how well she looks. Sometimes we all need a little reminder.

I checked in with Star and everyone was having fun at the convention. She told me to be careful, and I told her I loved her. I tucked my phone away in my clutch and focused. It was mission time, and we needed to get our hands on some drugs.

Constance was doing her best to walk in heels, but I had switched on my best imitation rockstar persona. I was serving a hard look and proud of it. The club was hidden away off the main strip because if you didn't know where it was you weren't getting in anyway. Our outfits would get us to the bouncer, but I would probably need my wallet to get us through the door. I had already stopped for cash on the way just in case.

The bouncer eyed us up and down, and I decided not to chance it and slipped him a hundred-dollar bill before he could say no. He tucked it in his pocket and adjusted his collar as he waved us inside. The inside was packed and loud, a local DJ was spinning custom mixes and really ramping up the bpm. I loved it, Constance was already uncomfortable.

We took a lap around the club, getting an idea of the layout and making sure the party boys noticed we were here. We needed to draw some attention to find a hookup but didn't want to get taken advantage of by the general creeps. I told Constance to relax and sit at the dark end of the bar to watch while I played the bait. I mostly needed her to make sure no one slipped anything in my drink when I wasn't looking.

I bought a couple girls drinks and danced with them for a little bit, really showing off and scanning the booths for anyone that might have what we wanted. Constance had already confirmed a dealer was pushing the stuff here. I suddenly realized I had no clue what the hell I was looking for, I had my weed delivered by a courier, what the hell did I know about undercover coke dealers?

Constance actually made it out to the dance floor after an hour of waiting and watching. I danced with her, and she started to really get into it. After a little dancing she leaned in towards me and I thought she wanted to kiss me, but she was just faking it to whisper in my ear.

"Booth in the back. Sleezy looking guy with the underage girls. Pretty sure he's our guy. How do you want to do this?" she asked.

"Honestly, I didn't think this far. I'm glad you spotted him, are you sure though?"

I turned to see the man she was talking about. He looked a few years older than us and was surrounded by a flock of girls that probably got in with fake IDs just trying to have some fun. He had a real sleazy vibe and was getting handsy with the two girls closest to him. I was always grossed out by guys like him.

"You could try asking him for some party favors, see what he offers." Constance suggested.

"Hm. Wait a sec, what is he doing now?" I said, tilting my head around her for a better view.

The guy was sprinkling a small bag of powder onto the nearest girl's shoulder and snorting it off with a rolled-up bill. His eyes rolled back in his head for a moment and then shimmered with energy. He got the attention of all the girls and held out his hand to show them little arcs of electricity between his fingers. The girls all gasped and cheered eager to participate in what he was showing them.

He leaned over and whispered to the young blonde beside him, and her face flashed with uncertainty for a moment before nodding as he guided her hand towards his crotch. I felt the heat rising inside my body.

"I've got an idea. I'll create a distraction and then you take care of him in the chaos." I said, clenching my fist and scanning the ceiling as I walked away.

"What do you want me do!?" she shouted.

"Improvise!" I shouted back.

I left her standing on the dance floor a little confused and made my way towards the bathroom. The club had to have a sprinkler system to be in code, but I couldn't see any fire alarm handles anywhere. I did, however, spot a few sprinklers in the mostly empty hall leading to the bathroom. There were a few people, but they were paired off in make out sessions and likely wouldn't notice what I was about to do.

I raised my hand, pointing a finger at one of the sprinkler heads and fired a small blast of blue flame. As soon as the flame hit the sprinklers the whole system blasted on, spraying water all over the club. The music cut off and the lights came on as the club manager urged people to exit the building calmly over the PA. As I had hoped, the various levels of sobriety mixed with sudden showers led to shrieks and scattering of bodies as they tried frantically to get out.

As I came back around the corner I checked for Constance and gave her a nod as we made eye contact while she scanned the club. She focused her attention on our mark and just as he was making a run for the door, stepped in front of him and delivered an uppercut worthy of Mortal Kombat. I could almost hear the announcer shout "TOASTY!" in falsetto. He hit the floor unconscious, and I rushed over to check his pockets.

I pulled a few packets of powder from his jacket, and then tossed his wallet to the girl he had accosted who was hiding under the table to stay dry. She was frightened but took it and stuffed it in her bag. We picked him up and carried him outside with us in the commotion and before people could ask, shuffled him to the alley beside the bar and dropped him in the trash where he belonged. We rushed back through the crowd to get to our car before anyone could say they saw us doing shady things in the club.

Once in the car, Constance quickly drove away and I checked the powder in the little bags. I had never done cocaine myself, but even I could tell the powder had an unsettling pink shade to it instead of the white color you might expect.

"Damn, you laid him out in one shot!" I exclaimed.

"I used to box for a few years after I graduated. Decided to quit before I took too many blows to the head. Still got a mean swing I guess." Constance grinned.

"You're full of surprises!" I replied.

"Well, I saw him getting handsy with those girls and felt he deserved it."

"Same, fuckin' sleazeball."

"What now? You said you have a way to analyze that?" she asked.

I nodded. Constance knew the story behind our magic from working with us, but I never told anyone about Cherry's ability to draw it out of people. I tried to keep most of her abilities a secret for her safety.

"Yeah, I'll take it back with me and I should know in a day or two if it's really the Opulentia, but I did notice the guy showing off a little bit of magic in the club so I'm pretty sure it's what we were looking for." I said.

"Alright, I'll drop you off at your hotel and then go tail him for a while. See if he can lead me to his supplier." Constance offered.

"Oh, great idea! Sometimes I forget you do this for a living." I said.

Constance chuckled and shook her head. She drove us back to my hotel and I offered her a quick hug before getting out, she grumbled but accepted.

"I'm not sure how deep this is going to go, but if we are going to start tangling with drug dealers you should get some protection." she said as I pulled away.

"I can literally shoot fire from my body…" I retorted.

"Yeah, but can it stop bullets? I've got some Kevlar back at my apartment I can bring you next time we meet up."

"Oh… right. Actually, I've got an idea about that. Star has some eccentric connections in the clothing world, I wonder if she can find someone to make me a suit!?"

"You… want a super suit? Like a comic book?" Constance stared incredulously.

"Less comic books, more sci-fi. I'm not trying to fight thugs in spandex, but I bet someone can work Kevlar into regular clothing." I replied.

"I don't think it works that way." she grumbled. "I'll bring you a vest, just in case it doesn't."

I chuckled and got out of the car. "Don't tell me you're all skill and no creativity Con!"

"Simple is usually more effective." she replied dryly.

I waved and headed inside, leaving her to do what she did best. I always felt that her general stubbornness and commitment to her job had kept her around longer than the other P.I.'s I had hired in the past. If Bach tried to take her out she would probably tell Death 'No.' and go back to work. She was reliable and had given us the most results so far. This was hopefully the lead we needed to figure this out once and for all.

CHAPTER 5

I decided to give Cherry time to enjoy her weekend with her friend before I would mention the drugs. I didn't want to spoil such a magical experience with my dirty business, and I didn't want to expose her friend Savanah to the weird world that was my private life. Cherry deserved as much happiness as I could provide as far as I was concerned. I bought myself a general pass on the last day so I could spend time with everyone too.

We got to see some a small concert from a local band performing anime theme songs in costume which was actually pretty neat. We hit the vendor hall and bought far too much stuff, but I had planned for that with the van. I was thrilled to see Cherry having so much fun, the girl was clearly in her element. I held Star's hand as we walked around and realized that I was still capable of feeling happy despite everything that happened to us, which was refreshing.

After the convention closed down we all took the shuttle back to the hotel to drop things off and go to dinner. We found a Mexican place with good reviews and stuffed our faces with various shapes and sizes of tortillas with meat, cheese, and veg. Savannah was gushing about the convention with Cherry in a rapid mix of speech and signing. A few times I heard her answer a question I didn't see Cherry ask, which confirmed my suspicion that she secretly communicated with her telepathically.

Savannah seemed like a good kid though that probably wouldn't cause any problems. I could tell they were very close. Cherry was a teenager now and probably starting to get feelings for other people. I wasn't sure if she had any kind of preference, though Star had mentioned she talked to her about some boy in one of her classes. It didn't matter to me who she was into, I was just curious what kind of talk I needed to have with her about keeping herself and her partners safe.

We spent the night in the hotel before driving back home so that everyone had plenty of time to rest and relax after the event. Just spending the day with them was more fun than I had expected and certainly more than I had in a while. It was really nice coming out of my depression cycle to all of this. Add in the trip to the club and the weekend was pretty solid all around.

Our room had a small balcony that looked out over the city and Star sat with me for a while outside. I packed a bowl and we just smoked and chatted for a while before bed. She told me about the panels she watched at the con, a lot of art and fashion related stuff during the day and then some horror panels in the evening. I told her about Constance destroying the creep at the club. We laughed and just enjoyed ourselves for the first time in a few months.

The day after we got home I had Cherry try to pull Opulentia from the cocaine, and sure enough she gathered a very small amount and burned it away. The power turned white again and seemed like a normal bag of cocaine. Part of me was tempted to try it, but I decided against it and flushed it down the toilet. I was well past my experimental phase with drugs, and not really in the best mental state to be introducing powerful stimulants.

I had given up drinking not long after we brought Cherry home. It took some effort, but I was in my fifth year of sobriety. I started going to therapy after the island to deal with the trauma and it helped a lot, but some things were never fully going to heal. My therapist suggested I try CBD for the anxiety which also helped some but we agreed marijuana might help more and so I started medicating with that to manage the darker thoughts. I would rather smoke some herbs to calm down than fall further into alcoholism especially raising a child.

Motion on the security camera caught my attention. A car was pulling up to the house that I didn't recognize. Cherry was in school, Star was out talking to some of her industry friends about my bulletproof suit idea, and Beatrice was helping Gerald with something in the garden. I felt my body tense up, but surely Bach wasn't going to be so bold to just show up at our house in the middle of the day, was he?

I fought the urge to rush up ready to fight and watched the monitor a moment longer. The car stopped and the back door opened. Callie climbed out of the back as her Uber driver opened the trunk to get her bags out. I let out a sigh of relief realizing I had missed the illuminated signage in the window and then smiled, partially because it wasn't a serious threat but mostly that my love had come home.

I rushed upstairs and met her in the hall as she came in the door. She immediately dropped all of her bags and we embraced. I started to cry tears of happiness to be holding her again. She laughed and squeezed me tighter. It was clear we were both happy for her to finally be home again.

"Trianna, what happened to your hair?" she asked after a moment.

"I cut it all off, it was time for a change." I replied, kissing her on the cheek.

"It looks great! Can you help me with the bags? I have lots of gifts for everyone. Is anyone else home?" she asked.

"Not right now, they should be back in a few hours. Just me." I said, picking up a couple of heavy bags.

"Ah, well I suppose you'll have to do." Callie chortled.

We carried the bags to the dining room table and then held each other once more. She always smelled amazing, and the scent brought back so many memories of the time spent together. A year isn't a terribly long time anymore but a year away from someone you love can still feel like an eternity. She tilted my face up with her finger and we kissed passionately. I practically melted in her arms.

Callie gently pushed me back against the wall and caressed my body as her hands moved downward. She scooped my legs around her and lifted me up so that we were the same height as we continued to kiss. I ran my fingers through her soft red hair and moaned as she nudged my head away to kiss my neck. There weren't many people that made me feel small and safe just with a kiss, but Callie knew just how to touch me and drive me wild.

I braced myself with my legs around her as she picked me up and set me on the table, pushing me onto my back as she took off my shirt. Her tongue danced across my skin eagerly exploring and teasing my breasts. I shuttered as she continued down and removed my panties. She rested the backs of my knees on her shoulders and plunged her tongue inside me as I quivered. I stroked her hair with one hand, while interlocking our fingers with the other.

Bliss and ecstasy took hold as she brought me to climax with her tongue and fingers after a few minutes. She still knew all the right spots to make me cum quickly. My whole body quaked as my leg spasmed on her shoulder. I moaned loudly as she stood up, still using her fingers. She quickly removed her dress and climbed on top of me so I could return the favor.

I positioned myself under her, feeling the warmth of her thighs on my face as she laid down to continue pleasuring me. We continued for a while, both orgasming a few times before finally taking a break. We both had been thinking about that for a while and were well rewarded for our efforts. I got up and brought us some water to cool us down while we caught our breath.

"Mmm… I missed you so much." Callie said, panting.

"Really? I hadn't noticed." I replied. "Not sure anyone has ever gone from the front door to between my legs that fast."

"I'd like a go with Star later too. I missed you both tons." she added.

"I'm sure she'll be excited for that. So, how was the trip? Learn anything useful." I asked, tugging my shirt and panties back on.

"Not much. I saw a handful of places I recognized. I thought I might have found a small city in Germany that felt familiar, but I don't speak German and most everyone there did. Good food though. I also went to some places in Italy, Greece, London, and Ireland. I think maybe my family travelled a lot.

Doesn't help me find anyone, but I had a lot of fun seeing the world. I really owe you a lot of gratitude, Tri." She said, grabbing my hand.

"You don't owe me shit. You saved me from that hell hole on the island, and you're family now. I'd give you the world if I could." I replied.

"In a way, I suppose you have. Maybe next time we can all go together and see even more of it." She smiled.

"I'd like that. Just as soon as I find and end to all this with Bach." I said solemnly.

"Any progress? I've heard some weird rumors about drugs while I was away, but I wasn't exactly looking for things. I thought I saw something on the news about someone levitating in a nightclub in Germany but when I tried to find more information everything seemed to vanish, and I wasn't sure I had seen it." she explained.

"You might have, actually. Matt's been tracking some activity worldwide with the drug cartels. There're a few different kinds of drugs that are laced with Opulentia making the rounds. Constance and I got our hands on some pink cocaine from a club in Charlotte last weekend and Cherry pulled the blood right out of it, same as you."

"You gave Cherry cocaine?! *Trianna!*" She shouted playfully.

"No! I held the bag and then flushed it afterwards! If she wants to experiment when she's a little older that's fine but I'm not going to just hand her a bag of coke."

"I know, I'm just teasing. Drugs seem like a strange play for Bach though. I remember he always wanted to make sure there were no impurities in his product. I don't know why he would want it diluted with recreational stuff." she said, trying to think through it.

"See, that's what I said. The whole thing's off, and I don't trust it." I added.

I explained everything I had learned while we carried her bags to her bedroom and unpacked. We agreed that nothing about it made sense yet, and that there was a bigger plan involved. Not long after we finished unpacking Cherry came home from school and we decided to surprise her. She wasn't aware that Callie had gotten back just yet.

I came downstairs and made her a snack, while trying to act perfectly normal. Cherry sat at the table doing some homework and mostly paying me no mind. Callie snuck downstairs and took the plate of fruit from me, carrying it over to the table.

"I don't care much for math. Looks like you've got the hang of it though." Callie said setting the fruit down.

Cherry was mostly mute, but now and then managed to make some noises. The doctor suspected her vocal chords had never formed correctly due to the conditions on the island. Today, however, in her moment of sudden realization, she managed to shriek a little with excitement before jumping out of her chair into Callie's arms. She cried too; we all did. My heart melted to see them together again, my little chosen family.

Star got home soon after, carrying a large paper bag full of groceries that obscured her view. She sat them down, looked up to see the three of us sitting at the table waiting, and screamed with joy.

"Ohmygod! Callie you're home!" she cried.

"So glad to see you too, Twinkle." Callie replied, standing to hug her.

Twinkle was Callie's pet name for Star, like the kid's song. It was the only thing she could remember of her mother, and it meant a lot to her. They hugged and kissed lovingly, and I could see them both holding back since Cherry was still in the room. Star and Callie loved each other just as much as either one loved me. I couldn't be happier with our arrangement.

We had set up boundaries and rules, all equally agreed on. Star and I were married because it had meant something important at the time but given the state of marriages in the modern world it was less about the official standing and more about sharing the moment. Callie wasn't interested in any kind of ceremony and being our girlfriend was more than enough for her. We all agreed that any one of us was welcome to date if we chose to, and only needed approval of the other two if they wanted to bring that person to our home.

I tried to date a couple of times but found that with my current goals and trying to raise a little girl, having two women was enough for me. Star casually dates amongst her clients and business partners but rarely anything physical. Callie made a few attempts but like me was mostly focused on her personal goals. We had each other, and it worked well. Cherry didn't seem to mind having three loving, caring moms either.

We sat around and caught up for a while, just enjoying each other's company. Beatrice and Gerald joined us for dinner as usual and Callie passed out gifts for everyone. She found little treats and trinkets in every city she visited and told us stories about the little shops she found. Cherry got the most, of course, toys and candy and books. Beatrice and Gerald were included as well, Callie brought them some nice Italian clothes and accessories which just made their day. Star got a couple designer purses and some candy, and I got some nice boots, some signed records for my collection, and an adorable cat pendant that looked just like my Echo.

After dinner we watched a movie together and enjoyed some of the candies Callie brought us. When it was over we sent Cherry to bed and told Beatrice and Gerald goodnight as they left. Star and Callie shared a glance and then made their way upstairs to Callie's room. I would have joined them if Callie had not asked for individual time. Three-ways are fun sometimes, but they can be cumbersome. We usually traded off partners for one-on-one time, and saved let threesomes happen spur of the moment.

I went back down to the basement to see if anything new happened while I was busy. I took a hit of my bowl from earlier and snacked on some pickles as I scrolled through the handful of reports Matt had sent over about the tattoo shops. Supply shipments started coming in regularly, most came from the usual shipping services, but a black van with heavy tinted windows was also making deliveries now. Unmarked boxes carried in on a hand truck by men and women in black hoodies, black pants, and dark sunglasses. Always arriving long after business hours in the dark.

The tattoo shops were open for business and seem to have steady bookings. People came and went regularly, and reviews seemed to be good. No big names from the industry but not many complaints from the clientele either. Several of the shops focused on serving gang communities and pumped out lots of different gang colors and designs, but there were some serving ordinary folks that just wanted decent ink.

It was interesting information, but still not entirely useful. I considered setting up an appointment at the nearest one so I could check it out, but I wasn't sure I was ready to risk getting more Opulentia forced into me. It likely wouldn't do anything, but there was also a small chance Bach was watching these places too and might recognize me. I wasn't taking it off the table, but I wanted to talk with Constance and my girls first. My phone buzzed.

Got something from our sleazebag.

Supply goes through a few hops and then leads to big crime.

Shipping containers, paid off dock workers.

Probably Triads.

Shipment comes in, different group picks it up for distro.

Caught wind of a meeting at the next shipment.

Want me to recon, or want to tag along?

High Danger.

When and where?

Georgetown. Tomorrow Night.

Meet me here, we'll take my truck.

What's for dinner?

B cooking?

Yeah, not sure what it is.

I'll be there. XD

K.

I wasn't entirely sure how Constance got this far in a week, but she had a lot of experience tracking drug related crimes in the past, part of why I hired her to begin with. She had a strong will, good moral compass, and was much more competent than anyone wearing a badge. I was a little concerned that I hadn't asked Star about my bullet proof suit, but needs must when the devil drives. I shook my head and thought for a moment, I didn't have a clue what that meant or why I thought it.

I was just about to look it up when I heard the door open to my soundproof room. I turned around to see Callie carrying Echo who was purring loudly.

"Brooding in your bat cave, Master Bruce?" she asked, playfully.

"I'm certainly not Batman, if I was half as good at being a detective as him this whole debacle would be over with by now." I replied.

Callie set Echo down on my desk and then sat herself down in my lap.

"Is that why you have Star looking for a super suit?" She asked.

"It's not a super suit! I'm not looking spandex and a cape! Just something with some extra protection that won't make me look like I'm ready for a raid." I explained.

"Sure. You'd look good in leather catsuit and mask." she teased.

"Probably, but that wouldn't help me hunt bad guys." I replied.

"Are you busy?"

"No, I was about to turn in. Plans with Constance tomorrow night in Georgetown, following up on the pink drugs."

"Good, I want cuddles. Star's waiting too. I hear you've been spending most of your time down here again. Tonight you will spend with us instead." she said, standing up and tugging my arm to get me out of the chair.

"Yes ma'am." I eagerly replied.

She led me up the stairs to our master bedroom with the California king bed, gently but firmly pulling me along. Since coming home with us from the island, Callie had developed this dominance about her that just made me melt. She knew what she wanted and was always very direct but never mean about it, and Star and I both just ate it up. Something about her eyes when she spoke made us want to do anything she asked, it didn't have to be anything sexual.

We changed into our comfy pajamas and climbed into bed together, Callie pushing me into the middle. Star smiled and cuddled up against me from one side, while Callie stretched her arm across both of us for a hug and then snuggled in as well. I relaxed instantaneously as a warm sense of safety washed over me. With those two women by my side, I felt I could take on anything the world could throw at me.

"I spoke with Ezra about your Kevlar clothing idea, and they said they could probably put something together that would work but they might need a few months to make it. Apparently it's a difficult material to work with." Star chimed.

"Are you sure you're not trying to make a super suit?" Callie asked.

"It's not a super suit!" I pouted. "I just want to look good and have some protection if I have to go up against goons with guns!"

"You realize you can just wear regular Kevlar with normal clothes right?" Star chuckled.

"No, I kind of want to see her commission a super suit." Callie teased.

"She would look really hot in spandex." Star added.

"You're both insufferable." I sighed.

"You're cute when you pout, too!" Callie said, brushing her fingers across my stomach and kissing my cheek.

I shook my head and accepted defeat. I thought it was a cool idea, but I guess it did sound a little bit like a super suit. I thought for a moment about getting one made and what it would look like. Maybe something red and bold like *Daredevil*, or something cute and tight like *Ghost Spider*. I'd have to make sure it was flame resistant too, but it could work.

"Now that we are all together again, I have something I wanted to talk to you both about." Callie said, sitting up in the bed.

"It really caught me off guard, but while I was out exploring my past I met someone."

"Someone you know from before?" Star asked excitedly.

"No…" Callie smiled.

She bowed her head, and blushed which reminded me of the timid and shy girl that we first brought home.

"You met someone… that you like?" I gasped.

"Yes. I was eating lunch at a café in London and kind of bumped into this guy. Well, I literally bumped into him, and spilt my coffee all over his fancy suit." She explained.

I watched the way she acted as she spoke, it reminded me of how she acted when we first started talking. We had been pushed together quickly during the trauma on the island, but there was a strong connection. After we got home, Star and I took her on real dates and showed her how our kind of relationships worked. She took to it quickly and really came out of her shell. Watching her now though, I could tell she was back in that early stage and had some real feelings forming.

"Well, tell us all about it!" I chimed in.

"Well, I apologized obviously, and he was really nice about it. He bought me another and we sat in the park and talked for a little while. He was also travelling to visit family and had stopped to spend some time in London. We talked for a couple hours before I had to leave, and then a couple of days later I saw him again at a bookstore." She said.

"He asked me to dinner, and I agreed. He has a really kind smile and the most beautiful eyes… I just couldn't say no."

"Oh you developed a crush real fast, huh?" Star teased.

"Yes. There was just something about his voice that drew me in, and he was a great dinner date. We had seafood at a beautiful little restaurant and then dessert from a nearby bodega." Callie said, reaching to the bed table for her phone.

She unlocked the screen and pulled up an image of them sitting on a bench eating pastries. The man was quite attractive, dark hair, glasses, and a kind face. He reminded me a little of Dan Levy, I could see why Callie was interested.

"We had a couple short dates between our trips, and I explained our relationship and our rules to him, which shockingly didn't seem to bother him. Then one night, as he walked me back to my hotel I gave in and let him kiss me." she blushed.

"Awww, how cute!" Star replied.

"I wanted to tell you guys about him, but then he told me he was almost done with his trip and was coming back to America. He asked if he could meet you both in person on his way back to work. He actually works in Richmond for an architectural firm. I told him it would probably be fine, but I needed to talk to you about it first. He's got another few days in London and then he'll be flying here and if you two want to meet I can pick him up." she said, blushing.

"You didn't tell him our address, or anything did you?" I asked.

"No, I knew you would be upset about that. I just told him what city we lived in. I don't have to bring him to the house if it's a problem..."

"No, it's fine. I trust you, and if you trust him then you are welcome to bring him here. What do you think Star?" I said.

"I'd love to meet him! He's really cute." she smiled.

"You guys are the best! I'll let him know right now!" Callie said, texting him immediately.

"You haven't even told us his name, Cal." I said, poking her gently in the ribs.

"Oh, gosh, I completely forgot. His name is James Mulaney."

We cuddled and talked about some more details of her trip, the places she visited, the food she tried, it was a wonderful night. We eventually drifted off to a peaceful night's rest.

CHAPTER 6

The next morning, we all stumbled downstairs for coffee. It was a relaxed morning as we unpacked Callie's bags for her while she drove Cherry to school. Star left not long after to have another meeting with Ezra, and I told her to tell them I was interested in their idea and would like to discuss designs. Star agreed and then sent me a text from the driveway that was just an image of my face crudely attached to a smutty image of the mom from *The Incredibles*. I sighed.

I decided I was going to take things easy today and try not to stress out too much before the mission with Constance. I went back to the basement, but not to my work computer. Instead I packed a bowl and plopped down in front of my gaming rig, ready to get stoned and escape reality for a few hours. I took a long hit from my glass piece and turned on my PS5 to play some of my new favorite game series: *Yakuza*. It was a fantastic series with an amazing cast of main characters, several of which were attractive inside and out. This particular game was an older one that had been remastered with updated graphics and the newer combat system.

I melted into my chair as the herb kicked in and let myself fully zone out wandering the digital streets of Kamurocho. The game location helped ground it in reality while the story and side quests ventured into the extreme and bizarre. Whether I was playing dress up and running a hostess club or fighting tattooed gangsters in the streets it was just tons of fun. Admittedly, I had gotten the phoenix on my back partially to express the flaming rebirth I experienced on the island, but partially because I loved the tattoos in this game series. I wanted to visit the game's locations when we took Cherry to Japan at the end of the semester.

Callie joined me after a few hours, she liked to watch me play games more than she liked playing them herself. We added a couch to the room so anyone could lounge and enjoy the space with me. Sometimes Star or Callie would just lay on the couch and read or scroll on their phones while I played games just so we could be near each other if we didn't feel like talking. Callie took a few hits of my weed too, which she didn't do often but said she wanted to really relax after her trip.

"So this guy just pops up from places in the city… just to get you to fight him?" she asked, coughing up smoke.

"Yeah, it's how he shows his love. I keep hoping they will just kiss in one of these games." I said, frantically pressing combos into the controller.

"This game is really weird." she added.

"I know! I love it!" I exclaimed.

Time passed, and eventually I got a text from Constance letting me know she was on her way and asking if she needed to bring anything. I had told her multiple times that she didn't need to bring things to have dinner with us, but she always asked. I don't think she was used to people being nice to her without expecting something in return. I told her she could bring some snacks for Cherry if it would make her feel better.

Callie had long since fallen asleep on the couch, and I gave her a gentle kiss on the head before heading upstairs. She grumbled and rolled over, a sure sign that she would get up in time to eat on her own. Star and Cherry had returned and were both watching TV in the living room as I emerged from the basement. I walked to the kitchen for a drink and said hello to Beatrice who had just started getting things together to cook.

"I've got company coming over, Constance is meeting me here before we go work on some things. Do you need anything to accommodate?" I asked.

"No, we'll have plenty. I always make extra in case anyone wants seconds and to make sure Cherry has lunch the next day." Beatrice replied.

"You're the best!" I said, taking a bottle of water and joining Star on the couch.

Cherry scooted over and gave me a hug.

Hey, Mommy! Did you have a good day?

"Yeah, I hung out with Callie and played some games. I'm waiting for Constance to come over so we can go do some work tonight." I replied.

Nothing too dangerous? I don't want you to get hurt without your super suit.

"You told her about the suit too?" I stared at Star, who burst out laughing.

You should get a red one that looks like Akira! You could even paint your motorcycle to match! It would be SO COOL!

Cherry grabbed my arm and bounced in her seat a little with excitement. I thought about it for a moment.

"That's much better than Star and Callie's suggestions." I said.

"Ezra said spandex and Kevlar don't mix anyway." Star added.

"Ha! Sorry to ruin your fantasy of sleeping with a superhero." I joked.

Gross. Cherry added.

"I could still make you something hot, maybe like *Captain Marvel's* outfit." Star mused.

Cherry mimed a gag, and rolled her eyes not impressed by her moms' flirty tones. She picked up her book and went to another room. I giggled and scooted closer to Star.

"We grossed her out being too flirty again." I said.

"She'll get over it, she did like the idea of you being a superhero though. She said you could just wear a leather jacket and jeans like Ghost Rider." Star replied.

"She told me to do all red like Akira."

"Both could work, and with a Kevlar vest underneath." Star said.

"She really just wants me to ride my motorcycle more I think. I told her I would teach her when she gets older." I said as the doorbell rang.

Callie emerged from the basement just in time to say she would get it, and opened the door to greet Constance who was mostly hidden behind a large brown paper bag.

"I told you we didn't need you to bring anything!" I shouted as she dropped it on the coffee table with a thud.

"I just brought some snacks and equipment for the mission. I brought that spare vest I told you about. What's B. cooking for dinner?" Constance asked.

"Pasta I think?" I said, realizing I hadn't asked.

"Perfect, I've been craving some good pasta for weeks!" Constance said as she sat down on the couch. "Here try this on."

I picked up the vest and looked at it for a moment. I wasn't entirely sure how it worked but it seemed simple enough. I undid the buckles and slid my head into the neck hole.

"Nope, got it on backwards, here." Constance chimed, offering to adjust it for me.

I spun it around, and she pulled the straps tight and buckled them in the back to make sure it was secure against my body. I stood up to see how it felt moving around.

"How's it look?" I asked, not realizing I was still wearing pajamas.

"Ridiculous, doesn't match your unicorn pants at all." Beatrice answered, setting plates on the dinner table in the next room.

We all laughed, and I undid the straps so I could remove the vest. Constance took it and set it on the coffee table next to the other gear she brought with her: binoculars, flashlights, a long-range mic, and some dark clothes.

"Fits like a glove though, should be good to go. You should change after dinner and get moving, don't want to miss the deal go down. I'll tell you the plan on the way." Constance said.

"Where are you guys going?" Star asked.

"The docks, going to watch some nefarious goods change hands and see who they belong too. Might get us a little closer to Bach." I explained.

"Oh, now I understand the vest. This is really dangerous, Tri." Star replied.

"I know, but it's what we've got for now. Matt's still observing the tattoo shops and hasn't seen any moves so hopefully the Pink Wiz gets us somewhere." I said.

"A shady drug deal at the docks… sounds like a movie." Callie chimed.

"You're not wrong, I almost though Constance was making it up." I added.

"Where do you think the movies get the idea? The docks are where stuff comes off boats for distribution, it ain't going to be full of pretty actors and lights but there's lots of people doing stuff they shouldn't on a regular basis. Rich people tend to be where the money changes hands, never mind the laws. No offence, of course." Constance explained.

"I mean, it's accurate. I'm rich and I'm going to be there to follow the money despite the dubious legality." I said.

"Unlike the movies, these are real gangs with real guns and real consequences. I don't know if this is a good idea." Callie said, a worried look on her face.

"That's what the Kevlar is for! I know it's probably a terrible idea, but I trust Constance. She's an expert and a professional on this kind of thing." I explained.

"I've scouted and observed many cases at these same docks. Helped bring down some human traffickers there six years ago. I know my way around, and where this meeting is going down we'll have a nice safe vantage point to watch and listen. Shouldn't get close enough to cause problems, and we'll have a quick exit route." Constance said calmly.

"Text us when you get there and when you leave. I'm going to be a mess worrying about you until you get home." Callie said.

"Don't do anything stupid. Come back to us." Star added.

"No missions on an empty stomach! Come eat, dears! I'm sure whatever miss Trianna has planned will work as long as she listens to miss Constance." Beatrice interrupted.

We took our places at the table and scooped portions of delicious pasta onto our plates. Beatrice made a fantastic five-cheese ziti and complimented it with fresh garlic rolls and sautéed veggies. She also set out a pot of seasoned meat-sauce to add for those of us that wanted it. Cherry and Callie both ate meat, but usually preferred to go without for most of their meals and we respected that.

We all ate a healthy portion, and Beatrice excused herself to prepare leftovers for Constance to take home after our mission. I went upstairs to change out of my pajamas into something more appropriate for the night ahead. I wanted to be covered but still able to move if things got hairy, so I slipped into some black leggings, all-black sneakers, a black tank top to wear under the vest and a black denim jacket with a hood to wear overtop. Unsurprisingly, metalhead that I was, I had a plethora of dark clothes ready to grab at a moment's notice.

Constance was already wearing a similar outfit: Black jeans, boots, a t-shirt, and her trench coat to hide her vest and gun holster. We certainly looked ready for a stealth mission as far as I was concerned, but my nerves were starting to get the better of me. I wanted to get high and calm them down but decided that I should be perfectly sober in case something went wrong. I could always smoke when I got home safe, I hoped.

We met downstairs, where Callie and Star were nervously waiting for us. I gave them both a big hug and I could feel them worrying about me. I was beginning to second guess the plan, but I had already set my mind to it and wasn't about to give up now.

"Should I come with you? Bring the thunder if something goes wrong?" Star asked.

"No, two people is enough risk. We don't want to be seen, and if anything were to happen to you again I'd never forgive myself." I answered.

"Now you know how we feel about you going. Don't make us come fight an army to get you back. I may not have powers anymore, but I know how to fight and how to shoot." Callie said sternly.

"I promise I'll come home without a scratch. Constance will too. We're just going to watch." I explained.

"And if Bach shows up?" Callie asked.

"Then I burn the whole place to the ground before he knows what hit him." I said, my voice cold and stoic. "Either way we will be out before anyone can get their hands on us."

"It's not their hands I'm worried about, but I trust you." Star said squeezing me tight.

"You bring her home to us in one piece, or else." Callie said, pointing her finger at Constance who visibly gulped.

"Yes ma'am. Not a scratch." Constance stuttered.

I gave Callie and Star both one more hug and a kiss for luck, helped Constance grab our gear, and lead her to the garage. I had a few options for vehicles, not as many as I used to before I stopped collecting, but still enough to fill our twelve-car garage. I had a thing for classic muscle cars and had quite a few in pristine condition that I liked to take to shows when I wasn't so busy hunting mad scientists for revenge. I figured most of them would be too loud to make a safe get away though and I had a better idea.

The very latest addition to my vehicles was an interesting one, and quite the opposite of my usual. Where muscle cars are loud and showy, my custom Rivian R1T was an electric truck that made almost no noise whatsoever. Each wheel had its own motor and gave it enough power to get from zero to sixty in three seconds. It was smaller than most modern pickup trucks too, but it made up for that with tons of space including several hidden compartments. I had the body reinforced and installed bulletproof glass in a fit of paranoia last year, all of which made it perfect for a stealth op. I opened the front compartment where an engine would normally be and started loading supplies.

"What the fuck kind of truck is this?" Constance asked, peeking into what she clearly thought was an engine bay.

"A Rivian, electric, fast, quiet. It's bulletproof too." I answered proudly.

Constance shrugged and climbed in the passenger seat. I unplugged the charge cable and then hopped in the driver's seat to start it up. The dashboard looked like something out of a spaceship in a sci-fi movie, which was honestly what convinced me to buy it in the first place. The custom sound system greeted me by name and the seats automatically adjusted themselves based on our weight.

"Holy shit this thing is cool." Constance said. "Will it buckle me in and give me a handy on the way?" she joked.

"Not yet, maybe the next model will." I chuckled. "So, what's the plan?"

"Head to the docks and I'll show you where to park. We'll have an easy way in through a side lot. I already paid off the guard there to let us in after hours. There's a flight of stairs that we can use to hop over onto the shipping containers and make our way over to where the meeting is going to be. Then we just lay down, set up the gear, and wait. Easy in, easy out." She answered.

"Impressive. What if we get spotted?"

"We shoot and run, it will take them a lot longer to get around to the side lot to try and follow, so we should be able to make it back to the truck and haul ass before they get close enough to stop us. If we need to lay low I know a few spots nearby we can dip into and wait them out."

I pulled the truck out of the garage and rolled through the driveway, punching the address for the docks into the built-in GPS. It would only take us an hour or so to get there, if I followed speed limits, which is slightly harder to do when you can't hear an engine running. The speedometer on the dash wasn't hard to see, but I was still prone to speeding a bit. We made it to the docks in forty-six minutes.

We pulled down a side alleyway and into a dimly lit part of the docks where a guard lifted the gate for us and left it open before walking towards the inner lots. Constance told me on the way that she knew the guard from a previous job here, and that he had helped her catch the traffickers that were loading women and children onto a boat to sell elsewhere. She only bribed him because she knew he had kids to feed, but he would have likely helped without it.

I turned and backed into a spot, leaving the truck facing towards the open gate for a quick exit. We climbed out and made our way up the stairs, over the rails, and on top of the shipping containers just as she said. We crouched while we walked to reduce the risk of being spotted but we were pretty high up. Constance led us over several containers to where I was told the exchange would take place.

There was a large nondescript boat docked nearby, and I could see a table and chairs set up on the deck through the binoculars. The wood was polished and decorative, and the tablecloth had intricate designs around the border, this was an expensive set up to just be sitting on a boat. I heard some motorcycles approaching, and Constance pointed to where the sound was coming from.

"Triad guards." She whispered.

I nodded and pointed out the table. She seemed perplexed by it as well but said that likely confirmed the meeting was happening here. A handful of bikes worked their way through the containers, several stopping in the loading bay by the boat. Men with suits and guns began taking up positions around the area. Constance set up the long-range mic and handed me an earbud so we could both listen in without being cut off from anything nearby.

Back on the boat, a finely dressed woman wearing an incredible traditional kimono emerged from inside and took a seat at the table flanked by several guards and a younger woman that began making tea. Shortly after, two black SUVs pulled up to the bay and parked, leaving their lights on. A tall man emerged wearing sunglasses and a smart suit, finely tailored. A few guards dressed in riot gear stepped out as well but remained by the car while the finely dressed man walked up the ramp and joined the woman at the table.

I watched him through the binoculars and tried to get a good look at him, but he was faced away from me until he sat down. I scanned his features, but after a moment I could tell it wasn't Bach. I studied him as best I could as he took the sunglasses off, and something felt familiar about him, but I couldn't place it. Maybe he looked like an actor or someone else famous. I was sure it wasn't anyone I knew personally. Constance trained the mic on them so we could hear the conversation.

"...tea is lovely as always. So to business, then. Do you have the amount my client is requesting?" the man asked.

"Of course, the price is more than acceptable. We will begin mixing just as soon as we get the product to our labs. Tell me, why does Bach send such a handsome and kind young man to negotiate for him?" the woman asked.

All the remaining hair on my body stood on end hearing a stranger say that name. I felt my internal temperature start to rise and did my best to keep calm. Constance must have sensed something and quietly shushed me, placing her hand on my shoulder to try and help maintain my composure so as not to blow our cover.

"It is you that is so kind, ma'am. Your hospitality's reputation precedes itself. My client has hired me to help alleviate some of the workload, he is a very busy man." the man answered with a polite smile.

I studied his face more, trying to place what was familiar about it but finding it hard to concentrate as my nerves were getting the better of me. I watched as the man gestured to the guards by the SUVs and they began to unload large security crates from the back. The man and woman stood up from the table as one of the boxes was carried up to them. The woman reached into the box and pulled out a vial of swirling red liquid that sent shivers down my spine. It was Opulentia, no doubt about it.

My neck flared with heat, and I gritted my teeth trying to suppress my rage. My mind raced with images, memories from the facility on the island where Bach was loading crates of this very liquid onto a helicopter after all my new friends were murdered. The way he smiled and went back to work as if we weren't even there. I shook my head to clear them but didn't realize flames were starting to form around my head and fists, and as I turned I saw my hood starting to catch fire. I reached up to pat it out and dropped the binoculars which clanged off the top of the shipping container and dropped to the ground below.

"Fuck…" I said.

"RUN!" Constance shouted, rolling backwards away from the edge of the container just as machine gun fire echoed through the still night air.

A bullet ricocheted off the edge right in front of me startling me with the sparks. I held out a hand and sent a beam of fire across the pavement, igniting one of the guards carrying the Opulentia who fell to the ground screaming. I took off towards the car and could hear motorcycles revving loudly as we ran. I glanced back just in time to see a large snake of water rise from the dock and slam down onto the shipping containers. The resulting wave nearly knocked us off, but we caught ourselves on the rail for the stairs and quickly leaped over and ran down to the truck.

We dove into the truck, and Constance pulled her gun from its holster scanning the area for anyone following us.

"Drive! North towards the highway!" she shouted.

I started the car and peeled off, but just as we reached the gate I saw the bikers approaching. Bullets pinged off the hood of the car, leaving scratches in the paint but were otherwise harmless. I sped up, racing right towards them as Constance kept fussing with the door.

"How do you open the damn window in this thing?!" she yelled, frantically mashing everything but the window controls.

I hit the auto-down button and she quickly put her arm out through the window and opened fire on the approaching bikes. They didn't swerve at first, holding steady to return fire.

Constance managed to catch one and he tumbled off his bike and I surged forward. The truck launched itself over the downed bike, barely missing its rider, and forcing the other three to swerve out of the way. I opened the sunroof and yelled for Constance to take the wheel.

She slid over into my seat as I stood up and out of the sunroof, the truck almost swerving off the road before she got it back under control. Actions movies always made that look much smoother. I saw the bikes catching up and dropped my jacket into the car, so my arms were free. Fire appeared in my palms as my tattoos flared with power and my eyes began to glow. I focused the flames into a ball in my hands and then raised them above me and threw the ball towards the bike, channeling more fire into it as it flew to increase its size.

The ball hit the ground right in front of the bikes causing the lead bike to swerve off the road and crash. I whipped the beam of fire across the road back and forth to catch the other two, setting their riders on fire and sending them careening into the ditch. I was too focused on the bikes and didn't notice the SUV approaching. It screeched out of a side road and pulled in right behind us before I had time to react. The man with the fancy suit leaned out of the passenger side and trained his pistol on me.

I brought the flames around towards the SUV but not fast enough. I didn't even hear the shot, but I saw the muzzle flash just before something hit me in the chest like a truck. I screamed and collapsed into the truck as the last of my flames forced the SUV to stop because the tires were ablaze. My chest felt like it was going to burst, and I gasped for air before passing out in the back seat as Constance shouted my name.

I opened my eyes, and my vision was blurry at first, but focused after a moment. I was in a dark room that I didn't recognize. I glanced around and realized I was lying on a bed in a somewhat sketchy hotel room. My chest was wet, and my first thought was blood. I looked down to see a shopping bag full of ice resting on my chest which now reminded me how much it hurt. I lifted the bag for a moment and saw a binding around the right side of my chest with some blood staining through. I gently lowered the ice back down and looked around. Constance was leaned up against the wall peeking out the window from behind the closed curtains.

I started to sit up and cried out a little which got her attention. She rushed over and gently urged me back down.

"Hey, hey, don't move. You've been shot." She said.

"How bad is it?" I asked resting on the dubiously clean pillow.

"The vest took most of it, but the bullet shattered, and some shrapnel cut clean through. Missed your lungs and other important bits, thankfully." She explained.

"Callie is going to beat both our asses." I chuckled which made me cough.

"No shit, I'm not sure who I'm more worried might show up outside."

"How long was I out?"

"A couple hours, we're holed up in a motel just outside of town. I don't think anyone followed us, but I've been keeping watch just in case." she said, lifting the bag to check my wound. She lifted the edge of the bandage and scowled.

"We're going to have to get you to a doctor. I've got enough credentials to keep them from calling the cops as long as we don't tell them how you got shot." she said.

"Hand me my phone, I've got a doctor I can trust. She can... help..." I started to fade again, my eyelids drooping.

"Tri? Trianna!? Fuck!" Constance shouted as I blacked out again.

This time when I woke up I was in a plush, clean smelling hospital bed for which I was very grateful. I hoped I had unlocked my phone before blacking out and Constance was able to find Dr. Pestoff in my contacts. She had been a friend of mine in high school, and I had helped her pay off some of her student loan debt, so she was willing to help us out. She was also the private practice doctor that examined Callie and Cherry when we got back from the island after some lengthy conversations and helped us work around a lot of the legal red tape of adopting Cherry officially.

When we tried to figure out Callie's lineage, she had processed the bloodwork and kept the results confidential for us so that the bizarre results didn't bring Bach's men looking for us. She was good people, and reliable, so I hoped that's where I was, and Constance hadn't taken me to the regular ER out of panic. If the cops got involved in this it might completely blow our whole lead on Bach, not that me setting his drug deal on fire had helped much either.

I looked around the room and noticed Callie and Star asleep on the rather uncomfortable hospital couch by the window. Moments later, Constance entered the room with Dr. Pestoff, and I sighed with relief. At least something was working out in my favor.

"Ah, you're awake. How are you feeling?" Dr. Pestoff asked.

"Better than before. How bad is it?" I asked.

Star and Callie had woken up to the sound of our voices and came over to stand by the bed as well. I smiled at them, and they both held my arm for support.

"You'll be fine in a few days. Shrapnel tore through your chest just above your lung, missing it by only a few centimeters. It bounced off your shoulder blade and out the back. No major damage, but it's going to be sore for a while. Wound was small enough that we didn't even need stitches. X-ray shows you are all clear with no shrapnel remaining inside. That vest likely saved your life, or at least your lung." She explained.

"That's great. I'll be fine until Callie kills me for doing something this stupid." I joked.

"I'll send a nurse in, with some meds, to remove your IV and you can be home before dinner if you like. I can also keep the room reserved if you want to rest here, but I have my suspicions you're not going to stick around." the doctor added.

"Make sure the bandage gets changed every 12 hours and gently clean the wound with warm soapy water and dab it dry, so you don't reopen it. No strenuous activity for at least a week. Call me if there's any bleeding or sign of infection." She said mostly to Star and Callie.

"We'll take good care of her doctor, thank you so much for everything." Callie said.

"I know you will, take care of yourselves too. Next time we see each other let it be a better circumstance, yeah?" Pestoff smiled and left the room.

Constance shuffled in next to me on the other side of the bed, not making direct eye contact with Callie. She was actually a little afraid of her. I grabbed Star's hand and squeezed it tight smiling up at both of them, partially because I was happy to see them and partially because I was high on pain killers, and everything felt great.

"I'm so glad you're alright." Callie said, leaning down to kiss my forehead.

"Why do we keep meeting with me in a medical bed?" I asked, a little deliriously.

"Because you're headstrong and have chaotic luck?" Star joked to lighten the mood.

"Probably right." I replied. "Constance, are you okay?"

"Yeah, I managed to avoid all the bullshit. I don't think anyone got an ID on us so we shouldn't have to worry about being followed." Constance said.

The door opened and Cherry rushed in with Beatrice in tow.

MOMMY!? I WAS SO SCARED!

"It's okay Cherry, Mommy's all right just be careful of my shoulder."

Cherry climbed gently into the bed with me and squeezed me with a hug. I held her to me, and wiped a tear from her face as she sobbed a little. Cherry had grieved her actual parents mostly in silence, driven on by the terrible situation we were all in, but it occurred to me that losing another parent would be devastating for her. I knew I needed to keep trying to stop Bach, but I had to try and be more careful. For Cherry, and all the other people in my life.

The nurse came and got me ready to leave, she tried to convince me to stay another night, but I decided I would much rather rest at home. We all needed to rest since the ordeal took a lot out of everyone. The drugs in my system hadn't fully cleared before we got home and I was back to sleep as soon as I hit the bed. I had managed to lose about four days since we went to the docks between passing out after getting shot and sleeping off the medicine from the hospital. I was lucid for some of it, but not much.

Constance had apologized to everyone and much to her surprise had been told that it wasn't her fault and Callie hugged her to help her feel better. Awkward as she was, it only made Constance feel slightly better, but she was relieved that Callie wasn't going to throw her in the bay or something. Star and Cherry checked on me periodically, but Beatrice and Callie kept an eye on me around the clock, bringing me food and water and changing my bandage. I had an amazing and loving family to care for me, and they made sure I couldn't forget.

CHAPTER 7

A few days after I got home from the hospital, I woke up to the news on our bedroom TV. Callie was sitting on the end of the bed watching. There was a report about several crimes around the US being committed by gang members using magical powers. I sat up despite the pain to see around her. Footage of a few crimes played while the anchor spoke about minor details. One sequence in particular caught my eye and I gasped.

A man came running out of a store he had presumably just robbed and was chased by security. He turned and held up his hand, and I watched parts of his chest tattoo light up just before lightning arced from his fingers destroying a magazine rack and causing one of the guards to drop in spasms like he had been tased. There was no denying that was an Opulentia-infused tattoo similar to the ones Khan and Bach had given to us.

The news anchors talked about twenty or thirty different events that happened in different cities and seemed to have no connection with each other beyond the magic they kept calling experimental weaponry. They didn't know what I did about Bach and the strange creature's blood. Callie had scooted back in the bed next to me to help support my weight but didn't take her eyes off the screen. She, too, understood the seriousness of what was transpiring, and I worried if I was too late.

I grabbed my phone and checked my messages for the first time in almost a week, and sure enough Matt had been sending information about this since just after we left for the docks. I had my phone on silent the whole time so as not to draw attention during our recon mission, so I had missed it entirely. All of the stories mentioned similar details about the criminals, visible tattoos that seemed to glow with energy just before the user unleashed some magical effect on whatever their scenario was at the time. Petty crimes mostly, robberies, muggings, a few fights but no casualties yet.

Matt was able to trace a few people that had been identified to some of the tattoo shops we were monitoring. Digging through social media posts, his team managed to find the designs and artists that did them. The tattoos themselves were your typical gang related tattoos with logos and words representing the communities these people had formed to survive the cities that gave them the need to live that way. The images, when examined closely, seemed to have overlapping lines that resembled some of the mystical symbols from the Opulentia designs.

Digging deeper Matt had found the original designs were being sent to these shops from an encrypted source. A single artist was creating these generic designs hiding the symbols and then having these gang owned tattoo shops push them as part of their cultural designs. I was curious if the artists doing the work had any idea what these symbols were or if they knew they were there. Perhaps this was just another layer of deception in Bach's overall plan that seemed to get more complex by the day.

I scrolled through reports and what little information there was about the known identities of people that had been caught. Repeat offenders, lots of petty and non-violent crime, some drug charges, the things you usually saw with folks abandoned by the social structures we all lived in. I couldn't find any mention of memory loss or severe personality changes, which seemed to indicate the tattoos were not pure Opulentia like mine.

The original process involved pure blood from that weird creature, and some twisted experiments that usually left the people with no memory of who they were, and an extreme submission to Bach and his plans. This almost felt like someone was trying to simulate Bach's experiment without knowing all the details, and I wasn't sure what was more unsettling. If this was just a copycat, do they have their own source or is this someone using Bach's supplies for their own gain and watering it down like cocaine? If it was the latter, was Bach still in on it, or was this some kind of diversion while he advanced his work?

I rubbed my head in deep though, running my fingers across the fuzz forming where I had shaved previously. I still had more questions than answers and the clock was ticking faster. The longer I spent trying to see the forest through the trees, the closer Bach was to his wild world domination scheme and now parts of it were in the public eye. The trail was growing cold again though, as Matt said he was unable to break the encryption hiding the source of the designs, but the team was still working.

I felt my body temperature rise a little, frustration about all this information was getting me worked up. I was lost in thought and didn't notice Callie was trying to talk to me.

"Do you want me to tell him not to come?" Callie asked, poking me to get my attention.

"Hmm? Who? Sorry I was lost in thought." I replied, turning to face her.

"James, the man I think I want to date seriously. He's in town already and wants to come meet my family. Should I tell him it's a bad time?" she asked again.

"No, no. This is important to you. I want to meet him too, see how he vibes with our polycule. I can put this aside for now, the leads have dried up again anyway. We can't let him know about Cherry's abilities though, not until we know he's safe at least." I said.

"I know, I talked with her this morning about it. It will be all signing communication while he's around. I'm going to go pick him up then, I need to change your bandage first though." she said with a smile.

We kissed and then cleaned my wound which was healing well. I was still sore as hell, and needed help changing clothes but after we got dressed I was able to get around fine on my own. We went downstairs and I sat at the dining room table with Cherry who was reading her book and snacking on fruit.

Good morning, Mommy. Are you feeling better?

"Yeah, thanks for asking. I feel quite a bit better and glad to be moving around. My butt was starting to hurt laying in bed all week." I said.

Mum says she's got a friend coming over. Is he a BOYfriend?

"Seems that way, you remember that means no showing off your wonderful abilities right?" I replied.

I know, I'll keep it a secret. Is he going to be my new Dad? she asked.

"I... I don't know. We all have to talk about that at some point. Is that something you want to happen?"

I like having three Moms. I wouldn't mind a Dad, but I would really have to like him first. If he's mean I wouldn't call him Dad.

"If he's mean to Mum or any of us, especially you, then he won't ever come back so you don't need to worry about that." I said, patting her on the head.

I think I'll just stay in my room and read. Can I go to Savannah's house tomorrow?

*Is Savannah just a friend or a **girl**friend?* I thought back to her.

I… I dunno. I'm going to my room now. Bye. She raced up the stairs and into her room.

I smiled knowingly. There were some kind of feelings going on there, and that was beautiful.

"Be back soon! Muah!" Callie shouted, blowing a kiss from the other room as she left.

Star sat down next to me with a plate of fruit and cheese to snack on. She gently hugged me and gave me a kiss on the forehead.

"What sent Cherry running so fast?" she asked.

"I asked her if she liked her friend Savannah. She got a little shy about it. She also said she wanted to stay in her room while James visits. I kind of also want to do that." I replied.

"I know your anxiety gets to you sometimes, but this is really important to Callie."

"Yeah, I know. I'm putting the effort in for her. Least I can do since she's been taking care of me all week. You two spoil me, you know that?" I said, leaning up against her.

"We love you silly, that's how this works." She said, and then paused for a moment to collect her thoughts.

"Did you see the news this morning?" she asked.

"Yeah."

"Do you think it's Bach?"

"It has to be related at least. Matt found some better images of the tatts; they seem to have *the symbols* hidden in them, but we can't tell if the artists doing them even know they are there. The design came in from somewhere else. They don't seem to work like ours though."

"So it's kind of like the drugs? Mixed with something else and made weaker?" She asked.

I nodded and stole a piece of cheese from her plate. We sat and discussed ideas for a little while, but none really got us anywhere productive. Eventually we moved to the couch in the living room and watched some more of the news. They cycled through stories but worked back around to the mysterious crimes. Supposed experts were interviewed claiming the people were using special effects to hide weapons on their person to make it look like magic, while other people speculated they were using secret military experiments that had been stolen.

A short time later I heard the front door, and Callie was entering followed by her new boyfriend. I stared at him for a moment, and there was a feeling of familiarity. I thought that I knew him from somewhere, something about his facial structure.

"I'm home! Star, Trianna, this... is James!" Callie said, interrupting my train of thought.

"Hello..." I said, staring at him.

"It's nice to meet you! I'm Star, this is my wife Trianna. Callie has told us so much about you, we're all very excited to have you visit." Star said, expertly taking control of the conversation.

"Ah, yes. Calliope has told me much about you both as well." He spoke in a gentle but deep voice. "Trianna, I'm sorry to hear about your accident. My cousin lost a finger to some firecrackers when we were kids, I know how dangerous they can be." He said.

His eyes moved to my wound, and there was a hint of interest, or maybe recognition, before he smiled and sat down with Callie on the loveseat across from us. I was still staring and had to shake my head to break my concentration, maybe I was just remembering him from the images Callie showed us. He looked like Dan Levy in person too, so maybe that was throwing me off, but I wasn't certain.

"Callie mentioned you all had a little one, Cherry I believe?" he asked.

"Yes, she's reading up in her room. We'll be sure to introduce you if she feels like coming down, you know how teenagers can be. How was your trip? Callie mentioned she met you in London." Star answered.

"The flight was delayed a bit, but otherwise it was a normal trip. I got home earlier than planned because I had some work to attend to in Georgetown." He explained.

"Callie mentioned you worked for an Architecture firm in… Richmond?"

"Yes, Firm Line Design, my father is the CEO now, but I have been working there a bit longer. He took over after years of running a firm in London. The board wanted me to be COO, but I have been considering changing career paths. I love to draw and draft, but the business side of the industry is very dull and unfulfilling." James said, reaching out to hold Callie's hand.

"He's thinking about starting his own firm where he can focus on his designs." Callie added cheerfully.

The chat went on for a while, we exchanged career information and all the boring small talk that type of conversation usually carries. I was never one for small talk, even though I had quite a successful business I could brag about, Star did most of the talking. She was always eager to discuss the workings of her fashion company and how she turned it into a non-profit so she could care for her employees since my success already paid for our needs. I couldn't shake the feeling that I recognized this man from somewhere though and stayed mostly quiet, contributing to the conversation only when necessary.

I wondered how much Callie had told him about our relationship, and what story she made up about how we met. If it was too elaborate, she hadn't shared any details with us, and I worried we might mess things up if we improvised an entirely different story. My worries were alleviated however as the conversation progressed that way naturally.

"Calliope dear, I don't think you ever told me just how you three met and came to be together? Such an... interesting arrangement surely has some kind of story to it." James said.

I picked up on the pause and recognized the slight judgement. Monogamous people rarely understood polyamorous relationships and often made fun of them, conflating it to twisted versions like cults and sister wives you see in the media.

"Well, I met Trianna first. We bumped into each other on vacation, which seems to be a habit of mine. I was on break from school and went on a cruise to the Caribbean, a gift from my aunt. While I was in port, I was walking on the beach and accidentally tripped over her while she was hiding under a parasol. As you can see, she's pale but absolutely beautiful and I just had to ask her for a date. I was only going to be on the island for a day and I didn't want to let anything pass me by. She agreed, and we had beautiful dinner together. We traded information and talked on the phone for a few months and after graduation, I moved here with her and Star." Callie explained.

I appreciated how she wove some truth into her story and explained enough detail that Star and I could improvise some details without completely derailing things. I hated that she had to lie to someone she clearly had real feelings for but given what we had been through, and how outlandish the details were, it was hard to be honest with anyone about everything.

"So Cherry is one of yours then, prior to the relationship?" James asked.

"We all adopted Cherry together about seven years ago. We had been together for a while and realized we made a great family unit and decided we wanted to raise a child." I said.

Why did he keep bringing up Cherry? I was getting a strange feeling about how he directed the conversation as we spoke.

"Do you have any kids?" Star asked.

"No, but I've always wanted to. I have just been waiting for the right partner to start a family." He answered, patting Callie's leg.

"So, I'll just come out and say it. I've never been involved in any sort of polyamorous arrangement. I assume there are rules and boundaries in place that I should be aware of, how exactly does this sort of thing work?"

"It's not all that different from any relationship. If you two date, then she's your girlfriend. She just also happens to be dating me and also my wife. Callie lives here with us, but she has her own room that she invites her partners into at her own discretion, and Star and I have our room as well. If things get more serious down the road we can discuss any changes to our living arrangements then. As long as you respect the space and our family, including our housekeepers, then you are welcome to visit. We are not a package deal for much else though. Just because you're dating my girlfriend doesn't mean you're dating me or my wife, those relationships would have to develop organically like any other. For now you can just consider us Callie's roommates if it makes it easier." I explained more bluntly than I had intended.

"We don't tolerate jealousy," Callie added. "My time with these two is just as important to me as time with you. I want to expand my polycule not replace it, so if that works for you then we can really see where this goes."

He sat back and nodded, taking in all the information we had given him. I could tell he still found part of it strange, but nothing came off as harsh judgement. Maybe this would work out for her after all. He did seem a little taken aback when I set the wall between Star, myself, and him, so it was possible he thought he had access to all three of us at first but understood and agreed to respect our boundaries.

We talked for a while longer about the details of how Callie and James met on their trip, and general worldviews. Beatrice brought us tea and lemonade and some light snacks while we spoke about topics I was finding more and more difficult to focus on. My shoulder was hurting, and I was still trying to figure out what was so familiar about him. He and Callie were cute together though, and I could tell she was happy and that was what mattered.

"Well, we should get going. We have dinner reservations in town later and I wanted to show James a few of my favorite places around here." Callie said.

"Oh, fun!" Star said, "I hope y'all have a great time. Will you be home later?"

"I'm not sure yet, I'll text you." Callie smiled.

"It was a pleasure meeting you both! I now see I have quite the shoes to fill as a partner for this stunning woman. Perhaps next time I can meet your daughter as well." James said, standing to join Callie by the door.

"It was lovely meeting you, too. You guys be safe!" Star replied.

I waved and couldn't help but notice he brought Cherry up again. I'm not sure why but it was really bothering me that he kept asking about her. Parts of the conversation certainly felt like he was feeling out his competition and trying to get a read on what we thought about him, but it seemed like he was comfortable when talking about Cherry, as if he knew things about her already. Callie is a proud mom and had probably already told him a lot about her, but the way he asked about her made it seem like he knew there was a secret he wanted to learn.

"He seems nice." Star said.

"He does, they seem happy together. Something was bugging me though."

"I could tell, you had that look on your face you get when you're overthinking something."

"When he walked in, there was something that felt familiar about him, but I couldn't place it. Why do you think he kept asking about Cherry so much?" I asked.

"I think he was just curious about everything in Callie's life. He seems to really like her, why do you think something's weird about it?"

"Hard to say. Could just be the drugs wearing off. Did you get any weird vibes from him? Like maybe we met him somewhere before?"

"No, I mean you were right, he does look like Dan Levy. His deep voice threw me off at first because of that. I kept expecting him to 'ask me thrice for a towel'." She chuckled.

I could tell she was making a reference to *Schitt's Creek* that mostly went over my head because I hadn't seen the show. She and Callie watched it together and had several inside jokes from it with each other. I loved watching them bounce lines off each other, it was really cute.

"Maybe that's all it was. I dunno. What are your plans for the rest of the day?" I asked.

"I have a meeting with Ezra in an hour or so, and then I'll probably grab some pizza on the way home and let B off to spend time with Gerald. Do you need anything?"

"Nah, I'm going to go catch up on things downstairs and see if anything new popped up with the tattoo cases. Might play some more games for a bit."

"I'd prefer you do that than work. You still need to rest. I don't want you to stress out too much and get yourself hurt again."

"I know, babe. I'll take it easy. I promise." I said as I leaned in and gave her a kiss.

I walked upstairs to check on Cherry and see if she needed anything before we sent Beatrice home for the day. She was sitting quietly by her window watching something outside.

He seemed nice, but you felt strange about him.

I paused in the doorway, taken aback by her comment.

"How... How did you know that?"

Sometimes I can sense what other people are feeling and thinking. I think it's similar to how I can talk to you like this. I can kind of read your thoughts, and if I focus really hard I can sort of feel what you feel. Why did he make you so nervous?

"I'm not entirely sure. He seemed familiar but I couldn't figure it out. You don't need to worry about that sort of thing though."

He kept asking about me, you were worried about my safety.

"I'm your mom, I'm always worried about your safety."

She turned to face me, and I realized she was floating, not sitting in the window. Her eyes had an eerie white glow to them and the air in the room shifted as she moved. I tilted my head in confusion, as this was certainly a new development.

"Cherry, honey. Are you feeling okay?" I asked nervously.

You feel concerned, but you also feel familiarity. You recognize something in me. Something from the island. Something that haunts you.

"Okay, you're starting to scare me. Why don't we just go have a snack and watch some TV together." I said nervously.

She was right. I did recognize something with the way she acted. The energy I felt coming from her as she floated there reminded me of the monster we fought and killed.

You fear me. Have you always been afraid of me? Do you think I'm a monster?

"No, baby, no! I love you! I'm only afraid of what could happen to you if someone else saw this kind of thing happening. I love you so much!"

I know. I can feel it now. Your feelings are confusing.

"I'm well aware, I have to deal with them all the time. What... what exactly is happening right now?" I asked, reaching out for her.

I'm not sure. This is the first time I've experienced this. I feel connected to something inside you. Like we are both part of something else. I feel something calling me from outside sometimes, something far away.

"How long has that been going on?"

Hard to say, weeks, maybe months. It ebbs and flows. Sometimes it wanes entirely to nothing. Sometimes I can almost feel someone trying to talk to me. Do you think there are other people like me out there?

The question hit me like a truck. Teenage hormones are one thing, magic powers are another. She was going through some intense changes and felt alone. My heart was breaking that I could only understand part of what she was feeling.

"I... I don't know, baby. There's a lot of things out in the world, a lot of different people. I suppose it's possible, but I couldn't tell you for sure." I said, hoping it would help.

If there are, I hope I can meet them one day.

"Me too, hon. Me too."

She floated into my arms, and I felt the air shift again. Her weight returned as she dropped and knocked us both into her bed. My shoulder surged with pain, but I didn't care. She needed my full attention right now and she was going to get it. I held her tightly as I could for a moment, trying my damnedest to let her know how much I loved and cared for her.

I'm bleeding.

"What!? Where? What happened, did you hurt yourself?" I asked frantically.

She looked up at me nervously, and blushed.

Down there. I'm bleeding down there.

She was having her first period. I sighed with relief, glad that it was just something natural and nothing bad had happened to her.

"Oh, that's perfectly normal sweetie. Come on, let's get you cleaned up and I'll show you what to do." I said, kissing her gently on the forehead.

I took her to the bathroom attached to our bedroom and let her take a quick shower to clean herself. I texted Star that we needed some extra period supplies for her now, and Star sent back a heart and a thumbs up indicating she was busy but got the message. I showed Cherry how to use a pad and told her we could try tampons later if she wanted to or get her a cup, whatever she felt comfortable with. After a little trial and error, we went downstairs to get a heating pad and some ice cream, the essentials.

We relaxed on the couch and watched some anime together. She picked out a rather interesting series, called *Kill La Kill,* that featured sentient clothing and made fun of a lot of the tropes usually found in other anime. It had a great mix of action and story, and I rather enjoyed it. We cuddled, ate our ice cream, and just spent time together. I would do anything for that girl, and right now this is what she needed me to do.

Later that evening, I carried Cherry to bed after she fell asleep on the couch. Star returned home with a bag full of options and some pizzas just in time to help me tuck her in. The poor thing was utterly exhausted, but I wasn't sure if it was from her period or the strange display of powers. They were possibly related, but there wasn't an easy way to tell. I sat down with Star to munch on our dinner and talk about what happened.

"She could sense our thoughts from upstairs in her room?" Star asked.

"That's what she said, she seemed to know how the conversation went, so unless she snuck out to eavesdrop it looks like she has advanced her abilities again. She knew what I felt about things though, not just what we talked about." I explained, chewing on a slice.

"Hopefully she can control it, and it's not just on all the time. That sounds like it would be awful. Can you imagine… feeling what everyone around you is feeling constantly?"

"I could think of a few cases where that might make things better, but in general that does sound really gross and really bothersome. I guess we'll need to keep an eye on her and see how she feels after her period ends. It might just be the hormones."

"Oh god, I hope she doesn't know when we are having sex, that would be traumatizing."

"Maybe we should wear tinfoil hats." I chortled.

"That's… I… Trianna…" Star said, exasperated.

I laughed at her trying to process the joke because I needed the laugh. We switched the TV to YouTube and watched our favorite content creators for a while to wind down and clear our heads. Several hours passed, and just as we were about to go to bed, the front door opened. Callie walked in carrying her things, dropped them on the foyer table, and then plopped onto the couch with us.

"Oh, I didn't think you would be home tonight." Star said.

"I… got nervous and made up an excuse to leave." Callie replied sheepishly.

"Nervous? About what?" I asked.

"We were having a wonderful date, great food, and good wine. We took a romantic walk around the lake, and then went back to his hotel for desert. After we snacked on some pastry we made out a little, and that's when I realized…. I don't know if I've ever had sex with a man." she explained.

"Oh honey. Well, consent is important and it's good that he respected your decision. Did he get upset or anything?" I asked.

"No, he was very sweet about it. I told him something happened with Cherry, and I needed to come check on her." Callie said.

"Ah, well whatever works I suppose. What's the problem though? You usually like trying new things." I said.

"I don't know, I just got nervous about it. I'm aware of how it works, I've just gotten used to being with women and I don't remember if I've been with a man or if I liked it at all. I don't know what I'm supposed to do." she rambled.

"It's not much different than when we use the strap-on." Star added.

"Yeah, men usually like to be in charge, and sometimes they just flop around on you until they finish. Sometimes you get one that really knows what he's doing and takes his time, and those are usually really nice." I said.

"Okay. I will try it next time. I usually like to take the lead, so I might have to figure something out to be more submissive I guess."

"Some guys like being dominated by tall curvy women though, so you might be in luck. I can't say I blame them; you make a really hot dom." I said, fanning myself a little.

"In an interesting turn of events, your escape story wasn't a complete lie." Star chimed.

"What do you mean, what happened to Cherry? Is she okay?" Callie blurted.

"She's fine. She got her first period. It got a little weird, but nothing bad happened." I answered.

"What got weird?" she asked.

"Well…" I started.

I explained everything that happened again with the levitating, mind reading, and the strange things she mentioned about being called by something beyond the property. That might have been the most concerning part to me. I was worried she might be reaching out to Bach or one of his weird creatures, but I wasn't sure how I would ever know the answer unless they started writing letters to each other. Dark magic pen pals seemed just as twisted as the people that write love letters to serial killers in prison.

I got a ping on my phone from the house security system, and a notice that something was moving in the back yard. I pulled up the cameras to check, usually it was just a critter or something. The camera feed showed the small yard and the path leading to the beach, but nothing seemed out of place. I panned it down to check the door, it was closed, and I remembered locking it earlier. A large moth fluttered by the camera, and I decided that was likely what had caused the alert.

"Something wrong?" Callie asked.

"Nah, just a bug setting off the cameras again." I replied.

"Cal, are you all worked up from your date? Do you need us to help you… relax?" Star asked, flirtatiously licking her lip.

"God, yes. I could have kayaked out of that hotel room on a river of my own making. I can't believe I chickened out while that turned on." Callie joked.

"Well, that settles our plans for the night. You head upstairs, I'll go grab the tin foil." I said with a grin.

Star groaned and grabbed Callie's hand to head upstairs.

CHAPTER 8

I woke up during the night to my phone buzzing again. I carefully climbed out from between the two gorgeous naked women in my bed with some reluctance and grabbed my phone from the dresser. It was the security system again, but this time it wasn't just a bug or critter. There was a person trying to pick the lock on the back door.

"Callie! Star! Wake up! Someone's trying to get in the house!" I shouted, rousing them from their sleep.

I charged out of the bedroom and down the stairs, temperature in my body rising. I could feel the heat on my neck from my tattoos starting to glow. I ran to the backdoor through the kitchen as fast as I could, eager to get there before the person made it inside. I made sure to flip on lights as I ran so they would know they were caught and maybe give up. Just as I reached the door, it swung open revealing a man in all black holding a set of what I assumed were lock picks.

"Wrong house, fucker!" I shouted, still running.

I used the momentum of my run to my advantage and leapt into the air. My still nude body flew directly at him led by my feet in my best attempt at a flying kick. I caught the guy in the chest and we both tumbled out the door. He was knocked back a bit and rolled but got to his feet quicker than I could. He started to run, and I quickly followed. Just as I got enough speed to start gaining on him, he spun, and I only barely noticed him throw something. I felt a sting across my ribs as I just managed to twist away from the flying object. I stumbled and then held up my hand sending a blast of blue flames flying towards him. The ball of fire hit him in the legs and caused him to trip a little, but he kept running with his smoldering pants.

"Get back here, coward!" I shouted, starting to run again.

He was moving faster than me now, but heading towards the beach, which would slow him down for sure. A moment later there was a bright flash and crack of thunder as the sand exploded beside the man. I knew it must be Star coming to help, and I pushed my legs to run harder. The man managed to keep his footing despite several more lightning strikes that couldn't quite hit their mark.

We raced onto the beach at full speed. I launched more fire at him but only managed to clip him. He was fast, agile, and determined to reach the water it seemed. I glanced past him to see a boat resting on the shore with another person waiting. Suddenly the man threw something else, this time larger, then a bright flash and loud bang erupted in my face. I tumbled to the ground disoriented and clutching my ears.

It took a few minutes for my vision to return and for my ears to stop ringing. Star was holding my head in her lap. I looked towards the ocean just in time to see the boat fleeing quickly. I slumped back against Star and tried to catch my breath.

"A fucking flashbang!? Seriously!?" I growled.

"Hey, you're bleeding. Are you okay?" Star asked, pointing at my ribs.

I wiped the sand off my hand on my leg and checked the wound with a few fingers. It was just a small cut, not very deep, like a cat scratch.

"Yeah, it's fine. I can't believe the bastard got away!" I grumbled.

"I can't believe you chased down a burglar in the nude…" Star chuckled.

She helped me to my feet; my head was still reeling from the grenade. We stumbled back up to the house, and I noticed a glimmer on one of the porch posts. I reached for it and found a small knife embedded in the wood. Instead of a handle it had a metal stem that became a ring. A kunai? Just what the hell was going on?

I brought the knife inside and dropped it on the kitchen counter. Callie met us with the first aid kit and started cleaning up the cut on my side.

"I don't think that was just a burglar. What kind of thief brings flashbangs and ninja weapons?" I said, pointing my head towards the kunai.

"That is bizarre, should we call the police?" Callie asked.

"Fuck no. I might be rich, but I'm not about to rely on those shitheads when I have the best P.I. money can buy already working for me." I laughed.

"Do you think it's related to Bach?" Star asked.

"Could be, he's gotten violent before when we got close enough. Maybe our little stunt at the docks hit closer to home than we thought." I said, wincing as Callie wiped some peroxide over my wound.

"I don't like the idea of anyone sending goons straight to our house, least of all him. Did you get a look at the guy? Recognize anything about him?" Star asked.

"No, he was covered head to toe. Did anyone check on Cherry?" I replied.

"Yes. She's sound asleep, I don't think she noticed anything at all." Callie answered, wrapping my midsection with a bandage.

"I don't think they will be back tonight; we might as well get some rest. I'll call Constance first thing in the morning to look into our ninja." I said, yawning.

"You're not getting anywhere near that bed until we get all this sand off of you." said Callie sternly.

"Relax, no one wants sand in the bed. I'll step out and rinse off really quick." I said, heading to the back door.

Outside we had built a little sand rinse shower for this exact purpose. It had two upper showerheads for rinsing your body, and a lower head for rinsing just your legs and feet. It had a filter system built into it that let the water drain naturally and collected the sand in a little compartment that we would empty back out on the beach. It was temperature controlled as well, so even rinsing off at night wouldn't freeze you.

Star joined me to rinse off her legs and feet and brought us towels to dry off, while Callie swept up the sand we got in the kitchen and pantry hallway. We eventually went back to bed, but I don't think any of us slept very well.

The next morning we all got up, got dressed, and made coffee before splitting off on our plans for the day. Star was busy with work, and Callie wanted to take Cherry to the museum to spend some quality time with her now that she was home again. They both really loved museums as many of the exhibits were new and exciting to them. I loved museums too, but I had work to do figuring out who our masked man was.

I grabbed my phone and headed downstairs to my command center. I pulled up Constance's number and dialed it. She would know by now that I hate talking on the phone, and receiving a call from me indicated a very serious situation. The phone only rang once before she answered.

"What happened? Anyone dead?" Constance asked frantically.

"Not yet. Someone broke into our house last night, and I have my suspicions that it might be related to Bach or the op at the docks." I explained.

"How do you mean?" she asked.

"I chased them down to a boat waiting on the beach. They winged me with a kunai knife, and then stunned me with a flashbang grenade."

"No magic though?"

"I don't think so, just ours."

"Anyone hurt?"

"I got a little scratch, but everyone's fine."

"Could have been a merc, someone with a ninja fetish. These chuckle heads love to create personas in the field. Sometimes it gives them away if you know where to look. Any markings on the blade?"

"I... don't think so. Hold on let me check."

I picked up the knife and carefully glanced over both sides. I couldn't see any markings or symbols, but the handle was wrapped in high quality blue silk.

"No, seems clean. Fine blue silk ribbon on the hilt though." I said.

"Hmm. Okay, I'll do some digging and see what turns up. You need anyone to watch the house in case they come back? I know some reliable muscle." she offered.

"Thanks, but I think I've got it covered for now. I'm going to keep an eye on the security system and then have Matt's team run live surveillance when I can't. Anyone tries that again and I'll light them up good. You find anything new on our mystery man from the docks?"

"Not yet. I thought I had something but came up dry. He doesn't seem connected to anyone else involved, which seems to me that he's in close with Bach, but I don't have anything solid to confirm yet. Could be another decoy." she grumbled.

I could tell she was getting just as tired of the dead ends in this case as I was. Every time we got any closer something happened to set us back or throw us off the trail entirely. Part of me wanted to crawl back in my bed and wallow in self-pity, but I wasn't quite ready to give up just yet.

"Let me know if you find anything, I'm going back down to the beach in a bit to see if I can find any more clues." I said.

"Sure thing. Later." Constance said and dropped the call.

I set the phone and the knife down and thought for a moment. I didn't have a clue how to look for mercenaries or even how I would try. I was pretty sure googling *'real mercenaries'* would just land me on some kind of watchlist. I decided to check the news and see what, if anything, had developed with the tattoo shops.

I checked reports from Matt's team and flipped through the news channels. I stopped on a major network with a headline about magic armed robbery.

"Gang related crime is on the rise, as more magic powered criminals committed more dangerous and bold crimes across the nation." The anchor spoke.

"In cities all across the US, reports are coming in of criminal activity with gang members robbing stores, homes, and even a bank wielding strange magical powers some say. Other experts suggest the criminals are using stolen experimental military equipment, but whatever the case may be we are seeing a surge in criminal activity with a strange magical twist."

I was always impressed at how nonchalant a news anchor could sound while delivering incredibly dark or absurd news like this. It could just be professional, but sometimes it came off as just completely disconnected from reality. They would speak calmly in the mostly the same tone whether they were covering a bombing or a new restaurant opening. It had to be intentional on their part. Maybe it was a requirement of being a news anchor.

I could feel my heart sinking as I came across more and more stories about similar incidents. Opulentia was hitting the street in full force, and it was wreaking havoc. I couldn't help but feel like I was too late, but I knew Bach still had to be stopped. If I could find a way to stop the flow from the source, maybe the world could heal itself from this. I just had to keep fighting, I thought, no matter what.

I turned the news off and went back upstairs and outside to check out the beach. I wanted the fresh air to try and clear my head some while I looked for clues about the attack last night. The beach was a bit of a mess. Blackened spots with shards of glass were scattered along the trail of heavy tracks where Star had struck lightning down around him. I was still trying to figure out how that had missed him, it should have been attracted to him before hitting the ground that close.

He had to be using something to dodge our abilities. I only managed to clip him with my fire, and even that didn't slow him down much. I walked all the way out to the shore looking for signs of anything the man might have dropped but turned up nothing. Anything this close to the water would likely have been taken by the tide already. I took some time to scoop up the glass and tidy the beach up a little while I thought about the series of events.

I couldn't shake the feeling that Bach had to have sent them. I didn't know why he wouldn't send his army of drones, or better equipped mercenaries at least. It wouldn't have been hard to mow us down with guns or just burn the house down while we were inside. He had to be toying with us, letting us know that he knew where we were but that he wasn't threatened enough to remove us from the equation. I growled under my breath as I finished cleaning the sand off my feet in the shower.

Defeated, I made my way back downstairs to listen to some music and think. I had to try and figure out something that would get us ahead of Bach's plan instead of just reacting to things after they happened. I knew there was a plan behind all of this, and if I could just put the pieces together I might be able to find enough of a pattern to let me guess the next steps and try to intervene. I turned on some bass heavy death metal, micro dosed some marijuana, and flopped on my couch to think.

I tried to gather my thoughts on what information we had so far. First, we know from the island that Bach has a huge stockpile of Opulentia and was already planning to distribute it in some way seven years ago. He told us at one point while trying to mess with our heads that he already had two other sources. He seemed to go to ground after that and we didn't hear anything major for a long time. He had to be doing something during all that time other than stalking us, but we had no information as to what.

Almost out of the blue we learn about the cartels distributing Opulentia laced drugs through their usual channels. Then just as we are following up on that, tattoo shops owned by those same gangs pop up all over the place. Then we find out the tattoo shops are getting mysterious designs from a hidden source that contain some of the mystical symbols Bach used to make his drones. It was just too much of a coincidence not to all be connected to something bigger, even if I couldn't see what it was.

I rubbed at my temples in frustration trying to fit all the pieces together. The drugs and the gangs had to be some kind of diversion. What if he was building an army, and using this as cover? If he can get enough chaos in the media and the world at large, it would provide a large distraction for him to make some kind of move. What was the end goal though? World domination? That was just a villain trope in comic books though, right?

Maybe he's trying to see how the government reacts to the influx of crime and the appearance of magic. The Opulentia on the streets currently seemed to be watered down, so maybe it was to see what the response is before making a move with the real deal. Testing the waters so to speak. Or maybe this was the whole plan, maybe he just wanted to be in charge of a network of the largest drug syndicates on the planet bringing him untold wealth to do who knows what?

Not knowing what the end game was really threw a wrench into the whole idea of figuring out what was coming next. It's not easy to jump in front of something when you can't tell where it's actually going. I pondered for a while, and there was something I thought of that could happen in a multitude of plans:

building an army. If he was able to connect to these tattoo shops putting this stuff on the street, it's possible this was used as a screening process for candidates that would react better to his conditioning.

I bolted up and jumped over to my computer to contact Matt. The secure line rang through for only a moment before his face popped up on the screen.

"Got something, boss?" he asked.

"Maybe. I've been trying to get a grasp on Bach's plan using all this open chaos and I had a thought that he might be recruiting people for an army. Can you check around the tattoo shops for missing persons and then try to reference that against the footage we have from the stores? Does that make sense?" I blurted.

"It won't be easy, but it should be possible. Any site in particular?"

"Probably one of the bigger city locations, where it might be easier to cover up someone going missing. If we can find some, we might be able to track them back to his facility somehow. Is there one close to me at all?" I asked.

"There's at least one in Charleston, and one in Columbia." He replied.

"Start with Columbia, if we can find proof of it happening I can get Constance to help me stake the place out."

"Sure thing. Oh before you go, I sent you a notice this morning about some strange activity outside one of our server houses last night. Something kept tripping the security system at one of the repair businesses, but if it was anyone trying to break in they never made it inside. I didn't see anything on the footage, but I prepared a server wipe protocol just in case."

"Someone tried to break in? I had something similar here last night too. Keep a close watch, up security if you feel you need to. I don't want anyone getting their hands on our work here. Hopefully it was just somebody trying to steal laptops again."

"We have brought up live feeds of all server farms here in the base, and I have the team checking it around the clock. If anything happens I will let you know." he added confidently.

"Perfect. Let me know if you turn up anything with the missing persons. If we can link human trafficking to this we might get somewhere with some official support."

"Roger that. I'll keep you posted." he said and cut the line.

I reclined in the chair and thought about what he said. If someone was trying to break into the servers, did Bach know about our whole operation to find him? Was he looking for ways to stop me or just trying to find me and spreading his resources around? I hoped it was as fluke, but it was troubling to say the least.

I felt my leg tapping rapidly, a clear indication my anxiety was spiking. I was working myself up a lot these days with one crazy event after the next. It was starting to take its toll on my nerves. I had been getting heated more often lately too, my anger jumping out at the drop of a hat. The way it happened at the docks nearly got me killed, I needed to make sure I could keep it under control.

It wasn't just anger that was heating me up, and I knew that. I was driven by vengeance, eager to put a stop to Bach's plan, and I think the beast inside me was feeding off that energy. Since we left the island I had mostly been able to make peace with the rage that the creature's blood seemed to amplify. When I let my power take control there was something animalistic about it, something primal. I was still myself, but I didn't feel completely in control.

I had spent months practicing using my abilities, training to fight Bach if I managed to track him down, but also trying to get a grip on the urges inside me begging for destruction. Star expressed similar feelings, but when she allowed her full power to channel out she said she felt an intense clarity, like she was suddenly in more control. After we talked her down on the island and brought her back, she seemed to be in harmony with her powers at all times.

I often wondered if it had something to do with which elements we attuned with when we were fused with the Opulentia. Star's storm powers turned her into a literal force of nature, commanding bolts of lightning like she's the next *Thor*. My fire was incredibly strong as well, the blue flames were much hotter than your average flame, and when I used them I felt like I was tapping into something older than the world itself. It almost felt like the power came from the chaos that created life on our planet, something primordial.

I took another hit and sank back onto my couch to try and calm myself down. I couldn't do much else until either Matt or Constance got back to me. I was tired of having to wait around all the time, but with nothing to go on I didn't have much choice. I closed my eyes and let the smoke and metal wash over me for a little while until I dozed off.

I often had strange dreams, especially since the island, and this one proved to be a bizarre one. I found myself floating in a dark room, weightlessly drifting along in a sea of nothing. Stars appeared, twinkling all around me but I soon realized they weren't stars, but eyes, watching me. Faces formed, blank expressionless faces all staring at me as I floated by.

A few began to open their mouths allowing blood to pour out into a great red river that flowed far beneath my floating body. I was no longer in a vast emptiness but falling from the sky towards a giant sea of blood. I tried to call my fire to me to slow my fall but found only wisps of smoke. I hit the liquid and burst up through the other side like passing through some kind of doorway. I crashed down on a solid floor in what looked like a warehouse, nude and dripping with blood.

The room looked like that warehouse scene at the end of *Indiana Jones* with rows upon rows of boxes on shelves. The eyes were now lights beaming down from above illuminating the boxes as they began to open by themselves. Long arms stretched out of the boxes, all various skin tones and absurdly long, reaching up to the tops of the shelves. Each arm was covered with mystic symbols glowing different colors as they continued to reach upwards, and then they all crashed down upon me.

I bolted awake; my phone buzzed with a security alert. The front gate was open on the screen and Star's VW bus was rolling into the driveway. I sighed and tried to shake off the weird dream. Something had to give soon, this kind of stress was going to eat me alive. I started walking back up the stairs and my phone buzzed again. This time it was Callie and Cherry approaching the house in my Dodge. Maybe I should see if Matt could fine tune the system to not flag our personal vehicles.

I reached the top of the stairs and turned into the hallway towards the living room. My phone buzzed again, before I even got it into my pocket from the previous alert. I glanced up to make sure I didn't bump into anything and that's when I saw him standing at the other end of the hall.

CHAPTER 9

Flames coursed around my body in a protective barrier even before I could cognitively react to what was happening. A blade rushed at my face, but the force of the rising heat was enough to throw it off course and made it sail past. I lunged forward, channeling my power with pure instinct rather than intent, and when my flaming fist connected with the man's chest it launched him clear across the living room onto the couch. I shook my head to regain my senses and it felt like I had taken control of my body from someone else.

Star, Callie, and Cherry entered through the front door together, and Star gasped as she saw me standing fully enflamed in our house. Before she could say anything the man jumped up from the couch high into the air and hung there floating. Callie shrieked, and unfortunately brought the man's attention to them. He held up his hand and I felt the air in the room shift as several kunai knives launched from his sleeve towards them.

To everyone's surprise, Cherry reacted first. She waived her hand and a burst of wind the knives changed course in mid-air, embedding them into the wall next to her. She jumped into the air and flew towards the man with incredible speed, the wind knocking papers and small objects from all the surfaces in the room. Her eyes were solid white as she hovered in front of him and held her hand in front of his face. I moved forward to try and intervene, but I only managed two steps before I heard the man let out a blood-curdling scream.

Cherry clenched her fist slowly, and drew her arm slowly backwards, pulling liquid from the skin of the screaming man. First it appeared to just be tears or sweat, but then it ran crimson as it poured out from his eyes, nose, and mouth. Callie screamed and covered her eyes and Star and I both ran to try and grab her down, but she was too high up now, lifting the man up near the fifteen-foot ceiling of the living room as she continued to draw blood from the man. After just a few seconds he stopped screaming.

Cherry let him drop to the ground with a disgusting thud as she collected the blood into an orb, much like when she removed Callie's powers. This was human blood though, not just the blood of the creature. It seemed to be nearly all the blood in his body swirling in the orb next to her. She lifted her other hand and channeled fire through it to cauterize it like a giant floating scab that she then dropped onto his lifeless body.

My flames had already dropped before I watched Cherry float back to the ground and stand over the man she had just killed. I ran over to her and just as I reached her, I watched color return to her eyes as they rolled back, and she collapsed. I just managed to catch her before she hit her head on the table. Star and Callie quickly joined me, and we all kneeled and held Cherry unsure what to say about what had just happened.

Callie used her foot to poke the body of the man, but he did not stir. Star just sat with her hand over her mouth, staring at the body lost in thought. I lifted Cherry and decided to carry her to her room. I could hear her snoring lightly as I walked. I felt tears running down my cheeks and as I laid her onto her bed I felt waves of emotions washing over me.

I was furious that someone had been in our home without me knowing despite my constant paranoia. I was shocked that my little girl had so quickly dispatched him and murdered someone in self-defense. I was terrified because I didn't know what to do with the body or how we could explain what happened to anyone. Most of all, I was ashamed. Ashamed that I had failed my family once again and let something terrible happen in our own home.

I wiped the tears from my face as I walked out of Cherry's room and headed back downstairs to the living room. Callie was rolling the body up in a sheet and Star had kitchen gloves on and was trying to put the large, coagulated blood ball into a trash bag. I pulled out my phone, opened the secure line, and called Constance.

"Hey Tri, what's up? You never call unless something's wrong." She answered.

It took me a few seconds before I could reply, I was struggling to find my voice again and fighting back my emotions.

"You there?" she asked.

"Ye.. Yeah. Something awful happened. Someone was in the house. Can you come over?" I finally managed.

"What?! Yeah, I'll be there in about an hour. Just gotta... fuck it. I'm on my way. Thirty minutes." She replied.

I could hear her rustling something and then slamming her car door before the call dropped. I collapsed on the love seat and watched as Star helped Callie tie the ends of the sheet closed around the body. They were focused, but I could tell they were in shock. I began to cry as I sat there watching the people I loved cleaning up another one of my messes. I felt like such a failure, like I wasn't doing enough, like *I* wasn't enough.

They heard me crying and sat on either side of me. They wrapped their arms around me, and we all sobbed together, the stress catching up to all of us. We sat there quietly sobbing and staring at the dead body, wrapped in an old sheet, laying on our living room floor, next to a trash bag full of its own roasted blood.

I almost wanted to laugh it was so absurd, this couldn't be what my life was turning into.

Roughly thirty-five minutes later, my phone buzzed, and I glanced at it to see Constance racing up the driveway in her black sedan. She pulled up to the house and rushed inside. Professional that she was, she just glanced at the body and then to the three of us and nodded.

"Are you guys okay? Did anyone get hurt?" She asked.

I shook my head.

"Where's Cherry? Is she okay?"

I nodded. "Upstairs."

"Do you have a boat?"

We loaded the body into the small motorboat in my garage. It was on a trailer attached to an ATV so that we could easily tow it down to the beach or to one of the public docks in the area. Constance grabbed a cinderblock from her trunk and some rope, I was always impressed with how she was prepared for damn near everything. I climbed in the boat while Constance started the ATV and drove us down the beach, backing the boat into the water so we could launch. I had bought the boat for fishing, but had only used it once or twice, and decided it wasn't worth the effort. I never would have thought I'd be using it to hide a body.

Constance climbed in the boat and began tying the cinder block to the body with the rope as I started the engine and we set off for deep water. She had me drive the boat for a while, maybe a mile or so away from shore, far enough that the body hopefully wouldn't just get caught in the current and brought in with the tide if the rope broke. We rolled the body up and over the edge, careful not to tip ourselves over and I just stared blankly as the figure vanished into the waves, hopefully to be forever lost at sea.

We sat in the boat for a little while under the moon. I was crying again, and I could feel the darkness closing in on my mind. I was spiraling into my feelings, and it wouldn't be long before the crippling depression took root once more. Constance sat across from me, smoking a cigarette, and looking out over the rolling waters.

"Want to tell me about the body we just dumped?" She asked, softly.

"I don't know much. He was in the house, didn't set off my security system. He attacked us, he…" I paused as I suddenly realized it. "He had magic."

"Tattoos?" Constance asked.

"I don't know, he was all wrapped up in black cloth like the last one. I couldn't see him, but he was using wind magic for sure before… before Cherry killed him."

"Cherry?!" Constance choked, nearly dropping her cig.

"Yeah, she had some kind of episode, probably out of panic. Her eyes went all white and she just floated up to the guy and killed him. Pulled all the blood out of his body, it was pretty horrific to watch. I couldn't stop her, it all happened too fast."

Constance took a long drag of her cig and then tossed it into the water.

"Mercenaries don't tend to show up on missing persons reports at least. We shouldn't have to worry too much about the cops looking for him, whoever hired him is another story."

"It's got to be Bach, right? I'm pretty sure he knows where we live, and I'm surprised he hasn't done more before now." I babbled, my mind racing with scenarios.

"It's probably not him directly, paper trails and all, but someone working for him seems likely. Could be we are spooking him with our progress and now he's trying to stop us."

"I should have killed him on that god damned island when I had the chance."

"If you really had the chance, you would have. You don't have time to beat yourself up over what-ifs, Tri. We need to focus on keeping your family safe right now."

I was taken aback by her statement. She was right though; Bach had never let me get close enough to stop him or I would have. I started the motor and ushered the boat back to shore. I was glad Constance was here to keep me focused, otherwise I might have just let the boat drift in the waves and carry myself out to die at sea.

Back on the beach, we wrestled the boat back onto the ATV trailer and hauled it back up to the back of the garage. Star was sitting on the back steps waiting for us, watching the stars to help clear her mind.

"Do you guys have anywhere safe you can go for a little while? Keep these guys off you for a bit?" Constance asked.

"I'm not sure where would be safer than here with our high-end security system and magic powers... unless we moved into a military base or something." I replied.

"Well, clearly things have been compromised here so moving around would at least add steps for anyone following you. I would pack some things and at least head to a busy hotel for a little while. Somewhere with a fair amount of traffic, lots of people with cell phone cameras at the ready. Its great deterrent for merc activity when everyone could be recording at the flick of a thumb." Constance explained.

"Yeah, we could do that I guess." I said. "Maybe we go back to Charlotte for a while, but then what? I feel like I'm just sitting around waiting for things to react to instead of hunting this asshole down."

"We're following every lead we have so far. We know something is happening at these tattoo shops now, shit's popping up all over the country and the government is starting to take notice. We might not have to do much if they catch wind of who's behind it all. They've probably already got the FBI digging. They're connected enough to the drug cartels to know something's been up for a while now, surely."

"The government's taking notice? So it's already that big of a problem..."

"Yeah, cops have been having a hell of a time dealing with the gang violence. It was only a matter of time before they started calling the feds for backup. I can't imagine it will be much longer before they start raiding the tattoo shops looking for answers."

"Maybe we should turn over what we have, help them along." Star added, leaning her head on my shoulder.

"I don't know if I want to reveal us to the government like that though. They'll want to know where we got the intel, and how we're connected. If they find out about our powers they could lock us up and experiment on us and we'd be in a whole new hell." I said.

"You're probably right about that. A couple people picked up in the gang raids seemingly vanished right after. Their families got loud about it at first, but something seems to have silenced them. Sounds like fed interference to me." Constance sighed.

"We're going to have to keep ourselves a secret for now, I'd rather die than be a lab rat again. I'd hate for any of us to be there again." I grumbled.

"What if we let Cherry take our powers?" Star asked.

"That would keep us safe, but what about Cherry. I don't think she can remove her own powers, and I'm not sure she'd want to. We sure as hell couldn't force her, she's growing stronger all the time, and I'm not sure we could control her if something happened. They'd be quick to take her, or worse just kill her outright to study the body." I said.

I rubbed at my temples, trying to relieve some of the stress my mind was under. Constance was right, staying here was dangerous. I needed to warn Beatrice and her family, but I wasn't sure what to tell them. In the years since the island, we had told them some things about what was happening, but I didn't want to scare them away, so we hadn't told them everything.

They knew about our magic and some of Cherry's abilities, but I never told them the full story of what happened on the island. They only knew that something terrible happened to us, and that we had barely made it home alive. I hadn't told them about Bach or his plans to distribute his vile creation across the world, just that we had been tricked by an evil man and experimented on. They took it in stride and kept loving us just the same as far as I could tell, but I always wondered if they would be safe staying with us.

"You guys need to get some rest. We can plan everything in the morning, how about I stay and keep watch on the place while you try to get some sleep?" Constance suggested.

"I'm not sure I can sleep, but I do need it. Thanks Constance, you're too good to me." I said, standing up and giving her a quick hug.

"Hey, I'm just doing my job. You can't pay me if you turn up missing." She joked to ease the tension.

Star grabbed my hand, and we walked up stairs together, leaving Constance to patrol and keep an eye out. Callie was leaning in the doorway to Cherry's room watching her sleep.

"She's out like a light, that must have taken a lot out of her." she said as we approached.

"Yeah, she'll probably be out for a while. Constance is staying to keep watch so we can get some rest too. We need to make plans in the morning to take off for a bit while we try to figure out why these people keep showing up here." I said.

"Yeah, I guess my dates with James with have to wait." she said, wrapping her arms around mine.

"I'm going to have to reschedule so many meetings" Star sighed.

I couldn't help but laugh. I could tell they were downplaying the seriousness of the situation to make me feel better. They both knew that our regular lives were on the line now, and yet they still were concerned about how I was feeling. Tears pushed through the laugh and I was sobbing again.

We walked to the bedroom together, and all climbed into the big bed still holding hands. Callie and Star managed to fall asleep before me, they were each exhausted I could tell. It took a while for me to calm my mind enough to rest, but eventually I gave in. It wasn't restful, but I drifted off to sleep on a tear-soaked pillow.

Morning came sooner than I wanted, and we all got up and began to pack up some things for an extended trip. I went to check on Cherry, and she was still sleeping peacefully, and I decided to let her rest while I went to speak with Beatrice about taking some time off. I made my way downstairs, and Constance was leaning against the counter in the kitchen scrolling her phone and sipping a cup of coffee.

"Morning!" She said with a smile. "I made coffee, figured you'd need it."

I nodded and grumbled something like a thank you, as I poured a cup. I stirred a cube of sugar into it to cut the acidity, and then walked outside. It was early morning, and the sun wasn't fully up yet. Gerald was already out mowing the lawn, but Beatrice was likely still at home, she usually came in after breakfast to work.

I walked to the garage and the ATV trying fruitlessly to not think about the body I had dumped in the ocean the night before. I unhooked the trailer and climbed on to drive down to the house we had built on the property for Beatrice and Gerald to have their own private place to live while still being on site if we needed anything from them. I was dreading the conversation I needed to have and was already trying to come up with ways to hide the truth.

I reached their house, a cute little place that reminded me of houses in fairy tales. It had a little fence and a flower garden. I half expected there to be a pie cooling in the window like a cartoon or something. I walked up to the door and knocked, waiting anxiously on the covered porch, listening to the rocking chair slightly creaking as it moved in the breeze.

Beatrice answered the door with a beaming smile, she was always so kind and loving.

"Oh, good morning Trianna, did you need something?" she asked.

"I just needed to talk with you for a little bit. Something's happened, and I'm worried you might not be safe here." I explained.

"Oh dear, please, come inside."

I followed her through the lovely home she and Gerald had made together, and my heart ached at the possibility they could lose it all because of me. I swore to myself that I couldn't let that happen, I wouldn't.

"So, what's all this about? Are you okay?" she asked, sitting down across from me at the dinner table with her own cup of coffee.

I sighed and tried my best to explain the situation. I told her about Bach and his shady organization from the island, and that he was responsible for what had happened to us. I told her that I had been trying to find a way to stop him from hurting anyone else but had been unable to find him. I explained now that we were getting closer he was retaliating and that he might send more people after us. She sipped her coffee and listened eagerly.

"I'm just worried that they might try to hurt you guys to get to me, and I don't want that to happen. We are going to leave for a little while, go somewhere else so that it's harder for them to find us. I'd like you guys to go somewhere safe too. I'll pay you still, but I want you to take the cats and get out of here for a month or two." I explained.

"Well, that's a whole lot to digest, but I'd be lying if I said I didn't notice something was wrong. Gerald keeps saying he thinks he seen someone while he's working but every time he goes to see there's nothing there. My sister lives a couple hours away, so we could go stay with her. What do I tell her about all this though?" she asked.

"Tell her that your boss got into some trouble and just wants to keep you safe. Don't tell her about Bach or our magic, it might draw too much attention if it gets into the rumor mill." I answered.

"Okay. I can do that. Gerald should be done mowing soon and he'll be wanting some lemonade, so I'll let him know what's going on. I'll keep those little kitties of yours safe, don't you worry about that. They love helping me clean house, so I'm sure they won't mind taking a little trip with us." She smiled.

"I can't tell you how much I appreciate you, Beatrice. You're such a sweet soul, I am so sorry to put you in danger."

"We all make mistakes, Trianna. Some are worse than others, but it's how we deal with them after that defines us. I know you will do what you can to make everything right. You protect your family how you know best; we'll be waiting for you to tell us when to come home." she said, patting my hand as she spoke and smiling that big kind smile of hers, "You can handle this; you always find a way."

I smiled back and gave her a big hug before heading back outside to ride back to our house. I waved goodbye and started up the ATV. I hated putting them out, but I was going to make sure they had anything they needed while they were gone. It was the least I could do for putting them in danger.

Back at the house, Star and Callie had gathered our luggage and packed up what they felt we needed to be gone for a while. We weren't sure how long we would need but if we ran out of anything we would deal with it later. I grabbed mine and stuffed it full of clothes, and then went downstairs to get my secure computer so I could keep contact with Matt from the hotel. I had built it in a case with a handle for easy transport for just this kind of emergency.

Callie went to Cherry's room and started helping her pack now that she was finally awake. She didn't seem to remember anything from the night before and we all decided that was for the best. We told her that we needed to leave because Bach was after us, and that was enough to get her on board with the plan. It only took a few hours to get everyone packed up and ready to leave.

Star had been at the table with her laptop looking for hotels and made reservations for a suite at a fancy place in Charlotte that did long term rentals. We talked out the plan, and decided that taking our vehicles might draw attention, so we rented a van and had it delivered so we could load it up and go. I passed the time waiting for it to arrive by picking up all the cats and loving on them since I wasn't sure when or if I would see them again. I had briefly considered bringing them with us but decided that if anything happened at the hotel we didn't want to risk losing them and so Beatrice was the best option.

The rental service dropped off our van and I signed the paperwork while Callie and Star loaded everything into the back. Cherry climbed in and started reading her book, and I stood in the driveway looking back at the house. I was so proud of myself when I bought it, and all the memories of the time we spent together in it came flooding back. I didn't want to say goodbye to my dream home, but it wasn't safe anymore. I had to stop Bach and only then could I come home again to my lovely house by the sea.

Constance joined us in the driveway, and we discussed details before she left. We planned to stay at least two months with the option to stay longer if needed. Hopefully our leads would pan out and we could catch Bach soon before anything else got out of control. Constance would periodically check the house to see if anyone else showed up and try to make sure nothing bad happened to it while we were gone. I still had access to the cameras, but I couldn't trust them as much anymore, and I needed to talk to Matt about that.

Everyone piled into the car, and we set off on the road. It would be several hours, and I planned to take back roads most of the way which made it longer, but it would also be easier to tell if we were being followed. Constance honked at us from her sedan as we pulled out of the driveway to begin our trip. I honked back and fought back tears. I really didn't want to leave.

On the drive we flipped through radio stations, listening to news reports about people using magic to commit all kinds of crimes now, and having fantastical shoot outs with police. Clubs were having to shut down because people were doing drugs and then using magic on the dancefloor, while at least two raves were raided by police due to people flying through the air or throwing fireballs in rhythm with the music. The world was full of chaos as the Opulentia made its way around, and it felt like things had gone to shit practically overnight.

Luckily, the drive was uneventful and no one seemed to be following us. We stopped for fast food and eventually made it to Charlotte without any issues. I had been here several times and was starting to know my way around. I barely even needed the GPS to find the hotel. We pulled up and parked so I could check us in.

We got a large suite higher up in the building with several bedrooms for everyone to keep their own space, something vital when travelling with a teenager. We all picked rooms and started to unpack, and everything felt surreal. It was like being on vacation, we were just going through the motions of being in a hotel, but instead of going away for a fun break we were fleeing our home and hiding in plain sight for protection. I was having a hard time getting my brain to cope with the juxtaposition of it all.

We settled in, and I flopped on the bed ready to stretch out and relax from the drive. I flicked ono the TV and it was already on the news station. There was a conference happening from the white house, and the president was getting ready to speak. The words scrolling the bottom of the screen read: *PRESIDENT MORALES TO ADDRESS CONCERNS OVER GANG VIOLENCE AND MAGIC.* I sat up, dumbstruck with my eyes glued to the screen.

The president walked steadily to the podium and began to speak. He carried himself with purpose and wore a focused concern on his face ready to read the prepared speech about the current situation in a way that they hoped would ease the minds of people across the nation.

"My fellow Americans. In recent days we have seen an explosive rise in violence across the United States, as well as the world. A mysterious drug has run rampant in the streets and is tearing communities apart. I would like to take a few moments to address and explain things as we currently understand them in this ongoing investigation.

"Witnesses at the scenes claim that gang members and drug users are committing these acts with the aid of some kind of weapon that allows them to perform feats of a magic-like nature. There are rumors that this drug came from an experimental military facility, and I would like to state first and foremost that this rumor is false. The United States Government does not have any programs dedicated to this kind of weaponry or pharmaceutical, and I can say with absolute certainty that we had no knowledge of this prior to these recent events."

"We are currently investigating the source of these outbreaks and what connection it may have to similar violence we are seeing across the globe. We are joining forces with other world leaders to determine the best course of action, but I have personally assigned a task force under the Secretary of Defense along with the FBI to begin addressing things here on American soil as quickly as possible."

"We do not know yet if these attacks are related to any terrorist organization or if they have ties to any of the world's governments at this time but are taking every step possible to get to the bottom of this. At this time, I have not yet decided to institute martial law as such extreme measures could potentially cause more harm than good, but I have decided to declare a state of emergency until we can gather more information on the situation at hand."

"I urge you as citizens to not consume any strange drugs or pharmaceuticals or any other unknown substance without direct advice from your physician, and to report any strange activity to your local police department. We are networking with police and state troopers across the nation to face this menace head on, and we appreciate reliable information that may lead us to the source. If you see anyone using these weapons or performing feats of magic for non-entertainment purposes please alert your local authorities. Thank you."

The voices of the press surged as the president finished his speech, but he simply waved and walked away with his entourage of secret service. The Press Secretary took the stand and began fielding questions as the camera panned through the crowd to see all of the officials and advisors present for the speech. My heart skipped a beat, and I gasped as the camera passed by a familiar face. Sitting off to the side of the stage with some members of congress was Bach, smug look on his face as he watched the press ask questions.

"No fucking way…." I said in utter disbelief.

Star and Callie had joined me halfway through the speech, and they reacted much the same way. None of us would ever forget that man's wretched face and there we were hiding in a hotel room miles from our home as he sat only a handful of yards from the President. I had spent seven long years searching for him, only to finally spot him on the news, clustered with politicians. I growled as my fists clenched, and I could feel the heat rising inside me.

My head was spinning as it tried to keep up with all the emotions I was feeling all at once. I wanted to scream, I wanted to puke, I wanted to hide. Just as I was about to succumb to rage, the power went out, the windows shattered, and broken glass scattered across my face.

CHAPTER 10

In the years since I escaped the island, I had spent some time getting in touch with my power. There was a force hiding deep within that was stronger than I could ever hope to be on my own, and it used to speak to me in my dreams. For months it haunted me, teasing me, reminding me of what happened to us in that wretched lab. I thought it wanted to take control of me for its own gain.

I found a trauma therapist, and actually went to sessions for a while. They helped me process a lot of what had happened, even though it took me a while to really open up. As I learned to process things, the voices began to ease away from haunting and started to seem conversational. After months of mediation, self-reflection, and therapy I learned how to communicate with it and discovered that it wasn't always trying to control, it was trying to empower. It wanted me to grow stronger and seek the vengeance I deserved.

For a time, I didn't trust it. I thought it only wanted to deceive me into giving in and letting it have control. Eventually I learned that it wasn't a malevolent force or some creature wanting to escape. It was me but an enhanced version of me, like some kind of powerful incarnation of myself. It was a representation of a more primal version that felt things more intensely and was focused on revenge. It scared me and so I buried it, and to my surprise it stayed dormant.

As I fell into depression I could feel it there, not taunting, not demanding, but waiting. It felt the sadness that I felt but stronger, it felt everything stronger. It was raw all around, and echoed whatever I was feeling which I found strangely comforting. It took time, but I eventually found peace with it, found peace with what I was now capable of with it. I knew if I ever needed to give in and let primal feelings take control, they were there, ready and waiting.

As the glass danced across my skin, leaving micro abrasions in their wake, I felt it call out to me. As the boots hit my chest and sent me careening to the floor, I felt it scream out. As Star and Callie all cried out in pain and confusion, I felt it reach for control. I took a breath, closed my eyes, and gave in to rage inside me.

It felt like letting go of thousands of pounds all at once. Everything that had been weighing me down for the last seven years broke free. Flames rose around me, my eyes rolled back in my head, and I felt flames burst from the sockets, but I could still see clearly. My skin grew tight and suddenly I couldn't feel the heat anymore. I glanced at my hands and found them encased in ash, my skin looked like a lava flow down the side of an erupting volcano with blue flames visible through the moving cracks on the surface.

Time slowed to a crawl, as I glanced around the room at the mercenaries that had burst through the window. There were six, a few had guns but were not using them. They had Callie and Star pinned on the ground next to the bed, and two were heading towards Cherry's room. Ropes dangled outside the window, and I could see a couple more people descending.

I stood up to my full height, and felt my body rise off the floor into the air. I hovered for a moment, and the mercs began to reach for their guns. Their faces were covered, but one's eyes were visible, and they were wide open with fear. I took another breath, and as I exhaled I let go of the last bit of emotion holding me down and closed my eyes.

It was over just as quickly as it began. When I opened my eyes again, I was standing in the middle of the room, water from the sprinkler system pouring down my steaming body. Charred bodies littered the floor, and most of the room and furniture was smoldering. There was one section of the room, directly behind me, that was completely untouched by flames. Star, Callie, and Cherry stood there in silent awe of what had just happened. I could hear the fire alarm blaring in the hallways.

Everyone rushed over to check on me as my head cleared. I took a moment to relax into the arms of my loved ones as they wrapped around me.

"We have to go, now." I said calmly. "Police and Fire are probably already on the way, and there's no way we can explain all this."

"Who are these people? Is it Bach?" Star asked.

"Not directly, but most likely. I think I have some idea what he's up to now, but we don't have time to discuss it, we need to go!" I answered.

"Well, I'm pretty sure you burned all of our stuff, but hopefully we can find the car keys." Callie said, searching through a pile of burnt rags that was likely her luggage moments earlier.

We dug around for a moment, and then I remembered I still had the keys in my pocket. I reached in and found them unharmed but a little warm. We managed to find our phones and purses mostly unharmed. Callie picked up her bag and was slapping out some glowing embers when she paused and began to tear at part of the pocket.

"What the fuck is that?" she said out loud.

She tore at the fabric and pulled out a small coin sized device with a small nearly unnoticeable light. A tracking device. We had been tracked the whole way here. Suddenly I could hear sirens getting closer from outside.

"Smash it and let's go! We'll check our shit in the car!" I shouted.

We raced down the hall, down the stairs, and out through the lobby just as the police arrived outside. There were people still evacuating the lobby, but most were standing outside and being ushered towards the other side of the road. We darted around the corner towards the garage entrance to hopefully avoid questioning. With all the magic related incidents popping up in the news, there was no way I was going to risk the police finding us in such a bizarre situation.

There were several people getting in their cars to leave, and I hoped it wouldn't stop us from getting out in time. If we were too erratic, it would just make the cops chase us down as suspects for the fire, which given that it was our room that was on fire, we likely already were. We piled into the car, and I drove through the garage as quickly as I safely could, while everyone else began to search their bags and clothes for any more tracking devices. The small line of cars ahead of us filtered out into the street and away from the hotel with no issue, and I followed suit. As I turned out I could hear one of the officers shouting for us to stop, and I could see them setting up barricades at the other end of the street. We had just made it.

I sighed heavily and wove through the city streets with no real destination in mind, just hoping to shake off anyone following us. I pulled out my phone and thumbed my unlock code through the freshly cracked screen. Once it unlocked I ran the security program Matt had installed to ensure the phone was secure and shut down any tracking while I called him.

"Matt, can you hear me? I'm in the shit, please tell me you can hear me!"

"Yes.. yeah Tri, I got you. What's going on?"

"We've been attacked by mercs at the hotel, I burned out the whole room to get away, but Callie found like a tracker in her purse. How do I see if our phones are being monitored?"

"Well yours should be fine with the soft I ran on it to build this secure line, but if you're worried about the others, they'd need to be properly examined. I can do it, but you'd have to bring them to lab, and if they're compromised... well that could lead to problems."

"No shit, any quick solutions? I need to come to you anyway."

"Bust them and throw them away? Or you could turn them off and wrap them in foil... might be enough until I can take a look."

"I don't have any fucking foil in the car, Matt… ugh fine I'll stop at the store. Call Constance and see if she can come for backup or send some muscle or something."

"Sure. Did you see the news?"

"Don't. Just fucking don't, I saw it. I'll see you in an hour or so."

"See you then, boss."

I ended the call and tossed my phone into the cupholder as I looked around for a grocery store.

"Doesn't look like there's anything else in the bags, do we need to do anything about the phones?" Star asked.

"I'm getting us some foil at the store, and we can grab drinks and snacks but we gotta be quick about it. Shut the phones off for now, then we'll wrap them up. Matt better not be pulling my leg with that." I answered.

Callie was holding on to Cherry, who was clearly overwhelmed by everything. I could hear her sobbing softly into Callie's chest.

"Cherry, baby. It's going to be okay. I'm going to get us somewhere safe." I said.

I know Mommy, it's just all so scary.

"I know baby, it's alright. It's fine to be scared. We're going to get through this."

You were scary too, but I know you were protecting us.

My heart sank. Despite her own abilities, Cherry was still a young girl, and I had just immolated a bunch of people in front of her. That was probably going to leave some scars. I bit my lip to try and distract myself, so I could focus on what I needed to do. I pulled the car into the store parking lot and found a space.

I released my seat belt and crawled into the back to give Cherry a hug. I held onto her so tightly, hating myself for making her watch that. I knew that she understood, but she shouldn't have to, she should get to live a normal life and not have to deal with this kind of bullshit.

I love you, Mommy.

"I love you too, Cherry." I said, kissing her forehead.

"We all do." Callie said, holding us both.

"Forever and always." Star added, resting her hand on my leg.

I wiped tears from my face and sniffled a bit to try and clear my emotions to go inside. I needed to put a stop to this before anything else got out of hand. We all took a few minutes to compose ourselves and then went inside for snacks and supplies. It was late, but luckily this store was open twenty-four hours, and we didn't have to rush. I needed to get some heavy caffeine and soon.

As we walked through the aisles my anxiety kicked in, and I felt like everyone was watching us, like they all knew what I had just done. Every time I looked around, I swore someone was staring or pointing, but there was hardly anyone even in the store. I knew it was all in my head, but logic rarely beats anxiety in these situations. I picked up a few energy drinks and protein bars to try and cover the basics of filling my stomach and keeping me alert. The anxiety and stress were already going to keep me awake, might as well be a little jittery too.

Star got some fruit and cheese, Cherry got some dried fruit and candy, and Callie got some nuts and smoothies. We all had different ideas of panic snacks it seemed. I started walking to the register but had to stop and go back for the aluminum foil that I had originally come in to get. I'm sure the overworked underpaid employee behind the counter probably didn't care but couldn't help but think this was a weird set of things to buy and that they would be questioning what we were doing. If they did, they didn't say anything other than an unenthused *'thanks, come again.'*

We walked back out to the car, and I tried my best to act natural while sneaking glances all around the parking lot for anyone watching. I was letting the nerves make me paranoid now, and that wasn't great. I needed to get to Matt so I could hide in the security bunker and ease my mind about being followed. Everyone else was tired and hungry, and I'm pretty sure Callie and Cherry were dozing off in the back seat as we drove. Star was staring out the window, and I could tell she was lost in thought.

"You okay babe?" I asked.

"Yeah, it's just a lot, y'know?" she replied.

"Yeah, I can't say that's what I was expecting."

"Why now?" she said.

"Huh?"

"Why after all these years of us hunting him, why does he show up now? Why does he send goons now? Seven years is a long time, so what's the deal?"

"Constance thinks we got too close and spooked him. We saw someone at the docks pushing Opulentia, but it wasn't Bach. I think he's got someone working the crime rings for him, I'm just not sure why. Maybe it's a distraction, maybe it's just easy money… dunno. I can't wrap my head around it all, but he's got something big in the works. What the fuck was he doing on TV with the president?"

"I'm not sure, but I don't like it. There's something really fucked up going on, and we have to stop him before it gets worse."

"Agreed. But if he's in tight with the government I'm not sure how we'll be able to get to him. As if his own resources weren't enough of a problem, he might make us look like terrorists if we aren't careful." I said, continuing to drive to the shop in a nonsense pattern to try and keep from being followed.

The computer shop was conveniently located downtown where it could be easily accessed by foot traffic, but on the end of the street so there was room for us to have our own parking lot.

The building was a restaurant originally, and during prohibition the owners built a speakeasy in the basement. We renovated it entirely into a sever farm and storage room when I first bought the property for the repair business, but after the island I converted the basement into a secure bunker for my team of digital investigators to use.

It was still mostly servers, but there was a main room that had been converted into a bit of a command center full of monitors and other things Matt used to coordinate our efforts on tracking Bach. He had a few people that worked with him sometimes, but we kept a lot of things remote so that if anything was compromised we'd lose less. Matt had been one of my best technicians when I first opened the repair business and had studied network security in college. I knew a fair bit about computers, but he made me feel dumb by comparison.

When I needed someone to set up and run a high-tech center that could help track Bach's through the net, he was an obvious choice. The sheer amount of data he was able to filter and process through even on his own was impressive, and then being able to add on leading a team of equally impressive techs was game changing. I was forever grateful for his continued efforts to provide digital security and investigation over the years. I'd be lost without him to say the least.

Everyone else had fallen asleep by the time I finally pulled into the parking lot of the building across the street from the shop. I didn't want to risk being followed directly to the base if they were still managing to do so. I woke everyone up and we took a moment to watch and scan around the area and the passing traffic to see if anyone was watching before we got out. Content that the coast was clear, we made our way to the shop, and I unlocked the door to let us all inside.

I locked the doors behind us and led everyone to the base entrance hidden behind a moveable rack of components in the storage room. I pulled a hidden lever and the whole wall shifted and then opened to reveal a security door at the end of a short hallway. It had taken a few expert craftsmen to make the wall look completely normal when it was closed but I loved how it made me feel like I had my own secret *Batcave*. No wonder everyone kept teasing me about a super suit. I entered the code to open the door and ushered everyone inside, then hit the button to close the wall and door behind us.

The room smelled interesting. It was a mix of electronics, air conditioning, and lemon-scented candles. This was a lobby of sorts, but there was new furniture and a bed, tapestries hanging on the walls, and a full-sized refrigerator. Next to a pile of bean bag chairs in the corner was a large bookshelf and a hundred-gallon aquarium that housed a handful of colorful fish and plants, and Cherry immediately dashed over to watch them swim around. I smiled at her excitement.

"I guess she's occupied for now. Looks like Matt made himself at home here." I thought out loud.

Through another small hallway was the command center. Maps hung on the walls with pins and photos from surveillance cameras, images of important locations and people that may be connected to Bach in some way. There were monitors everywhere on the massive circular desk in the middle of the room, and a wall of TVs on one side of the room that had continuous feeds of news channels and security cameras. The far wall had a series of workbenches and shelves full of components for security systems and computers, mostly spare parts in case anything in the main system failed.

"Welcome back to the bunker, boss." Matt's voice echoed from behind one of the shelves.

He was carrying some kind of device in a box over to the table. He set some things out, plugged them into a laptop and held his hand out.

"Phones?" he said expectantly.

"Oh, right. Here, I wrapped them up a few times. Hopefully it worked." I said.

I handed him them phones as Callie and Star found chairs to sit down. We were all exhausted from the day's events, and I could see it was starting to wear on them. While Matt began to unwrap and examine the phones, I gave each of them a hug.

"I'm really sorry all this is happening." I said.

"We knew this was a possibility from the start." Callie replied.

"We've always known this was going to be dangerous. I think maybe we got a little complacent over the years with nothing really happening." Star added.

"Yeah, this was a big shift. I'm a little worried that it's only going to get worse. Any word from Constance, Matt?" I said.

"Yep, she's on the way. Should be here in the morning. Said to tell Star she's got 'the package' with her." Matt said, more focused on his work than the conversation.

"Package?" I asked.

"You'll see." Star grinned.

"Phones are all clean, but there's ways to track smartphones that don't require direct connections. If you're really worried about it, I'd suggest leaving them off or replacing them. I have a few burners here we could set up the secure lines on." Matt said, handing us our phones.

"We probably should do that, don't want to risk it." Callie said. "Oh, I should tell Jason that I'm going to be out of town for a while."

"You didn't already?" I asked.

"No, I was too busy getting ready to leave, I forgot all about it. Would it be okay if I texted him? I don't want him to worry." Callie answered.

"Yeah, you should tell him something, so he doesn't call the cops. Gotta think of something to explain not being able to talk for a while, at least until we set up the secured lines." I replied.

"I can have them set up in a few hours, it's easier when I don't have to do it remotely. You guys should get some sleep too, you look like hell." Matt interjected.

"It's been hell tonight." I retorted.

"There's some cots in storage, not the most comfortable but they work. I've also got a twin bed out there if you want, I'm usually up all night anyway. Crime does more at night than during the day, and the team usually monitors daytime activity for me." Matt said, cracking open an energy drink.

"Yeah, I could use the rest. We're all pretty beat. Thanks Matt." I said.

We headed back to the other room, and stopped as we noticed something strange. Cherry was standing next to the aquarium with her hand on the glass. All of the fish were floating near that side of the tank, looking at her almost as if they were communicating. I tilted my head in confusion.

"Cherry?" Star asked.

The fish looked up and then went back to swimming through the tank like normal, as if we had interrupted them and they decided to look natural. Cherry turned to face us with a smile on her face.

The fish are really pretty! So many colors

"Were you talking to the fish?" Callie asked.

No, it's more like... feeling. We just kind of connected and had a moment. I could almost feel the water. It's peaceful.

"Alright then, dear. Let's get some sleep. I'm going to set up some cots, do you want one or do you want to have the bed? Or you could sleep on the beanbags?" Star replied.

I'll sleep here on the beanbags. I like the sound of the aquarium.

"Okay, goodnight hon." I said, giving her a kiss on the head.

None of us felt comfortable taking Matt's bed from him, so we all set up a cot and found some pillows and blankets. I wasn't sure I was going to be able to sleep, but not long after my head hit the pillow my eyes forced themselves shut, and I quickly dozed off.

CHAPTER 11

I found myself standing in the middle of a street, ruined buildings looming high overhead. The road was lined with destroyed cars and smoldering rubble. I looked above me and gasped, the sky was on fire. Behind black clouds, fire coiled through the air like nothing I had ever seen before. I heard gunfire and screams in the distance, but it was hard to look away from that terrifying sky.

Glancing back at the road around me, I noticed the bodies. Charred corpses and smoldering bones lay scattered at my feet. All of the faces were looking directly at me. A few bodies had their arms reached out in my direction as if trying to stop me. Had I done this?

An explosion rocked the ground, and rubble tumbled from the buildings overhead. I turned to look as a couple fighter jets soared by, dropping bombs on the next block over. The buildings near me began to crumble and I had to run to avoid being crushed as the explosions went off again. I ran as fast as I could, and then suddenly felt myself lift into the air. Blue flames swarmed around me, and I noticed my skin was molten and cracked again like when I transformed in the hotel room.

I floated above the city and saw the jets arcing around to fly towards me. Machine gun fire raced past me; they were trying to shoot me down. Instinctively I held up my arms, and massive beams of fire erupted from them. It wasn't just fire, it looked almost like some kind of radiation, bright and blue like *Godzilla's* nuclear breath. The beams raced towards the fighter jets and cut them like a hot knife through butter, causing them to explode into pieces that flew past me.

I was moving again, and I realized I wasn't in control of myself. I floated above the city, and I could see battles in the streets below. Soldiers were fighting against people flinging magic at them. Guns versus the elements in a display of apocalyptic fury filled the streets. I felt my arms connect in front of me with my palms facing the city. My body began to heat up, and blue flame swarmed me like an aura, then it all drew into me, and I could see my arms begin to glow.

I screamed, not wanting it to happen, but I had no control of my body. A massive beam of flaming energy erupted from my hands and in a moment, a huge section of the city, and the conflict within, was reduced to smoldering ash. The fighting went silent. There was no one left to fight, only charred bodies.

I bolted up in my cot, drenched in sweat, chest heaving for breath. The room was still and quiet, aside from the water in the aquarium and the resting breath of my family. I wiped sweat from my face and then stared at my hands. I had frequent nightmares since gaining these powers, but nothing quite like that. It almost felt prophetic if I believed in that sort of thing.

I climbed up from the cot and walked over to the fridge to grab one of my energy drinks wishing it was coffee instead. I didn't know if Matt had a coffee maker, given that he seemed addicted to energy drinks himself judging by the pile of cans in the recycling. I walked to the command center to see what he was working on and found him staring at the wall of TVs in disbelief. He had several of the screens working as a single display of a new broadcast.

"What's going on?" I asked, and he jumped a little.

"Shit just got real out there. The gangs are having turf wars in broad daylight." He answered.

I joined him to watch the screen as the camera cut to show footage from a city street. Police had a few blocks surrounded with barricades, but aerial footage showed a small war underway in the street. Gang members with guns were backed into a run-down community center by another gang that was clearly winning by using magic. They had people holding up walls of stone to block bullets while others sent fire and electricity into the building. The scene cut again to another city with a similar incident, and then another, and another. There were at least twenty active conflicts across the US of magic fueled gang on gang violence.

The reporter was doing their best to comment on the footage, but it was easy to tell they could hardly believe what they were seeing. It was only a matter of time before this would turn into riots, and the police were already preparing for an all-out war. SWAT vans were lining up and heavily armed officers were checking their gear ready to storm in when given the signal. It was chaos, and I could only stare open-mouthed at the screen.

This was exactly what I had wanted to prevent, and here I was stuck hiding in a bunker watching it play out on the news. Tears welled up in my eyes as a massive feeling of failure washed over me. Atlanta, Chicago, New York, Dallas, Los Angeles, Miami, all these major cities and more were experiencing just a taste of what the Opulentia was capable of, and it had resulted in destruction on a scale no one ever expected to see on the news. I stumbled back and sat down on the desk, tears streaming down my cheeks.

"We have word the President is about to speak on the rising crisis spreading through the nation." The reporter said, cutting the camera feed back to them in the studio.

"Let's go Live to the White House to hear what President Morales has to say."

The feed cut again to the podium set up in the courtyard outside the White House where the usual gathering of politicians and press were eagerly waiting.

"My fellow Americans: Today we have seen unprecedented chaos in the streets as gangs are openly warring in our cities trying to claim what belongs to our citizens. Violent turf wars are currently being monitored by police and I have already ordered the National Guard to intervene and ensure the safety of those living in these areas. I ask that you remain indoors and do not try to interfere with anyone involved in these terrorist activities taking place on our soil."

"We will be monitoring these events closely and tracking down those responsible. We have reason to believe that persons with strange magic-like abilities are involved and that it is related to a previously unknown narcotic substance. Anyone caught with this substance will be persecuted due to involvement in this matter of national security. I would advise anyone with information about these narcotics report to their local authorities so that we can begin removing this menace from our streets."

"The Department of Justice and I will be speaking on the matter, and we will decide if declaring Martial Law will be needed to end this plague of violence in our streets. I don't wish to see that happen, but we are considering any and all options at this point. Press Secretary Johnson has been briefed on the matter and will be fielding questions in just a moment. Before I leave, I want to say one more thing."

"I will not tolerate terrorist activity on American soil, and those responsible for this madness will be brought to justice. We will come for you, in full force."

Matt had circled back around to the desk and was bringing up footage on the other screens. The team had already tapped into CCTV footage from a few of the areas where the conflicts were taking place. The gangs using magic were all finishing up their battles with their rivals. Police were beginning to shrink their perimeter and with added support from the National Guard were encroaching on the scene after the violence began to die down.

I watched as the stone walls began to drop, replaced by swirling whirlwinds kicking up dust and debris. The gang dispersed into small groups from behind the dust screen and with small, concentrated bursts of wind and stone managed to break through the police line quickly with little resistance. The cops were unsure how to deal with magical foes and firing blindly to whirling dust pockets was getting them nowhere. A few fell and were immediately swarmed by officers, but most made their escape retreating deep into alleys in the city or prepared getaways.

"This, this is exactly what I wanted to prevent." I sobbed.

"Yeah… I know boss." Matt said, patting my shoulder. "I want to show you something."

I wiped my face and came around to the other side of the desk with him as he pulled up some images on the monitor. A series of images showing various images of what looked like secretive meetings. All of them featured the same man in a suit with dark sunglasses shaking hands with someone surrounded by goons. I stared at the images, the quality wasn't great, so it was hard to see details, but I was pretty sure it was the man Constance and I saw at the docks meeting with the leader of the Triads.

"Looks familiar, right? Check this out." Matt said, switching to some camera footage.

The video played and I instantly recognized my front yard. The man was standing in our driveway pointing towards the house, while another man was pulling a mask over his face. The mercenary that Cherry had killed for breaking into our home, he was facing away from the camera so we couldn't see his face before the mask was on.

"Can you go back, to when they showed up?"

"This is all there is. They just appeared, see?"

The man from the docks pressed something on his phone and the feed cut for just a second and both were gone suddenly, only the yard remained.

"They managed to alter the live feed somehow, which means they had physical access to the system at some point. Even if it was done remotely, they would have needed to physically add something to the server to allow access. I set that system up myself, there's no way in unless they got hands on it or come in from my station here which isn't possible. Maybe with some kind of ridiculously strong jammer device, but that feels unlikely given what they've done, it would be easier to just shut the feed off." he said, scrolling through the footage again as if he hoped to find something to prove himself wrong. "This is strange behavior. Why reveal themselves just before the attack?"

"To taunt me. That's Bach's style." I answered.

"Is that Bach?" Matt asked leaning to look closer at the image.

"No, it's the guy from the docks. Has to be working for him though, I don't know how else he would have access to the Opulentia." I said, pounding my fist on the table in frustration.

"He's been really busy the last few months, pops up all around the place. Probably using a private jet. Seems to be in charge of all the gang distribution. Maybe Bach is expanding the business and training a protégé." Matt said, sipping his drink.

"Bach's meeting with politicians while this guy is running the show and hassling us. What's the play here?" I said, thinking aloud.

"Palpatine." Matt replied.

"What?!" I laughed, almost spitting out my energy drink.

"Emperor Palpatine!" he exclaimed. "He's working both sides! He's causing the street level problems and then he's going to try and prop himself up as a solution so that he can get money and power from both sides and take control!"

"I... that's... fuck." I said, baffled. "What's the end goal then? Dismantle the government and become supreme ruler of the world? What is this a *Dr. Doom* comic?"

"No, it makes sense if you think about it, he's probably trying to run the long con and manipulate everyone until he's powerful enough to... I don't know, do some evil rich guy shit? Maybe he'll convince the government to sponsor his experiments and start turning prisoners into those drones you told me about."

My hand drifted to the symbols hidden in the flower tattoos on my neck as he mentioned the experiments and drones. I got a quick flash of his near mindless servants packing boxes full of Opulentia to load onto the helicopter Bach used to escape. Their brains scrambled into submission by Bach's twisted doctors in that wretched lab. There's no way he could get the government to sign off on that kind of cruelty could he?

A beep sounded from one of the other computers and pulled Matt's attention from the conversation. He tapped the keyboard and I saw Constance standing outside the repair shop's door smoking a cigarette and pulling out her phone. Matt buzzed the intercom.

"Hold on, I'll come let you in." his voice causing Constance to jump.

"Fuck! I was just about to text you." Constance replied.

Matt grinned and stood up to go open the doors for her, and I sat down in a chair to watch more of the news. As he walked away I flipped the main screens back to the news footage where the Press Secretary was finishing up questions after the speech. The press had been drilling pretty hard trying to comprehend everything that was going on. I scanned the crowd, and in the background as people were leaving I saw a young man in a nice suit with some medals on his chest approach a man in a very expensive looking suit facing away from the cameras. He turned to shake the man's hand, and just before he leaned in to speak to him I caught a glimpse of his face. Bach's face.

The bastard was still there, taking part in all the proceedings. Maybe Matt was right, maybe he was trying to convince them to let him get involved. Maybe he already was involved and was just biding his time. The camera began to zoom out from the podium as the questions came to an end. The young man, had to be military, gestured towards the White House and then led Bach towards it just before the footage cut. I punched the table again and could feel heat on my neck.

"Yeah, they're in there on the desk, ready to go." I heard Matt say in the other room.

Callie walked in a moment later and picked up her phone. She sauntered over to me and, sensing my stress, gently rubbed my shoulders and kissed my head.

"You're worked up this morning already? Did something else happen?" she asked.

"You could say that. Gang wars in the streets in broad daylight, the President threatening Martial Law, Bach once again sitting at a national address… yeah I'm getting pretty worked up. Everything I wanted to prevent is unfolding before my eyes, and I'm sitting here in a bunker with my thumb up my ass doing nothing about it." I grumbled, turning off the news feed and resting my forehead against her stomach.

"I'm sure we'll figure something out soon. There's no way he can keep getting away from us. I'm curious, what will you do when you find him?" Callie said, gently stroking my head.

"I don't know anymore. Originally I just wanted to kill him, get revenge for what he did to us all and hopefully put an end to whatever he was planning. Things have gotten so far though, I'm not sure that would stop it anymore. What if I'm too late?"

"It's never too late. We will have justice, one way or another. Matt said our phones are ready, so I was going to call

Jason, but I don't know what to tell him. What do you think I should say?" she asked, deftly changing the topic to distract me from my thoughts.

"Uh… hmm. Good question actually. Can't really say we're on the run from mercenaries, might be suspicious."

"Just a little." She chuckled.

"Tell him you're with us visiting some of my family for a while, maybe someone is sick or something. Don't let him try to talk you into giving him an address or anything. I know Matt said the line is secure, but I don't want to risk anyone getting a hint of where we are or might be going."

"You almost sound suspicious of him." Callie replied.

"I'm suspicious of everyone at this point. I don't know who we can trust. Matt showed me footage from the security cameras at the house, they had found a way to alter the live feed which is how they got in without me noticing. Everything's fucked and I'm still not sure where we should go. Part of me wants to stay here, but I don't want to compromise Matt. I've already put enough people in danger."

"You keep saying that you've done this, or you need to solve that. Why do you blame yourself?" Callie asked.

I was stunned by how direct her question was and sat back in my chair.

"I… I let him get away on the island. I let this happen, it is my fault." I said softly after a moment.

"It's not your fault. You were a victim, just like the rest of us. He unleashed that monster on you to get away, you didn't *let* him escape. You and Star destroyed that thing and saved us all. You became a hero in the middle of an otherwise hopeless situation. You can't shoulder this all by yourself."

"But… I… He…" I stammered, "You're right. It's just so hard to deal with. It's taken so long and feels like we've gotten nowhere, nothing to show for the effort. It always felt like he was a step ahead of us, but now it's more like he's miles away. I don't even know what his plan is after years of trying to track him down."

"He's an evil bastard bent on manipulating and exploiting anyone that will listen. There might not be a plan to uncover. He might just be seeing how far he can go with this just for the thrill of it. He's a sick and twisted man."

"You don't think he's got some goal in mind?" I asked.

"I'm not sure, I just know he's evil and needs to be stopped. It doesn't matter what his goal is, we have to stop him from reaching it regardless. I gave up my powers, but I can still help and I'm willing to do whatever I can." She replied.

"I know. You're a hell of a woman and I'm glad you're on my side." I said.

She hugged me tightly just as I heard footsteps approaching. Constance and Matt were making their way into the command center. Constance was Carrying a leather case, and Star was right behind them. I had to assume that was the package they had mentioned, and Star was eager for me to see what it was.

"Morning, Tri. Got a special delivery for ya, from Ezra." Constance said setting the large case on the table.

"No... you didn't." I gasped, looking at Star.

"Open it and find out." Star grinned.

I reached for the case and undid the latches, opening the lid to reveal... a normal looking set of clothes? There was a nice looking, cropped, black denim jacket sitting beside a pair of thick, dark brown, leather pants and a band t-shirt bearing the bloody logo of *Gorehowl,* my favorite metal band.

"What is this? Oh..." I said picking up the jacket.

It was much heavier than I expected, even with the studs and patches. I set it aside and picked up the pants which were incredible quality leather, but something felt dense underneath. Even the T-shirt felt thicker than it should as I set everything out on the table to see it all together. Under everything in the case was a pair of shin-high leather boots with metal plates down the front and sides. It was a goth-rock dream outfit to say the least.

"Ezra custom made everything themself. It's all lined with some kind of alloy and Kevlar to make it mostly bullet proof while looking like a punk rock bad ass." Star explained.

"You actually got me a super suit but made it *metal*." I gasped, totally stunned. "This is the most incredible thing I've ever seen!"

"They said it should hold up pretty well against blades and stray bullets, but you'd definitely feel it if you take a direct hit again. It should be better than standard Kevlar, and it's some kind of cutting-edge material a friend of theirs developed. This way you won't stand out as much in a crowd, provided that crowd is full of metal heads, but should still be safe from the neck down from another mercenary attack. Oh it's flame resistant too!" she added.

"This is amazing, ridiculous, and possibly the best gift I've ever gotten." I said, still a little shocked.

"I'm having them make some for the rest of us, but it's going to take a while. I figured since you're so headstrong, and have already been shot once, that you needed it as soon as possible." Star teased playfully.

I scooped everything up and ran to the bathroom to try it on. The clothes were noticeably heavier than they should be, but still fairly comfortable. The material felt fine on the skin, just a little weighted and I figured I would get used to that after wearing it for a while. They were even perfumed with the signature scent of Ezra's work, a mild hint of vanilla and lemon. I did my best to examine the look in the mirror and grinned from ear to ear, this was way better than a spandex catsuit.

I stepped back out to the main room and gave a little spin to show off the whole look. Callie clapped and Star whistled flirtatiously, Matt and Constance both nodded their approval.

"This is fucking awesome, babe! Thank you so much!" I exclaimed.

"You look great, Tri, but we've got business to sort out so let's get to it." Constance said, refocusing the group.

"Right, we need to figure out somewhere safe to move to and then find a way to stop Bach from wreaking anymore havoc out there." I said.

"He's holed up in Washington with the government, for whatever reason, but we can hopefully put a wrench in the works elsewhere. I managed to get a little more information on the merc that showed up at your house." Constance explained.

"They hit us again at our hotel last night." Star said.

"Yeah, I heard. Matt filled me in, glad everyone's okay. They seem to be an independent organization, as you'd expect from mercenaries. They have some ties to the Triads though, so that makes sense after the debacle at the docks. They have a few hideouts and bars they like to hang out in, but their leaders never really make public appearances. I'd say we could bust the doors down and try to pry information from them, but these kind of people would just swallow cyanide before answering any questions and while it would limit the number of them Bach has to throw at us, it would likely leave us with a bunch of bodies to explain to the cops."

"We almost had to deal with that already too. I meant to ask, Star, what name did you register the hotel under?"

"Scarlett Pugh and Florence Johansson." Star chuckled.

"That's ridiculous, and I love it. Hopefully that makes it harder to tie us to the room itself for now since we left it full of smoldering bodies." I said.

"The President is cracking down on anything magic related, so they might pull financial records, but with a fake name its possible you could explain it away. I'd call your bank and report the card stolen as a precaution." Constance said.

Star nodded and took her phone to the other side of the room to call her bank. She argued with them for a moment but seemed to eventually get what she wanted from them.

"I have a lead with the tattoo shops!" Matt interjected from his computer desk.

"What is it?" I asked.

"Missing persons reports near the shop in Columbia turned up a match with some of the footage. Geoff Bridges, twenty-four, reported missing by his grandmother. Ties to gang activity, but not directly involved in anything we know of, but he was spotted entering the tattoo shop about a week before he was reported missing. The team checked the footage several times, he went in but never left."

"Think they're holding people in the shop?" Constance asked.

"Hard to say, but he never shows back up on the footage and police haven't updated his report since. They probably gave up looking for him since he's black and has record." Matt added, showing clear disgust for the system.

"Well, I'm tired of sitting around doing nothing. I want to hit that shop and get some answers. We need to find a new place to lay low for now. I hesitate to book another hotel; in case we get spotted. You have any ideas Constance?" I asked.

"I've got a safehouse a couple hours out of town that I use sometimes. It's an old farmhouse, not much around. Used to belong to my uncle before he passed. Could set up there, it's got a few places to hide if anyone comes sniffing around too." She replied.

"Okay, here's my plan so far. We need to keep Cherry safe, so I want Star and Callie to take her to this safehouse and set up a base there. Constance and I will hit this shop and try to find out if they are keeping people there. Thoughts?"

"I don't like you two going in alone again, but I suppose someone with powers needs to keep an eye on Cherry." Star said with a sigh.

"We're not alone, we'll have Matt and his team watching us on the CCTV footage, right?" I asked.

"Sure. Oh, here, if you can get this plugged into one of their computers I can try to get into their internal security cameras if they have any. Maybe if the front desk has a system set up I should be able to get into the network." He added, handing me a USB drive.

"Perfect. Anyone else want to add anything?" I asked.

Everyone was solemn but in agreement, we had to make moves before things got any worse and this seemed like the best option.

"Constance, give them the address for your safehouse and then let's get on the road, it'll take us a few hours to get down to Columbia. Let's fucking do this!" I exclaimed.

I gave everyone hugs and walked them back to the rental across the street. We were all worried things would go south but had decided now was the time to act.

"You better come back to us in one piece." Star said.

"I will, I promise."

"Don't make us come looking for you." Callie added.

"I'll be in and out before they know what hit 'em. You two keep Cherry safe and away from all this mess. I'll be back as soon as I can." I replied.

I love you, Mommy. Please be careful.

"I will sweetie, don't worry. I'm going to find a way to end this all soon." I said, kissing her on the forehead.

Another round of hugs and goodbyes before I watched them drive away towards the address Constance provided. I was ready to get to work, but still had a few hours in the car before I'd get to do anything and was having trouble trying to reign in my eagerness. I walked back to the shop and Constance was already waiting outside. She handed me a set of earbuds as I approached.

"Matt said he's got these secured so we can be in communication with him once he gets there. You've put a lot of effort behind your speech down there. You don't have a clue what we're going to do when we get there, do you?" Constance asked.

"Not really, but I had to make sure they would get somewhere safe and not try to come with us. I don't want to put them in any more danger if I don't have to."

"Listen, I know I'm going with you, but the deeper we get in this shit, the harder it's going to be to keep everyone safe. We don't have the resources that the bad guys do, and it's going to be an uphill battle at some point. We might need Star to give us a bit more firepower along the way."

"I just… I don't want to lose her again. I don't want a repeat of what happened on the island. Besides, Cherry needs…"

"Cherry is more capable than you want to admit. She drained that guy like juice box, and while it's probably going to traumatize her, she's got the strength to save herself. I'm not going to ask you to bring her along, but maybe we don't need all our backup watching over her when she might be stronger than the both of you combined." Constance said bluntly.

"You might be right. Whatever our next move is, I'll consider it. For now, you and I have a shop to bust. So let's get on the road before any more of this goes to hell." I said bitterly.

CHAPTER 12

A couple hours of traffic later, we pulled into the parking lot across from the tattoo shop in Columbia. It wasn't easy to spot, and even with GPS it took us a while to find where it actually was. They didn't have any real signage outside; it was a low-key kind of place where you needed to already know where it was to get there. We sat in the car and watched the alley entrance for a bit to see what kind of foot traffic it was getting.

The entrance was a winding path behind a hedge just off the road on an already quiet back street downtown. There was some foot traffic, but mostly on the other side of the road where most of the business's main entrances were. This section was mostly the backside of the other buildings, service doors and dumpsters. It certainly wasn't a glamorous spot, but the shop property seemed to be well kept from what little we could see from the car. We dialed up Matt and connected our earbuds, ready to make a move.

"The gang here is tied to the cartels from Mexico, nothing big but after recent events they seem to be getting brought into the fold. Call themselves *El Diablos Rojo,* members have been spotted racing bikes and throwing fireballs to show off their new power." Matt explained.

"Looks like they were local boys that got scooped up as security for the cartel moving product through the club scene. Nothing in their records of human trafficking or anything like that, so odd they would be taking people if not for ulterior motives." He continued.

"I don't know what's going to happen if I walk through the front door. Bach might have them all watching out for me. Should we send Constance in first?" I asked.

"No offense Tri, but of the two of us you fit in more here. I look like a cop; you look like a punk." Constance replied lighting a cigarette. "I walk in there… I'll probably get shot on sight."

"Well, do we just bust in and start cracking skulls? What if there's some regular folks getting inked up?"

"Hey this was your plan, I'm just the muscle." Constance said.

"Fine, I'll go. Maybe I can talk up the person at the counter long enough to distract them and plug in Matt's drive so he can get a view from the inside."

I climbed out of the car and adjusted my jacket. Constance had a good point, I looked like the type of person that spent a lot of time in tattoo shops, because I had. I walked towards the entrance in the hedge and followed the winding rock path through a nice garden towards the door. The beds were full of bright red flowers, some were in painted pots that looked to be kids' artwork. Probably community kids helping maintain the plants.

It was pretty common for gangs to take care of the less fortunate in their territory. Often it was a way for them to make peace with their neighbors and try to keep everyone afloat in a system that ultimately failed them all. People turned to gangs for survival in an oppressive society, doing what they felt they needed to get by when the rest of the city abandoned them. Crime wasn't always a choice, but still ruined a lot of lives, and played right back into that system of oppression. It was a vicious cycle that gave people a lot of shitty choices to make.

I stepped through the glass door into a finely decorated lobby. Velvet carpet, leather seats, and an impressive collection of taxidermy and other oddities lined the walls. I could hear the faint buzzing of tattoo machines echoing from the back behind a bead curtain next to the front counter. A young woman with more ink than myself popped her head up and the sound of the bell ringing as I entered.

"Hello, can I help you?" she asked.

"Yeah, I'm back in my old neighborhood, wanted to get some jewelry. Maybe get a new piercing, you guys do walk ins?" I replied.

"Yeah, I think everyone is busy right now though. Our body jewelry is in this case here, and then we have a whole case over there with ear and face jewelry, also has our wood and bone options. What kind of piercing did you want?"

I thought for a moment, trying to come up with something else convincing to say if she kept talking. "Eyebrow, maybe two rings on each? What's that run these days?"

"It's usually fifty each plus jewelry for the face, but sometimes we discount for multiples. Jesse is our face piercer today, let me go see if she's going to have time for a walk-in. If you want to browse that's fine, otherwise you can have a seat over there and I'll be back in a few minutes." she said cheerfully.

"Ah great, thanks!" I said, watching her leave in my periphery.

As soon as she was through the curtain to the back I made my way back over to the desk to look for the computer. The tower was sitting right on the counter, and I quickly spotted an open USB slot. Everything felt too easy, but I pulled the drive from my pocket and plugged it in to the tower, only having to flip it around three times before it went in. I stepped away quickly and back to the case of jewelry.

"Alright Matt, I've slotted the drive into the computer up front. Work your magic." I whispered.

"Perfect, it'll take me a bit to work through whatever they have set up, but I'll get started now." He answered.

I walked around for a few minutes examining the various oddities on display. It was a really nice collection: taxidermy, wet and dry specimens, strange occult objects, crystals, all the things that made me feel at home in a tattoo shop. I was a weird girl that liked weird shit, and I liked being around other people that also liked weird shit. It was almost enough to make me forget that I was here to look for a missing person and track down an evil madman.

It was taking longer than I was comfortable with for the girl to come back, and I was beginning to worry that my cover had already been blown. I was trying to decide if I should leave or rush in through the back just as the receptionist came back with another woman.

"Hey there! I'm Jesse, I handle the face work here. Benny tells me you're looking to get a few eyebrow stabs today?" she asked cheerfully.

"Oh, hey, yeah! I haven't fully made up my mind if I want two on each side or just one, maybe two on one side. I was just popping in to see if you guys had time today or not." I replied.

"Yeah, for sure! So I have a few appointment today but I've got a little bit of time right now for walk ins, but I wouldn't be able to do four. I could do two probably before my next appointment gets here, and then if you still want four you can wait, or we can schedule a time for you to come back later this week."

"Okay, no two sounds great, maybe do them both on the left side and then I can think about if I want them on the other side after I see them."

"Sounds great! I'm going to go finish up back here with my client while Benny gets you signed in, and I'll see you in about ten minutes." She explained, and then turned back through the curtain.

"Here, I just need you to sign these, and then I'll need to see your ID to get you in the system. Have you gotten work with us before?"

"No, I'm just visiting from out of town. I used to live a few blocks from here and came to visit friends and wanted to see what popped up around town since I left."

"Oh cool. Well, we're glad you found us. Just a sec and I'll have those forms printed for you." she said, typing away at the computer.

She handed me a clipboard and a pen with a few documents to fil out, the usual consent forms and acknowledgements that you sign before getting work done. I wanted to use a fake name, but since I didn't have a fake ID with me I'd have to hope it didn't flag an alert in the system or something while I was here. Everything seemed fine so far though.

"I'm getting through the network now, there does appear to be a security system but it's going to be a little while longer before I can get eyes on you." Matt said quietly in my ear.

I handed over the forms and my ID and the girl took them without any questions. She began filing the information and I watched her face to see if anything strange was going to happen, but everything seemed fine. I suddenly had the realization that I was about to get a piercing on a whim just to take a look inside a shady shop. The last time I got pierced on a whim, I was still in my twenties and decided that I just absolutely needed my bellybutton pierced. I took that out a month later because I hated it, but I did actually kind of want these.

Jesse returned a short time later and beckoned me to follow her to the back of the shop where her setup was waiting for me. I glanced around, trying to get a feel for the layout of the building in case I needed to make an escape. The hallway was small and snaked through the building, giving plenty of room for curtained off rooms for the various artists and piercers working here. The back room looked to be an old garage that was converted into their workspace for anything that didn't require privacy.

Jesse was explaining her process for marking and preparing the area, sanitation and what not, things I've heard many times before and was only partially listening to as I looked around. Back here were more obvious ties to the local gang, art pieces with red devils and guns and things hung on parts of the wall, and there was an artist working on a sleeve for a client across the way and both seemed to have gang related work done. I was looking for any sign of the mystical symbol designs, but aside from some generic and probably culturally inaccurate witch designs there didn't seem to be any. Neither of the guys here had any that I could see, I figured that work was probably done elsewhere so as not to be so obvious.

"I have eyes on you, Tri, still working on getting feeds of the rest of the shop. There's layers to the network, this wasn't set up by amateurs." Matt said.

"What are you listening to?" Jesse asked curiously.

"Oh, nothing. It's just for my phone, I leave it in while I'm out doing stuff so I can have it reads texts to me if my hands are full." I said.

"Smooth." Constance chimed.

"Oh right on, I should do that for when I'm working so I don't have to change gloves so much." Jesse said. "Okay sit here so I can get a look at your brow and find the best spot in your anatomy for the jewelry to go. I'm just going to mark spots with a sharpie and then I'll get them cleaned off before I'm done. I'll let you check in the mirror if you like the placement in just a moment." Jesse said taking a closer look at my face.

I watched her glace at the artwork running along my head and neck, and she seemed impressed.

"This is some quality art on your neck, you get that around here?" she asked.

"No, this was done over in Asheville. My girl Danica runs her own shop, *Infinite Artworks.* She's a sweetheart, super talented, does fantastic work. She did this coverup on some… scars I had from a freak accident a long time ago." I answered.

"The line work is impressive; I'll have to check her out on IG sometime." Jesse replied.

"Got a few more cameras. Looks like main lobby, the bay you're in, a storage room, and a couple empty tattoo booths." Matt said.

I thought for a moment, all the rooms were closed off and had people in them as we came through to the back. I could hear voices or machines in each one that we passed.

"Seems pretty busy today, you guys stay booked up?" I asked curiously.

"Yeah, we got a full house today. Everyone's booked through the end of the month, owners have been pulling strings and pushing advertisements all over town. It's nice to see everyone getting quality work time. Alright, stand up and check the mirror for me, let me know if you like that placement."

"She said the place is full? Interesting. These could be hidden rooms I'm looking at. There's still a few devices on the network we haven't gotten into yet. I'll keep digging."

"Yeah these look sick, let's do it!" I said.

I sat back down in the chair, and she leaned me back to get a better angle. She started sanitizing my skin around the area, and then started lining up the needle. She had gentle hands and was laser focused on her work like a true professional. She pinched my brow just firmly enough to get my flesh where she wanted it and put the first needle through. It hurt, but only a little, and she was clearly very skilled. The jewelry transfer hurt a bit more, but still not bad. Before I knew it she had the ball on and was lining up the second needle. Another pinch, stab, and transfer more painful than the first but still delicate. I was impressed.

"And, just like that you're done. You did great, let's take a look at you. Go ahead and sit up for me." She said and started cleaning up her space.

"Yeah, that looks right. Take a look in the mirror and tell me if you're good with it while I get this cleaned up."

"Stall, I'm getting something weird on the cams. Maybe a warehouse? Feed's encrypted or something." Matt chimed in.

"It looks perfect… phew… I'm a little lightheaded though." I lied.

"Oh, that's perfectly normal. Go ahead a sit back for a few minutes while I finish cleaning up and I'll grab you some water. You want a snack too? Candy bar maybe?" she asked.

"Yeah, sounds great." I said slowly, leaning back in the chair trying to look weak.

"There's something going on downstairs. Five, maybe six guys with guns posted around a warehouse. Someone's being pushed into one of those booths, can't make out who it is. I don't see any windows; I think it's underground. Ask her what the building used to be, maybe I can find blueprints or something." Matt said frantically.

"Hey, what did this place used to be? It's been maybe ten years since I was here last. Trying to place it in my head." I said as she brought me my snack.

"Oh... I think before we took over it was an old automotive joint. Small family biz, it was probably run out of business by Jiffy Lube or Valvoline. Boss always calls this room the garage, and well, you can see the big doors over there." She gestured towards the big bay doors that were locked shut to seal off the room from the outside.

"Oh yeah, that sounds right. I don't remember the name, but I remember seeing those doors from the other side." I said.

"Auto shops usually have at least some bays under the floor for oil changes, could have expanded it into storage over the years. Theres another guy with the person downstairs, they have him strapped down but he looks unconscious. They are doing work on his neck I think it's what you were looking for. If you want to stop this you'll have to find a way downstairs."

I furrowed my brow, trying to figure out how to get from my chair to the rooms downstairs without causing too much of a scene. These people were just trying to do their jobs, I wasn't convinced they all knew what was going on.

"We've got a van pulling up to a loading dock on the other side of the building. I think it connects to the warehouse. More guys, big, looks like the gang colors on their clothes. Somethings about to go down, they seem worked up. You might be made." Matt chimed again.

I was going to ask the girl another question when my head started to spin. I was lying about being lightheaded before, but now I felt strange. I felt like I was slowing down, and as I looked around, I noticed the people in the room were all watching me.

"Hey, I don't... feel... so... good." I stuttered.

"Shit." Constance said, and I could faintly here her whipping the seatbelt off.

"Constance, I think she's been drugged. Get in there!" Matt shouted.

"On it"

"What's... the... big..." I stammered but each word was getting more difficult.

"Boss ain't gonna believe she just walked right in here." Jesse said to the man across the room.

"Coño gueva." the man replied.

My whole body felt hot and sweaty, but I wasn't sure if it was all from the drugs. I felt something bubbling under my skin and knew that my powers were trying to cook off the poison in my system. It was calling out to me, trying to keep me awake and alert. I decided to let it take over for a moment, clear everything out. I wanted to give these folks the benefit of the doubt, but they had played me the whole time.

"Qué chingados? She's burning, get some water!" the man shouted.

Flames burst out from my skin, and I felt myself lift off the chair. I felt in tune with myself again after a moment, like whatever they dosed me with was boiled out of my system before it could take hold. I was cognitive of the transformation this time, I felt it all happen and I was awake and aware as my skin turned to molten ash. It didn't hurt, in fact it felt liberating, like I was taking on an aspect of the flames themselves. Maybe that's what I would call it, an Aspect.

Constance had burst into the room, flinging the body of a guy that was in her way onto the floor, and she paused as she saw me in this new form for the first time. I could tell it frightened her, but she still recognized me. She pulled her gun and opened fire on the man across the way that had pulled a shotgun from under his table, catching both of his arms to prevent him from shooting, but not killing him. I wasn't sure I could show the same restraint.

I kicked the woman away from me, sending her crashing into her cart of supplies and knocking her unconscious. I looked around for a way to get downstairs, and just when I spotted a door, it burst open as several armed goons rushed out. I held up a hand and watched the glowing energy from my dream flow down the length of my arm and then blast a beam of flaming energy right through them. I shuttered at what I had done but knew that was just a part of this elevated power. The door smoldered and dropped off its seared hinges.

I flew through the air towards the door and sure enough it led downstairs. I could hear Constance hesitantly approaching from behind, unsure if she was needed. I could feel her fear like a sixth sense, but I also felt her determination. She was a professional after all, and she knew I was capable of extraordinary things.

I floated down the stairs looking for the warehouse and booths Matt had mentioned. I couldn't hear him anymore, perhaps I had melted the earpiece when I transformed. I turned the corner down another set of stairs and saw more goons approaching. I raised my hand and blasted them out of the doorway before they could even raise their guns. I could hear their screams of pain as I raced over them, I had apparently only seared off one of their arms. I was getting the hang of focusing the beams and had made this one smaller trying to hold back some of the destructive force.

I burst into the warehouse and felt a few rounds graze my leg, but it didn't make it through my new suit. I returned fire and put two more guys on the ground, but I was pretty sure I killed them. I wanted to drop the Aspect and show restraint, but I couldn't seem to wrestle control away from it no matter how hard I tried. I didn't really know how to, so I was mostly just trying to picture it going away in my head and chanting things like *'stop, stop, stop, stop, holy fuck you're killing people, just stop already'* to no avail.

This room was full of boxes and lab equipment that brought memories of the island flooding back to me. It wasn't completely the same, but so much of it looked like things I saw in Bach's heinous facility. There was no denying this was related to what was happening in the streets, Bach really was building an underground army from gang members. I had to put an end to this madness, here and now.

I found the doors to the booths Matt had told me he saw on the cameras and ripped the curtains off. A gunshot echoed out and I felt impact on my shoulder, but only slight pressure. I blasted the 'doctor' and then checked my shoulder, but it felt fine. Constance caught up and started unstrapping the man from the table. He wasn't awake, but he was breathing.

She propped him up on her shoulder and started to carry him back up the stairs, shouting something at me, but I couldn't really hear her over the flames I was filling the room with. I was making sure that everything in this wretched lab was reduced to ash before I left, and there was nothing that could stop me. A few more guys with guns entered through a side door but I blasted them away with one hand as I engulfed the last of the room with my other. The Aspect was incredibly powerful, and Even though I wanted to stop, I knew this had to be done.

Once I was satisfied with the flames rising in the lab, I flew back up the stairs and set fires in places around the shop. Constance had already made it outside, and the clients had escaped as well. I checked all the rooms to make sure on my way out but found no one other than a few Diablos that foolishly tried to shoot me. I made quick work of the few that were left, and then then set the lobby on fire before heading outside. I was sad to see that collection burn, but I had accepted that everything needed to go.

Once I made it outside and out of the garden, I felt a release as the Aspect dropped. I slammed to the ground, and it felt like I had been dumped out of a moving truck. Constance rushed over to pick me up and helped me limp to the car so we could get away before the authorities arrived to deal with the fire. I was losing consciousness, and I wasn't sure if I would make it to the car. I flopped into the backseat, and stared up at the upholstery as my vision blurred and then went black.

CHAPTER 13

Waking up in a strange bed, sore, disoriented, and completely unaware of how I had gotten there was something that happened far too often. I was in a small bedroom, the walls were lined with timeworn flower wallpaper from the late eighties, and there was a strong scent of stale cigarette smoke emanating from everywhere. A ceiling fan spun overhead, cobwebs and dust clinging to the edges as it pushed uncomfortably humid air through the room. The sheets with stiff with starch, I hoped, and more than a little itchy. It reminded me of spending the summer with my grandparents as a child, to get time away from my father.

I sat up despite the aches in my muscles and looked around the room. Old wooden furniture covered in dust and aging knickknacks lined the walls, and a single old glass window with peeling paint was cracked open to let a trickle of light and fresh air into the otherwise gloomy room. Putting the events I could remember together in my head, I guessed that Constance must have brought me to the old farmhouse she mentioned that she used as a safehouse when she needed to lay low. I wasn't sure how long I was out, but my body was stiff, and my stomach was growling so I decided I should find something to eat while I got my bearings. I carefully climbed out of bed and hoped that I would bump into someone as I shambled around.

I took three, maybe four steps away from the bed before I lurched forward and hit the ground. I managed to catch myself on my hands and knees but just as I did, I vomited. There wasn't much substance to it, but it burned and smelled rancid. This again reminded me of my past, waking up so hungover I could barely walk and puking my guts out on a stranger's floor. It had certainly been a while since I had to deal with that kind of embarrassment and was on the long list of reasons I put together to get sober.

I looked around for something to clean up with, but there wasn't much in the room. I was just about to grab the sheets from the bed when the door opened, and Callie rushed inside nearly tripping over me. She must have heard me fall and came to check on me like the natural caregiver she was.

"Oh, Trianna. I'm glad you're awake. Let's get you up so I can clean this." she said, lifting me to my feet and propping me against the wall.

"Thanks, I'm starving, how long was I out?" I asked.

"Two days. Everyone had just gotten settled in when Constance lugged you in here. She said you got drugged, immolated the shop, and then passed out in the car."

"Yeah, that sounds about right. I think they were watching for me… I heard them say something about the boss not believing I just waked right into the place."

"Maybe not your best plan. I'm just glad you're safe."

"I think I saved a guy. Yeah, I did, saved him from being run through Bach's experiments. They had him strapped to a table and were about to give him the neck tattoos."

"Well, that confirms your theory that he's using these places to build an army. Did you find out anything else useful?" she asked, wiping my face with a cold damp towel.

"No, I had to let the Aspect take control to keep the drugs from taking me out. It was like the power boiled it right out of me."

"The… Aspect?" she asked, confused.

"Yeah, I think that's what I'm going to call the transformation that Star and I do when we let the power take over and get really strong. It really takes a lot out of me though." I explained.

"Maybe we should sew a big 'A' on your super suit." She joked.

"I'm never living down the suit thing. They held up great in the heat though, I don't think I damaged them at all even when I transformed." I rebutted.

Callie finished cleaning up my mess and helped me walk to the kitchen to get some water and food. I eagerly gulped down a few glasses of water as I realized how thirsty I was, while Callie made a turkey sandwich with extra pickles. They must have gone to the store for supplies while I was out. I scarfed down the sandwich so fast I almost choked while Callie glared and me and shook her head.

"Thanks, I really needed that. Where is everyone?" I asked.

"Star and Cherry are outside poking through the grass looking for bugs. There's not much to do here, Constance is in town to get some stuff to try and get the cable back on, so we can have TV. Matt asked us to tell you he managed to pull a bunch of data out of the shop's computer and is looking for anything useful. Wanted you to call him whenever you woke up." Callie said, putting away dishes.

"Anything big happening with the outside world?" I asked, finishing a fourth glass of water.

"Hard to say, we don't get great signal here and with the TV down we've been a little cut off from things. I saw something about new groups of people forming to fight the gangs, other people that have magic, but my internet cut out and I couldn't open the article." she replied.

"Great." I groaned. "Just what we need, magic vigilantes taking matters into their own hands."

"Do you seriously not hear yourself right now? You're literally wearing a super suit while saying that out loud." Callie chortled.

"That's different!"

"Is it?"

"Well… yeah! I have a personal vendetta against the asshole that started all of this." I exclaimed.

"You don't think some of those people might feel the same way about the violence in their streets? Their friends or family being in danger, or worse going missing while the world tries to cope with the sudden emergence of magic powers?" she asked.

"I… but… no. I guess you're right. I think I'm having trouble dealing with the fact this isn't an isolated issue anymore. The world is literally changing before our eyes, isn't it?"

"It's scary. Imagine how it must feel to them, though. They don't even know where this all came from, what's causing these powers to exist." Callie said.

"Do you think anyone in charge has an idea? If Bach is getting close to the government, do you think he's revealed that he knows how it works?"

"Wouldn't they just arrest him on the spot if he did?" she asked.

"Who knows! He's got tons of money at his disposal, he could have bought his way into this and gotten some influential people on his side for protection. I don't know how any of this works!" I grumbled.

The back door opened, and Cherry and Star came strolling in with a small basket full of raspberries and cherries.

Mommy! You're awake! We found fresh fruit over near the pond!

"Oh those look delicious! I bet they'll make a great snack." I replied.

Cherry took the fruit to the sink, and Callie helped her start washing them off and setting them on paper towels to dry. I was impressed to see that Cherry was keeping herself busy and taking all of this so well. She had already been through so much, and I knew she understood everything that was happening better than most other people. Still, I was glad that she was able to keep enjoying being a kid even while we were on the run.

"Was beginning to wonder if you were going to wake up." Star said, kissing my head.

"I'm not sure if it was the drugs or the transformation, either way I was completely drained. How're you holding up?" I asked.

"I'm fine, annoyed that my wife keeps showing up passed out or beat up. Whatever the next plan is, I'm going with you and there's nothing you can do to stop me!" Star replied.

"Honestly, I'm not sure what the plan is, but yeah I think I need the help. Everything is spiraling out of control and each time I think we've gotten somewhere it just gets worse."

Can I help too?

We all stopped and turned to face Cherry, dumbfounded by her question. She just stood by the sink, eating some of the fruit that she had picked with Star.

What? I'm really strong too, I can do just as much if not more than you guys. I want to help so you don't get hurt!

"Cherry... there's no way I could possibly bring you along. I know you're strong, but this is really dangerous and you're still a little girl." I said.

I'M NOT JUST A CHILD! I KNOW WHAT HAPPENED ON THAT ISLAND TOO! I WANT TO STOP BACH JUST AS MUCH AS YOU DO!

The air in the room swirled slightly and there was a faint rumble in the ground that caused all the dishes in the room to rattle. I was afraid that we might have to deal with emotional and magical outbursts as Cherry got older, and I wasn't sure what to do about it.

"I know, baby... I-"

I'M NOT A BABY ANYMORE! STOP TREATING ME LIKE ONE! FUCK!

She stormed out of the room and back outside taking the thick presence in the air with her. I sat back in my chair a bit dumbstruck.

"I'll try to calm her down. She's going through a lot." Callie said, following her outside.

I picked up a couple berries from the counter and bit into them, savoring the tart juice as it burst. I wanted to keep Cherry safe and take care of her, since her real parents died on the island. I knew we couldn't let anyone find out about her powers because they might try to take her away and experiment on her, and I just couldn't let that happen. I wasn't sure how I was going to be able to do that if her hormone swings were going to trigger outbursts with her powers.

I was about to ask Star what she thought we should do if Cherry started lashing out with her powers when the whole house shook again, enough to cause a few dishes and things to fall and break on the ground.

"Ah shit…"

We rushed outside to find Cherry floating in the air, surrounded by swirling wind and debris. Lightning cracked, and bits of stone lifted up from the ground and floated around her as she hung in the sky above us. Callie was backing away, trying not to get hit by anything flying around. Walking towards her was like walking into a small tornado. I held my arm up to shield my face as I started to approach. I wasn't concerned about getting hurt, but I needed to get her down before someone reported the strange event.

There was a buzzing noise in my head like static, but underneath it I thought I could hear voices. It was too distorted to make out what they were saying, but none of them sounded like Cherry. I wondered if she heard this too, was this constant buzzing and cacophony in her head all the time? As I got closer the noise continued to grow louder and more coherent, it was starting to hurt, and I hoped that it was just some side effect of her letting out her rage. Was this what she meant when she said before that she heard something calling to her?

"Alright Cherry, if you want to be treated like an adult you need to come down here and talk like one. I understand you're upset, and that's totally valid, but we don't need to draw attention to ourselves with a tantrum like this." I said, still trying to reach her through the buffeting storm.

YOU DON'T HAVE TO TREAT ME LIKE A CHILD ALL THE TIME! I UNDERSTAND WHAT'S GOING ON.

"Fine. Then shut down the theatrics and let's talk. Someone's going to get hurt." I shouted.

She locked eyes with me, and I could see the pain behind her rage but there was something else there as well, as if she wasn't fully in control. She pointed a finger at me and curled it and I felt the ground tremble beneath me as a pillar of dirt and stone lifted into the air. I had to brace myself to keep from falling off while holding her gaze determined to snap her out of this. I could tell she was fighting something inside of her and I knew I had to help her I just wasn't sure how.

YOU'RE NOT THE ONLY ONE THAT HAS BEEN PRACTICING THEIR POWER TO GET STRONGER. I CAN FIGHT TOO! I KNOW I CAN!

"I know you're strong too, that's not the issue. I don't want to risk losing you! You're very important to me, you're important to all of us. I don't want to put you in danger."

I'M ALREADY IN DANGER. WE ALL ARE, YOU SAID IT YOURSELF. THAT'S WHY WE'RE OUT HERE HIDING FROM OUR PROBLEMS INSTEAD OF FIGHTING THEM HEAD ON!

"It's not that simple, Cherry." I said as she lifted me higher into the air. "This isn't one of your manga stories, it's not good guys versus bad guys. People's lives are at stake, the government is involved. If it was as simple as fighting the bad guy, I would have done it by now."

We didn't have to run away though. We could have stayed home and just fought off anyone that came to get us.

"No, we couldn't. What about Beatrice and her family? What about our pets, or your friends? These guys won't stop at trying to hurt us, they will try to hurt anyone important to us to draw us out. We had to leave to protect our loved ones, and if you don't calm down we're going to have to leave here too. Now please, let's go back inside and talk calmly."

I dropped to my knees on the rock platform as the noise in my head swelled again to the point I couldn't focus anymore. I clenched the sides of my head and struggled to keep from falling. Cherry began to lower me down to the ground, reforming the pillar into the yard where it came from. The sound began to ease off as I reached the ground again, but it was still present. I looked up at her and held out my hand to beckon her down hoping that she would calm down and let her powers wane.

Just as she was starting to float towards me, gunshots rang out. I turned to see two black vans pulling onto the property and some goons dressed in all black tactical gear wielding machine guns aimed at us. Star and Callie had jumped behind trees, and I looked back to Cherry to see if she was alright. I watched in awe as her skin burned away revealing dark stone crackling with energy. I suspected it was similar to how I looked when I transformed into my aspect, but she was different.

Cherry didn't control just a single element like I did, she controlled all of them and hints of each power was reflected in her new form. Her skin was stone like a statue but seemed to crack and shift as she moved. Lightning arced from the cracks in her skin, and her eyes resembled small pools of water. Her hair had shifted to flames that flickered with her movement. She dropped from the sky and hit the earth with force that caused the ground to tremble and ripple towards the mercenaries knocking a few off their feet.

I barely had time to react before Cherry was rushing towards them, and I called my aspect to try and stop things from getting too out of hand. Cherry was incredibly fast for someone seemingly made out of stone, and already had two of them men pinned down and knocked unconscious. A couple more vans pulled up from the other side of the house and goons were already opening fire. I blasted them with my fiery plasma beams, immolating them where they stood as Cherry pulled stones up from the ground to give us all cover. Star took on her aspect as well, the sky overhead churning with a rolling thunderstorm. *So much for not causing a scene*, I thought.

Callie pulled a pistol from her ankle holster and popped off a few rounds at one of the groups but paused and stared at someone in the back of one of the vans. She looked horrified, and I was curious what she saw but didn't have time to waste as Cherry was already jumping more guys on the other side of the yard. Bones crunched and shattered under the force of her blows and while I wasn't thrilled to see my daughter fighting grown men with guns, she was holding her own. I charged up another big blast of energy and melted through one of the vans the men were using for cover just as Star began to call lightning from the sky.

Bolts of raging natural energy crashed down from above striking the remaining mercs and causing them to convulse and drop to the ground. Callie stood up from behind the rock she was using for cover and fired a few shots into one of the open vans as it started to drive away.

"You SONUVA BITCH!" she shouted.

I raced around to support her and locked eyes with the man in the back of the van who sneered as he shut the door. It was the man that shot me, and then I realized why I recognized him. Callie emptied her weapon, but the van was out of the yard and started to pull away, and she just screamed and cried. It was James, her new boyfriend. I snarled with rage and took off after the van, using the amplified force of my aspect to propel myself faster than I could run normally. Cherry was right beside me, gliding through the air as if it were nothing.

I reached out towards the van and fired off a beam of flame to stop it, but just before it caught up, a massive wave of water dropped from the sky. It was like a tidal wave from the clouds themselves. The bastard was using Star's storm against us. I felt energy in the air and looked up just in time to see Star racing through the clouds, clinging to them with bolts of electricity that resembled spider legs sprouting from her back. She leapt forward and pulled a massive bolt down towards the van, but it swerved at the last moment to avoid being hit. Another massive tidal wave hit us, and knocked Star from the sky, and sent us both careening to the ground. I tumbled and rolled for a bit in the retreating water, unable to steady myself against such force.

Cherry was unphased, and simply parted the water as it neared her and raced through. The back door of the van burst open, and James was there holding some kind of strange gun-like device. He fired the weapon and a net swirled out into the air towards Cherry. I got back to my feet and leapt back into the air, channeling heat through my legs to lift myself off the pavement for more speed. Cherry met the net head on, and I heard it pop like one of those electric flyswatters, as she immediately dropped her aspect and fell to the ground unconscious. James now had a winch attached to the net trying to quickly reel it in, but I caught up just in time to blast the winch with a plasma beam, severing the rope and rendering the winch useless.

The van sped off, and James raised a hand to hit us with one final wave from the clouds to make his escape. Star had dropped her aspect and the storm was clearing, so it wasn't as strong as the ones before, but it was still enough to shake us off as the van got away. I skidded and rolled over myself, letting my aspect fade away as I tumbled to where Cherry had stopped moving. Star caught up a moment later, but with much more grace.

I pulled out my knife and began cutting at the tangled net, trying frantically to get it off of her. The rope was thick and had cables running through it that made it hard to cut, and just touching it made my hands feel like they were burning. Star helped me untangle it enough to get Cherry out and she was sleeping soundly, having been forced out of her aspect by the net. She was unscathed thankfully, and I picked her up to carry her back to the house.

We had gotten far enough down the road that we were in range of some of the neighboring farmhouses, and I worried that someone had watched all of that commotion take place in the street. Surely the sudden isolated storm and gunshots had drawn some attention and then they would notice the magical car chase literally blazing down the road. I had to hope that they would keep it to themselves or that they were too busy watching TV or something to notice.

I was still furious as I walked, and the more I thought about the situation, the angrier I got. Not only had James been working with Bach the whole time, not only had he shot me, not only had he broken my girlfriend's heart and lied to us all, but then he tried to steal my daughter. I decided that was probably his goal from the start, that night that we had him over for dinner and he kept asking about Cherry, he was probably already planning how to get to her. I was also increasingly angry that yet another evil man had wronged me and gotten away.

I finally got back to the house and Callie was sitting on the front porch sobbing. There was a broken necklace and locket laying on the ground in front of her, clearly a gift from him that she smashed to try and reconcile the feelings she was going through. Star sat down next to her to comfort her as I carried

Cherry inside to the couch so she could rest. I sighed trying to let go of my tension over what had just transpired.

I covered Cherry with a blanket and left her to sleep while I went outside to console Callie. She was crying into Star's shoulder when I emerged from the house and I sat down on the other side of her, wrapping my arms around her in a hug for comfort. Tears ran down my face as well, my heart ached for her knowing how much that had to have hurt her. She was really falling in love with him, and for him to turn around and not only betray her but try to kill her family right in front of her, I knew she must be devastated.

We all just sat there in silence for a little while, holding each other and sobbing, each of us trying to process our own thoughts and emotions about the situation. I stared at the ground, and my gaze eventually landed on the locket. It was a little heart, with some writing on it, but as I stared at it, I realized there was something poking out of the inside where Callie had stomped on it. I knelt down off the steps and picked it up, and I could see a small microchip inside and realized that he had planted another tracking device on her. She probably didn't think to let Matt scan it with our other belongings, and that was how James managed to find us all the way out here in the middle of nowhere.

I dropped it back on the ground and focused a small beam of fire on it until it melted away on the stone.

"I'm so sorry I put everyone in danger." Callie said.

"It's not your fault. We've been manipulated from the start. Bach just found another twisted way to get to us." I said, sitting back down next to her.

"I was really falling for him... I can't believe I was so stupid and let him fool me like that."

"You're not stupid, Callie. Love makes us look past certain things, and some people are really good at hiding their intentions. You brought him to dinner with us and none of us noticed. Hell he shot me, and I didn't even recognize him. It's easy to feel dumb, but it's not your fault." I explained.

"I'm going to go make us some tea to help us relax. That was all so stressful." Star said, kissing Callie on the cheek and heading inside.

Callie shifted her weight to lean on me and wiped some of the tears from her face. I just held her tightly and reminded her that it wasn't her fault and that everything was going to be okay. I'm not sure if I was trying harder to convince her or myself, but I wanted to make sure she knew that no one was mad at her, it wasn't her fault. I held her close and ran my fingers through her hair until she finally calmed down enough to stop crying. Star returned with some of Callie's favorite tea and snacks to help us all relax a little.

Not long after we finished and were about to head inside, Constance pulled up to the house and hopped out of the car looking befuddled.

"What the fuck happened while I was gone!?" she shouted, gesturing to the mostly destroyed black vans, dead bodies, and debris in the yard.

"It's a whole thing, Cherry was upset and then we got attacked by a bunch of armed mercenaries. Turns out we were betrayed and manipulated again." I sighed.

"And you're all sitting out here just having tea and cookies about it?" she asked, looking over the carnage.

"For now, yeah." I replied.

"Can I have some before we figure out how to hide the mess?"

"Absolutely."

We spent the rest of the day digging holes to hide bodies and pushing wrecked vans into the barn. The police never showed up, neither did the FBI, or any more mercenaries thankfully, so perhaps we managed to avoid being spotted somehow after all. Constance managed to get the cable working and helped Star cook up some burgers and fries for dinner before we all dozed off a little in the living room watching TV. The events of the day had taken a toll on us, and we were all exhausted. Cherry woke up just long enough to eat a salad and some berries and then dozed back off. I was sitting next to her and gently stroking her hair, glad that she hadn't gotten hurt.

I got up after an hour or two and walked around outside, checking if anyone was hiding out and trying to clear my head. I was lost in thought trying to come up with some kind of plan to put an end to all this but getting absolutely nowhere. I was tempted to just leave and try to deal with it all myself, just hop in the car and drive to D.C. and murder Bach in cold blood before he could cause us anymore pain. I'd probably go to jail for the rest of my life, if I wasn't gunned down on the spot, but at least part of the problem would be solved, and my family would be safe.

The more I thought about it though, it wouldn't work. I didn't know where he was, and even if I did kill him, his shady corporation probably had other people that would just step up and take control and make things worse. If I was going to end this, I needed to find a way to expose Bach and get the whole operation shut down first before it got worse. I didn't have a clue how to prove it though, I would have to find a way to show how he was connected to the Opulentia and if he's already courting politicians, he might be too insulated for it to matter.

I walked over to the porch and picked up the rope net that we had taken off Cherry earlier. It still hurt my hand a little to hold it, and as I poked around I realized there was a series of glyphs on some of the ropes and the weights that caused it to wrap around its target when launched. Holding on to the rope I tried to summon a little bit of fire in my palm, but it wouldn't appear. I let go of the rope and tried again and it worked fine.

"What the fuck?" I gasped.

Someone had managed to find something that made the effects of the Opulentia inert, and that's why Cherry dropped to the ground when it caught her. I thought it was just some kind of shock net, but there was more to it. If it was this effective on Cherry's massive powers, then it was more than enough to stop the folks using diluted versions of it, and now part of his plan was starting to make sense. He wanted to find people that reacted well to the trial dose and then capture them for experimentation, grabbing up candidates in broad daylight with the government's backing.

I walked back inside and flopped into the empty reclining chair. Everyone else was still asleep, and I desperately wanted to join them, but I knew my sleep wasn't going to be all that restful. I started to doze off but woke up anytime the house made a noise, paranoid that someone else had shown up to try and capture us. After a couple hours, I snuck outside again and smoked a bowl to try and ease my nerves enough to let me sleep. I needed to come up with a real plan, but I wouldn't get anywhere without some rest.

CHAPTER 14

I woke up to the sound of the news on TV, the reporter was listing cites that had broken out into all-out war between local police and waves of magic users. Footage of combat zones played out on the screen displaying people blasting police barricades with flames and rocks while riot teams circled around isolated users. It wasn't just gang members anymore it seemed, or at least not the ones we had seen before, they lacked the gang colors and symbols, and instead looked like party animals, frat boys, and youtubers.

The balance was tipped in favor of those with magic, but the police refused to back down. Part of me wondered how this would continue to evolve, maybe something good could come of this. If enough of the right people took advantage we could see massive shifts in the political world, oppressed people fighting a revolution. That would be ironic, wouldn't it? Imagine cheering on a magic fueled revolution while trying to stop the source of their power. I sighed and sat up in the chair.

Star noticed me moving around, and brought me a cup of coffee, her eyes glued on the screen as she entered the room. It was bizarre to say the least, seeing this much chaos happening in the world around us. It had only been a few weeks, but global chaos erupted nearly overnight, and world governments struggled to cope. There were reports from other countries that military forces were gathering and gunning down users in the streets just to make an example, and I wondered how much longer it would take until the US followed suit.

The reporter cut his ramble about the struggles as the feed shifted to a podium at the white house. The president was about to give another speech addressing the developing situation. I sat forward in my chair, eager to hear what he had to say. I was starting to sweat, nervous that at any moment I could be labeled a terrorist just because of what Bach had done to me on the island. I didn't have time to dwell on it as the president quickly approached the podium with a determined look on his face.

"My fellow Americans, and peoples of nations across the world. In the last few weeks, we have seen a sudden and massive wave of crime and people using experimental weaponry to wreak havoc on not just American soil, but in the city streets of the world at large. We have been monitoring the situation closely and have not yet found the true motivation behind these attacks, but you can rest assured that we are doing everything in our power to bring an end to the heinous terror in our streets.

As of this morning, I have created and staffed a team that will focus on dealing with this threat as we seek further information. I will now allow the head of that team to address the nation and field questions regarding their new team. Before I go, I again want to stress that we will not tolerate terrorist activity on our sovereign land and will put an end to this one way or another."

My chest felt heavy as I watched President Morales step back from the podium and hold out his hand to gesture someone to it to speak. The camera didn't adjust its position, so I had to wait with bated breath for them to enter the frame.

"Don't let it be him. Don't let it be him. Don't let it be him." I whispered, hoping that I wouldn't see Bach walk up to that podium. My hopes were immediately dashed as, sure enough, up walked the man I hated most on the entire planet.

"FUCK!" I shouted, punching the arm of the chair.

I watched in rage and horror as Bach approached the president, shook his hand, and then stepped up to the podium adjusting his finely tailored collar and expensive tie. He was smiling his best sleazeball salesman grin while adjusting the mic stand to a comfortable height.

"My fellow Americans, my name is Sebastion Artosis. I have been tasked with lending my extensive knowledge and experience with tech and engineering to find a way to end the plague of terror running rampant in our streets. My team and I have developed prototypes for a device that will allow us to easily subdue these magic users across the globe, and with the aid of local authorities return your daily lives to normal. We have already begun to dispatch teams across the United States to test these devices in the field, and initial testing has proven them to be highly effective and non-lethal. We hope that by subduing the targets rather than killing them, that we will be able to question them about their sources and put an end to the violence quickly and efficiently.

My teams will begin working with local authorities upon arrival, and I urge you citizens to remain indoors and away from any struggle as there is no guarantee these terrorists will not try and use you or your family as leverage when cornered. With the support of the Department of Defense and Homeland Security, we hope to have the devices finalized and prepared for global distribution to aid other nations around the world in putting an end to this madness. I have brought my head of engineering, Doctor Kevin Marlowe, to field questions about the device and our strategies for deployment. I must begin overseeing our team's deployment, but I promise to deliver results with expediency."

Bach walked away from the podium, replaced by a short man in a lab coat but I had already checked out. I grabbed a pillow from the couch and pressed it hard against my face and screamed so hard I thought my lungs would bleed. I knew this was going to happen, but it still hurt. Everything felt so futile in that moment, like I had already lost somehow. I knew deep down I had to keep fighting, but right then all I wanted was to give up and die. It felt like no matter what I tried from then on it wouldn't make enough of a difference.

I dropped the pillow and stared at it laying on the ground as tears streamed down my face. I felt Star's hand on my shoulder, her touch was warm and soothing, but it felt distant. I was spiraling and I wasn't sure if anything could snap me out of it. I thought about ending it all then. There were plenty of knives in the house, I could just rip open my veins and let my tainted blood run across the wood floors and be done with everything right then and there.

I collapsed back into Star's arms as she tugged me close to hold me as I continued to cry both from anger and sadness. Callie came and sat on the other side of me, holding my hand tightly for support even though they felt numb to me. Constance leaned in the doorway, frowning into her coffee while staring at the TV. I knew she was disappointed by the news, but I felt like it was directed at me, felt like I deserved it.

Just as I was ready to concede to my dark thoughts and break away from everyone in the room, I felt something else. Cherry, my wonderful little girl, climbed into my lap and wrapped her arms around me pressing her head up against my chest, and I could feel the tears on her cheeks.

We're all here, we all love you, you don't have to feel this way. We will find a way to stop all this. Please don't do it. Don't kill yourself. I love you.

I thought my heart would shatter as those words echoed softly in my head. She knew what I was thinking and came to comfort me. I was wallowing in my self-pity and remorse and letting my feelings get the better of me, forgetting that she could feel them too. I wrapped my arm around her, and felt my sobs begin to wane.

"I'm not going anywhere, baby. You all mean too much." I whispered.

"We'll find a way to end this. Come hell or high-water." Star said.

I clutched Cherry to me tightly and wiped the tears from her cheek. Callie and Star squeezed us both in a group hug and I could feel my doubts melting away. My love for these women had gotten me through everything in the last seven years, and it was going to get me through this next wave of bullshit as well. I had to hold on and see this through, for them.

We turned off the TV and gathered in the kitchen to eat breakfast and try to regroup our feelings. Constance had cooked up a hefty amount of eggs and bacon for us while I was still asleep. I chewed on some bacon and tried to think how we could end this now that Bach was directly working with the government. He was openly working against us now, and I had to assume that the device he was talking about had something to do with the net launcher they used when they tried to capture Cherry. I figured that I should see if Matt knew anything about the device or how it worked but wanted to finish eating before diving into anything else.

"Hey… Tri?" Constance grumbled.

"Yeah, what's up?" I replied.

"I, uh… I don't know how much more of this I can keep up with." she said.

"What do you mean?" Star asked.

"Well, I'm not trying to give up on you or anything… but I don't know if I got what it takes to go against the feds if they start looking into us. They've got some fucked up tricks up their sleeve, and I don't know if I could get us out of it." Constance replied.

"That's fair, no one's asking you to, not by yourself at least. You think you can still help with security and intel though?" I said.

"I work well with tracking down goons and street level stuff, I got connections and experience out the wazoo. Where I'm sitting though, we all just got labeled terrorists on national television and that's not easy to get away from. I don't know what Bach's got cooking, but he's got the D.o.D. behind him and already has it out for you, pretty sure your names are on the top of his list of problems to remove. All the bodies we been hiding? The goons, the mercs, what happens when they show up with badges and warrants?" Constance said, sipping her coffee.

"I… I don't know. Fuck, I don't know okay? I'm flying by the seat of my pants here, every time I think I've gotten ahead of it, something else bites me in the ass."

"I know, I know. I'm just thinking out loud. You've got a legitimate reason to stick your neck out for this, and I know that. I want to see this prick brought down too! I'm just getting scared that we're going to go down first." She said.

I had never seen Constance admit to being scared of anything, in the years we have worked together she's always proven to be resourceful and fearless in the face of anything despite all we've uncovered along the way. She had a right to be scared though, she was right too. The government backing our enemy was an absolute worst-case scenario, one that we hadn't prepared for at all.

"I guess what I'm saying is that I'm still ready to work, but I'm not sneaking into any government facilities or secret military bases. I'll hunt leads and do research all day, but I'm not going against the feds head on." Constance added.

"We have to expose him somehow. We have to find a way to show everyone that he's really behind all this and let everything crumble around him." Callie said.

"Yeah, I'm still trying to figure out how we're going to do that. I wanted to just kill him and be done with it, but it's not that simple anymore. Guess it hasn't been that simple for a while." I replied.

"Going to have to find a way to get the feds suspicious of him too, or they'll just shut you down for interfering. Proof or no proof. They're already working with him so they might already know he's behind it all and are just trying to profit off the situation." Constance said.

"We're fucked if it's that deep, but I have a feeling he'd want to stay ahead of that. He's not exactly the type to be used by someone else. It's far more likely he's using them for profit and as a distraction for his real plan." Star added.

"That rope yesterday, the one they launched at Cherry." I said, finishing my food. "It kind of hurts when I touch it, and the weights have lots of runes and symbols on it. I think he's found something that nullifies the effects of the Opulentia. I'm pretty sure that's what he's going to deploy with this team of his, and I think he's going to abduct people and try to convert them to his army. The problem I keep running into is… what then? What comes next?"

"Working with the government as cover so he can kidnap folks and build an army. Yeah, what the hell for? If he's already in tight with the politicians he can basically do what he wants." Star chimed over her coffee.

"Maybe that is what he wants. He wants an army of loyal servants he can use as fodder to keep up the appearance that he's hunting them down and cashing in tax dollars. Could it just be a demented profit scheme like that? I don't know what else it could be." I replied.

"That thing you said he dug up, the monster where the blood comes from. You think those things got anything to do with this?" Constance asked.

I paused and thought for a moment. I had almost forgotten about the beast that we killed back on the island. Devon told us that Bach dug it up somewhere, and later Bach mentioned he already had other sources for the Opulentia after we killed that one. Were there more of them out there somewhere?

"What if there's more of them out there somewhere, and he's building forces to capture them or contain them? We still don't really know what they are…." I trailed off.

"What if it's an alien invasion, and he's building an army to protect the planet?" Callie chuckled, trying to lighten the mood.

"I suppose we'd be damning humanity then by stopping him. Let's hope that's not the case and focus on figuring out what we can do as we go. If the mothership appears we'll have to go blast them out of the sky ourselves, I guess." I answered.

I pushed my plate aside and leaned back in my chair with the last of my coffee, turning to face Constance. I could tell she was still bothered by how things were turning, and I couldn't blame her. The whole ordeal was a shit show to begin with and only getting worse by the day. It didn't matter what our intentions were anymore, we were risking treason simply for doing what was right.

"Constance… If you want out, you can drop anytime you want. I love you as a friend, and I won't put you in harm's way if you don't feel up to it anymore. You've done more than I could have ever asked of you since we started working together and I'm eternally grateful." I said, catching her gaze.

"I… No. I'm still in. I've put this much work into all this mess, might as well see it through. I appreciate you saying that though. If I change my mind later, I'll let you know." she said in her usual gruff tone.

"You're a part of the team, and basically family at this point. Nothing's going to change that as far as I'm concerned." I said.

"Yeah, yeah. Don't get all mushy about it. I'm still not fighting any federal agents, but I'll keep putting foot to shovel where things need to be dug." she replied.

I stood up from the table and set my dishes in the sink, Callie was already beginning to clean up. I gave her a peck on the cheek, and she stopped me as I started to walk away.

"You okay? We can go sit and talk some more if you need." she said.

"Okay? Probably not, but I've got other things to worry about. I'm going to go call Matt and see if he's got anything else I can set on fire to make myself feel better." I smiled.

I patted Cherry on the head as I walked by, she was really special, and I hoped she knew it. She smiled and continued to munch on her fruit and read a manga that I wasn't sure where she had found but didn't feel like questioning at the moment.

Constance got it for me when she went out.

Right, she reads minds. I nodded and made my way to the front porch and sat in one of the rocking chairs facing the road so I could see if anyone was approaching while I pulled out my phone and brought up the secure video line to Matt. The line rang longer than usual, and I was starting to get worried when he finally answered, wiping powdered sugar from his face.

"Sorry boss, I was eating. What's up?" he choked.

"That's a loaded question and you know it." I said grimly. "You got any specs on that device Bach's talking about?"

"Not a clue, whatever it is they have it locked down tight. I've been digging through their system from the tattoo shop, and it just keeps going deeper. Every time I break encryption to a new part of the network I find another rabbit hole to fall down."

"Find anything useful or just potions that are going to make me giant?" I joked.

"What? Oh… Well, I had planned to tell you about the task force, but you were apparently unconscious when I found it, and by now you've seen the announcement on the news, so that's a bit moot. Other than that, I feel like I'm just jumping through loops of code following network connections to nodes that aren't even attached to anything else as far as I can tell. I got a few more camera feeds from other tattoo shops, but nothing we didn't already know. I keep hoping to find a way into their base of operations but I'm not sure these hubs even connect to it at all."

"So we're stuck with nothing but a target on our backs, and no leads to go on again? Fuck this is getting old. Why do the movies make this kind of shit look so much easier?!"

"Because the movies are written by writers, not coders." Matt replied bluntly. "We aren't completely out of leads though. I managed to track a cellphone making repeat connections to the Wi-Fi at one of the shops, and by checking it against the cameras found out it lines up with one of those mysterious vans dropping off or picking up something."

"Oh? Does that help us?" I asked eagerly.

"Every time it popped up, I pinged it until I got enough data to connect to it and track it's GPS, and while I'm not sure what it's driving to and from, I can tell you where it is and what it looks like." He replied.

"Great! Spit it out, what do you have?" I said.

"A warehouse, totally nondescript, downtown. The property lists the owner as classified, so it could be government related, or at the very least covered up. The van makes regular trips to pick up supplies and drop off the... packages."

"So it's where they're taking the abductees?! Holy shit! That's huge, why didn't you call me sooner!?" I shouted.

"I did, you were unconscious. I wanted to gather more intel on it before presenting it, but the whole place is locked down. I haven't managed to find a way into their network at all. I would probably need physical access again, and given how that went so well last time..."

"Hey, I made the connection, it was just the rest of the plan that went tits up." I grumbled.

"Still, I'm not even sure how you would get access to this one. I don't have a clue what they have inside or out. Other than magic drugs and kidnap victims at least. I'm not completely sure that they are keeping anyone there, it could just be a link in the chain."

"That's still better than nothing. Send me the address and keep digging. I'll try to come up with a plan, and if I need to come by and get another bit of tech from you, just let me know."

"I'll get something ready for you to pick up. Later boss."

I flicked the call off and rocked back and forth in the chair watching the road. I felt paranoid looking for anything and anyone that might be out to get us, but was it paranoia if it was true? A van drove by, an old Econoline, white with blue stripes, probably not one of Bach's. I glanced at the tire marks and scorched grass in the yard and frowned. I didn't have a clue what I was going to do, but at least Matt had a lead.

"Tch…" I scoffed.

I had been relying so much on everyone else around me to get anything done, I felt useless. Maybe I should just let the whole thing go, give up our powers and change our names, cash out my accounts and flee the country. Maybe we could go hide out on a beach in Mexico like in the movies, getting drunk and hiding from all our problems until someone from our past shows up and pulls us back in, or more likely just kills us. That fate was starting to seem inevitable anyway.

I reached in my pocket for my glass and weed, but the bag was empty. There wasn't even enough left for a real hit. I called a small flame to my finger and swirled it around the bowl to try and heat up any resin to make it easier to scrape. I kept a few paper clips in the sack for scraping just in case I forgot to buy more, and with a little effort I managed to get a small ball of sticky black residue and centered it on the screen. A red sedan raced past the house while I debated smoking the scrapings. I lit them with my finger, took a drag, and nearly gagged at the taste of skunky burnt eggs, but knew it would get the job done.

I held the smoke in my lungs until they started to burn and slowly let it out, watching the thick grey cloud slip from my lips. After a few moments I could feel the familiar fuzziness in my head as the THC started to take hold, it was easing my nerves but wasn't doing much for the racing thoughts. A black truck approached, and then continued past without stopping. I rubbed my face and pinched at my nose, feeling the numbed sensation to confirm that I was feeling the buzz. A blue truck sat in the road in front of the house, much to surprise.

I braced myself in my seat, unsure of when that truck had even pulled up. I felt the heat begin to rise on my neck as the passenger door opened and someone got out. They ran around to the front of the truck and picked up something off the ground, a turtle. I sighed with relief and let the fire inside me die down. I shook my head, I almost roasted innocent people for helping a turtle cross the road. I decided that I should go back inside before someone got hurt.

I walked to the kitchen and grabbed a bag of chips and a couple pickles to snack on and plopped down at the kitchen table. Everyone else had found something to do to keep themselves occupied, and I found myself envying them. I constantly felt that the world was ending, and it was almost paralyzing, but everyone else was just continuing to live their lives and adapting to the situation with ease. I wanted to scream or cry or hit the street and start burning my way through my problems, but everything felt fruitless. My mind was racing with different scenarios playing out in my head, all of them terrible. How did everyone else seem so calm with everything collapsing around us?

Star was sketching clothing designs in her book, Callie was tending the garden outside, Cherry had her nose buried in her manga, and Constance was tinkering with some of her surveillance equipment. I was just sitting at the table, stoned, and eating pickles to stay calm. Maybe I was overthinking it and everyone was just trying to cope in their own way while we waited for what to do next. My phone buzzed as if queued, it was Matt saying he had the tech ready for pickup if I was serious about trying to raid the warehouse.

I mulled the idea over for a few moments trying to decide if it was going to be worth the risk, every other outing had not gone well for me but if we didn't do something we would just be stuck waiting for the next attack. I should probably come up with a real plan and stick to it instead of just bumbling my way through everything and getting hurt. I was getting tired of getting my ass beat, shot, or whatever other nonsense they were going to throw at me if I stormed in alone again, but I was terrified of putting anyone else in danger. I had powerful allies, but they were still my loved ones and my deep-rooted desire to keep them safe made it difficult to consider bringing them along.

I walked to the den where Constance was cleaning her weapon. She had a towel rolled out across the table and her various tools and brushes meticulously laid out in front of her. I used to have a gun, and I never cleaned it properly like this. I watched several YouTube videos on how to do it, but ultimately was too lazy to do it and then I got magic powers and decided I didn't really need the gun anymore. Constance finished cleaning and oiling the components and expertly slid each piece back into place, engaged the safety, and started loading the ammunition into the magazine. I leaned against the doorframe watching her as she finished and put everything away.

"You've got that look on your face." she said glancing up for a moment.

"What look?"

"The look that says you're about to ask me to help you do something dangerous. Let me guess, you've got a lead on something from Matt and are ready to blindly jump headfirst into another situation without hesitation and will likely need me to dig you out of it?"

"I've been making you do that a lot lately haven't I?" I sighed.

"Yeah. I'm a private investigator, not a soldier Trianna. I know you pay well, and you've done a lot for me, but this is getting ridiculous. What if you don't survive this time? I'm just supposed to bring your body back to your lovers and your child and watch them grieve while the man we've been chasing gets away with everything?"

"Look... I know it's crazy but..."

"It is crazy, any sane person would have bailed on you by now. I don't know if it's worth it anymore. I'd love to see this asshole brought down, but I don't want to watch my friend kill herself trying to get to him.

"Well what the fuck am I supposed to do!?" I said, tears welling in my eyes. "I'm just some lazy bitch that won the lottery and got suckered into this whole mess and all I wanted to do was stop him before he could hurt more people and now everything has blown up out of control and the whole world has changed in just a couple weeks."

"I know, it's... it's a whole lot to take in. I barely believed you when we first met but after getting to know you I had no choice but to believe after everything you showed me. I barely had time to adapt to magic being real and then everything went to shit the further we dug into things. Hell, I almost feel like we are responsible for at least some of this going sideways." Constance grunted.

"I know… after we fucked up at the docks things really seemed to escalate."

"Yeah, I don't know if we spooked them into moving faster or what. Either way, I don't know if we have enough resources or manpower to get much further with this. The more we learn, the bigger everything turns out to be. Bach wasn't twiddling his thumbs the last seven years while we were looking for him, he was building an empire and romancing politicians. Things this scale usually take whole governments to combat, what the hell are we going to accomplish with four women, a super child, and a techno-wizard in a basement."

"You make it sound like the plot of a comic book."

"It feels like one with how outlandish and absurd everything is." she chuckled.

"You're not wrong. I totally understand if you want to walk away. I have to keep trying though. I have to stop this one way or another, even if I wind up dead in the process."

"Well then I guess I have to stick around."

"Are you sure?"

"Who else is going to drag your sorry ass out of the trenches when you black out?"

"Thanks, Con. You're a treat."

"I know. So what'd our wizard find?"

"A totally non-descript, mystery warehouse where the abduction victims are being taken after they get picked up."

"A *WHAT?!*" Constance nearly spat out her coffee.

"A shady, and possibly government owned building completely off the record, and Matt needs me to plug in another USB stick so he can hack into the network." I said, watching the vein in her forehead throb.

"That's big, but also maybe the most demented target we've had yet. Where is it?"

"Downtown, Matt's supposed to send the address. I think he's trying to dig up some more information about it, but everything been erased or hidden."

"That might actually work in our favor. Downtown means it's pretty visible and they aren't likely to have too many guards posted outside. Inside might be a different story, but they wouldn't want to draw too much attention to the building itself. They probably just have a few bodies with radios and a surveillance system that we could potentially disable."

"Why does this sound like something you've done before?"

"Not exactly, but I have *watched* places like this before. Also, I've been thinking about what to do with the vans in the barn. Pretty sure they are the same ones that they use to transport stuff, maybe we can use one."

"They're all pretty beat up, aren't they?"

"There's one that didn't seem to get hit with anything, might just need to clean it up a little, I'll take a look at it. I should be able to hotwire it and then we might be able to sneak in through the loading area, pick up some supplies and see what's in them, and you might be able to hop out and plug in Matt's toy somewhere. It's dangerous, but honestly not any more so than anything else we've tried."

"Yeah, that could work. You go check on the vans, and I'll call Matt again and see what he thinks. He might have some other gizmo to help out."

"We should bring Star with is us too." Constance added, packing away her supplies.

"What do you mean?"

"She could zap the building and kill the power, might give us a window to pull this off."

"I don't know… I don't want to put her in danger."

"She's already in danger, we all are. They came here once already, and I'm honestly surprised they played that card and haven't been back to finish up. Star is just as strong as you are, you can't keep them safe by excluding them all the time. What happens if someone shows up while we're gone, then she's stuck fighting them off without you. She's in danger either way, might as well bring them along and you can keep an eye on them."

"I suppose that means we need to bring Callie and Cherry too."

"We can't leave anyone here, that's for sure. Callie doesn't have powers, and Cherry is too young so maybe we can have Matt babysit them again for a bit. I get the feeling the mercs are going to come back with bigger guns and torch the place any minute though. I'd hate for them to be inside when that happens."

"Cherry got pretty mad that I haven't been including her. She feels like I'm treating her like a baby."

"Oh, she's already at that stage?"

"Yeah, I guess so. Maybe I do baby her, I just love her and want her to have the childhood she deserves."

"I don't mean to sound rude, but that ship has already sailed."

I frowned. "What do you mean?"

"She's been in the shit with you from day one. She saw all that mess go down on the island, and while you gave her several years of carefree living, she's still feeling like the weird kid. She's a bit of an outcast at school, she had like one friend that she can't even see right now. Oh, and her family is on the run from the magic police, she's not getting a normal childhood."

"You're right" I sighed. "I've fucked that up too."

"No, you've done everything you can. It's not a mistake on your part, it's just the reality of things. She's a ball of hormones and incredible abilities, and there's no amount of hovering around her that will protect her from that. You have to let her grow up."

"Constance... how are you so damn insightful all the time?" I asked.

"I made a living of observing people, psychology comes into play pretty naturally. I got really good at reading people. When you watch people all the time, you start to learn from them when they are going through the hard shit."

"So... Cherry's going to cheat on me with another Mom?" I joked.

"No, but she's going to lash out and demand the attention she feels she deserves if she's not getting it. You said she threw a big tantrum outside yesterday, showing off how powerful she can be. That's her asking you to listen because she doesn't feel heard under normal circumstances. It's excessive, and in our case dangerous, but that's what teenagers do. Maybe you should include her a bit more."

"I can't have her on the frontline fighting Bach and his goons, what if she gets shot?"

"That's not what I mean. She doesn't need to be your main soldier but giving her a supporting role where she feels like she can contribute might help her feel better. She loves you as much as you love her, and you do everything you can to keep her safe... you don't think she sees her power and wants to return the favor?"

I chewed on my lip and thought for a moment. Constance was probably right. Cherry knows her own strength and isn't afraid to use it. She's young but all the trauma she's endured has pushed her into an early maturity. I didn't want to risk driving her away by trying too hard to protect her. I wondered if Star and Callie felt the same way.

"Yeah… maybe we find something for her to help with, for everyone to help with. We're supposed to be a team right?"

"Now you're getting it." Constance smiled. "Go call the wizard, and let's get this show on the road."

"Why do you keep calling him a wizard?" I asked.

"I dunno, I heard it in a movie or something and it's been stuck in my head. Seemed to fit well enough."

I shook my head and patted her on the shoulder. I felt motivated again, she really had a way of revealing the bigger picture when I was stuck on something. I needed to focus my momentum on the task at hand and get ready to put together the details for a real plan, and to start I had to call Matt back and run things by him to see if he had any new information or suggestions. I wasn't relying on everyone because I was useless, I had my role to play. I was getting help from my team to fill what I wasn't capable of on my own, and that wasn't a bad thing.

CHAPTER 15

I called Matt and updated him on the plan so far, asking if he had found any more intel on the warehouse or if he had anything else we could use to make things go more smoothly. I had hoped he was secretly a gadget expert like Q from *James Bond* but that just wasn't the case. Matt excelled in a digital world where he was capable of running code to manipulate data and networks to get to things people want to hide, but creating incredibly niche and powerful technological tools and gadgets was not on his resume. He did, however, manage to find an original blueprint for the building which gave us a general idea of what could be inside, but it's probably that some things were changed or added over time. It wasn't perfect but it was better than nothing.

I called everyone else into the living room to discuss a plan. Constance had checked out the vans and, sure enough, there was one with no visible damage and it still had the keys in it. The idea was to go pick up the USB stick from Matt and drop Callie off with him to monitor communication while he prepped to hack into the system. Constance would get us near the warehouse and drop Star and Cherry off so they could sneak up to the generator in the back and try to knock out the power temporarily with a surge and give us a window to try and accomplish getting the drive into a computer. Then Constance would drive the van up to the loading bay and hopefully get us inside to pick up supplies, the power goes out, and we make our move in the chaos. It seemed feasible, but there were still many things that could go wrong.

We found a clothing store on the way back to town that sold work clothes and jumpsuits like the ones the van drivers wore making their deliveries at the tattoo shops. It would be pretty easy to stop in and grab everyone a suit that fit well enough to hide our identities at a distance, and so long as there wasn't any major check-in process to get into the warehouse it should suffice for what we needed. Everyone seemed thrilled to be included, and we decided it was probably our best shot and getting closer to putting an end to things. We packed up our things and loaded up my truck, Constance's car, and the van, since we all agreed it wouldn't be safe to come back here after.

As we picked up the jumpsuits, Star made sure that we got them just big enough to fit over our normal clothes. She wanted me to wear mine over the suit Ezra made for us and said that she had managed to get in contact with Ezra with measurements for the rest of us, even Constance. I was curious how she managed to talk Constance into giving her measurements but didn't press the issue. Ezra had been working on them since delivering my suit and had them ready to be delivered by secure courier to the store before we got there. I was impressed they managed so quickly, but Star explained that after my prototype it was easier to repeat the process. I wasn't sure I wanted to know what it all cost but knowing that we all had an extra bit of protection was comforting.

I felt like we were prepping for a movie heist, and I suppose in a way we were. The movie nerd in me couldn't help but draw parallels to the absurd things I've been living through the last seven years. At times it really felt like I had tripped and stumbled onto the set of some crime thriller or action movie, ready to blast may way through another adventure tracking down the villain that wronged me. As we continued to gather the gear we needed, it felt like we were joining the MacManus brothers on a mission and I had the sudden urge to find some rope.

A few hours later we were pulling back into the secluded back lot for the shop, we hopped out and pulled a tarp over the van and then weighed that down with some junk we found laying around to keep it hidden from anyone passing by. I glanced around the parking lot, but despite my paranoia telling me we were being watched, I found no one. I wasn't convinced, but if anyone was watching they were well hidden. I pulled out the keys and unlocked the doors to let everyone inside, still glancing over my shoulders. I just couldn't shake the sensation, I really wanted to get high and take that edge off, but I was didn't want to risk the mission. I then also remembered that I was out and couldn't do anything about it anytime soon. I contemplated looking for a local head shop and picking up some of the legal Delta8 stuff, but now wasn't the time for that. I needed to keep my head in the game and focus.

We entered Matt's hidden bunker through the secret door, and I sighed with relief at the familiar smell of incense and electronics. Matt had received the packages from Ezra and placed them by the backroom for us to grab and quickly change into the suits. They were all mostly dark denim and leather with the reinforced fabric weave underneath, and I couldn't help but think we looked a bit like a cyberpunk motorcycle gang. Everything fit everyone perfectly, and the sight of Constance all punked out almost made me burst with laughter.

Once everyone was settled into their gear we joined Matt in the command center to go back over the plan.

"I don't know if you'll be able to find a terminal as easily this time, but we don't have any solid information on exactly what is inside. There's bound to be something in place to help keep track of shipments and whatever else is going on, but I don't know if you'll be able to just hop in and out of the van in the time it will take for them to load up a shipment." Matt said.

"I've got a USB drive ready for you, and also some hidden cameras so you can discreetly record what's going on inside. If nothing else maybe we can gather some evidence to use against them."

Matt projected the blueprint of the building up on the wall, and while I hoped it would give us insight into the base of operations and really help solidify our plan, it was mostly just a big box, some catwalks and storage areas, a few bathrooms, a single office, and a break room. The blueprints were from the original construction, and it was just a hub for storing and loading for a small distribution center probably filled up only a few vans and small trucks per day. That business had gone under, and the property sold a few times to various people trying to profit from it but eventually was snatched up by a buyer with a redacted record. As much as some of this felt like a movie, this wasn't the elaborate pre-heist scene I was hoping for.

"I managed to pull the building up on satellite images with Google, and the roof looks to have some large cooling units installed, far more than usual for standard a warehouse building, so it's possible they are running tech in here and converted some of this to office space or something else. I found some old news clips talking about construction closing a couple roads, and in the back of the video it looked like they were taking trucks full of concrete out of the property, so it's possible they expanded downward and created a basement level, but most everything else since the current owners took over has been scrubbed."

"They're in the city, how would they make a basement?" Callie asked.

"It's not easy, but there could be an old aqueduct system or even part of the failed subway down there, or with enough money they could have just dug it out with heavy equipment and then reinforced the walls before the whole thing caved in on them. Without access to the records it's hard to say." Matt explained.

"Bach's got no shortage of money, and if the government is backing him that could give him even more to work with, we'll just have to poke around and see what's there for ourselves." I said.

"They have some kind of signal jamming setup, which would imply they have their own contained wired network inside. Without physically inspecting it I don't have a way of knowing how strong the jammer is, however, I can take a few hours to install a rig into the van that could potentially boost your gear enough that it could still transmit back to us here. It's not a guarantee but it should work in theory." Matt continued.

"Would that let you see our cameras while we're inside?" I asked.

"As long as the booster works and we set everything up correctly, then yeah we should be able to monitor and record the information here. I can link it with your phones and set up a network through the van with the booster..." he trailed off in thought for a moment, running the idea over in his head.

He stood up and walked over to a pile of equipment he had laid out on a table and rummaged through it for a moment before grabbing another box from another table and digging around for something. He pulled some cables and a little box and spun it around in his hand to inspect the underside and nodded approvingly.

"Yeah, this should work. It's possible they could ID the signal and shut it down, the government has some nasty tools, but it's worth a shot. With Callie assisting me here we would be able to monitor you guys while I'm trying to get through the network once you have the drive in a terminal."

"Hey, I'll be like a real 'man in the chair' for you guys!" Callie exclaimed.

"Were you able to find a good place for me to overload the power from the outside?" Star asked.

"It's not going to be easy, from what I can tell the backup generator systems are up on the roof also, and the only access would be from inside the building. However, there is a parking garage not far that is a couple stories taller than the warehouse.

You could use it as a vantage point and try to strike from afar. Can you do that? Does your stuff work that way?"

"Yeah, I can pluck lightning from the sky, it's pretty noticeable though. I might be able to try throwing some like Tri does with the fireballs. I guess I'll figure it out if we need it."

I can also do that if we need extra power.

"Oh yeah, both of us hitting it at once would definitely fry it!" Star replied.

"Hopefully they don't have any kind of lockdown security in place that will trap us inside if shit goes sideways." Constance chimed.

"I can probably melt through it if they do, but yeah, that wouldn't ideal." I answered. "So we need to prep the van with tech, and then we can go… do we have any idea what the schedule is like to seem less suspicious?"

"It's hard to say if they have a check-in system or not, but we have a rough pattern of when vans usually show up for supplies. We know there's seven locations that regularly use this warehouse, as well as a few others that only come when they have a person to deliver. Once we identified how they were transporting those, it made tracking things a little easier."

"Couldn't we just send this to the cops and have it investigated and shut down?" Callie asked.

"There's a few problems, one is how we got the footage and information in the first place, not exactly legal. Second problem: the local PD might take enough interest to investigate but as soon as things like 'human trafficking' get involved the feds come knocking and take over, then if Bach has their backing they will just make it go away. If this place is government owned, we get locked up on federal espionage charges as well as a long list of other felonies. The best we can hope for currently is to get enough intel to pass on to someone high enough up the chain that's already interested in taking him down. I've got no clue who that might be though." Constance answered.

"We'll need to learn just how connected and supported he is somehow, but for now we should focus on getting what we can here. I'd like to get started on the van so you guys can head out as soon as possible. The longer we wait, the worse things could get." Matt said.

"What do you mean?" I asked.

"Bach's started rounding up folks and making them disappear. Some of them are related to the gangs, but others don't seem connected at all." He said, pulling up some news.

The footage showed police and men in suits loading a few people into a van in cuffs, they looked like there was some kind of struggle.

"The raids started last night, but they've been hitting places all over the nation since." Matt said, swapping it for another feed.

More people brutalized and dragged into custody. A few people were tangled up in nets like the one they used on Cherry. The feed cut to another location where cameras were closer to the people being arrested, and my blood ran cold as I recognized some of the faces.

"No…" I gasped.

The text scrolling the bottom read: *POLICE RAID TERRORIST COMPOUND WITH CONNECTION TO WANTED PERSONS.* The *compound*, as they called it, was the farmland that I purchased for the other survivors that escaped the island, who were currently being rounded up into unmarked vans and taken from their homes. The camera zoomed in on one of the people struggling who noticed and began shouting to the screen.

"HELP! TRI, IF YOURE WATCHING! WE NEED HELP! ITS HIM!" she cried out before being stifled by the men dragging her into the vehicle.

"It's Reed…" Callie sobbed.

Reed had overseen the construction of the makeshift boat we used to escape the island and had sailed us all back to shore. She was tough as nails, but like most of the other survivors had given up her magic before even leaving the island. They weren't connected to the magic gangs at all, this was a message aimed directly at me. Bach had targeted me specifically and called me out by raiding the farm. It was bait, and I knew it, but I was furious.

"Let's get to work." I said sternly.

Constance and I spent the next six hours helping Matt install, configure, and test his boost rig inside the van while the others set up the cameras and got some pizza for everyone. Satisfied that the rig was as good as we could make it we covered the van back up and rejoined the others to get rest for the night. Callie and Star watched the news, Cherry found more manga to read, and Constance was busy double checking all the gear and cameras to keep busy. I sat down with Matt in the command center for a little while, just watching him scroll through all the data we had and filing away reports from the rest of our team.

"Hey, Matt." I interrupted. "You got any bud?"

"Yeah, I've got a little. Want to go sit on the roof and smoke?" He replied, not looking away from his screen.

"Fuck yes! I ran out and I just really need to relax before we do this. I'm strung the fuck out with everything happening."

"Understandable, boss. Come on."

He stood up, locked all the screens, and grabbed a small pouch from his makeshift bedroom. I followed him up the security ladder to the roof where there was a small pop-up tent set up with a couple camping chairs.

"I come up here sometimes to get some air or toke and just watch the city for a while." He said, flopping into one of the chairs.

"Why two chairs?" I asked, "Aren't you usually here alone?"

"Sometimes some of the team come to check on me. Having two chairs makes it feel less lonely even when no one else is sitting in the other." He explained, pulling out supplies from his pouch.

"How come you spend so much time here alone? Why not set up something to work from home sometime?" I asked.

"This is home, I decided not to renew my lease on my apartment last year when it ran out. I like being in the bunker, makes me feel safe."

He got out some paper and a grinder and started preparing a joint, my least favorite way to smoke but beggars can't be choosers.

"What about dates? You seeing anybody these days? Got a cute gal, guy or otherwise?" I asked staring out into downtown.

"No. I'm not interested in much of that. Everyone always wants sex, and I'm not that keen on it." He answered bluntly.

"Oh, I didn't know you were Ace, that's cool man. Sorry for assuming."

"It's fine. I keep a lot of that to myself, plus I like keeping busy and working with the tech here. I've always preferred computers and networks to dating anyway. Everything makes more sense that way."

"Well you're damn good at it. I don't know what I would do without you and the team backing me up. You and Constance have been literal lifesavers lately."

He nodded and finished rolling the joint using a water pen to seal the final step. He produced a lighter from the pouch and handed them both to me.

"Here, green's for you, boss."

"Aw, a gentlemen to boot." I smiled.

I lit the joint and puffed it a few times to make sure it stayed. It was strange using an actual lighter, but he likely didn't consider that I could just make my own flame. The gesture was symbolic, giving up the green hit on a bowl or whatever showed some general respect amongst those of us that liked to toke. I wasn't sure why, but when I first started smoking back in high school before moving on to alcohol my weed guy always told me about all the various quirks of how to smoke with other people. Hit it twice and pass it, don't put your lips on it, if you're using a bong don't draw more than you can inhale so it doesn't waste any, all the general etiquette.

"This feels different, right boss?" Matt asked.

"The joint?" I coughed and passed it back to him.

"No, the job. We've been clutching at straws for so long that something about this particular mission feels different. Bigger. Like there's more to gain, and maybe more to lose. I dunno, maybe I'm overthinking it."

"Oh, no, I'm getting that too. We've been getting closer each time, and everything is starting to get personal. It almost feels like we're going to war with him now. I'm steadily running out of places to stay, and probably hemorrhaging money. I haven't had the time to really track what we've been spending just trying to get away from his goons. I'm running out of favors to call in, and it seems like things are going to be over soon. One way or another."

"What if we lose?" Matt asked, letting out a cloud of smoke.

"I don't know. The world has already changed so much, but if we don't stop Bach I don't have a clue what he's going to do next. I wish I could just kill him, but he's insulated himself so much that I don't think that would help anymore."

"I never thought I'd see the world like this. People running wild in the streets with magic powers, televised gang wars, a magic defense team being created by the president, like... all of this is absurd. And here I am just trying to piece it all together digitally, working my own magic."

"Heh, that's why Constance calls you the Techno Wizard." I chortled.

"The fuck? That's kinda awesome though. Maybe I'll get a big pointy hat and a staff."

We laughed and joked about the concept of what a Techno Wizard could be as the weed took hold. We quickly moved away from the stress of the job and just relaxed on the roof watching night take over the city and laughing at each other's dumb jokes. I hadn't ever really seen this side of Matt; he was always hyper focused on his work, but I knew he was a good guy. I think he needed the smoke session as much as I did.

"We should probably head back down. They might be looking for us." Matt said.

"They're all pretty beat, everyone but Constance is probably asleep. But yeah, I could use another slice and some sleep myself. Thanks for this."

"No problem, boss. It's not every day you get to smoke at work with your employer and talk about the end of the world. Here." He said, tossing me a bag. "It's not much but should get you a bowl or two next time you need it."

"You're an angel. See you in the morning."

I tucked the baggy into my pocket and made my way back down into the bunker. I had been right, and almost everyone had passed out on the couch or one of the cots. Constance was sitting alone at one of the tables sipping tea and finishing off one of the pizzas.

"You sure about this? It's got red flags all over it for me." She asked.

"I'm not sure about anything lately, but it's the best chance we've got. Are you still in? I don't want to force you."

"Ah, I couldn't quit now. I'm too invested in bringing this shithead down. I'd love to walk away, but knowing he's abducting people and bringing them here for his sick experiments has my skin crawling and I've gotta do something about it. I just don't like our chances of getting out unharmed this time."

"Thanks for dragging me to safety, maybe I can return the favor."

"Let's hope not, I'd rather stay conscious for the whole trip." she laughed.

I patted her shoulder and grabbed a slice of cheese pizza before heading over to the couch and cuddling up against Star. She didn't wake up but shifted a bit to hold onto me while we laid there together. I couldn't shake the feeling that I was putting them all in danger, but we were past any alternatives. Bach was rounding up people connected to me and apparently had me labeled as Wanted. Trying to hide them anywhere else would just mean I wouldn't be there to help fight when someone showed up to take them away from me. I wasn't going to let that happen.

CHAPTER 16

I slept a bit longer than I meant to the next morning, but we still had several hours before we could hit the warehouse. All the stress of the last few weeks was catching up to me, and I was exhausted. I had spent so much time running on pure adrenaline just trying to stay ahead of things, I wasn't sure how much more I could give. I sincerely hoped this mission would be the break we needed to get to Bach and try to put an end to this nightmare.

Callie was in Matt's makeshift kitchen piecing together some food and coffee for everyone. Star and Cherry were working on a jigsaw puzzle and Constance was sitting with Matt at the desk going over the cameras again. I stumbled over to Callie and wrapped my arms around her waist resting my head between her shoulders.

"Morning sleepyhead! Coffee's almost ready."

"Mrrrr…." I mumbled back.

She twisted in my arms so she could hug me back and kiss my forehead, nearly smothering me with her breasts, not that I'd mind. It would be a decent enough way to go.

"Okay, let go the bacon's going to burn." She said, tickling my side to loosen my grip.

I reluctantly let go, but only because the promise of bacon was exciting. I washed my face in the sink to try to wake myself up a bit more while I waited for breakfast and then joined Matt and Constance at the computers.

"Anything change overnight?"

"Funny you should ask. I just got a report that the shop delivery we were going to use as cover is heading to the warehouse for a pickup in a few hours. A little earlier than we had intended to make a move, and it could blow our cover entirely." Matt said.

"Which is why we're going to hijack them when they get to the city limits." Constance added.

"Hijack them?" I yawned, confused but interested.

"We can set up an ambush pretty easily, disable the driver, stash the van, and then continue with our original plan. We can interrogate him a bit to see what kind of security we might be walking into or if we need a password or anything to get inside. It's honestly more helpful than harmful." She replied.

"Great." I said fighting another yawn. "When do we do that?"

"Now that you're up, right away. Grab your coffee and your keys, let's go." Constance said standing up from the table and holstering her pistol in her new jacket.

"Oh… fine." I grumbled.

I slipped into the rest of my suit, grabbed the keys to my truck and Callie handed me a bacon wrap and a thermos full of iced coffee. She kissed me on the cheek and wished us luck. Star stopped us on the way out to give me another, and Cherry hugged us both. It was surreal, like they were saying goodbye to us on our way to go to work at the office, not hijack an enemy vehicle in broad daylight.

Once outside I climbed into the truck, and looked over for Constance to hop in the passenger seat but she was getting into her car.

"We're not riding together?" I asked out the window.

"We need two vehicles to block them off. I'll call you for comms in a sec." She shouted back and then climbed into her sedan.

I had a sneaking suspicion that my Rivian was about to get beat to hell or worse but, we needed to get this driver for questioning. I connected my phone to the truck so I could answer her call hands-free.

"You hear me?" she asked.

"Loud and clear, let's get 'em." I replied.

"Perfect. Matt's sending you GPS, we're going to wait in an alley the van takes to avoid traffic and box them in. I'll park in front in case he tries to ram us. He'll have a hard time pushing this tank around before we get him in our sights. You close in behind and then get ready to blast the tires if he gets squirrely."

"Roger that." I said gulping at my coffee.

We drove to the edge of town and found the alleyway. It was more of a side road connecting a couple blocks without having to use the main road. Locals most likely used it to avoid the tourist traffic during work hours in the busy months. There were a couple vacant lots that we used to lie in wait for him to pass through. Matt had already pinged his phone from the tattoo shop and was feeding us updates on his approach. It wasn't long before the black van turned onto the road, and I casually pulled out behind him.

"I've got eyes on the van, I'm right behind him."

"Roger. Pulling out now." Constance replied.

Up ahead of us I saw her boxy sedan pull to the middle of the road and come to a stop. The van slowed down and then stopped a car length or so away from her, waiting to see if she was going to move. I slowly rolled right up behind him to make sure he couldn't back up, and let the heat rise in my body, ready to hop out and melt some tires. Constance hopped out of the car and drew her gun on the driver. I could see him putting his hands up in the side mirror, clearly confused and afraid.

I yanked the parking break to make sure the truck would stay in place and then bolted out and up to the driver's door.

"Open up, shit head. We've got some questions for you." I shouted.

"Holy shit, what's going on!? I'm just a deliver driver! We don't... I don't have any money or packages. It's all empty!!" He shouted back.

Constance moved beside me, keeping her gun focused on him while I reached through the window and opened the door. He panicked and tried to grab me, which was probably the worst idea he could have had in the moment. I flared my arm with searing blue flames, and he cried out in pain and shock as it burned his hands and when he let go I ripped the door open and slammed my fist into his jaw. He went limp and we pulled him out and around into the back of the van, which was in fact empty.

I checked his pockets for his phone and anything else of interest while Constance ran and grabbed zip ties from her trunk to bind him with. Aside from the phone I found a keycard and some candy but not much else. The keycard was blank except for the magnetic stripe on the back, so I wasn't sure if it was for drugs or the warehouse. Constance returned and we tied his hands behind his back and propped him up just as he started to come to.

"We know what you're up to, we just need to ask a few questions. Play nice and answer them for us and we'll let you out of this mostly unharmed." she said.

"Do you use this keycard to get into the warehouse?" I said, holding it up for him to see.

He was clearly panicked but realization was starting to set in, and he sighed.

"Yeah… yeah you have to swipe it to get the doors open its all automated. Listen I just needed a job, it pays well. All I do is transport packages for the tattoo shops."

"Yeah, and sometimes those packages have a pulse, right? We're on to you, bud." Constance said.

"I got nothing to do with that. I just drive the van."

"You know about it though, makes you complicit. You're just as bad as they are. Now, what's in the warehouse?"

"Supplies for the shops."

"What else."

"I…. I dunno, I don't!"

I drew flame to my finger and pressed it against his leg, searing a hole in the fabric and lightly burning his leg. "Try again."

"I don't know what all it is, labs or some shit. I just drive the truck and take stuff where I'm told! Everything downstairs is off limits. I got no clue I swear!"

"What's the security like?"

"What?"

"Security, numbnuts! Are there guards or cameras or anything up top?"

"Probably cameras, everything's automated. We drive in, stop in the paint and a remote forklift loads the supplies in the back. If we are dropping it off someone comes and gets it and takes it downstairs. I don't know anything else I swear."

"It. That's what you call the people you're abducting?" I scowled.

"It, the package, them, whatever. We're supposed to treat everything like product."

"And you're okay with that? Treating people like products?"

He smirked. "Look it's just a job. I was just following ord..mmph!?"

I grabbed his face, covering his mouth with my hand. I felt my tattoo's blazing with power and rage.

"Just following orders, huh? I seem to remember some other folks else using that excuse. Didn't end well for them."

I glanced back at Constance, who had already put her gun away and just nodded.

I turned my head slowly back and locked eyes with him. My hand began to heat up and he squirmed for only a moment before the flames emerged, melting the eyeballs from their sockets. I dropped his lifeless body to the side and jumped out of the van, slamming my fist into the side of it. I walked over to a pile of trash, leaned against the wall, and vomited.

Constance patted me on the back to help me calm down and then motioned to the van.

"We gotta go dump this somewhere. Can't just leave him in the alley. You good?"

"I'll survive."

"Let's finish this. We can unpack it later."

I nodded and let myself go on autopilot as we loaded the body into her car and covered it up with a blanket. I'm glad that Constance was there to keep things moving on the mission because I felt useless. She had already planned a place to dispose of the van just in case and so she drove it and parked it behind an abandoned junkyard she and Matt found. I just sat silently trying not to throw up waiting for her to return while visions of his face burning out played over and over in my head.

I'm not sure why I was affected so much by killing the man. Sadly since being taken to the island, he wasn't the first person I'd killed. He wasn't even the first person I'd killed since going on the run. Something about the way I had done it, so purposefully, while staring into his eyes and letting my rage take over, just sickened me to my core. What was I becoming?

Eventually Constance returned and said she was going to take the body somewhere to get rid of it, but I was barely listening. I just nodded and got in my truck to drive back to the shop and clean up. I felt disgusted and I hoped that the shower would be enough to make me feel a little better. I'm not sure how I made it back to the shop, I zoned out pretty much the whole way.

I stumbled through the building, into the hidden bunker, and into the little shower room. I cranked the hot water and stripped off my clothes. I locked the door so no one would bother me and then sat on the floor of the shower, staring at the grout between the tiles. I sobbed quietly, or maybe it was just the water flowing down my cheeks, I wasn't sure.

There's a difference between killing someone actively trying to kill you and killing someone you have already tied up and left defenseless. Self-defense is one thing but what I did in the back of that van was cold-blooded murder, and no matter how much I listened to the voice in my head saying he deserved it I just couldn't believe I had done it. Was that who I was now, or was the power inside changing me?

I've always had some anger issues, I'm pretty sure that comes in the standard package for children raised by abusive fathers that like to yell a lot, but since gaining these powers it's been on a whole other level. Anytime I got angry I could feel it boiling inside me, the fire begging to be released as if something else was fighting for control. Maybe it was the Aspect, the strange, enhanced form of my powers that seemed to be connected more to the blood of the strange creature that created the Opulentia. Whatever it was, it was starting to scare me.

I sat in the shower long enough for the water to run cold and only decided to get up after I started to shiver. I summoned a small amount of my power to warm up letting some of the water on my skin turn to steam and evaporate before patting myself off with the towel. I stood over the sink and stared at myself in the mirror. I barely recognized myself anymore.

My reflection shifted in the mirror to the young girl I once was. A full head of red hair hung around my bruised face, a single hanging lock of it stuck in the crusted blood from my nose. No tattoos or piercings yet, just wounds from my father's hands for being in the wrong place at the wrong time. Mascara filled tears inched down my cheeks and my brow furrowed with anger and pain.

I filled my hands with water and splashed my face, the image shifted again. I was a little older, maybe senior year of high school. My red hair was shorter, and I was combing it forward to cover a black eye gifted to me by my boyfriend after I accidentally spilled his drink at a party. My skin was covered in makeup hiding various other bruises and there was a small cut on my lip. Razor thin lines on my arm from cutting myself, just to feel it, stood out amongst the pale skin. My eyes were unfocused but full of deep rage as I wiped the mirror with a towel.

Another version of me stood there brushing her teeth and sniffing the mouthwash to make sure there wasn't any liquor in it. No visible wounds this time, but the hurt was still there as I contemplated driving my Camaro into the river on her way to her dead-end job. This wasn't long before I won the lottery and started this hellish journey. So much of my life was filled with misery and anguish.

The image faded into my current self just in time for me to punch the mirror sending spider lines across most of the surface. I stared at myself, the cold eyes of a murdered staring back at me and I wanted to scream, wanted to give in and burn the world down around me. I felt the heat rising and watched the hidden symbols on my neck begin to glow a pale blue. It would take no effort at all to just let go and destroy everything around me, but just as my thoughts began to swirl in my head there was a knock at the door.

"Babe? Are you okay in there?" Star asked.

I froze for a moment and then unlocked the door. She pushed it open, and I collapsed into her arms. Callie was there as well and held onto both of us as I sobbed.

"I'm… becoming… a monster!" I stuttered through my tears.

"Oh, Tri… you're not a monster."

"I just killed him like it was nothing, melted his head right out of his skull and I *wanted* to do it. It felt good in the moment but now I just feel sick. Why am I like this!? What's happening to me?"

Star and Callie wrapped their arms tighter around me to console me and we all fell to the floor in a pile as my legs just gave up on supporting my weight. They probably tried to say something to me to soothe me, but I was crying so hard I couldn't tell. I was scared, terrified that I was turning into someone terrible like my father. I sat on the floor leaning into their arms just repeating over and over that I didn't want to hurt them.

It took a while for me to calm down enough to compose myself and get up from the floor. Star and Callie sat with me for what had to have been an hour just holding onto me and telling me everything was okay. I had just completely melted down. After everything we had been through, killing that man was the push over the edge. The stress of all that had happened had finally caught up to me in that moment and it broke something inside of me.

Cherry had joined us on the floor at some point too, my whole family came to me in my time of need, and it made me think that maybe I wasn't as bad as I thought. They still loved and cared about me, even though I felt like a monster. Matt had even brought some tea over, and while it wasn't my favorite thing to drink I guzzled it down. Constance was just returning as well and so we were all together again.

I wiped tears from my face and gave everyone a hug individually. I apologized for the way I acted but everyone assured me it was fine and that I wasn't a monster I was just stressed out. I wasn't sure I fully believed them, but it was comforting to hear. I wanted to get high and go to sleep, but I knew we still had a job to do. We still had to raid the warehouse, and I wasn't going to let this opportunity go to waste.

Callie and Matt took their spots in the command center, loading up the comms and cams so that we were all connected back to them as we piled into the van. Everyone was focused and ready as we drove to the parking garage near the warehouse to drop off Star and Cherry. I gave them both a big hug and kissed their foreheads before letting them out. *I love you* we all reminded each other, just in case. I laid down in the back of the van and covered myself with a moving blanket to make it look like the back was empty if someone peeked.

Constance drove the van to the gate at the back of the warehouse and swiped the card in the terminal. There was an unsettlingly long pause before it buzzed and raised the arm to let us inside. I held my breath the whole time, sure that we had fucked up somehow and been made already, but we pulled into the warehouse without issue.

"In position and waiting." Star announced over the comms.

I sighed with relief because that meant Matt's booster had been enough to get past whatever they were using to jam signals. Constance rolled to the designated pickup area, hopped out and opened the back of the van so that I could quickly hop out before the automated system began loading supplies. I walked towards the back wall where the office and other things were listed on the blueprints, and sure enough there was a bathroom and some other closed unlabeled doors. At the end of the hallway was an elevator and a stairwell clearly leading underground.

"What do you think, check the offices or head downstairs?" I asked.

"Offices first, we don't know what all's underneath us. I'm not seeing any cameras around, but that doesn't mean they aren't there." Constance replied.

"Agreed, there could be terminals up here that would be easier to access than whatever lab is down there." Matt added.

"Roger."

I checked a few doors and of course they were locked, but I wasn't going to let that stop me. I placed my hand on top of one of the knobs and focused some flame inside of it, quickly melting through the aluminum handle and the locking mechanism. After a moment I was able to force the door open and found myself standing in a completely empty room.

"Fuck, nothing in this one."

"Van's getting loaded with a pallet of something, I'm going to have to move it out of the sensors soon. Try another one."

I moved to another door in the hall and melted through the lock to get inside but again only found a barren room.

"This is weird, right? Why is there nothing here?"

"The whole thing is a front for Bach's lab, so I guess they didn't need anything up here. They must run everything from downstairs." Callie said.

"I'm moving the van, wait there. I'll join you in a sec."

"Alright, I'm going to look in the bathrooms I guess. Maybe something is hidden in there." I said, unsure of what to do with myself while waiting.

I checked out the bathrooms and found toilets and sinks, they all seemed to work fine but there was no secret doors that I could see.

"Figures." I muttered.

Constance caught up with me back in the hall and we walked over to the door to the stairs. There was a card reader on the wall next to the door.

"Do you think our driver's card works on this too?" I asked.

"That's seems unlikely and rather unsecure for this kind of facility but might as well try it." Matt added.

Constance nodded and swiped the card. There was a beep and a green light lit up as the door unlocked and I pulled it open.

"The fuck?" Matt muttered, clearly unimpressed with the security system.

I shrugged and stepped into the stairwell. It smelled overly clean, like a hospital or doctor's office and it was well lit with overhead florescent lighting. I started down the steps and tried my best to walk softly but even our light steps echoed in the well because of how quiet it was. Constance drew her pistol and stood at the ready as I reached for the door handle.

I feel something inside.

I paused as Cherry's words echoed in my head. I didn't realize she could communicate from that range.

Something calling out... but I'm not sure for what.

"Well that's unsettling, but here we go." I said, pushing open the door.

We found ourselves standing inside a well-lit laboratory. I got a flashback of the lab on the island where Bach's scientists experimented on us and knew we had found the right place. I expected to see a large tank of Opulentia fluid and people strapped to tables, but this lab had something else. As I walked forward into the lab, I looked over the strange tubes of green fluid standing maybe ten feet tall with cables and tubes poking out of it. The room was cool, but the tanks were ice cold to the touch. There was something inside of them, floating in the liquid but the ones closest to the door were so small I couldn't make out what they were. They just looked like meatballs or something floating in something that resembled Nickelodeon Slime.

We walked further into the lab through what had to be fifty or more of the strange tanks, and as we neared the last row the objects in the tanks got larger and as I checked each one I got chills.

"Oh fuck… he's cloning the monster from the island." I blurted.

I leaned against the ice-cold glass of one of the tanks and observed the creature inside. It was the size of a toddler, but it was unmistakably one of the creatures Star and I had fought back on Bach's private facility island. The incredibly powerful Subject One monstrosity that tore up the entire facility and took all of mine and Star's combined strength to destroy.

"WHAT!?" Star shouted.

"There's tons of weird tanks in here with various stages of baby monsters. Holy shit, he's lost his mind!"

"Why are they bringing people here though? And where are they putting them?" Constance asked, looking around the lab for answers.

"Pop that drive in one of those computers and I might be able to find out." Matt said.

I had forgotten about looking for a computer, the sight of these creatures had startled me so much. I walked away from the tanks and up a small set of stairs to the desks and sure enough there were some computers running and displaying information about the vitals of the creatures in the tank. I slotted in the drive and let Matt get to work on his end while I poked around things in the lab.

It's them. The creatures in the tanks… they're calling out to me. They're… hungry.

"What do you mean?"

I'm not sure, they just feel hungry. It's only a few of them, but I can feel it all the way over here. It feels weird.

"Hmm… Does it feel like before? When you told me you felt something calling out to you back home?"

No… well, maybe. It's not as strong, but it is kind of similar.

"So there's probably more out there somewhere. Fuck." I muttered.

I flipped through pages on the desk, but it was just read outs of the systems monitoring the creatures and didn't make much sense to me. I sighed not wanting to leave empty handed and leave all the work up to Matt, but I wasn't getting much here. Constance motioned to get my attention and then pointed at another set of stairs going further down into the facility. I hurried over to join her and we began to descend once again.

These stairs went much further than the previous set and were much less clean and the lights were dim and looked old. The door at the bottom of the stairwell had a dingy glass window that we could just barely see through. On the other side of the door was a large platform and what looked like a rail system.

"Old subway?" I asked.

"Possibly, strange that it's connected to the lab." Constance answered.

We opened the door and stepped out onto the platform and lights flickered on to brighten up the room. At the far end of the platform was the elevator we had seen before and a few empty gurneys. There was a small control terminal that looked like it ran a trolley or something on the rails.

"It must connect to another location or something. I think this is as far as we should go for now." Constance said peering at the live track below the platform.

"Any luck getting into their system yet, Matt?" I asked.

"Nothing yet, it's hard to say how long it will take."

I walked over to the booth with the controls and had to resist the urge to start mashing buttons just to see what would happen.

"Why is no one here trying to catch us?" Constance asked.

"I dunno. This whole place is fishy. It reminds me so much of the island lab, but that had people in it running the experiments and shit. Do you think they knew we were coming?"

"It's possible, but I feel like they would have been waiting not hiding. I'm curious where these tracks go but I don't want to get trapped down here. I'm going to go poke around upstairs some more and see if I can find anything before Matt digs into the network." she said, walking back to the stairs.

"Okay, I'll be right the-" I started but cut myself off.

Something was coming on the tracks from the left side. I could hear the movement on the tracks and then suddenly lights started flashing from the tunnel and a subway car came barreling into view. Constance dove into the stairwell to hide but I was caught out in the open and decided to stand my ground. I was tired of the games and just wanted to get some answers.

The car slowed down as it approached the platform and I saw that it was fully open on the sides, no doors, or walls except for the front and back. A figure stood calmly centered on the platform. He looked up as the carriage stopped and smirked as I heard Callie gasp on the comms. It was James, her backstabbing sleeper agent ex-boyfriend.

"You." I growled.

"Nice to see you again. You're not supposed to be here." he replied.

I clenched my fists and felt my tattoos flare with power as I started to summon flames around me but before I could do anything James quickly stepped to the side and pushed the lid off of a barrel inside the subway car. He waved his arms through the air towards me and just as I had formed a ball of fire in my hand, a huge pillar of water rose out of the barrel and formed a wave that slammed me back against the wall. He drew the water back and then surrounded me with it lifting me off the ground and encasing me in an orb of water floating in the air. The son of a bitch was trying to drown me.

Gunshots echoed in the chamber and at least one caught James in the chest, but he stood unphased. He glanced over to see Constance approaching with her gun still drawn and focused on him and that was the gap I needed. I called to the angry voice deep inside of me and let my Aspect take control. The water began to boil around me and as I focused flames swirled across my body and I was able to burst the orb of water and drop to the ground as Constance shot him in the arm breaking his concentration.

I held out my arm and sent a beam of searing hot, blue, plasma flame at him but he managed to duck out the way at the last second and I watched it burn a hole in the far wall of the tunnel. He rolled across the floor and sent a stream of water under Constance's feet causing her to slip and fall and then sent multiple small waves slamming against me. The force of the consecutive strikes was pummeling me into the floor despite my best effort to hold my ground. The tile floor just made it incredibly difficult to brace myself without slipping.

I called more fire to swirl around me and then formed it into a shield to break the waves against which allowed me to get my footing again. I screamed with rage and flung a beam of fire at him once more, this time caching him in the chest and knocking him off the platform and back into the subway carriage. The water fell to the floor as well, and I could see him struggling to pat out his smoldering chest. It seemed he had some kind of armor under his shirt that protected him, but his clothes were ruined for sure.

I rushed over to the controls and slammed my hand on the buttons until I heard the car start to move again. Light began flashing and the carriage started to roll down the tracks further into the tunnel once more. James started to get back up but ducked down again as Constance fired a few more shots at him. The subway car raced out of view, and I ran over to Constance to make sure she was okay.

"You good?"

"Yeah, just busted my ass a bit. It'll bruise, but I'm fine."

"You two should probably get out of there before he calls for backup." Callie said over the comms.

Something is awake upstairs. I think one of the creatures got loose. It's hungry.

"Shit this just keeps getting better."

I helped Constance to her feet, and we rushed back up the long stairwell to the labs. The lab was filling up with a strange green fog and there were lights flashing from the computers up on the platform. I looked around and one of the tanks was shattered and the green slime was oozing out onto the ground and creating the fog, it smelled like a vile mixture of vanilla bean and transmission fluid.

"Should we kill the power?" Star asked.

"Not yet, I'll lose all progress getting into their system. I'm getting close." Matt replied.

"Do you have any eyes in here besides our cams?"

"No, but I've located their internal network and should be through soon, just try to get back to the van."

I nodded and turned to head back upstairs when something came leaping out of the fog and I felt claws trying to dig in through my reinforced clothing. One of the creatures was trying it's hardest to tear into me with tooth and claw as I struggled to stay upright.

"What the fuck is that!?" Constance shouted.

"Baby monster, long story!"

I shifted my hand under the stomach of the creature and produced a beam of plasma flame that quickly burned through the screeching beast until it went limp and dropped to the floor. I gagged on the horrid smell it made as it burned and had to fight back the urge vomit. I kicked it aside and then made a break for the stairwell leading back up out of the lab.

I don't know how, but I felt that creature die. It was really strange.

"We'll have to figure that out later, hon."

"Should we do something about the rest of these things? I feel like leaving them for Bach is only going to cause problems down the road." Constance asked.

I looked over the remaining tanks in the room and nodded. This could be a huge problem, and although Cherry was having a strange connection with them, I couldn't just let him grow an army of killer monsters that easily.

It's okay. Do it, I'm ready.

I lifted my arm and summoned as much of my power as I could muster and focused it into a beam and drug it across the room, blasting glass and goo across the floor as each tank burst. A few of the creatures squirmed and shrieked but fell limp after a moment, none of them seemed to be up and moving like the one that attacked me. I was curious how it escaped in the first place but didn't want to spend too much time figuring that out when James could be coming with reinforcements at any moment. I made a second pass with the beam just to make sure I got all of the tanks and their inhabitants and then joined Constance in the stairwell just as the sprinkler system engaged.

I think that's all of them. I don't feel any more here. I feel like I'm going to throw up though.

"Hang in there, kiddo. We're almost done here." I said.

The lab was erupting into flame, and I wasn't sure if the fumes from the tanks were flammable or not, but I didn't want to stick around to find out. We moved up the stairs to the warehouse where everything seemed calm. No alarms or flashing lights, no armed guards, just shelves full of unlabeled boxes and our stolen van parked near the exit. I was expecting resistance but then Star and Cherry likely would have seen something and reported it. I was relieved that we didn't find ourselves faced with federal agents and riot police as we climbed back into the van.

"I'm in the camera system. Shit, they've had eyes on you this whole time. I can see the whole warehouse, the lab, the tunnels… oh god there's multiple facilities connected here. It's hard to tell because there's so many camera feeds, but there has to be at least three labs connected to that subway system, maybe more." Matt rambled.

"Do they connect to the surface at the other locations?"

"I can't tell yet, but it's possible."

"Well, let's kill the lights and get the fuck out of here. Hit it, Star!" I shouted climbing into the passenger seat.

A moment later I heard a loud electrical pop like a transformer exploding and all the lights shut down right as we pulled out of the loading bay and headed back towards the street. I looked up and could see black smoke billowing from the roof that was probably going to attract attention, but we were already on the way out so it shouldn't matter. I was frustrated that they had caught us on camera, but James being there felt like he was waiting for us the whole time anyway and had lain a trap that just didn't work out for him.

"We're almost at the bottom of the garage!" Star huffed, running quickly down through the building.

We slid the van right up to the side entrance as they came racing out and dove into the back, pulling the door shut behind them. I could hear sirens in the distance, probably the fire department coming to investigate the smoke or possibly the sprinkler system was connected to an alarm. We took a winding path of back roads away from the building before heading back to base just to make sure we weren't being followed.

"I'm still getting camera feeds from at least two other locations, so it seems that building was isolated in terms of the power grid. The subway rails seem to be down for the moment as well. There's a lot to dig through here, and I haven't even got to the juicy bits yet. See you soon, boss" Matt chimed as we drove.

"Hey look, we made it out of a mission without you having to drag out my unconscious body!" I said to Constance, struggling to catch my breath.

"Yeah, you're still looking pretty rough though. You going to make it?"

"Oh you know… two birds… one… mrr…" I mumbled as I passed out in my seat.

CHAPTER 17

I woke up some time later to the sound of screeching tires and people shouting. I bolted up in my seat and glanced around to figure out what was happening finding that were currently racing down an old highway. The back door of the van was open, and Star and Cherry were currently fighting off a handful of trucks and vans full of armed mercenaries. Constance was shaking my arm to try and wake me up.

"Nice of you to join us, Tri. Shit hit the fan." She said, whipping the van around oncoming traffic.

"What the fuck?" I muttered, turning around to look out the back.

Star was in her aspect and energy was arcing along the metal edges of the van causing all the lights to flicker as she hurled bolts at the approaching vehicles. She connected with one and the engine immediately shut down and the van swerved into another pursuing vehicle knocking them both off the road. Bullets bounced off our van and Cherry pulled a large boulder over the opening to shield us all from the shots. I rolled my window down, called my aspect, and leaned halfway out of the window to get line of sight on our pursuers.

"Where did these assholes come from!?" I shouted, burning a truck in half with a beam of blue plasma flame.

"Not sure. They popped up and started shooting not long after you zonked out and they just keep coming. I'm surprised the cops haven't joined in yet." Constance yelled back, dodging another oncoming car.

"Road should clear up in a moment, police scanners show they are diverting traffic away from the area but that means you'll probably hit a roadblock soon." Matt announced in my earpiece.

"Cherry, do you think you can pull a large wall up from the ground?" I shouted.

Oh, that's a great idea!

She dropped the boulder she was using as a shield and sent it smashing into one of the vans and then hunkered down to focus. I was too tired to keep blasting for long but with Star's help we managed to keep the vehicles busy enough that they couldn't shoot at us accurately. I felt a strange density in the air as Cherry clenched her fists and started raising her arms. Our whole van lifted up for a moment as she pulled the ground up beneath us. We slammed back down on the road like we had just driven too quickly over a speedbump, but behind us a ten-foot-tall wall of dirt and stone erupted across the width of the entire road.

The vehicles chasing us didn't have time to react and most of them slammed into the wall sending dirt and rock flying while the ones behind them crashed into them causing a massive pile up as we raced away from them. Star and I dropped our aspects and flopped back into the van. Cherry pulled the doors closed and then sat next to Star, panting but otherwise unbothered. Up ahead the road was clear, but I could see flashing lights in the distance from the police barricade.

"Do we try to ram through?" Constance asked.

"We don't have much of a choice, they're blocking the only way off this road unless you think you can drive through the woods." I answered.

"We need something to make them scatter, I don't really want to kill any of them and pull more of a mess down on us."

I'll handle it.

Cherry climbed into my lap from the back and held her arms out towards the barricade.

Punch it, aim for the middle. I'll make a hole.

Constance nodded and floored the gas pedal as Cherry concentrated. I watched the barricade getting closer as suddenly the road split and lifted up between the two trucks in the middle and slowly began pushing them apart. Small pebbles whipped up in the air and bounced off the officers and their vehicles causing them to duck down for cover as the earthen walls spread the barricade just barely enough for us to pass through. Constance threaded the hole as best she could, but we were just a little too fast and the mounds of dirt scraped along the sides as we raced through, breaking off the sideview mirrors in the process. Cherry sighed and then fell back against my chest; she was exhausted from the effort.

"You guys need to ditch the van before anyone catches up. Sending your GPS a route that should be complicated enough, and Callie is enroute to pick you up." Matt said.

"We can't just leave it anywhere. Our prints are all over this van." Constance chimed.

"I'm sending you to an abandoned airfield, unless they catch up you should have time to burn it. Scanners are lit up, but it seems they've mostly lost you already."

"Let's hope that lasts, we aren't exactly inconspicuous." I said.

We wound our way through the outskirts of town at times doubling back and making circles to throw off anyone that might be following. We could hear sirens in the distance, but they didn't seem to have any clue where we were. We made it to the airfield and drove as far back as we could, navigating around a homeless camp carefully so as not to disturb them much. Callie showed up shortly after and as everyone piled into my truck I powered up and filled the van with as much flame as I could muster.

I jumped into the back of the truck and hunkered down expecting a massive explosion from the gas tank as we drove away but then I remembered the episode of *MythBusters* that debunked that. Black smoke billowed into the sky as we retreated safely into the city.

"Did the police ID us during all that?" Constance asked.

"Just Trianna, but she's already wanted for magical terrorism." Matt replied.

"Oh, fuck me." I said, clenching my face with my hands.

"Bach had you pretty low on the list of 'Persons of Interest' he released a few hours ago, but you were definitely on there. Things are going to get harder from here on out."

"Great. Hey, by any chance do you know of any property for sale in Mexico?" I asked, sarcastically.

"I... uh.. no. Would you like me to look boss?"

"That was a joke, Matt. I hope you're digging through the network that we just risked everything for access."

"Oh, right. Yeah there's a whole bunch of underground facilities linked together by that subway system which they seem to have expanded over the last several years. It leads out of Charlotte all the way down to the edge of Florida one way, and up to Richmond the other."

"Holy shit..." I gasped.

"Yeah, there's quite a lot to sort through, we can discuss it more when you get back."

"Alright, see you in a bit."

I pulled my hood up to cover my head as we rolled through the city to get back to the shop. I wasn't sure if my identity had been released publicly or not, but I figured it was better to stay as hidden as I could for now. As we drove I began to hear some kind of commotion from another part of the city. We stopped at a red light, and I watched a few blocks over as several people with magic were tearing up part of the neighborhood fighting against police.

I asked Callie to get us a little closer, and we watched as a van pulled up and some of Bach's drone soldiers emerged. They quickly subdued the targets with the strange net weapon we had seen before, the magic users dropping to the ground immediately upon contact with the enchanted net. I tried to stay down low so I wouldn't be spotted as we rolled past the police officers blocking off the road, but watched as the people were dragged into the vans instead of the police cars and taken away. It was surreal.

Travelling through large cities I had seen petty crimes before, but watching magical warfare play out in the street around normal everyday people really cemented the reality of the whole situation. Bach had permanently changed the world with his experiments and schemes. As we drove on I noticed signs hanging on businesses and buildings that said things like "No

Casters Allowed" and "Magicians will be Persecuted" and I just couldn't believe my eyes. Things were rapidly exacerbating in ways I never could have imagined.

We eventually made it back to the shop, and even as we turned down the road it was on I saw people protesting the use of magic in the city. We were living through a worldwide historical event, and I was unfortunately caught up on the wrong side by trying to stop it from getting worse. I was beginning to wonder if we could even stop things anymore, maybe the whole situation was so far gone that there wasn't a way to end it. I furrowed my brow with concern and deep thought as I climbed out of the truck and headed inside with everyone else.

The news was running on the TV when we got back into the bunker showing more footage of conflict across the US between people with magic and police or Bach's special forces. Much like what we had just seen down the road, the net launcher was stunningly effective every time it was brought out against their targets. The news caster mentioned the people being taken into custody, but the footage showed them being loaded into the unmarked black vans each time instead of police custody, just like we had seen earlier. Bach was just openly abducting people off the street and being praised for it like he was doing us all a great service.

Cherry and Star flopped onto the couch, still drained from our getaway. I wanted to join them but knew I needed to take a look at whatever Matt had found so far. Callie was already back in the command center ahead of me and Constance headed straight to the fridge and grabbed a beer. None of us had much to say, the adrenaline wearing off had us reeling from the mission in one way or another.

I rolled a chair up next to Matt who was currently setting up various camera feeds on the wall of monitors so that we could see more of what was happening at once. On another screen I could tons of files populating as Matt's malware worked its way through the encrypted files on the network helping the team locate anything of interest. Callie was poking around some of the information as well, but I could tell her mind was elsewhere. She was most likely still upset about watching James attack us in the subway.

I watched the camera feeds as Matt loaded them up on the different screens, and most of the rooms looked very similar to the building we had already been in. There were a couple warehouses, but there were mostly laboratories with strange equipment I couldn't fully make sense of. Scientists moved between different stations in some of them, fiddling with various liquids in vials or injecting things into other things. It was like watching B-roll on a science fiction movie about some rampant disease taking over the planet. I kept waiting for a narrator or something to explain the real-world problem the scientists were working on stopping, but that obviously wasn't the case.

One of the feeds was coming from a room full of tanks with the creatures inside of them like the one I had destroyed earlier. I could just barely make out the strange lumps floating in the goo, but I knew they were there. Looking over all the different feeds I felt my heart sink a little, Bach had accomplished so much in the last seven years while I grasped at straws trying to find him. There had to be at least seven facilities on this network, and who knew if there were more elsewhere.

"This is bigger than I ever would have guessed." Matt said.

"I wouldn't believe it if I hadn't just been there. This whole time we've spent looking for him and he's been right under our noses, literally."

"I've got people sifting through the data we've extracted so far, but I don't know what all they are finding. There's lots of medical records, I think related to the creatures, but I don't know enough to be sure. There's still parts of the network that we haven't breeched, and I'm curious because we haven't seen any sign of the people that have been abducted from the tattoo shops yet."

"I saw them taking people off the street earlier on the way back, do we know where they are being taken?"

"News reports all say 'into custody' but police chatter says otherwise. They keep referring to something called 'Quanta' or 'the Quanta base' but it's unclear what exactly that is other than something to do with Bach's new gestapo force."

"That sounds like something he'd come up with. He likes dumb names. It's not showing up on the camera's anywhere though?"

"Not yet, but like I said we're still digging in. There appears to be a link to at least one more location further north, but if it's on the same network we haven't cracked it yet. Their system is not well protected, but physical barriers can slow the process down. While each location generally shares communication, they aren't all linked to a single network but more like a collection of smaller networks with some being more connected than others."

"You'd think with all the money they had for these labs that they would have better security on their computers." Callie chimed.

"Well, most security systems are designed to prevent access from external sources, but since we physically entered the malware into their system on a local machine it bypassed a lot of the normal security, and I set it up to disable the local defenses first which makes it easier to get into the rest of the network because it looks like their own activity." Matt explained, sipping an energy drink.

I walked over to the wall of monitors and took a closer look at several of the rooms, trying to get a feel for what all was happening. Finally a screen popped up that had a face I recognized on it. James was standing in one of the labs, removing his burnt clothing and talking with some men in suits. He seemed aggravated and was barking orders at them, but there was no sound from the feed so I couldn't make out what he was saying. I could read enough of his body language to understand he was pissed off and taking it out on his subordinates.

"Oh we got… the fuck? Hold up boss, I just got some more cameras and this one is really weird." Matt said, tilting his head in confusion.

He pushed the feed up to the big monitor so I could see it better and I froze in place at what I saw. The room was entirely dark except for the center that was illuminated not by lights, but the creature positioned in the middle of the room. Large chains bound the arms and legs pulling the body into the shape of an X while suspending it above the ground. The bit of the floor made visible by the glow revealed runes and magic symbols scrawled all around the creature. The chest was spilt open and that was where the light was coming from, as well as the fluid in the hundreds of tubes running in and out of various parts of the body.

"That looks just like the monster we killed on the island, but bigger. What the hell are they doing to it?"

"Looks like they are either taking something out or putting something in, and I'm not sure which is worse." Callie added.

They are draining it, probably to make Opulentia. It's weak and in pain.

I hadn't noticed Cherry enter the room but looked at her curiously.

"Do you feel this one too?"

Yes. It doesn't feel like the others, but I can sense it. I think we are connected somehow. I don't know what that means. Am I one of these creatures?

We all paused and looked at her for a moment. Devon had told us that Cherry was the only child born to parents that had been experimented on, that something in the process seemed to make everyone infertile. But her biological parents, Cotton, and Daisy, somehow managed to reproduce. Cherry was born mute and as she grew she discovered that she could manipulate all elements, while anyone else altered with the blood of Subject One could only manipulate one. Her power seemed to grow with her and had extended into telepathic speech and now the ability to sense and feel other people or creatures.

She looked like a perfectly normal girl, but was there some kind of connection between her and these creatures? Did having two magically altered parents produce an offspring that was closer to the creature that gave us the powers? I had never considered it, but I didn't fully understand what these creatures were to begin with. Devon has mused that they could be demons or aliens but only confirmed that Bach and Khan had found them deep underground.

"You mentioned before you could feel the little ones, you even felt when they died. What did that feel like?" I asked.

Like some part of me also died, I felt sad and confused and then I wanted to throw up. I could almost feel pain, but it wasn't like I felt it myself. It's really hard to explain.

"You know, people say that Twins can feel each other's pain and emotions because they were so genetically close, but there's never been any conclusive science to back it up. Maybe since the magic came from those creatures you all have a connection." Matt added.

"She wasn't ever given the Opulentia, her parents were. She was born like this." I said.

"Oh… so she's genetically capable of magic, just like those creatures. Maybe they are some kind of proto humanoid or something and she's got the same genetic makeup because of how her parents genes formed to make her."

Am I going to turn into one of those things? Mom I'm scared.

"No baby, the little ones looked different remember. You might be connected because of your telepathy, but you're not going to turn into one of those things. I promise."

I can tell you're just saying that to make me feel better but thank you. I'm going to go back to my book and try not to think about all this for a bit.

"Sure thing, hon. We'll figure something out, don't worry." I said, kissing her on the forehead.

I was a little surprised that was enough to calm her down, but she was more mature than I was ready to admit, hell she didn't even call me 'Mommy' that time. I worried that the trauma we were all going through was aging her beyond her years, but I knew the only way to deal with that was to put an end to this madness. She was a good kid, and she was alarmingly powerful, which was another thing she shared with the creature we fought. That monster nearly killed us all had it not been for Star and I hitting it with everything we could muster.

I looked back at the creature on the screen, it was breathing but just barely. It didn't have the natural presence or intimidation the other one had, I actually felt bad seeing it like this. I watched the fluid glow in the wound and the tubes, and then rubbed the hidden symbols on my neck. Those tattoos glowed when I summoned my power, maybe that was the blood of the creature activating. I looked at the symbols on the floor and recognized some of them from the tattoo designs and some from the enchanted net.

"He's got a mix of magic symbols here on the floor, some that activate the magic and others that nullify it. What do you suppose that means?"

"I don't know shit about magic, but if I had to guess it probably has something to do with keeping the creature from breaking those chains and killing everyone around it like the one you fought before." Matt said.

He went back to typing and clicking away at his station squinting at the screen trying to filter what he was seeing, and I watched his expression change from focused concentration to surprise as he sat back in his seat for a moment.

"I found them. I found the people. Oh my god…" he muttered.

He flicked the image up to the screens and I stared in horror as I saw row after row after row of medical beds with people laying hooked up to glowing tubes with strange devices bolted to their heads. As I suspected, they were all being run through his process of making drones for his army, but he had streamlined the process. I traced all the tubes back to a machine on the far wall which seemed to be receiving the glowing fluid from the next room which I assumed had the creature inside. They were directly infusing the Opulentia into the people they abducted, while a few people in lab coats were tattooing mystical symbols on their neck and chest.

The symbols were similar to the ones Star, Callie, and I had but smaller and in larger numbers. I wasn't sure what the device on their head was, but figured it had something to do with the brainwashing they performed to make them obedient soldiers. Callie looked up from her thoughts and gasped, placing her hand over her mouth. She clearly recognized the procedure as well, considering she had once been a part of the recovery unit for people once they had been experimented on.

"Are you recording this?" I asked.

"Yeah, I've had to isolate some of our servers for storage, but I've been recording the whole time. If we can just find a way to link Bach to this footage we could potentially shut the whole thing down if we get the right eyes on it." Matt replied, staring at the footage in disbelief.

"Is that what he did to you guys?" Constance asked, stepping into the command center.

"Sort of. This is more refined that what we went through, but that's basically it." I said.

"This is monstrous. I... I can't believe what I'm seeing. You told me about the experiment on the island, but I hadn't pictured it like this."

"Yeah, and he's capturing more people by the day with those nets and his soldiers all on the taxpayer's dime."

"Alright, I don't care who we have to fight: the CIA, the FBI, Santa Claus, whoever. I'm ready to rumble. This can't be allowed to continue." Constance said determinedly.

I nodded in agreement. I had guessed something like this was happening but seeing it like that, seeing the scale of it all, was heartbreaking and infuriating. I was going to stop this, even if I had to burn it all down myself.

CHAPTER 18

We spent the next several hours watching the various cameras throughout Bach's facilities and waiting for Matt to break into the more sensitive data hidden in the network. A few times we saw people in suits, some of them obviously drones, bringing people on stretchers to the lab to be hooked up to one of the brainwashing rigs while waiting for their mystical tattoos. Once we saw James walk through a few of the frames and inspect some of the scientist stations or poke through the boxes of supplies. I asked what happened to the supplies we loaded into the van before we had to run, and apparently Star and Cherry had dumped them out the back to try and slow down the first few people chasing us.

I kept waiting for Bach to make an appearance and give us the connection we desperately needed to try and bring him down, but not once did we see any sign of him in the six hours we spent monitoring the footage. Given the ability of the rich to manipulate the legal system in the US, I knew we needed to have very solid ties between Bach and these facilities. Constance suggested that we should probably find a way to connect him with James since we had evidence of James running the facilities and that would be a good launch point for an investigation by an interested authority. Since we had committed crimes to get the footage from the facilities, they likely wouldn't be admissible in court but if we had enough connections otherwise it should be enough for the Department of Justice to investigate on their own.

It was time to put together a plan and hope for the best. Part one was to send Constance back to her specialization of being a private investigator and having her tail James outside of the facility to try and catch him meeting with Bach in some capacity. Once we had more specific details on the location of each facility we would be able to track where he was going anytime he left and have Constance ready to follow him and track him until he led us to Bach. Part Matt's team was busy capturing IP addresses to confirm locations of each facility, while the rest was focused on sifting through files for useful information as it was obtained. James seemed to be staying in Richmond, and so Constance loaded up and started driving north, as it would take several hours to get close enough to observe when he made a move.

Part two was to continue digging through their network until we found enough incriminating evidence to show that these facilities were responsible for the magic hitting the streets. We needed some kind of documentation that showed the supplies for the tattoo shops as well as the drug cartels came from Bach so that once we tied him to the facilities we could link him to the production and distribution of the Opulentia. We knew that James had been meeting with crime lords prior to the outbreak, but we needed evidence: bank records, receipts, anything transactional to show money changing hands for product, conversations or text messages that showed planned meetings or sales. This was going to rely heavily on our techs being able to find these things in the network itself.

Next, we needed to find a way to stem distribution by either shutting down the warehouses or eliminating the supply. We still hadn't isolated which facility housed the monster we saw, but that wouldn't be hard to figure out once all the locations were confirmed. I proposed that we raid the facility and destroy some of the warehouses and then kill the beast so that they could only make use of what they had processed already. It was likely that Bach had more product elsewhere, but this chain of labs seemed to be the distribution hub for the whole east coast based on what we had observed so far. If nothing else it could potentially draw Bach out of hiding and give us a chance to get our hands on him.

The final part of the plan was more ambiguous. We had to put an end to everything but if we just destroyed it all then there would be nothing we could use to convict Bach of his crimes. Matt suggested that we bypass part of the legal red tape and simply take the information public ourselves. It would implicate us in our own crimes, but if done correctly we could get enough attention on it that the government would be forced to react.

"How are we supposed to do that, though?" I asked.

"We stream it." Matt replied bluntly.

"What? How?"

"We'll have to set up multiple sources to keep from being taken down immediately but if we can push enough feeds out across all platforms then we should be able to put the evidence out there faster than we get banned. We can also publish the recordings on our own sites so that people can find it even if the streams get taken down."

"That seems like it would take a lot of resources and computers... How would we pull that off?"

"Luckily, we already have a massive server farm for the repair service that we could repurpose. I can have the team start setting up accounts and prepping the servers while we gather evidence. We could even have you streaming from inside the facilities if we build another signal booster."

I contemplated the idea for a bit, the court of public opinion was certainly powerful and with enough eyes on the situation it could lead us to our goal without having to directly work with the possibly compromised police and federal agents. I didn't fully understand how it worked, but as we talked through some of the details it seemed like we could practically force the information to go viral especially with the public eye already focused on the magic war in the streets. I agreed and set Matt and his team to purpose on setting everything up, Callie offered to help in any way that she could and together they got to work. We bounced ideas for a few more hours and by the end of the night we had a reasonable plan in place to put an end to things.

The next morning we really put things into action. Constance left for Richmond, and Matt and Callie began building another signal boost device for our raid on the facilities while the rest of Matt's team set up as many streaming accounts as they could manage without getting blacklisted. Star and Cherry went out for supplies, while I helped sort through the information we were pulling out of the facility servers. I was feeling a renewed vigor despite the voices in my head telling me we were just going to fail again and while part of me wanted to go back to sleep and just give up, I felt like we were making more progress than ever.

The work was quite tedious but also involved a lot of sitting and waiting, much to my frustration. The deeper we dug into the network the longer it took for Matt's malware to get through encryptions and gain access to the data we needed. It seemed most of the information we were looking for was either not saved on the computers in the facility or was sent elsewhere and deleted and had to be tracked down. Matt suggested it could be stored in a cloud server which would be harder to get into from the facilities themselves depending on how it was setup.

We did find tons of diagnostic reports and medical data for the clones in their tanks as well as some general logs about the experiments being run on the prisoners. Star and Cherry had returned with bags full of quick and easy to make foods and snacks and a mini fridge for more storage. Star also had managed to pick up a bag of weed for me from one of her contacts and I showered her with more than the usual amount of love and affection. Sitting for hours on end in front of live video feeds would be much easier with a bit of a buzz.

I snuck up to the roof to Matt's chill spot and packed a small bowl with the delicious looking flower Star had procured. I lit it with my finger and took a drag listening to the satisfying pops and crackles of the burning bud. As the smoke filled my lungs I looked out over the city and tried to just take it all in. I could hear sounds of conflict in the distance, likely another outbreak of violence between magic users and police. It was hard to fathom that most cities in the US, hell the world, were turning into war zones filled with small pockets of magical violence.

I had grown up on fantasy worlds and video games full of magic and fighting against oppressive systems and always dreamed of a world where magic was real. Living in such a world now I couldn't help but be disgusted by my own naivety, the real world was never as whimsical as the stories, and it figured that even magic would be tainted and contorted into something less extravagant and exciting. Sure, having magical powers was pretty amazing, but the damage it was wreaking on society was horrific and the process behind it even more so. Add in a heavy dose of capitalism and political corruption and even the coolest aspect of fantasy suddenly feels vile and morbid.

I took another hit as I watched a helicopter hover over the battle in the distance keeping an eye on the conflict below. A moment later a large chunk of concrete slammed into the rotors and the helicopter plummeted to the street below. Bach was killing people in the streets with his creation and getting paid to provide the solution without anyone knowing how much worse of a problem it was. A few of his special forces vans raced by on their way to the fight and several minutes later all was quiet again. I wondered how long it would take to clean up the downed helicopter and if Bach's people would be responsible for that or if it would be passed on to the city governments to deal with, though I was sure I knew the answer.

I took a final hit and held the smoke until my lungs burned. I slowly released it into the sky as I watched the clouds float by overhead. I never would have guessed my life would turn out like this. Going from living off scraps from a dead-end job to winning the lottery and completely changing my life for the better only to be manipulated, captured, and tortured by a mad scientist hellbent on changing the world for the worse. I chuckled to myself, that was my luck after all, I couldn't even live a peaceful life with tons of money without finding a way to fuck it all up.

My nose was going numb, and my face was beginning to tingle and so I put my bowl away and headed back inside. Star and Callie were watching the news and I could hear the anchor talking about the continuing conflicts around the world despite the efforts of the newly established Quanta Force and their rapid response to outbreaks. I paused and stared at the screen.

"Did they just say, 'Quanta Force'?" I asked.

"Yep. Apparently that's what Bach named his special unit of magic hunters." Star replied.

"We heard something about Quanta in the police messages about rounding up the magic users." I said. "Guess that confirms it. I'm surprised he didn't call it Paradigm just to fuck with us."

I continued into the bunker where Cherry was sitting at a table with a sketch book lost in a drawing. I poked my head over her shoulder to see and was shocked to see myself standing on the roof watching the helicopter before it crashed.

"What are you drawing, Cherry?"

Things I've felt lately. I think this was you just now on the roof.

"It certainly is. You got this much detail just from a feeling?"

Yeah, it's hard to describe with words but a little easier to put down as a drawing. I've got a few others, see?

She flipped over some pages and showed me a few drawings of strange creatures floating in goo, the large one suspended by chains and tubes, and piles of bodies left being carried to an incinerator. The lines were all hazy and scribbled but not without purpose, disturbing content aside the art was quite good and unique. The last page she showed was of herself standing with her hand up to the window across from a shadowy figure laying in a bed also raising one hand. The figure was fully shaded out with no visible details.

"What's this one?" I asked.

I don't know. I feel something or someone calling out for help, but I can't tell who or what they are. It's different from the creatures, more familiar but when I focus on it everything fades.

"Fades?"

Yeah, like I can't see them at all if I focus, I just feel it in the background. I think it's coming from one of the facilities like the creatures but it's too hard to tell.

I held the image up to get a better look, the room around the bed was clear and well defined but got distorted and fuzzy as it got closer to the shadow figure. It almost looked like a hospital bed, but I wasn't sure.

"Hey boss! You're going to want to see this." Matt called from the command center breaking my concentration.

I patted Cherry on the head and returned her drawing before walking over to join him at his desk. He was frantically cycling through screens of new video feeds from deeper within the facility as thousands of files and documents scrolled through another window.

"We just made a huge breakthrough and we're getting tons of information and new cameras. We've got research notes, experiment results, audio logs, emails and text messages, there's so much coming in, this has to be what we were looking for." he smiled.

I watched as he began filling out monitor wall with new angles, warehouses with people stuffing things into boxes, offices with scientists actively working on their computers and equipment. There was a room with several furnaces and people in hazmat suits pushing the dead bodies of the monster clones into the fire to dispose of them and it looked just like Cherry's drawing. Another room full of mystic symbols surrounding a suspended creature full of glowing tubes like the one before but with a more feminine shape and long thin patchy hair hanging from its head.

"Is that... a female monster?" Matt asked.

"It kind of seems that way… holy shit is he breeding them instead of cloning them?"

"Honestly that would probably be easier, but I can't say for certain without digging through their research. Whatever he's doing he's burning off the failures which might help us locate that particular facility. Even if they filter it, that smoke has to go somewhere."

"What else is there?" I probed.

We cycled through more footage until we eventually found an empty conference room and some offices. Inside one of the offices, flipping through paperwork and typing on a laptop was James. As we watched, his phone rang, and he answered quickly. There was sadly no sound for these cameras, but I could tell by his body language he was speaking to someone above his station. He nodded and gave several 'yes sir' 'no sir' answers and seemed generally uncomfortable as if he was being grilled about his work. It reminded me of performance reviews at my old job in the call center which immediately made me uncomfortable for a moment.

After the call ended James sighed, tossed the phone onto the desk, and flopped back in the chair clearly not thrilled about how the conversation went. He rubbed his face with frustration like he had just been asked to meet an unreasonable deadline and then slammed his laptop closed before grabbing his suit jacket and leaving the room. Whatever the conversation was, he was certainly upset about it, and we picked him up on another camera storming down the hallway and into an elevator. I quickly pulled out my phone and shot Constance a text message to let her know.

We got eyes on James.
Seems to be leaving in a bad mood.

I'm close. Thanks for the tip.

We got a ton of new data to filter, I'll let you know
if we find anything helpful.

K. Keep me posted.

We finished scrolling through all the available camera feeds and found ourselves with just over a hundred between the various locations which was quite a bit more than the amount of monitors we had, but we were able to get most of the more interesting ones laid out in a grid with several on each screen. Matt directed part of his team to start trying to determine the physical locations based on the connected camera feeds and the subway access so they could try to locate blueprints or maps for reference points. The rest of the team, us included, were going to start digging through the documentation and emails that we located to figure out more of what was happening in the labs and try to find connections to Bach or Quanta. Unsurprisingly, neither his name nor the Quanta force showed up in any basic searches but that didn't mean it wasn't there in some kind of code or something.

An operation of this size was naturally going to fall into some kind of corporate style ladder to stay operational and we only needed to decipher the hierarchy to figure out who might be talking to who. We started by looking for who was asking for results versus who was providing them, and then trying to trace those up the line until we found reports going to James or someone else of power. It wasn't easy work, and we spent several hours reading through correspondence before we made it past the head scientists' level. Nobody used names in any of the emails, and all of the handles were encrypted but eventually we managed to breakthrough and start compiling a list of the names.

We spent the entire day filtering through the data, only taking small breaks to use the bathroom, eat, or toke. Callie and Star joined in as well from time to time but also took breaks to play boardgames with Cherry and note how difficult it is to play against someone that can basically read your mind. The deeper we dug into the emails the more cryptic they became, but we started picking up a pattern of correspondence looking for a solution to the failed subjects. This seemed to refer to the creatures in the tanks not remaining stable while growing and either dying in the tank or needing to be put down because of trying to kill and eat the staff which happened at least once that we could confirm.

Someone higher up was pressuring that they needed a solution soon and the replies mentioned 'the girl' but never specified who. From what we could decipher, this girl was someone with powers, stronger than the usual experiments and drones, but was not in their possession currently. Following that string led us to conversations about research on the island prior to 'the incident' and I began to draw the conclusion that they were referring to either Star or myself. Bach had told us before that we had stronger reactions to the Opulentia than almost everyone else and that was partially why he tried to keep Star to himself, as she was one of very few to attune with lightning.

Sometime in the evening, as we were running out of steam for the day, I felt my phone buzz with a message. I grabbed it and flipped it in my hand to see the screen. It was from Constance.

Meet me outside, got something for you.

Outside? Aren't you in Virginia?

I don't want to ruin the surprise, but I think you'll get a kick out of it.

I hesitated, something about the message felt off. Why was Constance back here when we just sent her after James several hours away? I stood up from the table and started to head up stairs but stopped and stared at the message on my phone again. I wasn't sure why, but it just didn't seem like Constance sent me that message.

"Hey Matt, you can see outside in the parking lot, right?" I asked, turning back to the desk.

"Yeah, why? Something up?"

"Constance just texted me to meet her outside. Said she's got a surprise for me. Something feels off, can we take a look?"

"The fuck? Yeah, sure…"

Matt flicked up the local security system and an image of the parking lot outside the shop filled the screen. Sitting in the middle of the lot was Constance's car pointed towards the building with the lights on.

"Why is she here?" Matt asked.

"I don't know, but this is fucking weirding me out. I'm not sure that's Constance in that car, but I'm going to go check it out. Lock everything up behind me."

"Sure thing, boss."

"You're not going out there alone are you?" Star asked, having overheard the conversation.

"I was but maybe you should come with me. Something's wrong for sure."

My phone buzzed again.

Are you coming?

I set the phone on the table, glanced at the camera feed again, and then headed up through the shop determined to get to the bottom of things. Star followed but tried to stay hidden where she could still watch in case I needed back up. I opened the door and stepped out into the parking lot facing the car and holding my hand up to try and shield my eyes from the headlights in the dark.

"Alright, what's going on Constance? This is weird." I said.

The lights cut off and a figure was standing next to the open driver's side door, but it clearly wasn't Constance. As my eyes adjusted I could make out the shape of a man, a familiar one. It was James, shit eating grin on his face and his hands in his pockets. He opened the back door and pulled someone out of it and tossed them on the ground between us. It was Constance, and she was beaten up pretty bad.

"She better still be breathing, asshole." I said.

"She is, for now." He replied.

"What do you want?"

"I'm here for the girl. We need her to complete our research. I'm tired of playing games with you, so you can either hand her over peacefully or I can have Quanta down here in minutes to take you all in by force."

"You're not taking Star from me while I'm still breathing, so call whoever you want." I growled.

I felt the heat and anger rising within me as we locked eyes. The tattoos on my head and neck began to glow and I could see them lighting up the space around me as I got ready to call my aspect and destroy him.

"Star? I'm not interested in your wife you dumb bitch. I'm here for Cherry." he grunted.

"Cherry!?" I gasped. "What does she have to do with this?"

"She's the closest thing we have to a modern specimen and will catapult our research forward."

"You mean your breeding program for the monsters?"

"Sure, if you want to call it that."

"No way in hell, prick!" I shouted, and transformed into my aspect as I summoned a pillar of blue plasma flame under his feet.

He managed to jump out of the way before it hit him and as he ran he pulled a bottle of water out of his coat pocket and quickly ripped off the lid drawing the water out into a floating sphere. He turned and sent the water rocketing towards me in a small thin line with tremendous speed and though I managed to step to the side before it hit me dead on, it sliced into my upper arm and a small trickle of glowing blue blood emerged from the cut. I screamed and launched towards him, propelling myself with a controlled burst of flames that scorched the asphalt. Once I was a little closer I sent a beam of flames from my hand at him, but he managed to duck out of the way again.

He reached his palm downward and then clenched his fist as if grabbing something and I paused as suddenly the area was filled with an awful stench. I heard a noise and looked down by his feet as a manhole cover was forced open by foul liquid rising from the sewers below. He formed the wastewater into a wall and sent it flying at me like a tidal wave. I called a wall of flame in front of myself to prevent the disgusting mess from hitting me and focused on holding it there as it burned away the water and whatever was floating in it making the smell much worse.

I heard crackling coming from the shop and glanced over to see Star had emerged in her aspect as well, energy arcing across her skin to the ground. She flicked her wrist and pointed her palm towards James and the lightning raced across the ground in a ball and caught him dead on causing him to scream out in pain. I didn't waste any time and rushed over to him planting my fist into his jaw with as much force as I could muster sending us both careening to the ground as my feet slipped out from under me. We rolled and tumbled for a moment as he fruitlessly tried to prevent me from wailing on him.

All of my anger channeled through my fists that began to flare as I swung at him again and again. I eventually managed to straddle him and hit him a few more times leaving singed bruises along his arms and face. I got lost in the fury and rage and probably would have beat him to death then and there if Star hadn't shouted about the approaching vehicles. James coughed up some blood but still managed a smug chuckle as three Quanta vans pulled into the parking lot. I stood up and kicked him in the ribs before turning to face the approaching drones in suits armed with net weapons.

"Trianna von Drake. You are wanted for domestic terrorism, stand down or we will use force." a voice announced over the vehicle mounted PA system.

"Oh, that's a load of horseshit and we both know it." I shouted back.

They didn't respond with words but one of the drones fired their net at me and I sliced it in half in midair with a blast of fire.

"You'll have to do better than that!" I said calling more flames to my fists ready to brawl again.

"You are resisting arrest. If you continue to do so lethal force will be authorized. Stand down now!" the PA echoed.

"Fuck off!" I retorted, sending a beam through the engine bay of the van causing it to burst into flames.

More drone hopped out of the vans carrying actual guns and I had to dive behind Constance's car as they opened fire. I heard a loud thunderclap and felt the energy on the air shift as Star floated up and began to fill the sky with storm clouds. Lightning bolts crashed down onto the guns in the hands of all the drones simultaneously causing them to drop the weapons and spasm as they fell to the ground. I felt a few drops of rain on my face, and then I panicked as I realized what she had done.

Before I could even say anything, James reached up from the ground with both hands, gripped the air, and tugged every ounce of water out of Star's storm clouds into a massive wave that smashed into the parking lot bringing Star down with it. The force of the wave blasted the vans into the road and scattered all of us behind them. I tumbled and crashed into the side of the building so hard it knocked the breath out of me. Star was knocked out cold and thrown across into an adjacent lot.

James was on his feet, having routed the water away from himself and was walking towards me laughing. He reached out and pulled an orb of water around my face, again trying to drown me. I barely had time to catch a breath before I felt the water trying to force its way into my nose. I could barely see him approaching and then the water fell away from me as he grabbed my shirt and lifted me off the ground. He held his palm over my face, and I felt searing pain as he started to draw the moisture from my body.

I cried out and tried to summon my fire to defend myself, but I was exhausted and unable to focus through all the pain. My skin burned and my vision blurred, my mouth was drying out and I felt like I was turning into a husk when suddenly something struck James hard enough to knock me free from his grasp. I fell mostly limp to the ground and watched as a pile of broken concrete and rocks stood over me, picked James up, and threw him across the parking lot into the back of one of the vans.

I've got you, Mom. Hold on!

Cherry's voice echoed in my head as the concrete golem rushed over to the van, slammed the door shut and pushed it down the road until it started to drive away. The chunks of concrete collapsed into a pile, satisfied that it had done its job. A moment later Cherry emerged from inside the shop with a large bottle of water and began pouring it onto my face and somehow manipulating it back inside of me, rehydrating my wrinkled crepe-like skin. It wasn't comfortable but didn't hurt nearly as much as it did when James pulled it out of me.

"What was that?" I gasped.

I made a rock monster and beat him up so he would leave you alone.

"You made a… okay whatever. We have to check on Momma." I replied.

I turned and started to run to where Star had been thrown when I heard tires screeching and a roaring engine. I glanced back towards the road just in time to see the van's back door open and a net wrapping around Cherry instantly dropping her to the ground. James and a few drones leapt from the inside as I managed to find enough energy to blast a beam through the van, splitting int nearly in half. James and his goons raced over to

Cherry and started to drag her towards another van that was pulling up.

"NO!" I shouted, fearing that they were going to take my daughter from me.

My skin boiled away to magma as I felt the aspect take control stronger than ever before. I was nearly blind with white hot rage and my body seemed to move on its own. I leapt through the air and landed on top of one of the drones setting them ablaze as I lashed out at another with long tendrils of lava that slashed through the air like a whip. James and the two remaining drones dropped the net and bolted for the van, but I was faster.

I extended my arm towards the van and watched with confused horror as my fingers seemed to stretch and grow into fiery tentacles that grabbed the three men and flung them into the air letting them fall to the ground with a painful thud. One of my tendrils seared the face off of one of the goons, the other hadn't moved since they landed. James was scampering backwards trying to get away, trembling with fear at what he was seeing before him. I reached down with my other hand and sliced through the net allowing Cherry to scramble out and run to Star.

I recalled my finger tentacles as I approached James with murderous intent. I was no longer in control of my body, and I could only watch as my arm raised in front of me and melted into the shape of a long blade. The beast within, now fully realized, was about to brutally murder this man while I watched. The scariest part, however, was that part of me liked it, wanted it, craved it as if it was the only way to experience true satisfaction. I drew closer to him and aimed the blade at his chest, ready to plunge it deep inside of him, and then I heard the engine of the approaching van.

The impact sent me careening through the air and tumbling across the pavement just before I could disembowel James. The pain was bizarre and jarring. I never felt the van but as my molten skin returned to flesh I definitely felt every inch of the sidewalk. When I finally came to a stop, I did my best to ignore the scrapes and scratches and looked up to see what was happening. Cherry was tending to Star, Constance had been washed over by the door of the shop but still hadn't gotten up, and James was struggling to get to his feet as one of the Quanta goons tried to help him into the van that hit me.

I tried to lift my arm to blast them with flame, but I was so sore and tired that I couldn't. Suddenly, there was a loud crack and James cried out in pain and dropped to his knees clutching his shoulder. Another pop and a small hole appeared in the side of the van, another and blood spattered across the metal from James' other arm. Gunshots? I turned wearily and watched Callie approaching him, gun in hand with tears streaming down her face. The drone turned to intercept her, but she dropped him with another round.

"Callie, please…" James sputtered. "Let's be reasonable about this, dear."

"Fuck you!" Callie screamed back, taking a stance to steady her aim. "You lied to me, manipulated me, and then hurt my family! You tried to take our daughter from us!"

She braced herself in her stance and leveled the gun at his face. I could tell she was concentrating on keeping her arms steady against the well of emotions below the surface. Her face was a mixture of pain and determination, and I knew she had made up her mind about what she was going to do. Just as he tried to speak up again she pulled the trigger and splattered his brain across the side of the van.

CHAPTER 19

I woke up to a sharp pain in my leg and cried out as I lifted my head to see what was happening. Callie was lifting my leg to change a bloody bandage wrapped around a nasty scrape down the side of my leg likely caused by sliding across the pavement after being hit by the van. *Shit, the van, the bodies!* I thought. I tried to sit up but every muscle in my body ached so bad I flopped back in the cot despite myself.

Don't worry, I'm almost done cleaning up outside. Cherry's voice echoed calmly in my head.

"You need to rest. You're beat up pretty bad, but I don't think anything is broken. You'll be sore but you should be on your feet in a day or two if you take it easy." Callie said as she finished dressing my wound.

I glanced around the room trying to gather my thoughts. Star and Constance were both bandaged up and resting in cots nearby. We were in the bunker's living room, but the furniture had been moved around and it looked like a makeshift medical tent. Callie was tending to us all, checking wounds and replacing bandages as best she could with what limited supplies we had. She was focused on her work, but I could see the emptiness and hurt behind her eyes still processing that she had just shot and killed her ex.

I could hear scraping and rumbling from the parking lot above rattling through the walls and wondered what exactly Cherry was doing. There was a pause, and then a few slamming noises and something that sounded like metal crunching. Something heavy slammed into place and then what sounded like rocks being scraped along the ground. *What are you doing up there Cherry?*

I put all the bodies in the van, washed off all the blood and then burned everything, then I made a big hole and crushed the van into it and covered up all the damage, so now it looks like nothing happened. I don't think anyone saw us fighting or anything either. I'll be down in just a minute.

I was impressed, that was good thinking even if the act itself was a bit risky. One less thing to worry about at least, but now we had severed the link between Bach and the Opulentia operation as far as I knew. It was probably going to be harder to connect the dots without that one direct connection and that could thwart the entirety of our plan. I sighed and tried not to think about it, wanting to let my body rest and heal for whatever else lay ahead.

I dozed off for a few hours but awoke to Cherry and Callie asking if I was hungry. My stomach growled loudly in response before I had a chance to even nod. They helped me sit up and then handed me something I never thought I would want so badly: a fast-food cheeseburger. The smell of the greasy meat and cheese that wafted from the wrapper as I opened it was heavenly, perhaps partly because I wasn't even sure when I had eaten last.

There wasn't anything particularly special about the burger, it was your run of the mill franchise burger, but after taking the first bite I nearly moaned with pleasure. A little bit of grease ran down my chin as the tomato and pickles oozed into my mouth on a sled of melted cheese and mayonnaise. I had been eating fancy homecooked meals for several years and even if we ordered food it was usually from a high-end place. I loved to splurge on nice food whenever possible, but staring down this greaseball pile of processed food stuff nearly brought me to tears, so yeah, I guess I was pretty hungry.

I devoured the burger as if it were the last chance I was going to get to have one and let the nostalgia of childhood through young adulthood wash over me. It wasn't going to give my body many nutrients and was loaded with sodium and saturated fats, but I loved it. Classic American hedonism contained in a paper bag. Growing up poor I had eaten my fair share of cheap trashy food and once I got rich I thought I'd never want one again but there I was, hiding out in an underground bunker, licking the last of the ketchup and grease from my fingertips.

Star and Constance were awake and seemed just as enraptured by their food as I was, and I couldn't help but smile. Sometimes the simplest options are all you need. Cherry and Callie were sitting nearby opening their food now that ours had been distributed and I could hear Matt rustling through a bag of his own in the next room as he continued to work diligently on digging through our enemy's servers. It felt like the end of the night after a party where everyone was drunk, tired, and just filling their belly with something to soak up the alcohol before heading to bed. A bit of bittersweet nostalgia washed over me thinking about the nights I had just like that over the years.

We didn't have much more than Ibuprofen in terms of pain relief so I asked Callie to help me to the bathroom so I could turn on the exhaust vent and smoke a bowl. It was a struggle as my legs didn't want to support my weight and move at the same time, but we managed. I took a few tokes and handled my business while I was there before stumbling my way back to my cot with Callie's help again. Even as the THC worked through my system my body ached in protest of all the movement, and I supposed that was fair considering I got hit by a van.

I could have been in worse shape, all things considered. Something about my aspect's new form must have prevented my bones from shattering on impact, the van certainly hadn't taken it easy on me. It was difficult to remember clearly but I was fairly certain that my body had completely transformed into molten plasma and didn't revert to flesh until after I bounced off the parking lot the first time. Each subsequent bounce was what tore my skin up and left me bloodied, bruised, and barely able to stand. I was grateful for that much, but then I remembered how utterly out of control I was prior to that.

It seemed like every time I let my aspect take over it got increasingly stronger and more difficult to control, or maybe that was just me giving in to my anger. I was angry almost as much as I was depressed lately, and suspected the trauma played a large role in that. I was concerned that the next time I gave in, that I would lose myself completely and never come back from the burning rage that seemed to fuel my aspect's power. Maybe I should let Cherry take the Opulentia out of my veins before I did any real harm to myself or those around me. I was terrified at the idea of being powerless as we continued to take on Bach but was worried I might not have a choice if this was how it was going to turn out.

Matt roused me from thoughts with a few gentle taps on my shoulder, bringing my attention back to the world around me. He looked rather excited and grinned as I made eye contact with him.

"Come on..." he urged, "You're going to want to see this for yourself."

He helped me stand and I leaned on his shoulder as we walked back to the command center despite Callie's insistence that I stay in bed.

"This better be good, Callie's going to be cross with us." I said as he helped me drop into a chair and rolled me over to his computer.

"Oh, it's more than good. Take a look."

On the screen was a rather plush office with a large expensive looking desk covered in paperwork. Sitting at the desk angrily shouting into a phone was a man with a face I'd probably never forget for the rest of my life. Sebastian "Bach" Artosis was center screen in his chair berating someone on the other end of the line while pointing at various pieces of paper like they could see them. I growled under my breath on instinct and winced as I felt my tattoos pulse with power which caused my muscles to ache even through the slight numbness I felt across my body from the weed.

"I managed to get through the last of the network and it jumped me to a whole new location not physically connected to the underground facilities. This…" he gestured to the screen with one hand, "is Quanta's HQ."

"Holy shit, that's amazing! It's on the same network as the other places?" I asked in awe.

"No, not the same network but I did notice a lot of outgoing data heading to the same IP and managed to crack in after several hours of digging. That's not all, I found something really bizarre buried in the archives of the other facilities before I got into Quanta. What do you make of this?" He asked, pulling up a video file.

I leaned in to watch as the video began to play, it began with the sound of an old film reel and a black and white countdown that beeped as each number changed. I gasped with recognition as the black and white footage began, displaying a very familiar futuristic looking building at the end of a cobble stone driveway, set into the side of a mountain with a beautiful waterfall. A voiceover began playing, and the voice sounded like a World War II era newsreel announcer, all tinny and sharp. I recognized the building, I recognized the speech, and I couldn't believe I was seeing this message again. I explained to Matt as we watched that this was the video Bach sent me to trick us into coming to his little island and torturing us seven years ago. Sure enough, at the end of the video, there he stood arms raised in admiration of the building behind him as the Paradigm Corporation logo faded onto the screen.

"That's incredible, I can't believe you found this!" I laughed.

"I can't believe he's kept a copy of possibly the most damning evidence we could hope for tying him to the creation of Opulentia and starting the magic war. He'll be hard pressed to talk his way out of that, especially with the other footage we have of the warehouses." Matt beamed, clearly pleased that all his hard work was paying off.

"Alright, maybe our plan hasn't gone to shit after all." I said, glancing to the other monitor with the live feed of Bach's office. "Got you asshole, just you wait."

Bach's head rose towards the camera for a moment, and I panicked thinking that he somehow heard me but then I realized he was just exasperated by the phone conversation he was having. I hated that I felt that much fear and paranoia in that moment, that he still had that much power over me even as I grew ever closer to toppling his regime. I couldn't wait to see the look on his face when he realized that we had finally got what we needed to end him. Revenge was going to be sweet, though I wasn't sure any punishment would balance out what he had done to us and the rest of his victims.

I leaned back in the chair and thought about what it would be like watching the federal agents raid his facility as all his new political buddies turned their backs on him not wanting to be connected to the whole ordeal. I pictured the men in black suits walking through the aisles of bodies connected to brainwashing machines and finding the strange monsters they were hooked up to by the miles of glowing tubes. That thought bothered me however, what if the government didn't shut everything down? What if they decided to keep the monsters for themselves and just weaponize everything they found?

I mentioned the thoughts to Matt, and he reminded me that I had already planned to destroy the monsters when we went back in to stream the facilities. Something must have rattled that information loose in my head because I had completely forgotten that part of the plan. Probably getting hit by the van, or maybe it was just because I was high and paranoid. Either way, I decided to have him remind me of everything we discussed previously just to make sure I hadn't forgotten anything else important.

Satisfied that I hadn't forgotten anything else important I got up and left him to his work continuing to dig through the data we pulled from the network looking for any further incriminating evidence. I managed to walk on my own, which hopefully was a good sign that I wouldn't be down for long. I made it back to my cot and painfully collapsed into it, wishing I had asked for help getting in more gently. I groaned and shifted back into place, positioning myself so that I could see the TV hanging on the wall.

Callie was watching the news, and I found myself resenting how often we did that lately. It's hard to get unbiased news in the US unless you go online, all of the network stations linked back to just a small handful of sources that each had their own political ties and you had to try and decipher what was actually happening through whatever spin the network put on any given story. Sadly with the current state of things, televised news was our easiest option for quick updates on the war outside. I was still struggling with admitting it was in fact a war, it just felt so surreal to even think about. I always saw wars on movies and TV that were usually from the government bombing brown people with dubious reasoning, so the concept of there being a war on our own soil, let alone a few blocks away, was baffling.

The anchor was listing off locations and damage caused by continued conflict despite the effectiveness of Quanta forces dispatched across the states. They commented that it was almost like the number of magic users were rapidly increasing in response to the rise in captures, and I stifled a laugh knowing the truth behind that idea. I wondered how shocked these anchors would be when they found out Bach was running both sides of this shit show for personal gain the whole time. I'm sure they would just babble off the information like it was perfectly normal in that weird voice and near monotonous inflection that all news reporters use while not actually showing any real emotion about the situation.

I backed up my train of thought for a moment after that, trying to think about Bach's motivation for doing all this. Back on the island Devon had told us that Bach had this twisted idea that we should dismantle the various world governments and unify the entire population of the earth under a single government to put an end to conflict and prepare for other threats. I didn't think to ask then, but I had to wonder just what other threats he was so concerned about that he would be willing to go this far. Was he doing all this out of fear of an alien invasion or something else absurd?

Then again, maybe it wasn't absurd, after all I had magical powers thanks to the blood of some strange unidentified creature that Bach dug up somewhere, maybe it was an alien and he found proof that more were coming. I had to at least consider the idea, especially knowing that he had two more of the damn things strung up in his labs. I shuttered at the thought and then wondered if by stopping him we were leaving ourselves open to an invasion force from beyond the stars. I wanted to laugh but honestly I wasn't sure what was possible anymore.

My state of disbelief was only deepened when I looked up to see my own face plastered on the news next to footage of a burned hotel room. WANTED FOR TREASON was spelled out under my face in bold letters as the reporter cut to this new story.

"Fuck." I said, leaning up for a better view.

"Triana Von Drake, owner of Scurvy Dog Computing, an online computer repair service, has been identified as being involved with the rise of magic-fueled violence spread across the globe. Miss Von Drake may be responsible for distribution of the strange drugs that started this whole mess and is currently wanted under suspicion of treasonous acts and domestic terrorism." the anchor spoke as I groaned.

"Great, just what we need. Now we're going to have Quanta and the feds kicking in the doors of my shops looking for us. We're going to have to get our asses moving before we get thrown into federal prison or worse." I sighed, sitting up in my cot despite the pain.

"I don't know if we can pull this off." Callie said, "We've gotten our ass handed to us every time we've made any move and you three are barely in any shape to run and hide from the feds, let alone raid Bach's facility again."

"You're not wrong, but we don't have much of a choice either. I'd rather die trying than just give up and roll over."

How can they say this is your fault? How do they get to just lie like that? We don't have anything to do with this, we're the victims!

"That's what money and power get you, I'm afraid." I answered, "With his government connections it was only a matter of time before he put a direct hit out on us like this, and he can spin things however he wants. He's got footage of us in the warehouse from the security cameras, he probably doctored it to look like we were responsible."

That's not right, though, it's not fair!

I frowned, wishing I could explain it in a way that wouldn't upset her, but I just couldn't find the words. I was upset also and had already seen this coming. I knew the minute I lost control in that hotel room that it was going to come back to haunt us, I was just surprised it took as long as it did. Cherry clenched her fists and slammed them on the couch, not willing to accept the injustice of it all so easily. My heart ached that she was having to learn this all the hard way, she was no doubt terrified that she was going to lose her family. Again.

We decided to turn off the news and just listen to some music for a while instead. Matt started beefing up the security systems to prepare for when the feds came looking for us. We had already isolated the bunker to its own network separate from the shop above and it was incredibly difficult to find the hidden door without knowing it was there. We made sure to keep our security cameras up on the monitors at all times to see if anyone was trying to enter the building or snoop around. I still needed a few days to sleep off my wounds and get ready to go back to the facility and I just hoped that we could stay hidden long enough.

CHAPTER 20

Three days passed without issue as we hid in our bunker waiting for the world to end around us. I was up and moving with minimal issues, my wounds had all been superficial and it was mostly exhaustion that was keeping me down, but I had managed to get plenty of rest. Star was looking better as well, but Constance still hadn't stirred much. James had nearly killed her before dropping her at our door and she only got more banged up in the fight in the parking lot. She woke up a few times to eat and use the bathroom but hadn't said much more than a few grunts even after we got the swelling in her face down.

Matt had finished his boosting device and purchased a slightly beat up van to install it in with his own money because all of my accounts had been frozen the moment I was labelled a terrorist. We were running on fumes in terms of resources but luckily Matt was frugal with his money and was able to keep us supplied with necessities, and I promised to reimburse him entirely once I had access to my accounts again. Assuming of course that we didn't all get arrested and or killed in the process.

We had seen a few feds come looking for us at the various shop locations but none of them had been so bold as to break into our current location that was still 'closed for renovation' according to the sign hanging by the locked doors. I had found enough supplies to put in piles around the shop so that it actually looked like something was being done to the place and really sell the idea. It looked as if we had to suddenly stop working on things due to a lack of funds or something, which lined up well with the frozen accounts. They probably suspected that we had fled the city again, or maybe managed to get out of the country.

Luckily for us this seemed to be convincing enough that they hadn't set up a surveillance unit near the building, which I thought was odd considering James knew exactly where to bring Constance, and that Quanta had already been here once before. I wasn't going to complain about reduced complications while preparing for what could easily become a suicide mission, however. Any spare time we had, when not working on the van, was spent reading through emails and documents pulled from the various computers on Bach's network. I couldn't make sense of most of it aside from the various complaints and orders to speed up progress in various projects.

We eventually started noticing patterns and managed to dig up blueprints and map out the extent of the facilities, placing each one on a full-scale map to see just how much ground it covered. As we suspected, it was their main supply hub that connected unmarked and classified locations along the lower east coast, stretching from Virginia all the way down to the Florida border. We came across messages indicating that a similar system was under construction in the northeast, and another on the west coast. These other locations didn't seem to be built yet, nor have any labs attached that we could find which seemed to indicate that our plan to hit the distribution chain on this side should dramatically slow things down.

As we dug deeper we started finding correspondence with a highly encrypted account that was constantly asking for updates and progress reports from the various departments. I couldn't prove it, but I suspected it was from Bach. We couldn't breech into his system yet, we still only had access to the security cameras, but we managed to find the recipients of his messages within the facility network. I was busy trying to find if the source of the two creatures was mentioned anywhere and if they had the means to acquire more, when Matt grabbed my attention with a gasp.

"Look at this, boss." he said, flicking up a chain of emails on the monitor between us.

As I read through the messages my eyes widened and I felt the ever-present burning rage deep inside me start to rise to the surface. The chain of messages was related to the creatures in the tanks, and our encrypted account was quite upset at the repeated failures of the new specimens. The scientists were trying to explain the delicacies involved in combining genetic material from the two creatures and trying to successfully breed the offspring externally but were unable to convince their superior that it was nearly impossible. One person insisted that they would have better results if they were allowed to observe the creatures natural mating process, but that idea was quickly shut down from all sides as they were informed of the incident on the island.

About halfway through the chain, James was copied in and involved in a plan to try to stabilize the breeding procedure. The scientists were instructed to prepare for a new experiment injecting the genetic material into a separate live host for the initial incubation, and that James was going to provide the new host. Digging further through these messages we uncovered that this new host was supposed to be Cherry. I had to stop myself from slamming my fist through the keyboard with anger.

The encrypted account postulated that Cherry was in some way similar to these creatures having been spawned from failed experiments and since she was born with an array of powers they could likely use her to stabilize the process. They had apparently tried to replicate Cherry by forcibly breeding other people, but found that their subjects were all infertile, much like Devon had said back on the island. Cherry's birth had been some kind of fluke altogether, and it resulted in her incredible ability to control all aspects of this new magic. I was confused how Bach and James knew so much about Cherry though, and then I remembered that James had bugged our house must have gleaned the information that way.

I was disgusted that Bach wanted to use my daughter for his sick experiments and even more so that he seemed to see no issue with forcibly impregnating a fourteen-year-old child with genetic material from a horrific monster. There wasn't a single person anywhere in the conversation that had a problem with it either. The only problem they seemed to have was that James was unsuccessful in capturing her so they could begin. I growled and swore under my breath, they better hope that I never found out who they were.

I decided I needed to take a break and calm down. My body temperature was rising, and I was sure that my blood pressure probably was as well. Callie was changing the bandages on Star's back, she had gotten cut up worse than I did when James pulled the water from the sky and I was worried that she might need to see an actual doctor, but she swore she was okay. They were absently listening to the news again, and as I walked by to head to the roof for a smoke break I saw they were reporting on a sudden increase in Quanta troops around the US.

I stopped to watch as the scene changed to a podium set up on a stage with the Quanta logo hanging on the wall behind it as a cluster of press and other folks gathered waiting for someone to speak. I groaned, sure that Bach was going to walk out on stage any moment, and of course I was right. He was wearing an impeccably tailored black suit as usual, blindingly shiny black shoes, and pristine white gloves. As he took his place at the podium and raised his hands to shush the crowd I noticed the Quanta Force pin on his lapel and had to physically strain to keep my eyes from rolling out of my head. He was so full of himself he might as well start printing catchphrases onto bright red ballcaps just to draw more attention to himself.

"Greetings fellow citizens of America. I stand before you today with news of our progress with the continuing Magic War in our streets. As you all know, this war has caused unprecedented damage to our homes and communities and placed a nearly unbearable strain on our police and local governments. As we continue to root out the cause of this violence, I have put in motion a plan to help reduce that strain.

We have been recruiting a large number of skilled and experienced individuals to our ranks in Quanta to tackle this growing foe, and I'm pleased to announce that we have dispatched troops all across the US starting with the areas with the highest concentration of conflicts. These troops will be exchanging shifts on a twenty-four seven patrol to reduce the outbreak of violence in our streets. If you see or suspect anyone of using magic, you can contact these men and women directly and they will assist you to safety while they address the situation. You will have the option when calling 911 to be transferred to a Quanta dispatcher to report criminal magic activity should you not feel safe seeking out our agents in person.

We have made hundreds of arrests with the help of local law enforcement so far, and with the help of these new agents and the vigilance of our fellow citizens, we hope to bring an end to this conflict in the near future. We have identified a number of key targets we believe to be responsible or at least connected to the source of this war and will be enacting measures to capture them in the coming weeks. I urge you to keep an eye out for anyone that may be connected to magic users and to report any suspicious activity as soon as possible to help us bring an end to this war.

My press secretary will be here momentarily to address any questions you all present may have, as I have many important matters to attend, but I wanted to make sure to deliver this message personally. Quanta and the Department of Defense are working tirelessly to keep our citizens safe without the stress of bringing military personnel onto our streets. We will put an end to this threat and return peace to our lives. Thank you."

Bach strolled off stage, pausing briefly to whisper something in the ear of the press secretary before disappearing into a crowd of suits and sunglasses. *What a fucking clown!* I thought. I groaned loudly in disgust and continued on my way to the roof to smoke and think. It wasn't easy climbing up the ladder with my muscles still burning and aching, but I needed the fresh air and a moment to myself.

I eased into the chair on the roof trying not to acknowledge the pain in my body. I looked out over the city as I packed my glass piece and sparked a flame from my finger into the flower. I couldn't decide what was going to kill me sooner, the strange rage monster hiding deep inside me or the stress from everything slowly eating away at me. I exhaled a cloud of thick smoke and watched a plane pass by overhead and felt myself wishing that I could be on that plane, flying away from all my problems.

"Hey babe, wanna talk?" Star asked, sliding into the other chair.

I jumped a little, I hadn't heard her coming but it was nice just being near her. We hadn't spent much quality time together in weeks since we started running and just hearing her voice in a calm setting made me want to melt. I reached over and held her hand, grateful for the sensation of feeling her skin on mine.

"I don't really want to talk, but I probably should." I said.

"I get that. Everything's so fucked lately. I miss us, miss you." She said, squeezing my hand gently and rubbing her thumb across my skin.

"Yeah. It feels like ages since we've been able to enjoy each other's company. I don't fully understand that, considering we've been together through most of it, I don't get why it doesn't feel the same."

"Because we've not really been together. We've been near each other, but we're so preoccupied with everything else that we haven't been together." she replied, "I can tell you've been slipping into the dark place again though. I can't blame you with all that's happened, but I just wanted to check on you."

"No, you're right. I've been feeling disconnected from myself. I'm burning myself at both ends trying to fight and keep us safe, but I just feel like crawling into a hole and never coming out." I said, feeling a tear roll down my cheek.

"It's hard, keeping up with the world crashing down around us. You're not alone though, Tri. We're all still here with you. I'm still with you. I still love you just as much as I always have."

"I love you too, I just… I don't know how to stop feeling so worthless. I feel like this is all my fault, like if I hadn't ever taken us to that stupid fucking island that we wouldn't be in this mess right now. The world's going to hell, people are dying all around us, I'm a murderer and I just… I…" I sobbed heavily.

"It's not your fault, Tri. We both chose to go to the island, but we didn't chose to be manipulated and abused. You didn't do this, Bach did, and most of this probably still would have happened even if we never went to the island. You can't keep trying to bear the weight of that. He's an evil man, and he was going to do evil things regardless."

"We have to stop him though. We might be the only ones who can now."

"Yeah, you might be right about that much. We are in a unique position to do something about it, and I know you'll find a way to finish this. You're one of the strongest people I know, and I've always known you would do great things."

"I'm literally wanted for treason and domestic terrorism." I laughed through my tears.

"We know that's bullshit, but it is kind of cool. I'm married to one of the most dangerous people in the world! Ooh, the allure! The intrigue!"

"Stop," I blushed. "Be serious."

"Okay, okay. I just wanted to make sure you're holding together. Once this is over I think we need to see a therapist and really dive into what happened to us on the island, and everything since. I don't want to lose you to that dark place you keep circling."

"At this rate, I might not live long enough to fall into that pit anyway."

"I mean it, Tri. I'm worried about you, so is everyone else. We can see you struggling, and we all want to help."

"Thanks, I know you all care. I just wish I could get the damn intrusive thoughts in my head to understand too."

"Is it bad?"

"What?"

"The thoughts and urges."

"Fuck. Yeah, it's pretty bad. I'm constantly fighting the urge to give in and end it all."

"I'm glad you haven't."

"Me too."

We sat in silence for a moment, neither of us really sure what to say to the other, but both grateful to be together. I offered her the bowl, but of course she declined. She wasn't a fan of smoking the flower directly, on the rare occasions she did partake, she preferred a vape or an edible, so it wasn't so harsh on her throat. I took another hit, and we watched the city together. It was quiet, for a city, and for the first time in a long time I felt actually relaxed.

I stood up, and helped Star get up from her chair. She stumbled forward and I caught her, holding her firmly but not tight enough to hurt. She held me back and we stood locked in an embrace on the roof, gently sobbing together. She leaned her head back and baited me in for a kiss with her beautiful blue eyes and I quickly obliged.

The moment our lips met I felt my worries melting away, and as we kissed I felt every ounce of stress leave my body. I knew it was temporary, but it was an oasis of relief in a sea of stress that I was long overdue for finding. I felt a crackling of energy on the air and then felt the ground disappearing below my feet as Star gently lifted us into the air just a few inches. The hair on my body was standing on end and I got goosebumps as we floated, letting the moment wash over me and relishing every second.

I couldn't tell exactly how long we spent like that, but when we finally landed the sun was going down, and we decided to sit and watch the sunset together for the first time in a very long time. We sat up on the edge of the roof, bodies as close together as we could get them, until the cool of the night began to creep in and we decided to head back downstairs and find something to eat. Callie met us at the bottom of the ladder and gave each of us a stern, motherly look letting us know that she didn't approve of us climbing up to the roof in our current state before hugging each of us tightly and walking us back to our cots to rest.

"Ah... you're back." Constance chirped, "I hope you love birds weren't getting to nasty on the roof for everyone to see."

"No, we're too old for that nonsense." I replied. "Glad to hear your voice again, how are you feeling."

"Like some asshole pulled me out of my car and nearly beat me to death with my own gun, before dragging me across state lines and dumping a swimming pool on my head."

"That's surprisingly accurate."

"I figured. Where is the sonuva bitch anyway?" she asked.

The room went quiet, and Callie calmly stood up and walked back to the command center to avoid having to have that conversation.

"Oh. I see."

Don't worry, Aunt Connie, I hid the bodies this time. You can just rest.

"Well, can't complain about that I guess." she said, wincing as she lay back down in her cot trying not to move too much. "What's the next move?"

"We've got the rig built and installed in another van, so we can send a few people into the base again and start streaming. We have quite a bit of damning evidence dug up too, so it's just a matter of getting to them before they get to us." I explained.

"Perfect. If you don't mind, I think I'm going to sit this one out."

"I expected as much. I just glad you're still breathing, Constance."

"You and me both! I thought for sure I was going to wake up dead."

"I don't think that's possible."

"I'd rather not find out just yet."

We all laughed painfully, trying not to exert our pained bodies, but enjoying the moment of lifted spirits. We all relaxed for a bit, and Callie eventually came back to bring us food and change our bandages again. I knew we needed to talk to her about James, but I wasn't sure if she was ready for that yet. I placed my hand on the back of hers when she came to me, and I leaned in to whisper in her ear.

"I know it hurts, and that everything feels awful. Just let me know when you're ready to talk about it." I said softly.

Callie stared off into space for a moment and then wrapped her arms around me and began to cry. She tried to say something, but she was sobbing so hard that it only came out as nonsense. I gently shushed her and just held her in my arms so she could let it out. I knew how it felt to murder someone I felt was evil but had no connection to, I could only imagine what it would be like to have been in love with them. I hated that she had to deal with this, it was another item on the long list of things I felt responsible for despite knowing otherwise.

"I don't know if I'll ever be ready." She said, finally calming down enough to speak, "I did something awful."

"You did what you felt was right in the moment, and you did it to protect your family. You don't need to beat yourself up for that." I said, trying to comfort her.

"I know, but that doesn't stop me from wanting to vomit every time I think about him, because all I can see is the flash from the gun and his brains all over the side of that damn van." she said, fighting back a wretch as she spoke.

I nodded and held her close. I knew what that was like, all I had to do was close my eyes and I could see the face of the man melting in my bare hand in the back of the van we stole. Something about being that close to death was haunting, maybe it reminded us too much of our own mortality and how at any moment it could be us on the other end. Whatever it was, it was heavy and hard to process and so I just did what I could and let her get it out.

It took a while, but eventually she calmed, and we all managed to relax and rest for a while. Everyone was acting like their normal selves again, in spite of everything that had happened to us, we still managed to enjoy spending time with each other. Beaten but not broken, tarnished but not destroyed, we still found time to laugh and love. That's what real family was, I thought, and after I was robbed of that as a child I was glad to have it.

I often thought about my childhood when things were getting exceptionally bad in my head. The way my father would beat and abuse me almost made me feel like I deserved what was happening to me now, like I was always worthless. It took a lot of effort to understand that what happened to me then was not my fault, and it was taking a lot of effort now as well. As I lay in my cot thinking about this, something clicked and I realized that I felt the same way, and that I could get over it the same way. It wasn't my fault, just as everyone had been telling me, something just clicked and now I understood, now I agreed.

It wasn't my fault. These were things that happened to me not because of me. I didn't do anything to make my father beat me or scream at me or any of the other awful things that he did to me, he did those things because something was wrong with him. I didn't do anything to make Bach stalk and manipulate me, I didn't do anything that made him kidnap me or my family and experiment on us, he did those things because he was twisted and evil. It all seemed so obvious once I made the connection, and I couldn't help but feel a little dumb for not realizing it sooner. It wasn't my fault, and I was going to make him pay for making me believe that it was.

CHAPTER 21

My eyes popped open, and I found myself standing on the shore looking out to sea. The air smelled of salt and rotting fish as a cool breeze brushed over my skin. A gentle tide rolled in gently caressing my feet and causing me to sink down into the sand a little with each wave. I heard a few gulls screaming overhead and I debated running out into the water. I had loved the beach ever since the first time Star took me there on a whim before we started dating, and just being here made my heart melt.

I wasn't sure how I got to the beach, and just as I was having that thought I felt heat growing stronger behind me. I turned and found myself face to face with the molten blue form of my aspect that had emerged in the parking lot. I actually wasn't sure if it even had a face, the head seemed blank except for the ever-shifting flow of plasma and blue magma. This close the heat should have been peeling my skin off, but it felt comforting.

"We've grown." it said, words echoing around us, "We are stronger than ever."

"Your power is intimidating. I don't feel like I can control it."

"Because you cannot."

"Why not? Are you not me?"

"I am you, but I am separate. I am fury and vengeance, I protected you. Protected them."

"Then why can't I control you? Why do I have to sit back and watch while you decimate everything in your path?"

"You must learn. True power is earned."

"I didn't earn these powers. They were given to me against my will, forced into me."

"You were given the gift, now you must learn to use it."

"What if I don't want to?"

"You must. It is the only way to save them."

"You don't think I can beat Bach without you?"

"Perhaps, but what if he is not the only enemy?"

I was getting upset and feeling as if they didn't think I was capable without them, but the question refocused me.

"What do you mean?" I asked.

The sky overhead began to streak past, stars racing by leaving streaks in the sky. I watched in awe as day turned to night, night turned to day repetitiously in seconds. The tide rushed in and out and after a few moments the beach looked familiar. It was the beach we launched our raft from to escape the island. I turned and could see Bach's compound and as I blinked we were standing near another version of myself, beaten and bloodied.

I watched myself giving every ounce of strength I had left to blast a massive beam of fire at Subject One, only breaking through its shield once Star joined me. Neither of us had mastered our aspects yet, but there were hints that the power lurked under the surface. I watched as our combined energy finally managed to obliterate the creature and then we both dropped to the ground exhausted. Killing that monster was only the solution to one of our problems, we shifted again back to the beach, and I watched Bach's helicopter flying away and wished I had enough energy left to blast it from the sky before he could escape.

"You mean to say that I will fight more of those creatures?" I asked, turning to face my aspect once more.

"Perhaps. You will need my strength if you do."

"I saw the other two creatures, they are husks of their former selves, surely they won't pose as much of a threat. They were hanging by chains and tubes and looked nearly dead already!"

"What if more emerge? What if he has an army of them? You need my power! You need me to take control and protect your family!" the aspect flared, and I felt it emit a large wave of heat.

"Why? Why can't I do it on my own?"

"You are weak! Bruised flesh and brittle bones. I am BETTER, FASTER, *STRONGER!*" again the aspect flared its power as if trying to convince me through force.

I stood my ground and stared into the featureless face, not letting myself be intimidated. I was tired of giving in and letting others control me, tired of sitting back and doing nothing while everyone else did all the work. I built a team for support, but I wasn't powerless.

"I am not weak." I said, but the sound came out like a squeak.

"Weak!"

"I'll show you who's weak!" I shouted, and balled up my fist as I lashed out at the aspect. I connected with the molten head of the figure and passed right through it feeling my skin burn away to ash and bone.

"You are flesh, flesh is weak, therefore you are weak! Embrace my power, become strong!"

"I DON'T NEED YOU!" I screamed, feeling my throat burn like it does after a concert.

I lunged forward striking out again and again until my arms were nothing but charred bones and then I dove for the figure and fell through it onto the ground, all of my flesh melting away from the bone. I looked down at my organs and tried to scoop them back inside me but the fell like ash between my fingers. I stood up and turned to face the aspect, but it was gone.

"Embrace that anger, let it make you whole again, make you stronger." the voice echoed in my skull.

I looked down and watched the smoldering blue liquid rise from the sand, coiling its way up my bones and hardening them. It continued the whole length of my body, and I began to feel whole again. My body reformed around my bones. My flesh returned comprised of the molten blue magma of the aspect. I felt powerful like never before. I flexed my muscles, bending and dancing across the sand leaving little puddles of glass behind each step.

I felt light on my feet as if I was made of flame and could flicker my way through the air, and so I did. I raced across the beach with intense speed, my body fading in and out of view with each step. I turned and ran out to sea leaving a trail of ocean mist blasting into the air behind me. I spun, directing my speed upwards, and floated into the sky pushing my way through the clouds higher and higher until I could see the edge of space.

I tucked in my arms and legs and let my body solidify and drop back towards the earth. I reached terminal velocity and spread my limbs to slow my descent as I watched the tiny island grow towards me. Just before I hit the ground I sent a blast of heat and fire ahead of me controlling my fall and lowering myself gently to the ground. I felt my heart pounding in my chest, the adrenaline surging through my veins. I felt unstoppable.

"Perhaps you are ready…" the voice chimed once more.

My heart continued to pound, and my chest ached . It was hard to breathe. My head spun and I clenched my chest. The aspect from dissipated leaving my normal fleshy body behind. I wanted to vomit.

"What is happening?" I sputtered between pained breaths.

No answer.

"Fuck!" I cried out as my chest felt like it was going to cave in on itself.

I thrashed on the beach slamming my chest with my hand trying to force my lungs to work but as I lay gasping I felt my heart stop. I was dying, my body was unable to contain the power of the aspect.

"Weak."

I woke up in a pool of sweat. My hand surged to my neck to check my pulse out of fear. It was a bit frantic, but it was there, and I was relieved. I climbed out of my cot and grabbed a bottle of water from the fridge, chugging it down to quench my parched throat. I welcomed the cold, crisp sensation of the water filtering through my system and told myself it was just a dream.

CHAPTER 22

I woke up again a few hours later as everyone was getting up for the morning. I had gone back to sleep on the cold floor partly for fear that my body might burn away in my sleep, and partly that my cot was still damp with sweat after my nightmare. My back was stiff, and my muscles ached, but I felt much better than I had the night before. I got up and started cooking some eggs and bacon for everyone and to prove to myself that I could still do things for myself.

The dream had shaken me, and I wasn't sure what to take away from it. Sure, the aspect was immensely powerful and capable of great things, but I couldn't help but feel that it wasn't meant for the human body and the end of the dream seemed to indicate that it might kill me if I wasn't careful. I decided that I would only use it again if it was absolutely necessary. It was risky and I didn't want to literally burn out before I brought Bach to justice.

I helped Matt put the finishing touches on the signal boost rig and prepare our equipment for streaming our raid of the facility. With James dead it was likely that Bach would need to break away from Quanta and enter the facility himself which would give us the link we needed for evidence. We also still needed to hit the warehouses on the subway line and try to stop more product from getting out, and I decided that Star, Cherry, and I could each hit one simultaneously and really kick the hornets' nest. The rail system connected three locations and travelled pretty quickly so we should be able to get to each of them, do the deed, and then regroup to head deeper into the compound and try to find Bach. Callie would accompany us to keep the rail car tied up so that Bach's goons couldn't use it, while Constance and Matt manned the computers.

Matt and I went over what information we wanted to include in the stream before it started, and I decided I wanted to record a message and make use of my newfound notoriety. That combined with the Paradigm video and the live footage should be more than enough to bring the whole operation crashing down. I did my makeup and cleaned up my suit a bit and then stood against the wall of the bunker while Matt set up a camera to record.

"My name is Trianna Von Drake, and I'm wanted for domestic terrorism." I began. "You might be wondering just what I have to do with the magic wars and what my plans are. Well, I'm wondering the same damn thing. You see, I didn't have anything to do with all this until Sebastion Artosis kidnapped me and my fiancé and experimented on us, trying to brainwash us into being one of his mindless drones."

I held up my hand and summoned a small flame in my hand as I spoke.

"I was manipulated, abused, and forced into being able to use magic against my will. He did horrible things to us on his private island before we managed to escape and destroy his labs. Sadly that wasn't enough to stop him, and he slipped away from us bringing his demented magic drugs to the rest of the world. I've been chasing him for the last seven years trying to prevent this all from happening, and now I'm going to put an end to things before he makes us all into his slaves."

I clenched my fist and snuffed out the flame for emphasis as I spoke, staring directly into the camera hoping that I came off as sincere as possible. We recorded a bit more audio to tie into the Paradigm video, but I felt that I had gotten my point across. Matt queued everything up so that he could play the clips at the start of the stream once we were ready to begin. I hoped it would be enough, it had to be.

We started packing our things, we didn't need to bring much but I wanted to bring some medical supplies and other things in case we needed to patch someone up on the run. Matt had made a few smaller portable signal boosters that would help us connect to the one in the van as we moved further into the compound. We loaded them into backpacks that we could easily carry and drop as needed once we got inside, all we had to do was find an outlet and plug them in and then Matt would handle the rest.

"You're probably going to find an ambush waiting at the warehouse." Constance said, leaning against the wall for support. "Given that we hit it once before they're probably expecting us to come back."

"Yeah, but it's a risk we'll have to take to get back into the facility. We've got armor and powers, fingers crossed that's all we need."

"Cherry doesn't have armor." Constance replied.

Sure I do. Cherry said.

She reached her arm to the stone wall, and we all watched as part of the stone melted off the wall and coated her arm. She pulled it away leaving a small hole in the wall and then slammed her arm against it to show that it was solid.

Should be good enough.

"Are you sure you're okay with doing this? We can change the plan, leave you here if you're scared."

I'm not scared, I want to help. We need to stop this before anyone else gets hurt.

Maybe it was a mother's intuition, but even though her voice was disembodied and not actually attached to any vocal chords, but I could hear her voice waver ever so slightly indicating she was scared even if she didn't want to admit it.

"It's okay to be scared, I'm scared. There's lots of things that could go wrong, and I don't really want to go there or bring anyone with me."

I know. I can sense your fear. I want to be brave like you. I'm really strong, I know I can help!

"You are very strong, and you're very brave. If you are sure you want to go with us, I won't stop you."

I want to go. I can do this.

"Alright, then its settled. You're tagging along and I'm going to tell you exactly what to do. Besides, there's something that will need to be done once we get there, that only you can handle."

What is it?

I leaned down and whispered my plan into her ear, and her face lit up with surprise.

Are you sure? she asked.

I nodded.

Okay. I can do that. We just have to get close enough.

"I'll handle that part, just wait for my signal." I tousled her hair with my hand and then finished packing my things.

We were on the road within a few hours, heading through back alleys and side streets to try and avoid detection by anyone that may have watched us leave the shop. Callie was driving since she was the least suspicious looking despite the visible neck tattoos that occasionally peeked out from behind her hair. Star, Cherry, and I all sat on the floor in the back away from the windows with our hoods up. I couldn't help but feel like we were in a heist movie preparing to break into a vault somewhere, only we were trying to steal attention rather than money.

A few times we had to use the main roads, and I was convinced that we were being followed. I held my breath and prepared to start blasting if they drew weapons on us, but the suspicious cars always turned into a parking lot or down another road before getting too close. It was an anxious ride, but we made it to the parking garage next to the warehouse without issue. We made a few laps and then cruised up to the second floor to keep a low profile while we checked our comms one last time.

"There's a handful of Bach's drones in uniform stationed outside the loading dock of the warehouse, four, maybe five. At least two have the net guns." Constance chirped over the comms as we circled the garage pretending to look for parking.

"Inside the warehouse they have a few more on patrol, I don't see any nets but that doesn't mean they aren't there. There's three waiting on the subway platform as well, looks like they just have regular shotguns, which is still concerning."

"Where are the net guns outside, in relation to the entrance?" I asked, trying to visualize the scene beyond the wall we currently hid behind.

"One on each side of the bay doors, and I think I just spotted a third walking the perimeter, but they keep disappearing behind stuff."

"Those are our priority targets," I said, turning to face the others, "We take them out first, and then we can deal with the rest. Star and I will go first and hit the ones by the bay, Callie you and Cherry come in behind us and look for the third. Don't pull any punches but save your energy we've got a lot of these guys to get through."

The whole van suddenly shifted as if something heavy suddenly landed in the very back. We turned expecting an attack but found ourselves staring at a fully stone version of Cherry with her arm out the window pulling cement from one of the pillars in the garage.

What?

I shook my head, and we raced out of the parking deck onto the street and then barreled through the arm blocking the entrance to the loading bay. A few gunshots bounced off the outside of the van, but Star and I quickly dove out of the back and spun around to face the bay where the net guns were waiting. We each sent a blast of energy at them and dropped them before they had time to realize exactly what was happening. Two gunshots clapped behind me, and I looked over my shoulder to see Callie wielding Constance's pistol as she dropped the third net gun.

The other drones were swarming near the bay door to keep us from getting inside, but that made them easy targets as suddenly several large chunks of concrete came flying out the ground and slammed into their skulls. Cherry smirked, and they all fell limp to the ground as we climbed back into the van and drove it inside the warehouse. A few blasts from a shotgun peppered the side of the van but didn't manage to break through. Cherry pulled some stones in from outside and slammed them into the head of the drone that fired at us, and his body dropped behind the van as I hopped out to deal with the rest.

This warehouse had already been mostly emptied out since the last time we were here, but there were still a few piles of boxes for the goons to hide behind. Or at least there used to be before I set them all on fire and then Star and Callie picked off the troops as they ran from the flames. I heard a net gun launch and spun around just in time to see the net approaching and then get blown off course by a huge gust of wind from Cherry's palm. I fired a beam of blue plasma through the goon wielding the launcher and started running for the stairs.

We had cleared the first two sets much more quickly than I expected and I hoped that we could continue that moment as we moved through the compound. We carried our signal boosters on our backs ready to plant them once we reached the next set of labs but first we had to deal with the drones waiting in the subway tunnel. I jumped the last flight of the stairs and rolled through the doorway onto the platform, keeping low in case they were waiting to fire on us as we passed through. A few shots blasted over my head, and I quickly answered with a wave of fireballs that slammed into an invisible wall between us. One of the goons was holding a forcefield of wind in front of the group as the other two cocked their guns and got ready to fire again.

I focused a more concentrated beam this time, but again it was diverted by the wind, and I felt a peppering of buckshot across the side of my body, but none made it through my reinforced clothing. I felt my body hair stand up and then smelled ozone on the air as Star caught up and sent a crackling ball of lightning skittering along the wall and ceiling around the barrier and into their bodies. All three of them spasmed and one of them managed to shoot the other as he jittered, blowing off one of his legs. Callie raced over to the control box, and I picked up one of the shot guns to bring with us just in case.

A few minutes later we heard the trolley approaching quickly, flashing lights appearing in the tunnel.

"Heads up! There's someone on that car!" Constance informed us.

I turned and managed to duck at the last second as a rock came flying straight for my head from the man on the trolley car. Cherry bolted forward using the weight of her stone covered body to knock the man to the ground before he could attack again. He struggled for a moment and then actually lifted her up into the air and tossed her back onto the platform, his control over the stone a bit stronger than hers it seemed. I was already sliding across the tile towards him before he turned back to us, and I jammed the shotgun straight into his stomach and pulled the trigger. I shoved his limp body off the car onto the ground next to the tracks below, leaving only a bright red smear across the floor as we all clambered on ready to continue the mission.

It would take us about six minutes to reach the next platform, even with the impressive speed of the trolley system. I suspected Bach had used some kind of maglev system like the bullet trains in Asia. We had to hold the rails and brace ourselves as Callie jammed the controls to maximum speed, all except for Cherry in her heavy stone armor who seemed to be thoroughly enjoying the ride.

"There's a handful of people waiting at the next platform. Net guns, shotguns, machine guns, the works."

"Callie, take the car past the platform a little bit and then back up once it slows down. I've got an idea!" I shouted.

I clenched my fist and watched the skin burn away to the molten stone form of my aspect not ready to call on its full potential just yet but wanting a bit more oomph. I held it out in front of me, aiming to the side of the car where the next platform would be and started focusing as much blue plasma into my hand as I could muster before we got close. I had to time this just right, and I watched for the approaching platform in the dark tunnel ahead of us. The lights started flashing to signal our approach and I sent a huge beam of plasma straight ahead, using the moment of the trolley passing the platform to drag it across the waiting enemies.

The brakes squealed as we started to slow down, and then we reversed back to the platform. A huge line of burnt stone and ash split the platform visually in two. The top seemed perfectly normal, but the bottom half was covered in smoldering bodies. My plan had worked, and I tagged Cherry's shoulder letting her know it was time for her to shine.

"You know what to do baby girl: stay alert, fuck shit up and Callie will be back to pick you up ASAP." I said.

She nodded and stomped off the platform and up into the stairwell to start tearing up the lab and warehouse as we rocketed to the next stop. There were less people waiting on this platform, but they opened fire with machine guns as we approached. Constance had already told us they were there, so we had hunkered down behind the short walls of the car and Star filled the room with electricity quickly dropping the goons. She gave me a quick kiss on the cheek and raced up the stairs. I heard energy crackling and popping over the comms as she had already started fighting.

There's more of those little creatures here. Cherry said. *I'll take care of them.*

"Atta girl!" I said, holding on to the rail as we shot towards my platform.

"They've got something big waiting for you boss, be careful." Matt said nervously over the comms.

"What is it?" I asked.

"Not sure, they are loading it off a cart… holy shit is that a mini gun!?" Constance shouted.

"Callie, stop before we get there, I'll go on foot so I can use the tunnel as cover." I shouted back to her.

"I'll do my best!" She started fussing with the control and levers again.

The brakes screeched and we stopped just before the sensors for the lights, and I leapt off, carefully dodging the rails and pressing myself against the tunnel wall. The cart started up again and raced back towards the first platform to pick up Cherry once she was finished. I snuck to my platform and could hear the gun starting to spin up and get ready to fire. I was certain Ezra made a fantastic bullet proof fabric but didn't want to risk testing it against that kind of heavy firepower, especially considering I still felt the impact of the shotguns.

I reached the edge of the platform and twisted around so I could try to peek out and see where everyone was positioned. They had set up the turret smack in the middle of the platform and were waiting for us to come into view but didn't spot me. I coiled my finger over the edge of the platform and focused my flames into a small pinpoint beam that set the clothes of the gunner on fire causing him to freak out and pull the trigger as he flailed around. I fell back behind the wall and listened to the chaos as thousands of rounds sprayed across the far wall and the platform.

Once the bullets stopped I popped out again and blasted the next closest goon to keep them away from the big gun. Two more came racing out of the stairwell but I had jumped up on the edge of the platform and already sent a wall of flame to spoil their day. I rushed over and shot them both with the shotgun to make sure they stayed down.

The first warehouse is up in flames and now I'm taking care of the creatures in the lab. I feel bad for them, but I know we can't save them.

"I'll be there in five." Callie announced.

I started up the stairs to the lab to work on my end of things. We had finally gotten enough information from the cameras and labs to determine this building housed both of the big creatures and I needed to destroy them to cut Bach off from his supply of Opulentia. Hopefully he didn't have any more stashed away anywhere else. Star's voice called out over the comms.

Signal booster planted, awaiting pick up.

"I found a bunch of the medical beds, but nobody is here. It's like they all packed up and left." she said.

"I've got Cherry and we are heading back to you Star, when you're ready." Callie announced.

"Okay, I still need to hit the warehouse but that shouldn't take long. I can already hear the thunder outside."

Everyone was handling their assignments with ease, but that was concerning. Why was there not more of a fight? Did they know we were coming? Surely by now they would have more of their forces deploying to defend the base. I furrowed my brow as I climbed the rest of the stairs, trying to figure it out. As I reached the top of the stairs there was a loud pop, the comm device in my ear sparked and I had to yank it out to keep it from burning me. Then the lights went out.

"Fuck." I muttered under my breath. I knew it was too easy.

I heard movement, and then three impacts on my torso. I glanced down and saw three kunai partially embedded in the reinforced fabric of my clothing, just like the ones the mercenaries had used when they broke into our house. I barely had time to make the connection before the foot connected with my face and slammed me to the ground. I tried to grab their leg and bring them down with me, but they kicked me again and then backed away.

The floor lit up as the tattoos on my neck started to glow. I was back on my feet just in time to block a punch. I could see him now that I had illuminated the space around me, and I was able to make out the general shape of his dark clothes. I could barely make out his fierce eyes over his face mask, they were cold and focused ready to bring me down. He was wearing a dark karate Gi and had metal bracers guarding his wrists.

"Are you seriously dressed like a fucking ninja!?" I shouted jumping behind a nearby table to get some more space between us.

"It makes a clear statement." he replied with a calm raspy voice.

"So does this!" I said, and let the fire inside come pouring out of my mouth.

I expected it to hurt more and singe my lips, but I didn't feel a thing as the blue plasma beam erupted from my mouth and burned across his shoulder ruining the arm of his ninja clothes.

Maybe he should have gotten a flame-resistant bullet-proof suit instead, I thought. He ducked out of the way of the rest of the blast and flipped the desk at me which made me trip and stumble backwards into the wall. A second later a hard fist was buried in my abdomen knocking most of the breath out of me.

I knew how to fight, and I was decent at it in a general bar brawl kind of fight, but this was a trained killer, and he was apparently trained in kicking my ass, specifically. I caught his elbow in my sternum and another fist to the side of my bare neck which hurt far worse without the padding of my armor. I decided I had no choice but to call on my aspect to survive and hoped that it wouldn't kill me in the process. I dropped to the ground to narrowly avoid another strike and slid across the floor under a desk as my skin melted away to reveal the bright blue liquid magma form from before.

He was not prepared for that, nor the lashing tendrils that extended from my arms as I came back to my feet. He instinctively blocked with his arm and the tentacle wrapped around his armor and I could feel it burning through the metal. He undid the binding with his other hand and pulled free just as I burned all the way through. I jumped over the table and then rolled to the side as he drew a katana and lashed out at me. My whips retracted and then my arm extended and formed into a blade, and I realized that I wasn't just watching this play out like before, I was in control of my actions and holding my own.

Our swords met, and I felt the hardened steel begin to heat up and go soft as I pressed my fire blade against it. There was a quick shift in our position, and I felt something hit my stomach and could just barely feel the tip of something sharp trying to work through my armor. He had drawn another weapon and stabbed me in the gut but couldn't quite get the force he needed to drive it home. I backed off and tore free, lashing out with another whip from my other hand and managed to catch the exposed wrist, causing him to scream with pain as I left him with a smoldering cauterized stump.

He didn't slow down however, and closed the distance quickly pushing me back as he struck out at me with the shorter sword in his other hand. I wasn't sure how durable I was in this form, but he really wasn't the person I wanted to test it against. I channeled flames around me in a tornado and then sent them spiraling through the air around me forcing him to fall back. I immediately blasted him with a beam directly in the chest and he slid backwards across the floor from the force.

I expected him to fall to the ground with a smoking hole where his ribs used to be, but he stood his ground. I cut off the beam and stared curiously as he reached up with his remaining hand and tore off the Gi, revealing a leather doublet covered in mystic runes. I recognized a few of them from the nets. Of course he had magic dampening armor, I thought.

"No, fuck you! We're done!" I shouted and leapt on him.

He blocked and slashed at me with his sword, but it went wide, and I managed to grab him by the face. I closed my eyes and looked away as I filled his skull with fire until his body fell away from it and blood pooled at my feet.

"Should've put some on your mask, asshole." I said, dropping my aspect and sitting on a table nearby to catch my breath.

I was cut off from the rest of the team without my earpiece and I still needed to plug in the signal booster. As I picked up the bag and started pulling things out I remember that the earpiece connected to our phones and so I pulled it out of the bag as well. I plugged in the device, and it whirred to life while I held my phone to my ear.

"Anyone there? My earpiece got busted…"

"We read you, boss." Matt answered.

"I've got Star and Cherry on board. We picked off a few more goons and are heading your way. Be there in ten!" Callie reported.

"Nice moves, Tri!" Constance added.

"Thanks, I wasn't expecting to fight a damn ninja today."

"First time for everything I suppose. You got more goons up in the lab waiting, but only five or so. However, you're all over the police scanners and reports are coming in that Bach and a bunch of Quanta forces are heading your way." Constance replied.

"So everything's going according to plan then. Time to kill some monsters."

CHAPTER 23

I raced through the rest of the lab, incinerating drone soldiers as I went. They didn't put up much of a fight compared to the merc ninja. I was thankful for their ineptitude because I was already feeling worn out and still had a lot of ground to cover. I was careful not to damage too much of the lab here so that we could stream it later on, after I killed the creatures.

I recognized the layout of the building as I moved through it from the old blueprints and simple maps we put together from the cameras. I just needed to get through the double doors up ahead and it should lead out into one of the large medical bays full of prisoners. A gun shot echoed through the hall, the bullet grazing my cheek as I turned to see the drone standing at the other end. I put him down quickly, and then ran back to take his gun since I had lost my shotgun in the fight earlier.

I walked through the double doors and got hit with a medical tray. It stung but wasn't very hard. I turned and looked at the scientist holding the tray with fire burning in my eyes, and I'm pretty sure he pissed himself. I shot him in the leg and left him to be dealt with later. A few others scrambled through the exit, and I just let them go, not wanting to slow myself down.

I walked through the rows of people strapped into stretchers with heads encased in strange machines, hooked up to glowing red tubes. The tubes ran to different machines and then along the floor to a large machine in the back of the room where I was heading. On the other side of that wall was my first target, I just hoped it was still incapacitated as I wasn't sure I had the strength to fight one of those things by myself. I was stronger now that I was on the island, but it took so much to bring Subject One down and I wasn't sure I could pull it off.

I walked up to the solid steel vault door and was unamused to see a small keypad off to the side.

"Matt, this doors got a code lock on it. How the hell am I going to get inside?"

"Try... 46295." he answered.

I plugged in the code expecting it not to work, but it beeped, and I heard the electronic lock click. I turned the handle in disbelief.

"How the fuck...?"

"The idiots wrote it down in an email." Matt laughed.

I tugged the huge steel door open. it was heavy and the air that rushed out smelled like sulfur and rot. I covered my nose with my shirt and tried not to gag. The moment I stepped into the room I felt strange, as if all my powers suddenly vanished, which was probably true given that the entire room was lined with mystical symbols and diagrams.

The creature was suspended in the center of the room, a few feet off the ground. The thick chains attached to the manacles around it's wrists and ankles stretched to opposing corners to hold it in place. I couldn't imagine what it took to get this thing in here and strung up like that, but I needed to focus instead on how I was going to kill it. I tried to summon my flames but stopped as I immediately felt dizzy and had to brace myself to keep from falling over. I held up the pistol I had taken from the drone and wondered if it was going to be enough.

I walked around to the front of the creature, and I could just barely hear it breathing weakly as it hung there. I felt bad for it, seeing it like that. Sure the last one I saw had been a rampaging monster, but this felt different like a wounded animal caught and suffering in a trap. It was up to me to put it out of its misery.

I pressed the gun against its forehead and pulled the trigger. The eyes bolted open, and a faint cry of pain echoed in my head. I could see its muscles tensing against the chain and stepped back in case it suddenly found the strength to break free. I tried again, firing a small burst of shots into its skull causing blood to spray from the wound, but the creature still struggled, and I felt a heavy uneasiness wash over me.

"Well, that's not working… what now?" I muttered looking around for options.

I looked at the large glowing wound in the creatures chest and could see the tubes were attached directly to something that resembled a heart. I reached in through the gaping wound and started yanking the tubes free and throwing them to the ground. The creatures blood was glowing a bright orange color, but as I freed the last of the tubes from the heart the color faded to a dim pale green. I stuck the pistol up against the slow beating heart and fired three more rounds. The glowing blood spattered on my face as the heart burst and after a few seconds it stopped beating and a low groan escaped from the creature as it's last breath left it's lungs.

I walked out of the room feeling a bit like I had just hit a dog with my car. As soon as I was free of the symbols and back into the main room my face started burning from the creature's blood and had to wipe is off with my shirt. It felt like boiling hot cheese from a pizza roll straight out of the oven. I held up my hand and summoned a bit of flame just to see if I still could before letting it flicker out as I started walking towards the next steel door.

I felt that all the way back here. You just killed one of the big ones didn't you?

"Yeah, I didn't like the way it felt either."

The other one felt it too. It's sad.

"Great… well better this than suffering through whatever the feds would do to it if I just left it hanging there."

The door had another keypad, and I heard Matt giggle from my phone in my pocket as the same code worked again. I pulled the door open, wretched at the smell, which was somehow worse the second time, and stepped inside. Again the symbols around the room drained me of my power and it was like that feeling you get in your stomach when an elevator goes up just a little too fast. I took a moment to steady myself and then set to work pulling the tubes out of the heart of the second creature.

I pressed the gun to the large glowing heart and pulled the trigger, but nothing happened. I was out of ammunition.

"Fuck me…" I sighed.

I walked out of the room and went back to the other lab where I had fought the ninja and pried the wakizashi from his remaining hand. I didn't like how clammy his skin felt as I pulled at the fingers, but I needed something sharp, and this was the first thing that came to mind. I trudged back through the medical bay glancing around for more enemies, but everything was quiet. I wasn't sure that I liked that, but I continued on back into the chamber with the remaining monster.

I positioned myself under the chest again and pushed the sword up through the wound and began to slice through the various arteries attached to the heart. The creature stirred briefly, but much like the other it fell silent and then moaned as the air retreated out of its lungs for the last time. I shuttered at the sound of death echoing around me as the heart fell onto the ground. I couldn't help but wonder if I had done the right thing. Surely a quick death was better than continuing to be farmed for their very essence. I plunged the sword into the heart and left it behind in the chamber, glad to be done with the ordeal.

I heard footsteps from behind as I was pushing the large steel doors closed again and turned to see Callie, Star, and Cherry had finally caught up with me. We hugged and then stood in silence for a moment looking over all the bodies in the medical bay.

"There's so many... I know we saw them on the camera but it's so much worse seeing it in person." Star said.

"It feels like being back in the lab on the island, but much worse." Callie added.

She wasn't wrong. Just being around all of this equipment and knowing what it did brought up all the traumatic memories of being tested and probed and abused at the hands of Bach, Khan, and his team of mad scientists. The process that we went through was much rougher around the edges, but it had clearly been streamlined for efficiency here. Most of it seemed automated now, allowing the whole lab to be tended by just a few individuals.

"Okay, we've destroyed the warehouses and killed the monsters. Now we just need to get to Bach and finish this. Callie, you should hang back and get ready to start streaming this medical bay when we give the signal. The rest of us will head to the last stop on the subway and hopefully be far enough north that we can intercept Bach when he comes looking for us."

"When do you want the stream to go live?" Matt asked.

"As soon as I have Bach's attention so he's too busy to try to shut it down. He's going to have to deal with me if he wants to stop it."

"Police scanners say they are being told to form a perimeter around the facilities but not to interfere with you guys otherwise. Quanta is dispatching their elite team with Bach to come deal with the situation, so it looks like you ruffled his feathers enough." Constance added.

"Perfect. Let's get this show on the road." I said, and we all nodded in agreement.

We made our way back to the subway tunnel and I mashed the controls to send us forward to the last stop where we would make our final stand. It didn't matter now if they had access to the trolley, we were going to be escorted out as either corpses or heroes by the end of this. I still felt gross about killing the creatures, but that was fading away to the dread I felt about facing Bach again despite having spent the last seven years looking for him. I wanted revenge, I wanted justice, I wanted to throw up.

It took fifteen minutes to pass by the remaining two stops between us and the Richmond facility. The highspeed maglev trolley carried us to impending conflict with no interruptions and just as we neared what I thought was the platform for the last facility I noticed the tunnel kept going.

"Matt, I thought you said Richmond was the third platform from where we were."

"It is, you should be at the end of the tunnel soon."

"Well the tunnel keeps going, pretty far from what I can see." I said, slowing the trolley to a stop at the platform.

"I suppose they could have expanded it to a new location, but I don't think I have eyes there. Maybe it connects to one of the Quanta bases?"

"Do you have eyes on Bach?" I asked.

"No, we haven't seen him since he left that office, just guessing that he's heading your way." Constance replied.

"Alright, I'm going to see where this tunnel goes. Maybe we'll run into him."

"Hopefully not at full speed, I don't want to know what that trolley would do on impact" Matt replied.

I shook my head at his joke and pushed the controls to move the trolley again, but it wouldn't budge. I tried again, backing up a little but it simply stopped at the platform again and wouldn't go any further. A light started blinking on the controls near a section of the panel that looked different. I poked at it with my finger and realized it was a hidden compartment. I pushed it open to reveal a key in some kind of switch down inside the panel. I turned the key and then hit the controls again, and the car lurched forward deeper into the tunnel.

About ten minutes later we reached another platform, but it wasn't well lit. It seemed older than the other platforms and the layer of dust on everything indicated no one had been here in some time.

"An older part of the subway system?" Star suggested.

"Based on speed and time… You're somewhere up near DC most likely. Hard to say where you are exactly, but I'd wager this connects to something related to Quanta like an emergency exit." Matt replied.

"Well that sounds promising, let's see where it goes." I said, putting my phone back in my breast pocket and stepping onto the dusty platform.

We walked over to the gate, and we had to strain to pull it open, further confirming this had not been used in a while. The metal hinges squeaked loudly as we pulled it open and then shut it behind us. The short hallway led to a stairwell that went up several flights, much further than the ones we had used so far. The lights got brighter near the top, so we decided to start climbing. By the time we reached the top of the stairs we had to be above ground level I thought, but it was impossible to tell through the cement walls what was on the other side.

"Oh, I just found the jamming software!" Matt announced, startling me as I approached a door, "I have it shut down, we shouldn't need to worry if the boosters are working now. There's some other things here too, I'll keep digging."

"Try not to scare the shit out of me next time!" I scolded.

I checked the handle on the door, and it frowned as I discovered it was locked. I held the metal firmly and focused some flame into the core of it, melting the locking mechanism. I pushed the door open, and we found ourselves standing at the end of a long, carpeted hallway with florescent overhead lighting. An old, faded exit sign hung above door with cobwebs hanging off one side, wherever this hallway led it was just as unused as the stairwell.

It was deafeningly quiet as we moved down the hallway, and it reminded me of an old office building like the one I used to work at before I won the lottery. There were a few empty offices along the way, but the emptiness of it all made me nervous because it all felt like a trap. I heard Matt muttering to himself on the comms and then he spoke up again.

"Oh shit, I got another camera network." he said, frantically tapping at his keyboard, "You're in a Quanta base just outside of DC I think."

That's convenient… I thought.

"How can you tell?" Constance asked.

"See the logos, these are corporate offices…"

"I'm not there with you Matt, you'll have to give us some guidance here." I said.

"Oh sorry, I spotted you on the cameras which is bad. They know you're there now, but the floor you're on is totally empty. Ah fuck, there's a whole lot of people waiting for you on the next floor… hold on." He said over more tapping, "I see him. I've got eyes on Bach!"

"Where is he?"

"Having coffee by himself in what looks like a ballroom. Three floors up from your currently location if these are labeled correctly."

"We're raiding his compound and he's just sipping coffee? The pompous prick." Star growled.

"He knew we were coming." I said, "Start the stream. It's go time."

CHAPTER 24

The first floor was completely empty, as Matt said. It looked like it was mostly for the lobby and some inconspicuous public facing offices, likely to give the appearance nothing nefarious happened here. We moved through the vacant hallways until we found the stairwell up to the next floor. There was an elevator but that seemed like too obvious of a trap and I didn't want to risk getting filled with lead as soon as the doors opened.

The building appeared to be built like a maze, a single stairwell would only go up or down a single story despite Matt telling us there were at least five floors and a few basement levels aside from the subway tunnel. We were forced to weave our way through each floor that was likely filled with enemies or traps just to get to the next, and everything started to feel like we had been intentionally led there. I wasn't sure of what, but Bach was up to something. I frowned and gestured for everyone to stay low as we approached the door leading out into the second floor.

"They're waiting for us, and they know where we're coming from." I whispered, "We're going to have to go in hard and fast and find cover."

I can go first and fill the room with a little bit of everything. If we're fast enough my armor should hold fine.

"It's risky, but we might be out of options. We have to get up to the next floor."

We all sat in silence for a moment reading the mixture of fear and resolve on each other's faces. We all knew it was the best chance we had at moving forward. I held up my fingers and started a countdown and everyone tensed up, ready for action. As soon as the last finger dropped I kicked open the door and hoped for the best.

Cherry blasted into the room and chaos erupted with her. Wind, fire, stone, water, and electricity whirled through the room tearing up anything that wasn't nailed down. Guns fired, bullets ricocheted, and bodies were tossed around. Star and I followed and summoned our aspects, wanting to dump as much power into the wall of enemies as we could manage.

I raked beams of blue plasma through tables and bodies while Star filled the room with a lightning storm. Cherry buffeted the drones with hurricane force winds, and I even saw a few people get flung out of the windows in the far wall. A few nets were launched but couldn't make it through the extreme fury of our combined attacks. Moments later we were the only people still standing, and Bach's drones were reduced to scattered bodies on the floor.

Star and I dropped our aspects to conserve our energy and Cherry released everything but her pock-marked stone armor. I started looking around for a weapon I could bring with me when I heard footsteps approaching. A few drones were charging down the hallway with net launchers at the ready. Cherry and I each blasted them with beams of fire before they could get close enough to take a shot. I turned around to look for more, and then my heart nearly dropped out of my chest.

Standing at the other side of the room was Star, paralyzed with fear as a man in dark clothes held a very large knife to her throat. He looked like something out of an action movie, rippling muscles, focused eyes, shoe polish war paint. I half expected him to start monologuing in an Austrian accent. Cherry started to move but I held out my arm to stop her as I saw the knife inch closer to Star's jugular.

"If you harm her, there isn't a force in the world strong enough to stop me." I said coldly.

"We'll see about that." the man smirked.

"What's the game, big guy?" I asked.

He didn't answer, but instead pulled a syringe from his pocket with his free hand, ripped the cap off with his teeth and quickly jabbed Star in the neck. Her eyes rolled back in her head and her body went limp in his arms. Every muscle in my body tensed and I felt my skin melt away as my aspect activated in perfect synchronicity with the guttural scream emerging from my throat. I was already running before she hit the floor with my fist cocked back ready to strike with all of my weight behind it.

Within seconds I was lashing out for his face, but I felt my fist connect with something hard, much harder than his head would be. A slab of stone had risen up to meet the blow from nowhere. My molten punch blasted through the stone sending shards of it scattering across the floor as the man simply leaned back away from me. Something hit me in the stomach knocking the wind out of me, it almost felt like getting hit by a truck but I had an idea of how that actually felt. I doubled over and then something else hit me in the back just as hard. I slammed to the floor and could smell the carpet burning underneath me. I rolled to the side and glanced up to see the man had coated his arms with stone to hit me, and that's when I noticed the tattoos running up and down his neck.

I gasped, trying to refill my lungs, and then forced myself to my feet so I could dash away from him and gather my thoughts. He slammed his fists together causing the stones to spark from the impact and then charged at me ready to fight. He was bigger and stronger by leaps and bounds, but I was thankfully faster on my feet. He rained his fists down at me, but I managed to twist and roll around them, deflecting a few with my now molten blue hands.

"Cherry, get Star to safety!" I barked, sliding under the man's legs to avoid another barrage of attacks.

Already on it. We're in one of the offices.

I could hear the fear in her disembodied voice, for all her strength she was still young and afraid for her mothers.

I stood up quickly, dragging my magma arm blade up the man's back but finding only a stone slab in its place. The slab split in two from my cut, and then both pieces slammed into me sending me flying across the room. I tumbled for a few feet until I hit a desk and finally stopped. I looked up hoping to rush him, but he was already in my face bringing a heavy rock fist down. It caught me in the shoulder and likely would have broken it if I weren't in my molten form. It still hurt like hell though.

I rolled away again and then lifted myself into the air, summoning tendrils from my other hand and trying to bind his legs. As soon as I wrapped one, he reached down with a stone hand and gripped the tendril, yanking me towards him. Before I could get away he landed an uppercut to my chest, and I thought I felt my ribs shatter. I wrapped my legs around his arm to keep from falling off, struggling to focus through the pain. I held on as tightly as I could and drove my blade arm through the stone shielding his forearm and watched as it melted through the stone and found flesh.

He yelled and tried to fling me off, but not before I severed the arm completely. Partially charred blood poured out of the stone armor as it fell to the ground, and I lunged forward turning both of my arms to blades and driving them deep into his torso. We locked eyes and his held a look that resembled admiration, like I had just given him a glorious death, gratitude even. I rolled mine, spread my arms, and sliced his body in half. I fell backwards letting his body drop in front of me as I released my aspect and just lay on the floor desperately trying to catch my breath.

Everything hurt, but I was reasonably sure nothing was broken. My aspect could really stand up to a lot of abuse apparently. I could feel my heart racing, and it was hard to catch my breath but eventually it came to me. Maybe my dream was coming true, and the aspect was burning me up from the inside every time I used it, I thought. Cherry came rushing over to me after a moment, with a bottle of water from her pack.

Mommy? Are you okay?

"Yeah, baby. I'm just exhausted. Where's Star?"

She's still asleep. I think he tranquilized her, but she seems okay otherwise.

"Well, that's not ideal but at least she's safe. Should find a closet or something to hide her in case any more goons show up?"

I locked the office she's in. Come on, can you stand up?

"Probably." I said, guzzling the last of the water.

Cherry helped me to my feet which surprised me by supporting my weight. I expected to collapse again, but everything felt steady.

"We lost comms for a few minutes there, but damn. That was intense, Tri. Are you sure you're alright?" Constance asked.

"Am I sure? No, but I'll manage. Do we still have eyes on Bach?"

"He's still waiting on the third floor, has barely moved the whole time."

"Figures." I stretched, trying to make sure I could still move everything, "Is the stream running?"

"Yeah. We played your video and the Paradigm video. Callies been walking around the medical lab showing different stages of the experiment. We lost a handful of streams but managed to get a few back up. We've had millions of viewers between the different streams and the chats are going nuts trying to figure out if it's real or not."

"Can you patch in any of my fight with Rocky here?" I asked, "Maybe that'll ease the doubt."

"Yeah, I'll work some of my magic and push it out. What's your plan for Bach?"

"I'm going to ask for a cup of coffee and try not to kill him with it before the feds show up."

"Be careful boss, I can't tell if he has any traps waiting for you up there." Matt said, and then paused, "Holy shit… he just pulled out a chair on the other side of the table and poured a cup of coffee."

"I guess I should get moving then." I said, brushing myself off and walking to find the stairs.

Are you sure about the plan?

I paused for a moment, then nodded and kept walking.

CHAPTER 25

(The following interlude is an approximation of events.)

Vanessa poured herself a glass of water, sat down at the dinner table with her plate of tepid leftovers from the microwave, and turned on her tablet. She had spent the last forty-eight hours in her office at the Department of Justice. She removed her keys and laminated ID badge from her pocket and placed them in the basket on the table so she would remember them in the morning. She looked at the picture of herself under the logo and read her name and title in her head.

Agent Vanessa Thompson, Internal Affairs.

It wasn't the job she wanted, especially after spending most of her time in college studying psychology, but her boyfriend at the time encouraged her to swap her major to law and with him, and she followed along. Years later she finds herself as a single mother of two working for the government rooting out corruption, which felt like an uphill battle in D.C., but it paid well enough to keep a roof over her kids' heads even if she wasn't always around to enjoy it with them. She always kept pictures of them on her desk to remind her of why she continued to suffer through the monotony of her days. Lately, she wasn't sure it was enough anymore.

She had uncovered a few big cases not long after joining the department, but since then she's been pushed around and left with the shit cases that no one else cared to work. She found out later one of the guys she took down went to college with her supervisor's supervisor and while she couldn't draw any other connections, she still suspected foul play. It left her digging through case files and resignation letters from people only to find them missing from everything but the pension accounts if she had questions. Conveniently, lots of people could just disappear from the government if the FBI felt like stepping in, which just made her job even harder.

The reason she had been spending so much time at the office lately was that she got gifted the wonderful task of setting up the accounts and doing all the paperwork for the new Quanta Force project the President had created to deal with what the media had dubbed the Magic Wars. People running loose in the streets with some kind of stolen technology or something that let them shoot fireballs from their hands or lift rocks with their minds seemed absurd at first, but as the weeks went by and things escalated she began to worry about the safety of her family. Soon after the team was formed, bizarrely quickly she thought, her supervisor slammed the folder on her desk and told her to get to work. She had no time to object or ask for clarification and had to try to log the personnel into the central database all on her own.

She had a secretary, but recent budget cuts meant that she had to share them with a few other people in the department and often just did it herself. On several occasions she scheduled at meeting with Mr. Artosis to discuss ways to streamline the data she needed but he routinely rescheduled for ridiculous hours only to cancel later. She was tired of dealing with *his* secretary who insisted on talking in circles anytime she brought up possible openings in his schedule. She had finally gotten an email with the staffing roster two days ago, and half of it was corrupted and unusable.

The bureaucracy of if it all was not the only problem the Magic Wars were causing for her either. As a parent of three kids, one sixteen, one ten, and one five, the sudden appearance of magical abilities has them constantly babbling about hypothetical situations that could be solved or made worse with some exaggerated version of the abilities. It wasn't much different than anything else they saw on TV to be honest, with the exception that now it felt less hypothetical. One such conversation echoed from the next room between the youngest two as Vanessa tried to finish her dinner, when suddenly there was a hush followed by a strange old sounding voice on the television.

Vanessa stood up and walked over to the threshold to the living room and leaned against the wall to see what the kids were watching. They loved to watch people play video games online, but this was different. The footage looked pretty old, it was in black and white and even had some chunky film grain. The voice of the announcer cracked and popped with a tinny noise like a really old coil microphone.

The video looked like an ad for a sideshow or something, a woman manifesting fire balls and juggling them, a man climbing bolts of energy from a tesla coil. The scene shifted to a laboratory of some kind showing well-to-do people watching over a group of scientists working on something before it faded to black. A large building appeared set into the side of a cliff near a waterfall, and a man she recognized stepped into frame. Mr. Artosis was standing in front of a lab on her television advertising the creation of magical abilities.

"Fuck…" she muttered, and her phone started vibrating with multiple messages and notifications.

She rushed to gather her things, ignoring the messages on her phone. She already knew what they said. As she was rushing out the door she saw another face she recognized on the television. Trianna Von Drake, domestic terrorist, was giving a speech about something but she didn't have time to stop and watch.

"Find something else to watch guys, this isn't for kids!" Vanessa shouted, running out to her car.

Her phone was ringing now, and she couldn't ignore it anymore. She answered and spent the entire ride to her office listening to her supervisor explaining the situation to her that she already understood. He almost sounded upset that she was the one assigned to Quanta, and he demanded that she figure out what was happening and why it was being streamed all over the internet. It was an excruciating twenty minutes back to the office.

CHAPTER 26

Cherry and I carefully climbed the stairs to the third floor, expecting to be ambushed by something at any moment. I glanced around but there didn't seem to be any cameras or goons with guns hiding anywhere. Bach had something else in mind, and I was sure it would be accompanied by some villainous monologue. It would at least give me a great opportunity to slam my fist into his flapping jaws.

Cherry crouched down and pressed herself against the wall to stay hidden as I prepared myself to enter. This was the culmination of a seven-year obsession. I couldn't deny that, even if it was a justified one. On the other side of that door was the man himself, and I felt an underlying fear and trepidation as I reached for the handle. I looked down at my hand and saw it trembling. I took a deep breath and clenched my fist, steadying myself for what I knew had to be done.

The door swung open as I exhaled and sure enough, there at the other end of a large banquet table was Sebastion 'Bach' Artosis. I could already feel the heat swelling inside me as I watched him stand up to greet me.

"Ah, the Lady von Drake. How delightful to see you again after all these years." Bach said tipping his head in a light bow.

"Fuck you."

"Now, now. Is that anyway to greet the man that changed your life forever?" he smirked. "You should thank me! Think of how boring these last seven would have been without me."

"Thank you? For manipulating us? For abusing us? For *experimenting* on us? Why the fuck would I thank you for that?" I said, walking slowly to the chair he pulled out for me.

"Always so brash. I gave you power beyond imagination, and you surprised even me with what you were able to do with it. Your transformations are just stunning!"

"You forcibly altered my DNA with the blood of those creatures against my will."

"Against your will? I seem to remember you paying for the service and signing an agreement for the full treatment plan. Perhaps you should have read the fine print."

I sat down at the table, giving a side eye to the coffee and pastry sitting next to me. I remembered this from the first time we had a conversation about Opulentia, the pastry had secretly contained our first dose. The rest of the table had plenty of food on offer, just like it had back then. He was trying to send a message.

"I was naïve, sure, but that doesn't mean what you did to us was acceptable. You kidnapped us, tried to brainwash us. When that didn't work you tried to kill us!"

"Is that what you remember?" He asked, taking his seat, "I recall a different series of events."

"How so?"

"I offered a free trip to two young women to stay in my private resort to discuss a business opportunity. They agreed to join my tests, and then when things got a little intense they chose to start destroying my very expensive equipment rather than asking for a break. They murdered several of my staff, and then proceeded to rally a small army and destroyed my entire lab all because they were unsatisfied with their purchase but gave me no opportunity to fix it."

"That's a load of bullshit, and we both know it."

"They nearly destroyed my entire business, and even tried to wipe out an endangered species I was protecting in the name of science. I was forced to relocate and rebuild elsewhere to maintain my research and my livelihood, and they proceeded to stalk me for seven years."

"You really think you can just gaslight me about all this, that I'd just apologize to *you* for what you did to us?"

"You should. After all of that, the women had the audacity to track down my new locations and start destroying everything all over again. I'm just an honest businessman, a scientist, a philanthropist, trying to make the world a better place."

"Better? You've nearly destroyed civilization and the world is on the brink of world war three... How disillusioned can you be?"

"Amusing, let's all listen as the wanted terrorist deflects with baseless accusations."

I slammed my fist on the table, spilling the coffee as the tattoos on my neck flared with power.

"Ah, there she goes again. Letting her anger get the best of her and breaking my things."

"Shut up."

"Acting like a wounded little pup, lashing out at the world around her."

"Shut. Up."

"Placing the blame on everyone but herself."

"SHUT THE FUCK UP!"

"Never taking any responsibility for her own actions and trying to make me the bad guy!"

"FUCK YOU!" I shouted, flaring up my power and taking on my aspect.

"There it is! Look how glorious you've become thanks to me. The human body is so weak, and yet now you've found a way to transcend, turning your fragile form into something more!" Bach stood up and clapped as if watching a performance.

I hadn't fully transformed, not letting the rage deep inside take control, despite how desperately I wanted to lay into him with it. My ashen skin shifted and glowed with the power underneath the surface, ready to erupt at any moment.

"I commend you for your efforts in pushing the limits of the Opulentia. Without you showing me such beauty and power, I never would have known it was possible. Never would have thought to seek a deeper connection, and yet here we are. Oh, have I got a surprise for you, my dear..." he smirked.

Bach held up his hand, summoning his red-orange flames and slammed it into his chest. A wave of fire washed over him, and I watched in horror as he too transformed. His suit jacket burned away to reveal bare arms that burned away to ash before my eyes. The flame extended up his arms and neck as he titled his head back letting it burn away his face leaving only a flaming skull like he was the fucking *Ghost Rider*.

"You see, you two aren't the only ones capable of pushing your limits. I've grown a lot in the last seven years as well thanks to you and realized my own powerful transformation."

"Oh shut up already!" I shouted, lunging forward, and planting a flaming fist directly in his lower jaw.

I put every bit of my strength into that blow, letting years of emotion pour out of me into my fist, and he just stood there and took it like it was nothing. His arm flickered and suddenly I struggled to breathe. I glanced down and saw he had me by the throat and was lifting me into the air. I struggled for a moment, but his grip was too strong, and I had to think of something else. I bent my legs up and slammed them into his chest, extending them and breaking free of his grasp, flipping in the air before landing on one knee.

I snapped my head up ready to attack, but a tailored leg struck me across the face and sent me tumbling across the floor. How the fuck was he so strong? I held my hands close together and started concentrating a ball of plasma between them and then thrust it forward sending a beam racing towards him in the blink of an eye. I gasped as he held up a flaming hand and caught the blast, sliding back a few inches as he braced himself against the force of it. Something flashed, and then a bright red beam of fire ripped through my plasma and caught me in the shoulder, causing me to scream out in pain.

I knew I had to fully transform to even have a chance, but I worried that it might kill me before I could stop him. I decided quickly it was a risk I had to take. I focused on the rage in the back of my mind and let it wash over me, and it answered gleefully. In a second I was once again in the molten blue body of my full power. My heart raced and I felt the adrenaline pumping through me as I charged at him. He tilted his head, and I wondered if he knew I could transform twice.

I hit him square in the chest with both fists, putting all of my weight into the blow and sending him crashing into the table, scattering food, and igniting the silk tablecloth.

"Impressive." He said, returning to his feet.

I was already rushing him again and this time caught him in the chin with an uppercut that lifted us both into the air. He twisted and blasted me with a fireball that threw me off balance and we crashed to the ground at the same time. He got to his feet first, but I lashed out at his legs with molten tendrils erupting from my left hand. He just barely managed to jump over them, but it gave me time to shape my other arm into a sword and charge at him.

To my surprise he met my strike with a flaming blade of his own. We slammed together, each pushing with all of our strength to hold our ground until our faces were just inches from each other. He laughed, clearly enjoying himself. I blasted a beam of blue plasma from my mouth knocking him back a few feet. We clashed blades over and over again, neither able to land a strike or giving up any ground. The sprinkler system went off suddenly as the fire on the table was getting larger.

We stood a few yards from each other, catching our breath as the water from the sprinklers sizzled against our flaming bodies. Bach reached up and hit something on his chest and I thought I heard something but couldn't make it out over the noise of the sprinklers. He reached down with one hand and grabbed at the air. A ball of water rose from the floor as if he had grasped it. My eyes widened with realization of what he was doing, and I charged trying to keep him distracted.

He flung the ball of water at me with obscene force and then yanked the water under my feet causing me to stumble back and hit the ground. Water rushed up my body and swirled around my head and I struggled to catch a deep breath before it fully encased me. My vision blurred as the water boiled around my molten flesh. Suddenly something hit me hard in the chest, Bach was crouched on top of me. I felt the water trying to force its way into my mouth, but it couldn't get past the heat.

Bach slammed his fist into my chest, trying to knock the air out of me so that I would be forced to inhale the water. His foot had my blade arm pinned, but my other arm managed to slip free, and I wrapped tendrils of flame around his throat, pulling him backwards off of me. I focused and then screamed sending a pulse of fire from my entire body, evaporating the last of the water circling my head. I reshaped my blade arm into more fire whips and lashed them around Bach, pinning his arms to his body and started to pull trying to lift him and slam him into the ground but for some reason he wouldn't budge.

Glancing down I saw he was holding himself to the ground with the water, pooling it around his legs and using the suction to keep his body in place. His vest was burning away, and I noticed something shiny like metal peeking out from behind the burnt fabric. I slid a set of tendrils down to his legs to try and burn away the water and lifted the other set to his throat tearing away the last of his vest. His chest was covered in new tattoos and a strange device with glowing tubes that pierced into his chest where his heart was. I recognized the tubes from the lab, they looked just like the ones attached to the creatures. He was pumping fresh Opulentia into his veins.

I must have spent too much time thinking about what that meant, because he suddenly broke free of my grip and hit me with a massive wave of water, and then blasting me with a beam of concentrated fire as I stumbled back against the wall. Wave after wave hit me, pinning me against the wall when suddenly a flaming blade stabbed through my shoulder. Bach loomed over me, flaming skull inching closer to me as I cried out in pain. I reached up and grabbed him with my flaming tentacles once more as we locked eyes. I felt my strength fading but held on as tightly as I could.

Cherry, now! I thought.

Alright, here goes nothing!

The door next to us cracked open slightly, but Bach did not turn away from me. Cherry poked through the door, a determined look on her face as she concentrated. Bach's flames started to flicker out, and the flaming skull returned to his shocked face as Cherry pulled the Opulentia from his body. The flaming blade disappeared from my shoulder just before my aspect faded away. I felt my heart racing in my chest, and I thought it would explode at any moment. My body twisted and every muscle ached as the Opulentia was pulled from my body as well. Cherry maintained her focus and continued to draw the tainted blood from us as we cried out in pain and collapsed on the ground by the door. The wound in my shoulder had cauterized from the flame blade, but as Cherry began pulling the Opulentia from my body, it reopened the wound, and blood began to drop down my arm.

"No…NO! WHAT HAVE YOU DONE!?" Bach cried, his body contorting on the ground as the last drops of his power drained from him.

I laughed despite the pain as Cherry held the ball of congealing blood in the air and surrounded it with flame, reducing it to ash. The sprinkler system shut off, or finally ran out of water as she stepped into the room and placed her hands over my wound. A flash of heat emitted from her palms, and I screamed as she cauterized the wound. My heart was still pounding in my chest, and I worried it was too late. I thought if Cherry pulled the aspect out of me that the strain on my body would go with it, but it seemed that I was wrong.

I still managed to get up to my knees, and crawl towards Bach who was writhing in pain on the ground as well, the machine in his chest seemed to be malfunctioning without the Opulentia. I leaned over him and slapped his face to get his attention.

"What… what did you do? How is this possible?" he sputtered.

"I had an ace up my sleeve, and now it's all over."

"I'll kill you for this, you stupid bitch." He gasped, "I have more, I will raze everything you've ever loved to the ground."

"No, I don't think you will asshole. I've spent the last seven years planning this exact moment. I've wanted nothing more than to kill you and put an end to the madness you've caused. I longed for this moment, so I could watch the life drain from your eyes and finally have my revenge."

"That won't stop what I've accomplished." He laughed. "Killing me… solves nothing."

"I know. That's why I'm not going to kill you. I've informed the world of what you've done. I've shown proof. Any minute now, this whole operation is going to come crashing down around you. And as much as I'd love to kill you, I'm going to hurt you more and make you watch."

"You're nothing, no one, how could you possibly end what I've created?"

"You'll find out soon enough. But for now, " I said, drawing back my arm. "Lights out, fuckface!"

There was a satisfying thud as my fist met his face and he fell unconscious. I felt a crack in my knuckles and a sharp pain through the nerves in my right hand. I hit him so hard I must have broken something in my hand. I was much more concerned about the numbness creeping through my left arm, however. I reached into my pocket, falling onto my back to rest, and pulled out a small baggy full of aspirin. I popped a handful in my mouth and swallowed as many as I could manage.

"Cherry, go find Star and Callie and get the fuck out of her before the cops show up."

I don't want to leave you, Mommy. You're dying, I can feel it.

"I'm fine, baby. You guys need to get back to the tunnels, try to collapse them behind you so they can't follow you."

But your heart! Mommy, I'm scared.

"I know, baby… but you have to go! You have to get away, so they don't take you. They'll experiment on you, hurry run!"

Cherry gripped my hand, and I felt her tears dripping on my face. My head was swimming, my pulse was racing. Maybe she was right, maybe I was dying. I felt calm, even as my hands and feet went numb.

"GO! BEFORE ITS TOO LATE!" I shouted.

I felt her hesitate, but after a moment she bolted for the door. I heard her footsteps echoing from the stairwell, as I stared up at the ceiling. The lights were flaring like fireworks in the night, colors shifting before my eyes as my vision blurred. I tried to hold up my hands, but they wouldn't move. I thought my ribs were going to burst open from how hard my heart was pounding. I thought I heard voices, but they were muffled and alien. Then everything went dark.

CHAPTER 27

I don't remember much of the next few days. I get flashes of someone lifting me off the floor, and then getting strapped to a stretcher. Lights flashing overhead, wheels bumping underneath me, being loaded into an ambulance. Part of me was scared that I was being taken to one of Bach's labs to get thrown back into his sick experiments. I wanted to fight, wanted to break free and run away, but I couldn't move at all.

I tried to give in to it and just let death take me so that *he* couldn't. I couldn't stay awake long enough to do anything about it though. I remember a mask, the smell of oxygen, the sting of a long needle. Most of everything blurred past me like I was trying to watch it through the window of a moving car in the heavy rain.

Eventually I woke up in a hospital bed with a tube down my throat. I heard machines beeping, and suddenly Star and Callie were there grabbing my hands and yelling for the nurse.

I blacked out again for a while, and then woke up again in another room, no tube this time but my throat still hurt. Cherry, Star, and Callie all hovered around me smiling and crying.

"Where's the funeral?" I asked, weakly.

"Thankfully, you're not ready for one just yet." Star said, hugging me as best as she could with me being strapped to a bed.

"Where am I?" I asked.

"You're in the hospital, under police observation." Callie said.

"What the hell happened?"

"You had two consecutive massive heart attacks, and basically died on the operating table. They just barely managed to keep you alive." Star sobbed.

"Ah, well fuck. That explains the chest pain. What do the cops want? Am I still a wanted terrorist?" I asked.

"Not exactly, they want you for questioning but in the week you've been in here they did a lot of digging into Quanta. Bach and some of his connections already got arrested. I think they just want to hear from you why you were there on the floor next to him when the feds showed up."

"Heh, figures. So I'm still in hot water, but the stream worked?"

"Yeah, it looks like it worked just how we planned."

The door to the room creaked open, and a woman with long curly hair dark skin speckled with patches of white stepped in holding a cup of coffee. She looked like she hadn't slept in a week but was holding it together.

"Glad to see you're awake, Mrs. von Drake." She said, standing next to my bed.

"Who are you?"

"I'm with the Department of Justice's Internal Affairs, my name is Vanessa Thompson." she replied warmly.

"Internal Affairs? Aren't they the ones that look into crooked cops and shit?" I asked.

"Correct. I've got some questions for you about a Mr. Artosis, head of the recently disbanded Quanta Force department. Do you feel up for a quick chat?"

"Normally I'd pass, but I can't say no to a pretty face." I grinned.

"Well she's feeling better." Star and Callie sighed.

Vanessa and I spent hours discussing everything that had happened over the last seven years. I told her about everything starting from the mysterious tablet we got in the mail. I told her about the experience he promised us, the way he lied and manipulated us into agreeing to be his playthings. I told her about the refugees hiding on the island and how many of them sacrificed themselves to help us survive and escape. I told her about the monster Bach had used to create the Opulentia and his sick brainwashing lab turning people into his own personal army. I told her everything about the island, except for Cherry and her powers.

We shared some hospital food, and I told her about the years I spent trying to track Bach down after the island, and how I wanted to stop him before something like the exact scenario we found ourselves in could happen. She took notes the whole time as I told her the full story, she must have filled up two of her little notebooks from her jacket pocket. I expected her to be angry with me, accusing me of treason or whatever, but she was kind and supportive through the whole conversation. I felt relief as I spoke, finally being able to talk to someone about what happened to us was liberating.

After I finished, leading up to the heart attack in the ballroom she thanked me for everything and left me her card. I expected her to cuff me, but she insisted I needed to stay in bed and rest. She told me she would be in touch if she had more questions, but I never heard from her again. I never heard from any kind of law enforcement after she left. I spent a few weeks in the hospital recovering and waiting for them to arrest me, but they never came.

Matt and Constance came to visit, bringing some food and congratulating me on finally getting our man. Beatrice and Gerald came to see me also, happy to know that they could return to our home without being attacked by mercenaries. I was thrilled to see everyone and felt a huge weight lifted from my shoulders just knowing that they were all safe. I had somehow managed not to destroy the lives of my loved ones after all.

I watched the other side of things play out on the news while I rested in the hospital. Quanta Force had been completed shut down and disbanded like Vanessa said, their remaining troops had been arrested and were undergoing treatment to try and undo the brainwashing. Bach and a handful of politicians had been charged with conspiracy and a list of terrorism charges, and there was a long list of other world governments that also had charges against him. They had a hard time getting information from him during his trial, as his jaw was wired shut to heal after I busted it. My arm was in a cast, I had broken my hand and fractured my wrist, so I was glad to see it did some damage to him as well.

EPILOGUE

It took several months for all of the Opulentia to be rounded up and destroyed. Some of the drug remained in circulation, but over time the supply ran out without Bach's underground network pushing more for the cartels to distribute. The war zones cleared out pretty quickly, Homeland Security took the net weapons from Quanta and rounded up the last of the ring leaders who all turned out to be working for Bach. After about a year, the world had returned to the way it was before, nobody was seen using magic in the streets anywhere. There were a few rumors of soldiers using magic in small conflicts from time to time, but it was hard to say if it was true or not.

Eventually I was released and was able to return home to my family. I had burned through most of our fortune tracking down Bach and putting an end to things. I sold off the last of my computer repair businesses elsewhere and gave Matt the one he was living out of so that he could do whatever he wanted with it. Constance took her final paycheck from me and then took a long overdue vacation through Europe. She still visits from time to time. Star, Callie, Cherry, and I all returned to somewhat normal lives with our cats after things calmed down.

Cherry eventually built up the courage to ask her friend, Savannah, on a real date, and I drove them to the movies once I could walk on my own again. I worried about Cherry and her powers. It was possible that she was one of the only people left on the planet that could use magic, Star had given up hers not long after I got home from the hospital. She assured me that she could keep things under control and that I wouldn't have to worry about another big tantrum ever again.

We never told anyone about Cherry's power when talking about the island, even as people tried to interview us for news articles about how we ended the Magic Wars. I was always scared that the government or someone would take her from us if they found out. We all agreed to keep it a secret forever and if anyone asked about our powers disappearing, we just said they faded after the creatures were killed. As far as I was concerned, we were free from the magic and everything that came with it.

I started attending therapy regularly to help with my depression and anxiety. I didn't stop smoking weed, but certainly cut back quite a lot as I worked through my trauma. It was a long and painful journey, and I found roots of it going far beyond the island into the abuse I suffered as a child. Eventually I could see light at the other end and really started to recover.

~~~~~~~~~~~~~~~~~

I often sat and reflected on how my life had transpired. After processing the grief and the trauma, it was nice to look back on certain things with a new perspective. I found ways to forgive myself for things I had previously seen as my fault. I forgave my many perceived failures and accepted that making mistakes was just a part of life. I looked back at my time on the island for what it was and accepted that I had done everything I could. I made up for it later, and I forgave myself for being so harsh about not stopping things sooner.

There were lessons to be learned from everything that happened, and I liked to think that I was picking up on at least a few. I held up a finger and for a moment tried to summon a small blue flame, but smiled when none came. I could hear Star and Callie sleeping in the bed behind me and watched through the window as Cherry and Savannah snuck out of the house onto the beach. They were young and in love, and I was glad to have been a part of that.

I gently stroked Echo's fur as she purred beside me. *It's late, I should get some sleep,* I thought, but I knew I wouldn't be able to sleep for a bit. I was too caught up in my own thoughts. It
~~~~~~~~~~~~~~~~~

was bizarre to think about how quickly the world changed, and how quickly it returned to normal, even though I knew it was never going to be the same. For a brief moment, the world knew magic in a whole new light, tainted as it was, it was real. I grieved the people lost to the Magic Wars and hoped that their loved ones could find peace now that it was over.

I thought about it for a moment and realized that, even though I grew up poor and abused, even though most people would never even know my name, I had managed to change the world for the better. I had made a difference despite all the times it felt hopeless to even get out of bed. I hadn't done it alone, but I couldn't help but feel accomplished. I smiled and packed a fresh bowl under the stars, sitting in a chair on my balcony, watching the waves roll up on the beach.

Finally, I had found some peace.

A NOTE FROM THE AUTHOR

Wow, what a ride it was putting this all down on paper! To think this all started with a silly idea about a magic pill.

I've always dreamed of telling stories to the world, and so seeing my first book in print and in stores really filled me with more emotions than I could put into words. And now here I am, putting the finishing touches on my second book. There's so much of me poured into these characters and their journey that I can't help but be sad to say goodbye. I was able to process many things of my own personal story through these books and bringing it to an end is bittersweet to say the least.

From here I plan to move on, I want to explore new ideas and themes and settings, but I suppose part of me believes this world could be revisited at some point. Trianna and her family hold a special place in my heart and I'm grateful to them for letting me work through my baggage. I'm grateful to you as well for allowing me to tell this story within a story and I hope it was at least entertaining along the way. Thanks for sticking around for the ride.

I hope reading this story, spread across these two books, helps someone out there get through whatever dark place they might be in, as it did for me to write it. It's easy to get lost in that cold darkness, and maybe this can serve as a light to find your way out. Sometimes we just need a bit of escapism to put things into perspective. Whatever you're dealing with, even if we never meet, just know this: I believe in you, I'm proud of you, and I love you.

- Codi Morrigan Lokken

Please consider leaving a review wherever you purchased the book from if possible, and also on my website (www.authorcmlokken.com). It really helps get more eyes on my work, and considering I'm doing this all myself with nothing but scraps I need all the help I can get!

9 798988 431176